PRAISE

Poisoned Blade

"**A worthy sequel**, doubl[...]
and surpassing *Court o[...]*
world-building....**A tense, dramatic adventure**, raising the
stakes and the potential for drastic consequences as the story
barrels toward its conclusion." —*Barnes & Noble*

"Blends **emotional intelligence, passionate idealism,
and realpolitik** in a plot ending at the cliff's edge of
revolutionary change. At once **nuanced and thrilling—
a worthy sequel.**" —*Kirkus Reviews*

"Jes makes for **a worthy heroine, as bold and daring
as she is endearing**....The characters—heroes and baddies
alike—are **vividly real**, their motives and emotions often
fierce but always recognizable." —*Booklist*

"[Jes] **will remind most people of Katniss Everdeen**....
The book deals with issues of family loyalty, standing up for
one's beliefs, and self-discovery." —*VOYA*

"**Stellar description and pacing.** [Elliott's] eye for
detail is **extraordinary**, and descriptions of court life are
very evocative." —*Teenreads*

"**Fans won't be disappointed.**" —*Bustle*

"Anyone who thinks Young Adult fiction can't successfully
handle themes like a culture's endurance in defiance of
colonialism, the myriad socio-economic factors leading
toward revolution, or racial and/or gender inequality, needs
to **read these books.**" —*Fantasy Literature*

PRAISE FOR

★ "Jes will remind readers of fearless Katniss with her skill and strategy for games. But it's the fascinating descriptions of traditions, royal interactions, and, of course, the intensities of the Fives that will enthrall readers most of all. Let the games continue!" —*Booklist* (starred review)

"Kate Elliott's magic and mastery is better than ever. *Court of Fives* enchanted me from start to finish."
—MARIE LU, *New York Times* bestselling author of the Legend series and the Young Elites series

"Features a gripping, original plot; vivid, complicated characters; and layered, convincingly detailed worldbuilding. A compelling look at racial and social identity wrapped in a page-turning adventure." —*Kirkus Reviews*

"Simply amazing....This book will not fail you."
—GAIL CARRIGER, *New York Times* bestselling author of the Finishing School series

"Jessamy is a loyal and strong female protagonist who fights against injustice. This trilogy opener will be a hit with readers who love action-packed fantasy adventures." —*SLJ*

"Haunting. Epic. Impassioned. Layered. Breathtaking. This isn't just a novel; it is a coup d'état of the soul. Prepare to be ravished." —ANN AGUIRRE, *New York Times* bestselling author of the Razorland trilogy

"Highly entertaining and fresh.... This book is a winner." —*VOYA*

A **COURT OF FIVES** NOVEL

KATE ELLIOTT

LITTLE, BROWN AND COMPANY
New York · Boston

Little, Brown and Company
Hachette Book Group
1290 Avenue of the Americas, New York, NY 10104
Visit us at lb-teens.com

Originally published in hardcover and ebook by Little, Brown and Company in August 2016
First Trade Paperback Edition: July 2017

Little, Brown and Company is a division of Hachette Book Group, Inc. The Little, Brown name and logo are trademarks of Hachette Book Group, Inc.

The publisher is not responsible for websites (or their content) that are not owned by the publisher

The Library of Congress has cataloged the hardcover edition as follows:
Names: Elliott, Kate, 1958– author.
Title: Poisoned blade : a Court of Fives novel / Kate Elliott.
Description: First edition. | New York ; Boston : Little, Brown and Company, 2016. | Summary: "Now a Fives Challenger, Jes travels the countryside to compete against adversaries of similar skill levels, using the opportunity to search for her missing twin sister, Bettany, only to be thrown into the center of the war that Lord Kalliarkos—the boy she still loves—is fighting against their country's enemies"— Provided by publisher.
Identifiers: LCCN 2015042248| ISBN 9780316344371 (hardback) | ISBN 9780316344364 (ebook)
Subjects: | CYAC: Social classes—Fiction. | Sisters—Fiction. | Contests—Fiction. | Love—Fiction. | Racially-mixed people—Fiction. | Fantasy. | BISAC: JUVENILE FICTION / Fantasy & Magic. | JUVENILE FICTION / Action & Adventure / Survival Stories. | JUVENILE FICTION / Girls & Women. | JUVENILE FICTION / Love & Romance. | JUVENILE FICTION / Social Issues / Prejudice & Racism. | JUVENILE FICTION / Social Issues / Self-Esteem & Self-Reliance. | JUVENILE FICTION / Sports & Recreation / General.
Classification: LCC PZ7.1.E45 Po 2016 | DDC [Fic]—dc23
LC record available at http://lccn.loc.gov/2015042248

ISBNs: 978-0-316-34438-8 (paperback), 978-0-316-34436-4 (ebook)

Printed in the United States of America

LSC-C

10 9 8 7 6 5 4 3 2 1

For Rochita Loenen-Ruiz,
who carries a light on the long journey
so others may find the path

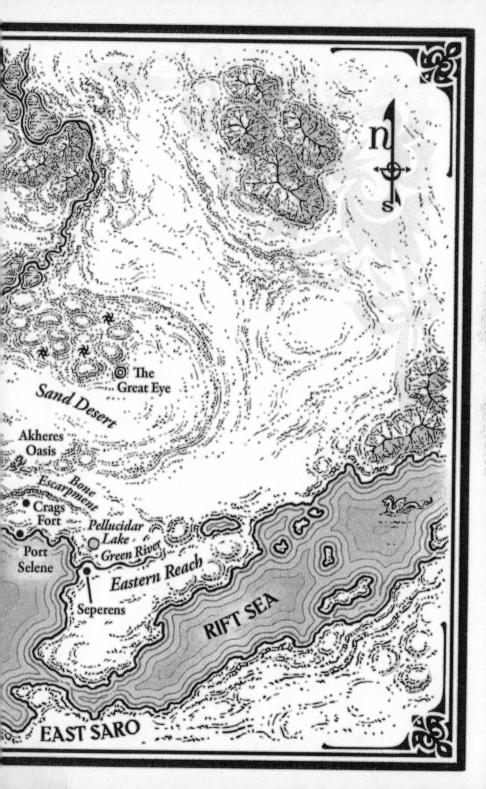

N

S

Sand Desert

The
Great Eye

Akheres
Oasis

Bone
Escarpment

Crags
Fort

Pellucidar
Lake

Green River

Port
Selene

Eastern Reach

Seperens

RIFT SEA

EAST SARO

1

no one must suspect what I plan to do tonight. I should stay in my bed, content with the place I've earned for myself as an adversary in Garon Stable. I should.

But I don't.

In darkness I swing my legs off my cot. My toes brush the stiff straps of my leather sandals, which I remember to shake out in case a scorpion has decided to rest there. Nothing stirs that I can hear, and it is too dark to see. I have to go now before it's too late.

After lacing up my sandals I creep to the end of the cot. A cedar chest stores the few garments and necessities I possess. I finger through the folded cloth and gather up my formal parade livery, roll up the garments, and tie the bundle atop my head beneath a headscarf.

The canvas curtains that divide the barracks into eight cubicles scrape the floor as I push past them. I wait, alert for any sound from one of the other four women who live here. They are adversaries too, competitors who run the Fives, the most popular game in the land of Efea. Running the Fives used to be all I dreamed about. Now that I have what I've always wanted, I should be ecstatic.

"Jes?" Mis whispers from the next cubicle. "Is that you?"

When I run the game of Fives, one of my strengths is that I know how to act decisively with a strategy already in my head.

"Just have to go to the latrine," I whisper back, hoping she doesn't hear the tremor of emotion in my voice.

She speaks the words I know she was desperate to say all evening at our victory feast, but was too kind to say in front of everyone else.

"What will happen to Lord Kalliarkos now that you've defeated him on the Fives court?"

"What happens on the other side of the wall in Garon Palace has nothing to do with adversaries like us." The lie pours like tar from my lips.

"I'm sorry. I know you really liked him. The attention of a handsome and friendly highborn boy must seem irresistible. But after a while you'll see it's better to stay as far away from Patron lords as possible. Even him."

A stone of foreboding lodges in my throat. I can barely force words past it. "I know."

I hear her roll over on her cot and yawn. "May you have a quiet rest, Jes. If you can sleep after all the glory you won with your victory today."

She says nothing more, and I steady my breathing, trying to calm the restlessness that plagues me, but it twists in my gut like shame and dread. If I don't do this while I still have the chance, I'll never be ready to move forward into the new life I've earned for myself.

Outside, a sliver of moon illuminates the stable yard, where adversaries hone their skills and fledgling trainees hope to become good enough to compete in the game of Fives. Here in Garon Stable everyone sleeps, but from over the wall drift the sounds of revelry and laughter as the highborn celebrate my unexpected victory, which has brought prestige and profit to Garon Palace. My victory also destroyed the dreams of Lord Kalliarkos even though that was never what I intended.

I don't expect him to forgive me. I just need to make him understand that I didn't have a choice. I can't bear to think of him leaving, maybe forever, if my last memory of him will be the terrible look of betrayal on his face, so similar to the expression my mother had when my father left her.

I creep into the bathhouse, where I probe my way into the outer changing room and past a curtain into the washroom. By patting a hand along the wall I find shelves and grab a folded towel to grip in my teeth. Although I could easily climb the wall, the keen-eyed sentries who patrol its top would catch me, and of course I would be turned away at the palace gate if I tried to walk in directly.

However, the two compounds—the palace and its Fives stable—do join in one place. They share the waters of a soaking pool because it is so expensive and time-consuming to heat.

I sink until the warm water reaches my neck, then edge into an underwater tunnel. By tipping my head back I get just enough room to breathe as my forehead and nose scrape the stone ceiling.

The wall between stable and palace measures five paces wide, because the palace is also a fortification. As soon as I pass into the pool on the palace side I stand up. No scrap of light illuminates the chamber, and I slosh a little, trying to get my bearings. On the palace grounds the victory party roisters along. Voices are raised in a famous song about the bird-haunted ships that brought the first Patron king from the broken empire of Saro to the fertile land of Efea that gratefully awaited his rule.

After I climb out of the pool I use the towel to dry myself, untie the garments from my head, then pull on my parade uniform and rebind my coiled hair under my headscarf, which now has slightly damp ends. A girl who looks like me would never walk the grounds of Garon Palace, but from a distance, at night, people may mistake me for a palace servant because of my clothes. All I lack is a mask to conceal my face, but I'm pretty sure the servants of Garon Palace don't wear masks inside the walls.

Easing through the last curtain takes all my courage. I immediately hide behind a statue of Lady Hayiyin, Mistress of the Sea, on the bathhouse porch, pressing my body against the smooth carving of the long straight hair that falls from the goddess's head all the way to her feet. Through dry lips I mouth a prayer asking for her aid to not be caught, just as sailors might plead to come ashore safely through a storm-tossed sea.

As I reach my place of calm focus I risk peeking out from behind the statue to examine my surroundings. To my right a walkway leads through a strip of garden toward a huge pavilion lit by a hundred or more lanterns and filled with a chattering crowd of highborn and exceedingly well-dressed Patrons. To my left benches shade away under a spacious arbor laced with the night-blooming jasmine for which I am named. For two breaths I inhale its intoxicating scent.

Then, to my horror, I realize two people stand entwined in the depths of the shadows beneath the arbor. By the cut of their clothing I can guess that one is a woman and the other a man. Whispered endearments float on the breeze, snatches of words catching at my ears.

"...of course no one suspects, beloved." I hear the woman's voice clearly. "I've made sure of it. Beyond anything else, no word of our meetings must reach Esladas. His honor means more to him than anything."

"More than you and your exalted rank? Have you not snared your new husband's simple affections with your sophistication and wit so that he will indulge all your wishes?"

"Why should I care if he indulges me at all as long as he obeys? It is an arranged marriage far beneath what is due to me." The woman's sneering tone sears my heart. This must be my father's new wife, Lady Menoë. "It is bad enough I have to bear his child to satisfy Uncle Gargaron. I will do my duty so they won't get suspicious. But I am not going to pretend I care about the affection of a rustic provincial risen far above his ordained place."

My hand twitches, and I grip the fabric of my jacket to stop myself from grabbing a bucket of water from the porch and dashing it into her condescension.

"I hear someone," the man says.

Tensing, I slide a foot back, ready to escape into the bathhouse.

"Go," she whispers.

The man hurries into an adjoining garden lush with towering shrubs and bloom-kissed trees. Menoë steps out into the marble forecourt and turns her face toward the moon as if drinking in its light. She doesn't even glance toward the statue that conceals me.

Menoë is an alluring flower garbed in bright colors. She has the pale golden skin of a person descended from the Saroese, who conquered Efea five generations ago, whereas I am the ordinary brown common among people of Efean ancestry. Her straight black hair has been looped and twisted into an elaborate hairstyle of ribbons, beads, and bows. The beauty of her eyes is enhanced with a painted tracery of wings flaring out from the corners. In daylight she would resemble the statue of Lady Hayiyin, a goddess who looks nothing like me.

Brisk footfalls alert us to the presence of a man coming from the pavilion, attended by a servant bearing a lamp and a guard in formal livery. At the sight of Lord Gargaron, I shrink even more behind the statue because I am sure he can somehow sense I'm here no matter how silent and hidden I remain. Yet I can't help staring at the man who rules my life. Garon Palace is his. Garon Stable is his. If he finds out I have crossed the wall, he could easily have me thrown into the mines to work until I die. But the truth is, even as my heart knots itself into a writhing coil of loathing and fear, a part of me enjoys the contemptuous way his thin smile greets the young woman who just ridiculed my father.

"Menoë, surely by now you comprehend why you of all people cannot be creeping out of a public gathering as though you have something to hide. Our allies and enemies alike have only just stopped calling you a butcher and a whore. For our plans to succeed, you must conduct yourself in a way that is absolutely above reproach."

She raises a languid hand. "Uncle Gar, how can you criticize me when it is Kalliarkos who has almost ruined everything by demanding to run the Fives? He's the one who disgraced Garon Palace with his laughably poor performances. I even hear people say he fell in love with that brawny Efean girl who beat him today. That would be just like him, so pathetic!"

I clench my hands rather than leap out from behind the statue and claw her face off.

Gargaron's expression and posture sharpen, and for an instant I think he has spotted my slight movement, but his gaze never leaves her. "Do not presume to lecture me. You still have a tongue because I saved it for you. You are a stupid, stupid, selfish girl. Are you pregnant?"

Her lips quiver. "I can't know that yet. I've only been married to that flour-stained baker's son for five days, Uncle."

She disgusts me, but in a way I welcome her mockery because I don't *want* her to like my father, not now and not ever.

Gargaron adjusts one of the meticulous folds in the wrap of his keldi. "If I had pity to feel for anyone, Menoë, be sure I would spare none for you. For all his low origins, that flour-stained baker's son is now *General* Esladas and an exceptional man whose skill we would be foolish to ignore."

"He lived with a Commoner woman for twenty years as if she were his respectable wife! To think the hands that touch me have touched such a creature! We both know *you* would never take a Patron woman as lowborn as Esladas into your bed, not even as a concubine."

He slaps her. The blow resounds with such a snap that I recoil, my back hitting the wall with a thump that claps as loudly as a shout in my ears. My lips move in a silent prayer to the gods that no one heard the noise or noticed the flutter of the curtain next to me. But the highborn care only about the scene enacted within the aura of golden light from their lamp. What lies in the shadows means nothing to people like them.

She presses a hand to her cheek and sucks in a breath.

I hope it hurts.

"If you dissolve into girlish tears I will lose my respect for your cunning and initiative," Gargaron says. "You must be strong because your brother is weak. Kal has fled the party. I need you to go fetch him back."

She smiles as prettily as if he is her dearest uncle and she loves him very much, but a viper would look kinder. "What if he says no?"

He shakes his head with a dismissive frown, as if her question disappoints him, then turns his back in deliberate rudeness and walks away. The servant and guard follow.

She glances around, probably searching for the mystery lover she was embracing in secret, then hurries after her uncle.

The long, tight sheath gown she wears constrains her legs, giving her the mincing walk that Patrons consider the mark of a well-bred woman.

I suddenly realize that I don't know where to find Kalliarkos, but she does. I grab a bucket from the porch and follow, keeping my head down in case they look back.

"What if he says no, Uncle?" she repeats peevishly to his back.

Lord Gargaron does not even pause to let her catch up but rather casts his words over his shoulder. "Tell him he need only attend until Prince Nikonos departs. After that he may go sulk in his pavilion for the rest of the night and indeed soak his head in a vat of his tears for all I care."

"You say the cruelest things about Kal! Sometimes I think you don't like him."

"He's a likable boy, as we all know. I want everyone to see the two of you enter the festival pavilion together, side by side, to remind them that you both have blood every bit as royal as that of the reigning king and queen."

She stops dead as he keeps walking toward the pavilion with his servant and guard. For a moment she twists a dangling ribbon between her fingers. Then, with a dainty shrug, she cuts down a different path toward a set of small pavilions half-hidden in the garden.

Before I can bolt after her, a servant carrying a jar emerges from another path, surprising me. I set down my bucket, bending over my sandals to hide my face, and speak in the perfect Patron diction that my father insisted his daughters learn. "Curse this strap for coming undone again."

No one hearing my voice alone would guess my mother is a Commoner. A scent of urine and feces wafts from the servant's jar as he hurries past without a glance. I wait until the footsteps fade, but by then Menoë has vanished in the shadows. If I've lost her I may never find Kal.

I set the bucket under a bush and stride quickly down the path I think she took, looking all around to try to spot her. At night the garden glows with a soft glamour of lanterns set atop stone pillars. Trees arch over the path, stars peeping through interwoven branches. Off to one side, amid a mass of bushes, fireflies dance among the leaves. In the Efean language we call them spark-bugs and say they each carry a little bit of life-force, but in this Patron garden they are trapped inside glass cages.

Lady Menoë's mocking voice startles me, coming from so close that without thinking I grab for an overhanging branch and swing up into the sheltering darkness so I don't stumble into her.

"Kal! Are you crying over your wine? How gauche."

"Shut up." His harsh voice is almost unrecognizable. In the last seven days I thought I had come to know it well.

The branch gives me the height to see across a bend in the path. Three small pavilions stand in a row, each raised on stilts and with a long balcony. A familiar shape leans against the railing of the nearest balcony, wine cup in hand, head bowed as he ignores his sister waiting on the path below. His slumped posture marks him as a defeated man. Soldiers dragged before their conquerors might stand so, bent and shamed.

She fans herself as if the short walk has overheated her. "Uncle Gar sent me to fetch you back to the victory party, my dearest brother."

"Stop it."

"True, you are my only brother so naturally you have to be my dearest brother. You are therefore also my most detested one, aren't you?"

"Leave me alone."

"Did you really fall in love with a Commoner? Kal! I'm ashamed of you. How could you even consider it?" Her fan whips back and forth with such agitation I am surprised the nearby flowers don't break off. My cheeks flame with embarrassment because I'm afraid of what he might say in reply, considering what I did to him.

He says nothing.

"There's a reason no Commoners are allowed on these grounds, not even as servants masked to hide their ugly faces. You didn't really kiss a mule like her, did you?"

His head snaps up. "They are people just as we are people, no different from us."

"You don't really believe that. You're just saying it to shock me."

"How could I shock you, Menoë? You're the one who murdered your first husband."

Murdered her first husband?

Alarm flares, a hundred questions crowding my mind with such force that I stop paying attention to my precarious position poised on the branch. My foot slips; my body tips backward.

I turn the fall into a flip, landing on my feet on the path with a thump.

In a sharp voice Kalliarkos says, "Did you hear that?"

"Of course I heard it! I know what nasty things people whisper behind my back! You don't have to remind me!"

I sidle forward and peer around the trunk of the next tree in time to see her reach up and rap him on the calf with her closed fan. "You're so dull and predictable, Kal! You pretend to be everyone's friend instead of a prince. Now be a good boy and come with me to the festivities."

In answer he tips the wine cup and pours liquid right down onto the intricate architecture of her hair. Ribbons droop, sagging with moisture. With a shriek she flings her fan at his head. He shakes the cup over her back to make sure not a single drop remains.

I want to crow in triumph. If we were still fellow adversaries, comrades in the stable, I would slap him on the back in congratulation. The need for silence and secrecy galls me.

Yet she surprises me by doubling over in a shockingly coarse burst of laughter. The violent motion tangles the ribbons and the strings of beads. As she straightens, her hair looks like a wild nest instead of a splendid work of art.

"I'm not going back to the party," he says.

"Defy Uncle Gar all you wish, Kal. It's sweet, even if it's pointless."

She licks a smear of wine off a finger and sashays away around the pavilion with her tangle of hair raised high. With a glance over her shoulder she flings a last retort like a final arrow shot in battle.

"You couldn't have won your Fives trial anyway. You're not good enough to beat her."

I wince.

He wrenches away from the lovely night vista over the garden and stalks back through the open doors into a lamplit chamber. I dash from tree to balcony. Grabbing the edge, swinging up, and climbing over the railing takes but a moment. I drop into a crouch in the shadows and peer into a room decorated with masterfully painted murals of war. In one scene, spears pinion three soldiers. Each wears the badge of one of the three kingdoms of old Saro, the remnants of an empire: a kestrel for

West Saro, a hawk for East Saro, and a peacock for Saro-Urok. Their dying bodies arch over a cluster of flowers whose white petals are turning red as blood waters them.

Kalliarkos gives his empty wine cup to an elderly servant, who hands it to a younger servant, who sets it down on a side table inlaid with ivory and gold. In the elaborate court clothes worn only by palace men, Kal looks handsome, but then again he looked handsome in simple adversary's gear. His coarse black hair is cut so short it stands straight up. His lean body has the confident posture of a person sure of his footing on a Fives court, but his eyes narrow as he clenches his hands.

I did this to him. I ruined his life.

"My lord," says the elderly servant, walking toward the balcony, "I will just close the doors now that you are returning to the festival pavilion."

I scramble to the back corner of the balcony, leap to grab hold of the overhanging roof, pull to get my upper body onto the gentle slope, then swing my legs up so I lie right along the edge.

The servant's footfalls pause. "Did you hear something, my lord?"

"Just the wind. Keep the doors open."

"But—"

"I'm not going back to the festival pavilion."

"But my lord, your sister said—"

"Leave me."

The door opens and shuts. Lord Kalliarkos walks out onto the balcony and looks to each direction, then out over the path, and last of all glances up to the roof.

"I thought it might be you," he says without a hint of welcome, staring at me with hard, hopeless eyes. "What can you possibly want? You and I pledged we would stand by each other, and then you cut my throat."

2

I **drop to land** beside him, and he immediately steps away from me.

"Kal, I just came to explain what happened."

"I think it's pretty clear what happened. You knew that if I lost I would be forced to join the army and become a pawn in my uncle's plot to put my sister and me on the throne. Which is the very last thing I want. So either you've been conniving with my uncle all along or you just couldn't stand losing, even knowing what would happen to me. Is there something I'm missing? Oh, yes. *Lord Kalliarkos* or *my lord* is the proper address."

The clipped arrogance of his tone infuriates me, especially after we once whispered secrets to each other. "I thought you would understand, but I guess I was mistaken. You can't possibly believe I've been conniving with your uncle. He's the one who threatened to send me to the mines."

"And you're the one who said it was time for me to act as the prince that I am. You should have known that if I'd won I would have been able to stay in the palace and protect you. I would never let my uncle condemn you to the mines. But apparently for all your fine talk you never actually believed I am strong enough to stand up to him."

I blink about five times. The accusation stings because I'm afraid it's true.

"I really thought you believed in me," he adds.

"It's not that simple." This isn't going at all as I had planned—I would explain and he would be understanding. Navigating a Fives court seems far easier than trying to negotiate his bitter anger. "Surely you understand that your position as a Patron lord makes you far more secure than I can ever hope to be. Because I have a Patron father and Commoner mother I have no legal standing. Garon Palace basically owns me."

"I'm aware of who you are." His gaze flicks up and down my body as if he is remembering the kisses we shared, but instead of softening, he tenses and looks sharply away, like he's mad at himself for thinking of me in that way. "Or at least I thought I knew your heart."

If I can just reach past his anger, I can make him listen. I'm sure of it.

"What happened on the Fives court was a choice I made for my family. You know how close my mother and sisters came to death, how unsafe they still are because your uncle will kill them if he finds out they are alive. And I don't even know where Bettany is!"

My voice breaks as a rush of emotion overwhelms me. I've held off truly thinking about her, holding my fear in a corner of my mind where it can't distract me, but now it thrashes out like a monster going for my throat.

His tone softens just a little. "Who is Bettany? Ah, I remember. Your twin sister, the missing one."

I rub at my eyes. "She and Mother's household servants were taken away by Garon stewards when I was brought to the stable."

"Yes, and if I wasn't being forced to leave I could help you find them. Did that ever occur to you? Because I know you, Jes. You may say it's all about your family, but once you get it in your head that you have to win, you can't see any other alternative. You *won't* see it. You just go for the victory tower no matter what it means to the people around you." His voice grates.

"Gargaron *ordered* me to win. He would have had me sent to the mines otherwise, and my mother and sisters can't survive without someone providing for them. I defeated you to protect them in the only way I knew how. You have no idea how vulnerable we are because you'll never be that vulnerable."

I realize I've raised my voice just as if I have the right to yell at him, so I add, stiffly, "My lord." It comes out mocking, even though I don't mean it to.

He strides over to the side table with its cup and bottle. Picking up the cup, he weighs it in his hand, and for an instant I think he is going to throw it at me, so I brace myself to dodge. The Kalliarkos I used to know preferred smiles to frowns, joking words and friendly pleasantries to surly glowers. That Kalliarkos has vanished, leaving this one with his rigid posture and pinched mouth. He is still the handsome lord everyone must notice, but I desperately miss the staggering sweetness of the smile he once turned on me.

He doesn't speak, so I hastily go on. "I shouldn't have come. I don't know what I was hoping for. What's done is done. I'm just sorry it ended this way."

He turns the cup in his fingers, glaring at the delicate flowers painted on white glaze. "I do not regret breaking them out of the oracle's tomb, if that's what you're worried about. What was done to them was blasphemous. But you used me to rescue them, and in exchange you did not help me when I most needed you. The worst of it is that I was so sure we were in this together." He looks at me, gaze searing. "I trusted you, Jes! And then you did this to me."

"But I didn't expect to be running against you at the victory games. You have more experience and should have gone in a later trial. I didn't have time to prepare or think about us running against each other until I was out on the Fives court."

His brow wrinkles as he contemplates my words. The straightforward way he addresses me hits me all over again just like the first time this handsome Patron lord spoke to a girl like me as if we were equals.

"You're right. My uncle must have bribed the officials."

His considering tone melts my caution.

"Exactly! How can either you or I protect ourselves against a man who can bribe Fives officials and holy priests, when such bribery is against the law? Besides, I couldn't lose to you a second time. Everyone would have known I threw the trial to let you win."

With a snap he sets down the cup and our brief harmony winks out as quickly as a candle flame drenched in water.

"You've never thought I was good enough, have you, Jes? Even when you were encouraging me."

"You're a good adversary," I say stumblingly.

"But never as good as you, the one they are grooming to become a champion. I know what everyone thinks of me, why they'll never give me a true chance to show what I can do. I'm nothing more than a pleasant but overly friendly featherweight who can't be anything more than my uncle's puppet!"

A man clears his throat. "My lord, what you make of yourself is up to you," says a familiar voice.

Absorbed by our argument, neither of us has noticed a person enter from the front porch. The man wears a general's cape and carries a general's baton, but it is his air of command that compels the eye.

"F-Father?" I stammer, utterly taken aback by his arrival.

Kalliarkos is no better. Despite his being a prince and my father having started life as a baker's son from a provincial hill town in the kingdom of Saro-Urok, Kal flushes exactly as might an overawed fledgling just beginning his training for the Fives and suddenly being introduced to a famous and admired Illustrious, the champions of the game.

"General Esladas. I did not expect you to come to my pavilion."

"Lady Menoë asked me to personally request that you return to the festivities."

"And you obey my exalted sister as might an obedient dog, General?" Kalliarkos snaps.

I grimace, expecting a harsh reply, but Father shows no change of expression. His tone is remarkably mild. "My lord, you will become what others expect of you if that is what you believe of yourself." Father certainly has a gift for talking to angry young men that I utterly lack. "Or you may determine your own fate through your decisions and actions. As it seems my daughter has."

I stand to attention because I am a soldier's daughter and I have been caught out in a place my father told me never,

ever to go. He walks over to me and rests a hand on my shoulder. When he brushes his fingers along the damp coils of my hair, he notices how bits of my headscarf are wet and the rest is dry.

His eyes narrow. He has figured out how I got in.

"Lord Kalliarkos, if you wish to make an issue of your attendance at the festivities, then by all means refuse to return there. But if to be gossiped about is not what you seek, then I might humbly advise that you return, make an entrance with Lady Menoë, and walk one circuit of the pavilion."

The mention of Menoë reminds me of her meeting with her secret lover. "Father, I saw—"

"Silence, Jessamy. I'm not finished." Again he turns back to Kalliarkos. "Greet the guests and well-wishers who have come tonight to congratulate Garon Stable on its strong showing in the victory games and to celebrate your departure for the Eastern Reach and the war. Greet Prince Nikonos in the manner appropriate to two royal cousins meeting at a festive gathering. Afterward you can safely retire, having done your duty, and be left alone until morning. We sail at dawn."

Finally Father's gaze flashes to me. I have his eyes but otherwise few people would guess we are related. He is Saroese, a short, compactly built man with light golden-brown skin and straight black hair. I look more Efean, like my tall, beautiful mother with her tightly coiled black hair and dark brown skin.

"Meanwhile, with your permission, my lord, it is long past time for my daughter to leave Garon Palace and return to Garon Stable, where she belongs," he finishes.

For the first time since I have known him, Kalliarkos's lips curl in an imitation of a thin smile that reminds me of his uncle. "Do you not trust her with me, General?"

A tic disturbs Father's right eye, the signal that he is suppressing annoyance. "I would never doubt your honor, my lord. But you and I are expected elsewhere. War is a fickle business, and this may be my last chance to bid her farewell and offer some words of necessary fatherly advice. May I have a moment alone with Jessamy?"

As much as I love my father, I do not look forward to the scalding lecture he is about to give me the moment we are alone, but I will stand straight and take it, as a soldier does.

Kalliarkos's gaze flicks from me to my father's stern expression.

"No, I believe you may not speak to her privately, General. You and I will return to the victory party immediately. As for you, Spider"—Kalliarkos brusquely calls me by my Fives name—"you can wait out of sight until we are gone. Return to the stable as soon as no servants are about to see you. If they spot you they'll carry the tale to my uncle, and none of us want that."

He opens a double door that leads into a sparsely furnished

24

bedchamber strung with netting so night-biting insects do not bother the one who sleeps within. My skin flushes as I look at the bed. Kalliarkos pauses. Our gazes meet.

We made promises to each other. I see them in the blush shading his face, in the way his lips part as if he means to whisper that he still cares for me. Did he refuse my father permission to speak with me privately in order to spare me the scolding? Is he trying to help me?

My breathing quickens. My cheeks could not possibly burn any hotter.

Father clears his throat.

Kalliarkos hastily shuts the door, crosses to the other side of the room, and opens a door into an office with a desk and a shelf of scrolls. As soon as I step into the office, he shuts the door, closing me away from them. In darkness I breathe the air of a room where Kalliarkos has lived.

War is a fickle business, my father said. I may never see Kal again, and things are so broken and unresolved between us. A tear seeps from my eye and trickles down my cheek, but I scrub it ruthlessly away. Crying won't change anything. I have to stay focused, keep my head in the game.

The door to the entry opens and closes as they depart for the nearby festival pavilion. Even inside with the doors closed I hear the muted babble of a hundred merry voices filled to the brim with satisfaction and triumph. I will never belong in a gathering like theirs. I'm a Commoner, an outsider, someone who will always be excluded from the most exalted ranks.

I know what Father was going to say: *He's not meant for you, Jessamy. No prince of Saroese ancestry was ever meant for a girl like you.*

Maybe Kal and I were both foolish when we thought we could be together. Maybe we should never have kissed. But any way I turn it, I can't see that it was wrong except by the way other people measure what is right.

And isn't that exactly what Father said to Kal?

You may determine your own fate through your decisions and actions.

The memory of Father's voice jolts me into recalling that I never had the chance to tell him about Menoë. My father is smart enough to have heard the rumors about her first husband's death and to realize that his new wife cherishes no affection for him, but he can have no idea she is betraying him with another man. Her behavior dishonors their marriage and humiliates him. I could never forgive myself if something terrible happens to him on account of her backstabbing and treachery when I might have warned him.

I know I am supposed to leave the palace right now, that I can't get caught here. But Father and Kalliarkos sail at dawn. This is the last chance I'll have to alert Father to what is going on behind his back. And even though things are over between us, even though I know better, it's also my last chance to see Kalliarkos. Maybe he was trying to protect me from Father's anger.

There is one dangerous way I might enter the pavilion, if I dare to take the risk.

And I always dare.

3

In the dark room I straighten my formal parade clothing and check my hair to make sure nothing is out of place, everything neat and tidy, as an adversary training in a palace stable must be at all times. I am no longer a lowly Novice. Successful adversaries can walk anywhere in Efea and be greeted as victors, because if Patrons love anything, they love a winner. The crowd has cheered my name at the Royal Fives Court during the victory games; the king and queen themselves watched the new Challenger Spider defeat Lord Kalliarkos and two other experienced Novices.

That makes me someone. I just need a plausible excuse.

I open the door and walk into the chamber as the startled servants gape at seeing a person like me in a place like this.

"Escort me to the festival pavilion, if you please. Is it not the usual custom to celebrate an adversary's victory with a public display of the winnings I earned for the palace today?"

By walking right past them I make it out the door onto the entry porch before they shake out of their shock. I pretend not to hear them call after me as I clatter noisily down the steps, making no effort at stealth now that I am charging into a party I am forbidden to attend.

The festival pavilion has no walls, only carved pillars that support the roof and eaves, painted with the horned and winged fire dog that is the emblem of Garon Palace. A rousing rush of chatter teases my ear, and the bright clothing of beautifully dressed highborn Patrons catches my eye as I approach down a side path between shrubs of white jasmine and stalks of purple betony. The women wear long sheath gowns glittering with embroidery of silver and gold thread. The braids and loops of their long black hair have been built up into fashionable tiers from which dangle strings of pearls and glass beads. The men wear the long formal wrap skirt, and formal vests of fine silk.

The noisy rumble of talk stills. People turn toward the shadows where I approach. But they aren't looking at me.

Wearing a sullen frown that seems wrong on his once always-smiling face, Kalliarkos steps into the light beside his sister. She has repaired her hair to display a cascade of silver ribbons and changed her gown to an undyed silk so simple in its line, and so ostentatiously unadorned with embroidery, that she makes all the other women look pretentious. My father stands near them, hands clasped behind his back, his expression as blank as if he has no thoughts at all.

Menoë's tinkling laugh sparks above the silence.

"Are you guests all still here? Come to bid Kal good-bye as he marches off to war?" Her derisive tone carries easily over the expectant audience, which is no doubt hoping for a scandal or at the very least something scrumptious to gossip about tomorrow. "Here he is! I have brought my darling brother to receive your accolades and good wishes. I am *sure* that with my brilliant husband, General Esladas, to guide him he will prove to be a mighty warrior and a dazzling strategist."

Kalliarkos stares straight ahead. Father steps up beside him and, with the easy patience of a man who has outlasted battles far more brutal than this weak mockery, he beckons to a servant to bring gold goblets for brother and sister. These contain the nectar that only the nobly born are allowed to drink. For himself he snags an ordinary glass goblet filled with cloudy-white palm wine and raises it in the traditional salute of military men.

"Under the eyes of the three gods who shower fecundity, martial prowess, and justice upon our ventures, let sister and brother prosper as Efea prospers. May all the undertakings of Garon Palace and its noble patroness, Princess Berenise, bloom as fields after the spring flood. Let my sponsor, Lord Gargaron, stand high among the lords of the land as he sends his precious nephew to the Eastern Reach to battle our implacable enemies, this unprecedented alliance between the kings of East Saro, West Saro, and Saro-Urok."

His audience enthusiastically hisses and stomps to show its hatred. When the noise dies down, Father goes on.

"May the gods judge these kings who once kept faith with our rulers and have now turned treacherously against us."

The gathered Patrons salute with the required response: "As the gods will it, so will it be."

They drain their cups.

A man dressed all in gold—the color of the royal palace—steps out of the crowd with a laugh. He is Prince Nikonos, the popular younger brother of the unpopular king and queen, and a soldier like my father. Because of his exalted rank he leads the Royal Army of Efea on behalf of his siblings.

He raises a golden cup. "To the glory of Lord Kalliarkos and his military career!"

A wave of dizzy revelation overtakes me. His distinctive, rich voice is that of the man who was embracing Menoë earlier in the garden.

"Dear cousin Kal, may your trials in battle end better than your trial at the Royal Fives Court today."

The taunting words fall like hot spikes, and the Patrons go so still that I can hear every scrape of a sandal on the marble floor. People look at Kalliarkos, wondering how he can possibly answer this blatant ridicule delivered by a prince pretending to chuckle as at a shared jest. Kal's cheeks redden under the assault. Even Father looks stymied. He cannot cross weapons with his commanding officer.

Fury boils up so strongly it sweeps me forward. I stride into the pavilion with the confidence of a victorious adversary, pulling all eyes away from Kal's embarrassment. Servants and highborn folk alike make way, for they cannot help but goggle at the brawny Efean girl who dares to walk in their midst. Kal goes even more red as the Patrons murmur with glee, sensing disaster or maybe an ugly fall as on the Fives court.

"Isn't that the adversary Spider who defeated Lord Kalliarkos today?"

"Look how tall she is!"

"She vaulted from Novice to Challenger in one trial, and gave Garon Stable something to brag about after all this time as the least victorious palace!"

"Did you see her flair and timing? She'll be an Illustrious someday, mark my words."

A man cuts in front of me and halts me with his thin smile alone. He extends a hand and I take an instinctive step away as from a scorpion, but Lord Gargaron never intended to touch a person like me. He gestures like an orator, demanding the crowd's attention.

"So! I have summoned my newest Challenger, whom you all know as Spider. I am sure you saw her triumph this morning at the victory games at the Royal Fives Court. Take a good look now, and start placing your wagers, because I predict she will rise from Challenger to Illustrious faster than any adversary before her." His gaze snaps to me like fire to tinder, offering no mercy and plenty of punishment. "As long as she does not fall and break her neck with those unexpected spins she uses."

I stand my ground, but it isn't easy not to run. This is the man who buried my family alive in a tomb so that Father could never find them. If he discovers that Kal and I rescued them, he'll not rest until we are all dead. What if my deeds are somehow written on my face?

My expression stays a mask. I wait for the whip to fall.

"Let the adversary known as Spider kneel before Princess Berenise and accept a share of the winnings she has earned with her victory today. A pretty stack of coin, as you can imagine, for the king and queen shower rewards on those they favor and scourge those who anger them, do they not?"

Kalliarkos's grandmother sits on a couch lavishly embroidered with vines and butterflies. The gold fabric of her gown proclaims her royal blood. Her hands are folded on her lap to display long nails painted in alternating red and orange. With a *tap-tap-tap* of her cane, she beckons.

But when Kal walks over to stand behind the couch, I hesitate.

"Spider!" Lord Gargaron's caustic tone hits like a slap. "You cannot wish to insult Princess Berenise by refusing her summons, can you?"

I approach cautiously. She has the look of a person who has just opened a treasure chest and isn't sure if the contents are precious or merely trash. Although she is a tiny woman, the weight of her regard presses me down to my knees before her. What she thinks of me I cannot guess as she measures me from the top of my scarf-covered head to the puddle of my jacket's skirts on the floor around me. Even kneeling, I do not have to look up very far to meet her eyes, and then I realize I ought not to look such an exalted person in the face at all so I look away.

My glance falls again on Kalliarkos in time to catch him suppressing a smile, eyes crinkling as if he is inexplicably pleased by the meeting. I instantly know that he is remembering a joke he made comparing my ambition to that of his formidable grandmother.

For an instant or forever I can't hear, as joy roars like wind through my flesh. However angry he is, I'm sure he doesn't quite hate me. If I am putting this all behind me, then I shouldn't care.

But, oh, I do care. I do.

"Spider," says the old princess. I must wrench my attention back to her, for to snub her would be the stupidest thing I could do. "You have brought distinction on Garon Stable by leaping from Novice to Challenger in your first trial. I am pleased to present you with a full half share of the winnings."

The gathered Patrons gasp at this shocking generosity, since usually only Illustrious receive a half share while lesser adversaries—Challengers and Novices—are glad to accept a quarter or tenth share respectively.

"The coin will be delivered to your trainers tomorrow. It is my recommendation as a businesswoman of some renown that you immediately deposit it in the Queen's Bank for safekeeping."

A general laugh greets this unexceptional statement, which of course is not advice but rather a command I can't disobey. Her brilliant gaze flashes to Kal with a warning, for he is staring at me. I sense a light in his face that makes me tremble. Surely he knows my feelings for him haven't changed.

She pitches her voice so that everyone can hear. "You were given your chance at the Fives as I promised, Kalliarkos. Now the gods will it that you take your turn with the army, like your noble and courageous father before you."

He stiffens, shoulders tight, aware of the people watching and listening and judging.

"I wasn't given a fair chance! I needed more time to train, like all real adversaries get," he retorts in the voice of a spoiled lordling, exactly the sort of behavior I would have expected from a young man like Kalliarkos before I actually got to know him. Now his tone makes me cringe.

"Don't be childish, Kal," she replies. To my horror, she turns to me. "What do you say, Spider? Would more training make a difference in my grandson's prospects as a competitive adversary?"

I did not expect this deadly spin of the Rings—using me against him—but I won't be bullied. "Of course more training makes a difference to any adversary's chances in competition, Exalted Lady."

Implacable, she goes on. "You didn't answer my question, Spider. Only truth serves a prince. Else you are nothing more than a flattering courtier seeking preference and favor with false honey. Can he defeat you on the court? Yes, or no?"

"No," I murmur in the hope only she will hear.

But everyone hears. Kalliarkos holds his ground, jaw rigid, chin high. Around us people cover their mouths to hide smiles and laughter as mortification deadens his face.

I wish my tongue had fallen out of my mouth before I was compelled to speak.

Lord Gargaron runs his lord's whip through his fingers as he considers me kneeling on the hard floor.

"Here stand father and daughter under a roof where neither could ever have hoped to walk," he says in a voice that flows as smoothly as oil. "Learn from their example, Kal."

"What do you mean?" Kalliarkos glances from me to his uncle as if he is finally seeing the chain that links Gargaron to me.

"She cleverly used you to gain the attention of people who would not have looked at her otherwise. Now the whole city knows her name, just as General Esladas has reached the pinnacle of a distinguished military career, the only lowborn general in the Royal Army. You would do well to emulate father and daughter's bold and cunning maneuvers. They have climbed the ladder of ambition without regard to what—*or whom*—they had to leave behind on their way up the victory tower."

Shame burns in my heart as Kalliarkos studies the gold victor's ribbon tied to my jacket, the most visible mark of my newfound success.

"Is that why you did it, Jessamy?" he asks in a low, hoarse voice.

"Of course not! I told you why!"

Lord Gargaron presses the whip to my cheek, the lash flicking against my mouth to sting me to silence. Kalliarkos sucks in a shocked breath. Father takes an abrupt step toward me.

"General, the tide turns at dawn," says Gargaron with a brusque nod that stops Father in his tracks. "You and my nephew must be on the ship."

"If I may be permitted one last word with my daughter, my lord."

"No, you may not. It is time for you and Kalliarkos to leave. Efea is in mortal danger, however peaceful it may seem to us here in the royal city where life goes on as usual. War does not wait."

Emotion shudders through Kal's body as he struggles to accept his uncle's pitiless words. He looks at his grandmother but she nods with cold finality, sealing his fate. At last he walks away, not looking back, just as I did not look back on the Fives court.

Father meets my gaze. All my life, every time he left home to go to the wars, I've known each farewell might be our last. I nod to let him know that I will fulfill my obligations, strive to excel, and protect my family. He nods back and follows Kalliarkos, two men headed for the dangers of an unpredictable war.

As I rise to follow, two guards step up on either side to block my path. Lord Gargaron has anticipated me.

Truth is the most brutal defeat of all.

This morning I thought I would be part of Kalliarkos's life, that we would be together. I was so sure.

I was so wrong.

And now he is gone.

Lord Gargaron taps me with the whip. I am almost as tall as he is, but I feel small when he presses the hard leather knot up under my chin into my throat.

"What precisely you thought to accomplish by entering palace grounds that you are expressly forbidden from, I do not know, but do not pretend you came here to collect your winnings." His whisper scalds terror right down to my bones. "You do him no favors by stoking a fire whose flames can only distract him when he marches into battle, as he will soon. He and your lauded father are leaving to fight, Jessamy. Never before in the history of Efea have the three old Saro kingdoms combined against us. If your father cannot defeat the invaders, then all Efea loses. If he does not win, he dies. If our army does not win, Kalliarkos dies. Is that what you want?"

"Of course not, my lord." I dare not look away from his flat stare.

He adjusts the whip to prod so painfully that I can barely breathe. "Reflect on their urgent situation as you consider your own. You remain an adversary in Garon Stable on my sufferance. I have a great deal of prestige and money riding on your ability to make a swift climb up the Fives rankings and bring glory and applause to Garon Palace. The day you stop winning I will have my stewards send you to the mines where we send criminals to die in the bowels of the earth. Do you understand me, Jessamy? Win, or die."

Whatever hatred boils in my heart, there is only one answer I can give.

"Yes, my lord."

4

After the blare of the trumpet announces dawn, the adversaries of Garon Stable line up on the training ground for our morning practice. Trainees so inexperienced they have not yet run in public trials are called fledglings; they stand in the back ranks. Novices are the lowest of the three ranks of competing adversaries. They take their places in the second row, lined up in order of their number of victories. Out of respect they leave an empty space where Kalliarkos used to stand. Two days ago I stood at the end of their line because I was the newest and least experienced Novice, but after yesterday's victory I am not sure where I belong.

Still, when my friends Mis and Dusty and Gira and Shorty nod encouragingly at me, I take my old place with them.

Dusty punches me on the shoulder.

Gira elbows me. "You're looking taller today, like having a famous name stretched you out."

Shorty falls in with the needling: "You need to work on your grip strength before you start getting cocky, Spider."

I force my lips up in an answering grin because I am happy to be with them, I truly am, and I don't want them to think otherwise. But I can't rid my mind of the vision of Kal's rigid back as he walked away. His grandmother knew exactly how to trap me into saying the one thing that would hurt him most.

Mis squeezes my hand as if she guesses what a turmoil my thoughts are in, and gratefully I squeeze back.

In the front row stand Challengers—Garon Stable only has four—and our sole Illustrious, Lord Thynos, who happens to be Kalliarkos's actual uncle, unlike Gargaron, who is related to Kal through Princess Berenise's marriage.

Our trainers, Darios and Tana, walk up and down the ranks, looking us over.

"Garon Stable had a good showing in the victory games yesterday," says Darios. The old Patron man has spent his whole life involved in the Fives; what he does not know about trials and obstacles and Fives strategy could fit into a drinking cup. "Lord Thynos managed a solid finish, coming in second at his Illustrious trial. His strong performance gilds Garon Palace's status at the Royal Court. As you naturally recall, our own Spider won the first Novice trial of the day."

The others stamp their feet amid whistles and cheers. I try

to keep my face expressionless but I can't help but bask in their approval like a lizard in the sun. So gratifying!

Darios goes on. "By doing so she brings glory and honor to Garon Palace. As is customary, any Novice who wins a Novice trial at the Royal Fives Court immediately jumps to Challenger status even if she doesn't yet have the ten victories usually required. Therefore, Spider, move forward to the front rank."

Mis elbows me, and Dusty punches me on the shoulder again. All the impressed fledglings stamp enthusiastically a second time, for the newest trainees surely hope they will make such a sudden mark on the Fives as I have. Only one person in the fledgling ranks stares grimly straight ahead: the young woman named Talon. With her pale skin and straight black hair bound up in a topknot, she is the only girl of pure Patron ancestry I have ever seen training for the Fives.

I take in a deep breath and walk forward. I am acquainted with Lord Thynos, of course. He has taken an interest in me because of my skill, and he also risked his life and his reputation to help Kalliarkos and me rescue my mother and sisters from the oracle's tomb. He's not my friend, but I think I can count him as an ally, someone who will help me find Bettany.

Darios goes on in a solemn voice. "As you all know, Lord Kalliarkos has left our ranks."

Everyone glances at me, then away.

"Duty has called him to the defense of Efea against our most bitter foes, the armies of our ancient enemies from old

Saro who have attacked our eastern borderlands. Let us offer a prayer. To Lord Seon, the Sun of Justice, that the gods' will shall prevail. To Lord Judge Inkos, that the worthy receive their just reward. To Lady Hayiyin, Mistress of the Sea, that the wind and the waters favor the righteous."

We answer in response: "The gods' will shall prevail. The just shall receive their reward. The gods favor the righteous. As the gods will it, so will it be."

But a dark fear washes through me. What if the gods will it that our army loses? What help can our prayers be then? Father always said to pray to the gods only after making sure all your preparations are sufficient to the task.

What if the gods will it that *I* lose? To protect my family I have to win because they need all the money I can funnel to them. To win I have to prepare. I have to keep my head in the game because the moment I lose focus I will be crushed.

Darios leads the entire stable of adversaries in the long warm-up known as menageries, a sequence of moves designed to make stronger and more flexible all parts of the body. It flows from one animal to the next: cat, ibis, elephant, snake, dog, falcon, bull, wasp, jackal, butterfly…

The butterfly is a soul given substance. I think of my mother. What if she isn't recovering from the terrible events we barely survived? What if she is dying and I'm not there to help her?

"Spider!" A baton whacks my rear end hard enough to

jerk my attention back to the training court. The other trainer, Tana, wags the stump of her missing left hand in my face. "Keep your mind on the court."

I wrench my thoughts back to the pavement on which I'm standing. We have finished the menageries while my mind wandered. All the other adversaries have gone to take a mug of water while I stand here staring at nothing.

"I'm ready," I say.

"Are you?" Tana is Efean, and although Darios is Patron-born and thus her social superior, she runs Garon Stable because she trained Lord Thynos from fledgling to Illustrious. In the Fives all that matters is skill and victory. Not even a prince can defeat a lowly person with no legal standing, one like me, if he isn't actually better. "You may think it an honor to jump from Novice to Challenger so quickly, but in truth you've just made things harder for yourself."

"I understand."

"I'm not sure you do." The disapproving angle of her mouth reproaches me.

I go to the dining shelter, drink chicken broth for strength, and afterward take my place beside Lord Thynos on the training ground. The four Challengers with us are all Efean men, but I know only Inarsis, a strong, confident man of my father's age who used to be a soldier. He is Lord Thynos's closest friend, as odd as it may seem to see a highborn Patron lord and a Commoner act as equals.

Tana trots over to us. "Lord Thynos, if you would, please pace the six of you through several warm-up runs on the Fives court. After I've run the fledglings through drills I'll be doing specific exercises with Spider." She pauses to frown at me, making sure I am listening. "She's not ready to compete at Challenger level. She won yesterday only because the Royal Fives Court was configured in a way that emphasized her skills and gave her an advantage."

Lord Thynos and Inarsis glance at each other as people do who know each other well. Neither looks surprised. The other three Challengers, listening in, don't look surprised either.

"I'm ready to run at Challenger rank," I blurt out, because it infuriates me they think I'm not. Because I'm pretty sure Lord Gargaron *did* illegally interfere with the trial, and the idea that I was given an unfair advantage makes me even angrier.

"We shall see." Lord Thynos leads us to the practice court as if we are a squad of soldiers following him into a skirmish. "Spider, you start at Trees. Nar, on Pillars. Pythias, you start at Traps. I'll begin at Rivers. Gelos, give the start signal. Sotades, you turn the water clock."

In the game of Fives, four competitors called adversaries race through a Fives court, made up of five obstacles called Pillars, Traps, Trees, Rivers, and Rings. The first to climb the victory tower and snatch the victor's ribbon at the top becomes the winner.

I trot around the exterior fence of the practice area and

chalk my hands at the gate. The court is divided into four quarters, each with its mandated obstacle: the maze of Pillars, the balance skills combined with the pitfalls of Traps, the climbing posts of Trees, and the moving steps of Rivers. In the center Rings awaits, a cunning and complicated mesh of the other four. The configuration of each obstacle changes with every trial, so you can never learn an obstacle by rote. Each time, you have to figure out what kind of variation has been set up, and what will work best to complete it quickly. I'm strongest on Rings and Traps and weakest on Trees, which is why Thynos has started me here: to rub in my face that I've jumped up the adversaries' ladder too quickly.

I'll show them I've not been given something I don't deserve.

Yet as I stand before the entry gate with its canvas flap hiding the obstacle beyond, I remember how Kal would glance at me during training and smile invitingly....

The *shweet! shweet!* of a whistle jolts me.

This is where I belong now, not wallowing in wishful thinking about a boy I can never have.

I push past the flap and immediately see that the posts in Trees have been configured into jumping ladders, rope climbs, and a sloped wall with movable pegs, tests that emphasize upper body strength. Most experienced male adversaries will beat me on Trees, but the Fives court includes such a blend of obstacles that physical strength alone won't give you victory, much less move you from Novice rank to Challenger. The best adversaries need strength, speed, explosiveness, balance, acrobatic ability, intelligence, pattern-marking, and a sense of rhythm, as well as a head for tactics and an absolute willingness to take chances in a decisive manner.

By the time I complete Trees by reaching the resting platform, I see that Thynos, Inarsis, and Pythias are already on to their second obstacle. After they complete their first obstacle, adversaries decide in which direction to continue. Now that I'm done with Trees, I can head into Traps or Rivers next. All I need to do is defeat one of my competitors to prove myself worthy of being called Challenger. I can't defeat Thynos, not yet, and Pythias has entered Trees behind me, so I run to the entrance to Traps and go after Inarsis because he's older, and as far as I know he's not competed since he left the army.

Traps includes balance beams, rope walks, tipping rope bridges, gaps to leap across, and always one "trap" that you have to figure out and negotiate properly or you'll lose time going back to the beginning. There are two paths you can choose between: the longer "low road" is straightforward but takes time, while the "high road" offers a shorter but riskier route because you'll fall farther and thus hurt or even kill yourself. When taking the high road in practice, everyone trains with pads and spotters beneath to catch falls.

Because we are running a warm-up Inarsis takes the low road, as I should. The trainers haven't yet laid out the pads for advanced training, and there is no one to spot me. But I climb straight up to the high beams and ropes. I relax my way across the slack rope, sinking into my center, the wide strip of cloth pressed hard against the soles of my feet. I'm way up here with nothing to catch me if I fall, and it feels like flying, sun on my hair and the heavens wide above. My smile is as big as the sky because the thrill of challenge chases all heavy thoughts out of my head.

I step easily off the slack rope and spring up to the highest beam. From way up here, three times my height to the ground, I can look all around the Fives court: Thynos has already finished Pillars and is entering Traps behind me. Pythias is almost done with Trees. Over on the basic equipment where Tana is working with the fledglings, she has stopped to stare.

At me.

Keep your head in the court, I remind myself.

When I glance down, I see Inarsis below me, clambering upside down along a fisherman's net. He can see right up to where I stand poised on a beam no wider than my hand. There's a gap between the end of this beam and a landing platform. It's a dangerous jump, the thing I'm best at.

I wait for him to finish the net because his next test is crossing on a tensioned rope. Catching his eye, I grin an assertive challenge. Then I swiftly calculate distance and arc, take six steps for impetus, and launch as I pick a focus point on a stationary object. This is the moment: the vertical leap, the tuck into an airborne somersault, the moment I open up and hit one foot in front of the other, eyes still on my targeting spot. My landing comes unbalanced, tipping into a slightly off-kilter crouch. I have to touch fingers to the platform to brace myself, but it's not bad for the first spin of the morning, a trick many Challengers would never try at this height even in competition.

Best of all, my leap disturbs Inarsis's concentration. He wobbles on the rope, loses his balance, and drops the arm's-length distance to the ground. Cursing, he turns to head back to the gate to start over.

I call down the traditional Fives taunt. "Kiss off, Adversary."

He flashes the kiss-off hand-sign over his shoulder and adds an even ruder flourish.

No time to rest. I get out of Traps before Thynos passes me, but he is gaining. In a real competition the losing adversaries stop as soon as the victor grabs the ribbon but in training we keep going to measure ourselves against the lines on the water clock. After scrambling through Pillars, Rivers, and Rings I arrive to the victory tower third, after Thynos and Pythias, and lean panting against the rungs as Inarsis trots up behind me in last place.

"Well played." He eyes me with the look of a soldier checking out an opponent's weapon. "You rattled me. It won't happen again."

Just as I open my mouth to reply, Lord Thynos rests a fist on my shoulder. "That was idiotic, Spider. Don't ever take the high path in warm-ups."

Tana One-Hand stalks up, looking ready to spit. "Spider! Haven't Darios and I made it clear we only train on the high equipment when the ground is fitted out with padding, nets, and spotters?"

"I don't like to lose."

"If you stupidly injure yourself in practice, you can't win. I'm pulling you out to work with Talon on the horizontal ladder."

"Let Inarsis supervise the two girls," commands Thynos.

Tana nods agreement. She may be head trainer, but Thynos is a highborn Patron lord so she has to obey.

I follow Inarsis out on one of the covered trails that cut between the obstacles. In a low voice he says, "I hear you barged into the festival pavilion last night. Don't try anything like that again. Do you understand?"

If he were my father I would accept the rebuke, but he isn't. "I thought Princess Berenise hired you to protect Lord Kalliarkos. Why didn't you sail with him and my father to the Eastern Reach?"

He doesn't even blink. "Because the Royal Army does not allow Efeans to serve as officers."

"You hold the rank of general."

"Yes, but as I explained to you before, it was only a battle-field promotion they had to give me after I personally killed the king of Saro-Urok and led the army to victory when all the Patron officers were dead or disabled. Never forget how quickly I was discharged and replaced by inexperienced Patrons. The Royal Army includes but a single regiment of Efean men allowed to serve only as lowly foot soldiers, little better than servants. We Efeans will always be nothing more than Commoners to the Patrons who rule us. You'd do well to remember that instead of having stars in your eyes about certain young men."

Does everyone feel obliged to admonish me about Kalliarkos? I push back.

"You're awfully good friends with Lord Thynos considering he is as nobly born a Patron as anyone. And you're more of a Commoner than I am!"

He yanks me around to face him. He has a hatch-work of scars along the right side of his face, although I'm not sure if the injury is a legacy of battle or a whipping.

"You may be the daughter of the lauded General Esladas, you may have charmed the crowd with your victory yesterday, but when the Patrons whose speech you parrot look at you they do not see the daughter of an honorable Saroese man but rather a bastard daughter of Efea."

How dare he scold me! He's not better than me. "I can become an Illustrious, if I win."

"Your presence on the Fives court proves my point exactly. No proper Patron girl would ever run the Fives, and certainly never compete."

Off to one side, Talon works hand over hand on the

horizontal training ladder, building up arm and back and grip strength while allowing her injured ankle to rest.

I tilt my head toward her. "Why is she here then?"

"That's none of your business. Now, listen closely. Stay out of Lord Gargaron's way. If he hears even a whisper of rumor that your family escaped the tomb, he will not rest until he finds your mother and kills her. After that he will hunt down whoever rescued them and turn all of us—you, me, Lord Thynos, and even Lord Kalliarkos—over to the High Priest, who will execute us."

"I know that!"

"No, you do not. Had you known it, you would not have entered Garon Palace last night in pursuit of a prince who stands far out of your reach. He's not for the likes of you, Spider." He pauses to let the jab sink in. From the court a whistle blows to begin a new practice trial for Thynos and the other Challengers. "You and I are going to have a little race to remind you that you're not as good as you think you are. Now!" He barks his order like an officer. "Five circuits of the horizontal ladder!"

Before I realize I mean to respond I slap my chest twice in the signal our father taught his girls, the same signal he teaches his soldiers to indicate "I hear and obey."

Inarsis's gaze softens with a glimmer of amusement.

By the time I finish five circuits up and back along the horizontal rungs, the sideways rungs, the twisting rungs, the tipping rungs, and the walking poles, Inarsis has passed me twice simply by climbing around me. He's so strong he makes it look easy while I sweat and grunt. All the while Talon sits on a bench with her injured ankle elevated, watching us with an unreadable look on her beautiful face as one of Darios's assistants applies moist seaweed wraps.

When I finally drop down, huffing and puffing, Inarsis taps my shoulder. "Go again, Spider. Five more circuits. Don't touch the ground."

I make it to three before I have to pause on the rungs and hang by my knees to rest while pounding on my spasming forearms with my fists. My knuckles throb, and I can barely open and close my hands.

Upside down to my eyes, Thynos and Inarsis walk up to me, standing one on either side as I flip down to the ground between them. I brace myself for criticism that I've earned for not finishing the second round of circuits. But that's not what I hear.

"By the way, I saw your mother last night. She's weak but improving," says Inarsis in a low voice.

A wave of relief crashes through me, succeeded immediately by a burst of frantic energy. "I'll sneak out to see her this coming Rest Day."

"No, you won't," says Thynos. "Because of your rash behavior last night, Gar has assigned stewards to watch your every move out of the compound. You must stay away from your family."

"I can't! I have to give my prize money to Mother."

Thynos shakes his head. "Didn't you understand what Princess Berenise said? The gold will be delivered this afternoon to Darios as a courtesy, but in fact it will be placed in a holding account for you. That way the princess and Lord Gargaron will be able to keep track of exactly how much of your winnings you are spending. If you draw out too much they'll know something suspicious is going on."

"Of course I won't take it to my mother all at once! I'll pretend I'm spending money on myself and slip a small amount to her every week."

"Impossible." Thynos makes a gesture toward the horizontal ladder so that anyone watching us will think we're discussing the Fives. "We simply cannot risk you going to see them until after Gar leaves town to make his usual yearly circuit of the Garon estates."

"When will that be?"

"In three months."

"I can't wait three months. What if she needs money now? Besides that, the Garon stewards took my twin sister, Bettany, together with the household servants. I have to find her."

"No, you don't." Thynos's tone makes me uneasy. "I forbid you from visiting your family, Spider. We can't risk Gar finding out, because we will all die if he does. Inarsis and I will deal with your family and household. You will stay put here. Do you understand?"

I want to clench my hands in frustration but they're so stiff and painful. "Yes."

Thynos nods and says, more loudly than he needs to, "Don't start at a dead hang. Keep your arms bent."

"But I did!" I protest.

"Did I give you permission to speak, Spider?"

He breaks off as a steward dressed in the gold and purple of Princess Berenise's personal household approaches. The woman hands him a folded and sealed square of papyrus, which Thynos opens and reads. His brow wrinkles. His eyes crease as his mouth turns down in a frown.

"What's wrong?" Inarsis rests a hand on Thynos's forearm.

Thynos scratches an eyebrow. "I don't know if anything is wrong. It's just odd. Princess Berenise wants to see me immediately. She never summons me this urgently."

He strides away with the steward, leaving Inarsis and me behind in a harsh reminder that palace business has nothing to do with the likes of us.

"Finish the set, Spider," Inarsis says.

By the time I stagger into the dining shelter for the midday meal my body might as well be a bag of wheat punched so many times the seams have begun to split and the grain to spill. I gulp down water, then grab my tray of food and drop on the bench beside Mis and opposite Gira and Shorty. Talon sits at the other end of the table, with us but apart from us. I'm so exhausted I can't decide whether I'm starving or no longer hungry, but the stewed chicken, millet, and greens taste better and better with each bite.

"They forgot to tell you that Challengers have to train twice as hard as Novices," says Shorty with a laugh.

When the bell rings for the afternoon break, I wash with the other women, go to my cubicle, and lie down on my cot. After all that time gripping bars my hands feel like they've been pulled apart and sewn back together.

But pain has never bothered me. I can work through pain to get to the victory tower. Every way I turn these Rings I see the same thing. Feigning obedience is the only strategy that will allow a person as powerless as I am to build a base from which I can eventually launch my own attack against the man who destroyed my family. As long as he can harm us, we'll never live in peace.

The canvas curtain that separates my cubicle from the corridor ripples.

Mis sits on the end of my cot and pats my knees. "Is Lord Thynos riding you? I thought Garon Palace would be happy to have someone win the glory you did yesterday, but sometimes people get envious if they feel their toes are being stepped on."

"They just want me to do well. I don't mind. I want to train hard."

She chuckles. "I've never met anyone so fixed on one thing as you, Jes. Have you told your family yet? I guess your father already knows. Are you going to see your mother and tell her the news?"

Lord Gargaron has torn from me even the simplest act of trust. None of my new friends know that my mother is supposed to be dead in a tomb, and they can never know. But I can't talk about her being alive either. My mouth is stopped up with all the words I dare not say, like I'm choking on pebbles.

"You miss her, don't you? You're homesick." In her sad smile I see the kind heart of a decent person.

She leaves.

If I could rub the ache of anxiety out of my heart I would, but I can't know for sure my mother is healing until I've seen her for myself, which means sneaking out to see her. And no matter what Thynos says, he and Inarsis have no reason to care about Bettany and our household servants. Whatever emergency called him to Princess Berenise has probably scoured Bett from his exalted highborn mind.

I can't confide in my friends without compromising their and my family's safety. Both Father and Kalliarkos are gone, and Thynos and Inarsis have cut me out.

The only person I can rely on is myself.

5

On the evening of Sixthday, also known as Rest Day Eve, Mis, Gira, Shorty, and I gather to walk down to the Lantern District to see a play. Last time we four did this I left them to meet Kalliarkos and rescue my family. Now I have to figure out a new way to slip away from my friends without making them suspicious.

As we leave the gate I nod politely to the guards, and they grin back. "Don't drink too much, Spider! You need to keep your legs under you for your next victory!"

"Don't let it go to your head," says Gira as we stroll down the King's Hill.

"Don't worry. I won't let it go to my head until I become an Illustrious."

We all laugh.

The setting sun spills gold across the sea. Boats bobbing atop the quiet waters fade into twilight and flicker like spark-bugs as sailors hang lamps from their prows. The main avenues of the city flare lamp by lamp into life as the queen's royal lamplighters kindle the night-lanterns.

On Rest Day Eve all the theaters run evening performances. It's the most crowded night of the week, but with the bulk of the king's army having marched east, fewer people than normal pass under the West Gate of the Lantern District. We have plenty of room to walk along the district's streets hung with colorful banners advertising the plays on offer this month. Just as I had hoped, there is enough time for us to shop along a lane of clothing stalls, where I buy an inexpensive ankle-length linen dress in the sleeveless, straight cut that has always been the fashion in Efea.

"Why do you keep looking back?" Mis asks as we stand at a food stall stuffing ourselves on a Patron delicacy of fresh pancakes wrapped around a paste of chopped almonds, dates, and cinnamon.

Fortunately my mouth is too full of the sweet, hot filling to reply, because I have spotted two men wearing the Garon Palace badge depicting a horned and winged fire dog. Although they don't seem to be paying attention to us, I am sure they are following. We are easy to spot: Commoner girls wearing long sleeveless jackets that mark us as members of a palace household. We also wear the fire dog badge to indicate our affiliation.

A group of Patron men I've never seen before approaches, and we four stiffen, wondering if they mean to offer an affront.

The eldest steps forward as the others whisper at his back. He has the muscular arms of a laborer but wears his hair long and bound up atop his head in the style of old Saro. He even speaks Saroese with the accent of old Saro, not the way Patron folk who have grown up here in Efea speak it. "Are you that one called Spider, who won the first trial at the Royal Fives Court in the victory games?"

I swallow. "I am."

He nods at his companions, and they give me the kiss-off gesture familiar to every person who runs or watches the Fives. Here on the street it can be a mortal insult, or a sign of respect.

"Well run, Adversary," he says. "You're one to watch with those spins and flairs. We'll be cheering for you."

He pays for all our pancakes, and they go off without asking a thing in return.

Gira whistles under her breath, Mis giggles, and Shorty shakes her head. The Patron woman cooking the pancakes offers us a second round at half price because the exchange has drawn attention to her stall.

We are still licking our fingers when we reach a theater entrance spanned by a banner painted with an overflowing cornucopia and the title of its play: *The Cupbearer's Calamitous Contract*. We pay our coins for the entry fee and a folded banana leaf filled with roasted chickpeas to keep us fed during the long play. Tonight, even with soldiers and mercenaries gone, Patrons pack their sections. Some spill over to sit in the tiers assigned to Commoners, who have to give way. Patrons love this popular comedy about the deified Serenissima the Third, called the Benevolent, and how her kindly but often misunderstood interventions help her frazzled royal cupbearer set to rights his disordered household.

Commoners aren't as fond of the play. Mother refused to allow Father to take our family to see it and explained why in a gentle tone that left him speechless and us girls open-mouthed. Part of me wants to see the infamous scene, played for laughs, in which the cupbearer keeps comically forgetting which of his Efean servants he has just chastised so ends up whipping all of them multiple times, but I've already made my plan. As the actors launch into the traditional introductory hymn, sung after the opening acrobatics, I'll excuse myself to go find a toilet. The play runs so long that I should be able to race through the city to the West Harbor District, check on my mother, and get back in time for the final hymn in praise of our current rulers, Kliatemnos the Fifth and Serenissima the Fifth. The pancakes make a perfect excuse: I'll say the rich fare upset my stomach.

Stagehands carry out the many lanterns that light the stage, while we sit in dimness illuminated by just enough light to mark stairs and tiers. Attending a play at night, with stars glittering above and oil lamps burning below, casts a glamour over the tales told before us, making them seem bolder and more vivid than our own lives.

Horns toot a fanfare as acrobats flip onto the stage in advance of the actors. Two tiers down a few latecomers arrive to annoyed murmurs. Despite the gloom I recognize a tall, muscular young man by his shorn head and surly grimace.

Ro-emnu! The Efean poet jailed for writing a scurrilous play that, the censors claimed, murdered the reputation of the royal family. He helped Kal and me rescue my family from Lord Ottonor's tomb, but then he kidnapped Ottonor's holy oracle and abandoned the rest of us beneath the City of the Dead with no light and no way out. I haven't seen him since.

A jolt of anger energizes me. I leap to my feet and shove my way past seated spectators just as Ro-emnu and his three friends bolt down the stairs and bound up onto the proscenium. He turns to face the startled audience, arms outstretched, as his companions run to the curtained entrances to block any actors who might try to come out onto the stage and interrupt him.

In an alarmingly powerful voice he shouts:

With what dull minds do you seat yourselves to hear these lies?
Friends! Do not listen to false tales fed you with your mother's milk.
Hear my words! There will come a day when truth will bloom,
Not this pestilent flower whose venom has infected your very blood.
Benevolent, do they call the queen named Serenissima the Third?
She killed her father and her brother and her brother's infant son!

All this she did so that her weak-willed uncle, whose reins she held,
Could become the kingly horse that pulled the carriage of Efea,
And she mounted as queen upon him!

The Patrons in the audience begin to jeer as the Commoners sit in stunned silence. His words burn like a poisoned blade.

"This is your ugly history! The truth you've buried beneath the tombs of your dead! Hear my words! Heed my call! Efea will rise. Efea will rise! *Efea will rise!*"

A censor and four entrance guards—required staff in every theater in the Lantern District—push forward to arrest the interlopers. A number of fist-shaking Patron men leap up to follow them down. The furious Patrons in the audience surge back and forth, throwing food toward the stage as Commoners cover their heads.

Ro-emnu has vanished into the rumble of acrobats. I catch sight of him slipping behind a curtained exit. A shower of roasted chickpeas patters to the ground all around me and bounces off my back as I jump up onto the stage, dodge through the tumblers, and follow him into the theater-house. Guards push in behind me, their shadows rippling along the walls like monsters.

"Where did the criminal go?" they shout.

Almost invisible in the darkness, a tall form creeps up a ladder that leads to the aerial walkway, which the actors use for tricks and devices that dazzle the audience. The guards haven't yet seen him. I grab a dangling rope and climb hand over hand to the walkway, marking his stealthy progress as I ascend. He's so busy keeping an eye on the guards searching below that he doesn't notice me swing up right behind him as he makes for a second ladder.

On the floor, a pile of clothes rumpled up to look like a body bursts into flame. As the guards shout and converge on the fire, he glances back to make sure no one is following him. With a curse he sees my shadowy form. Bracing himself for a fight, he raises a fist. His broad shoulders give him breadth and solidity.

"Keep going," I say, making ready to leap backward if he swings. "You must have an escape route already planned. Did you soak the clothes in oil so they'd burn?"

"The sullen schemer. I should have known." He grabs the second ladder, which spears up into the shadows concealing the eaves. "While they're dealing with the burning clothes I'm going out through a trapdoor on the roof."

"I'm coming with you."

"No, you're not."

"Stop me."

With an angry grunt he begins climbing. I'm right behind him, wishing he would move faster, because the guards are going to look up very soon.

A hinge creaks. Air curls in from above. He pushes up and out. I follow, sliding onto the flat roof beside him. As he lowers the trapdoor behind us, I look around. There are two ladders hammered lengthwise along the rim of the roof, from which actors can be "flown" as winged spirits or courageous birds along the front of the proscenium. In the seating tiers the agitated crowd is pushing and shoving, trying to get to the exit, everyone shouting, children crying, half the lamps extinguished so darkness makes things hard to distinguish. A horn blows in the distance, the summons for the city militia.

I'm so furious at the memory of him taking the last lantern and abandoning us in the dark of the buried ruins beneath the tombs that I can't keep my mouth shut.

"How dare you leave my mother to die under the tombs!"

"Shh!"

He crawls away into the darkness toward the far side where an alley runs between two theater walls. To my amazement someone has strung a rope ladder high over the alley between the two roofs to make a bridge: his escape route. But he hesitates. We are a long way up, far enough that a fall will break bones or even kill.

"Surely an audacious poet like you isn't scared?" I chide, mocking him. A swift tug on the rope indicates it is securely fastened. The guards will search up here very soon, and I can't afford to get arrested, whatever happens to him.

"I was supposed to meet a confederate up here," he says. "To disengage the rope so the guards can't guess how I got away."

"Well, that's piss-poor planning, isn't it? Or maybe a conniving, dishonest person like you doesn't have any loyal friends."

"You're one to talk about loyalty, Jessamy Tonor. Especially since it's Jessamy Garon, now that you're a high-and-mighty adversary running for the Patrons as a harnessed *mule*." He practically spits the word.

The urge to shove him off the roof surges through me so hard that I flatten a hand against his chest. "Call me what you wish, poet, but never, ever insult my mother by using that word to describe the children she gave birth to."

He tenses, and I brace, and then he gives a one-shoulder shrug as he relaxes. "No insult was intended toward your honored mother."

I snort because I can appreciate a good comeback. But I don't take my hand off his chest. It's like pressing into rock. With lightning swiftness a plan forms in my head, of how I can use him to help me. "I'll stay here and cover your getaway if you'll swear by the gods to tell me where I can find you to arrange recompense."

He glances at the rope ladder bridge, presses a hand to his eyes, then drops it to meet my gaze. His eyes have the intensity of a person smoldering with banked anger, waiting to erupt. "All right, it's a fair exchange. But I won't swear by Patron gods. I make an oath by the Mother of All that on Rest Day afternoons you can find me at the Heart Tavern in the Warrens."

I would be shocked at his swearing an oath by invoking the Mother of All, the outlawed old goddess of Efea, but voices clamoring from the proscenium grab my attention. "Where is that?"

"If you can't find it, you don't deserve to find me. The watchword for entrance is 'Efea will rise.'"

"What does that even mean?" But as I say the words, I sense through my whole body the vibrations of people searching inside, their hands grasping ladder rungs, feet testing the aerial walkway, lamplight drawing closer and closer to the trapdoor....

"Go now!" I command.

Muttering a string of curses under his breath, he grabs at the rope ladder and, like a big awkward bug, begins crawling across. I would laugh if I weren't wishing I could kick him along faster. As I feel along the hooks that secure the ladder I berate myself for the impulse that drove me after him instead of for the West Harbor District under cover of the turmoil.

The moment he hisses out, "I'm safe over," I unhook the ladder and let it go. The ropes swing down and hit the far wall with a slap. He reels it in and crawls away across the opposite roof as I drop over the side of the building and, hanging by my hands, search out a toehold in the wall.

Fortunately, these popular theaters aren't sleek marble buildings like the temples and the Archives. Efean masons love to build patterns into their walls, using regular courses of brick interrupted by four-pointed star shapes and stylized flowers. The protrusions give me easy toe- and fingerholds.

I climb down into the alley serving as a firebreak between the two theaters. A file of city militia runs past on the main street, and a moment later I see my friends hurry in the other direction. Praying they will get away without any further trouble, I use the shadows to strip out of the palace livery with its badge and into the nondescript sheath of a dress that I just bought. With my old clothing folded into a net bag and slung over my shoulder I slink out the other end of the alley.

The guards searching the streets pay no attention to a Commoner girl like me as I make my way through the food carts and merchandise stalls of Lantern District's night market. After passing under West Gate to the Avenue of Triumphs, I walk briskly down the broad avenue toward the harbor. The disturbance not only has swept away the men following me but gives me an even better excuse to be missing for some time without anyone thinking it odd.

Women sweep up horse dung into a wheelbarrow. Servants carry bundles on their heads, headed for home or on evening errands for their Patron masters. My racing heart has finally slowed although Ro's speech beats time in my head like an echo of my footfalls. Did Serenissima the Third really kill her father, brother, and nephew in order to install a weak-willed uncle on the throne beside her as Kliatemnos the Third? Or is the insinuation merely a story Ro-emnu has made up, as with any theatrical play that entertains us with lurid murders and assignations?

But Ro is a poet, and in Efea the gods give poets a special dispensation—and obligation—to tell the truth. One of

Mother's elderly servants once told me that before the Patrons came and began bricking up holy oracles alive in the tombs of the lordly dead to whisper prophecies, it was Efean poets who spoke the divine word. What nags at me most is how Ro bound his oath to the Mother of All. The Patrons forbade Her worship when they conquered Efea, and it is against the law to give Her offerings or to build any kind of altar or temple to glorify or recognize the old goddess.

There will come a day when truth will bloom.

The memory of his voice makes me shiver, its raw passion more chilling than an oracle's hoarse whisper. What did he mean? What does he hope for?

Efea will rise.

6

West Harbor is where ships from all across
the Three Seas off-load trade goods and afterward
fill their holds with Efea's grain, cloth, paper, perfume, glass,
and precious oils used for cooking and lighting and medicine.
It's lively in the West Harbor District in the evening, with
sailors from every shore of the Three Seas awaiting their next
tide, stevedores still unloading cargo, and drunks vomiting on
the street in front of taverns.

Father never brought us girls down here, so I have no idea
where to go to find the Least-Hill Inn, where my mother has
taken shelter. Roaming bands of foreign sailors give me the
eye, and a few blurt out rude suggestions when I ask for directions. I have to slap away more than one groping hand before
a sympathetic oyster-seller points me down a dim side street.

The Least-Hill Inn has a brown door, its sign lit by the night-lantern required by law of each household. Inside I find myself in a run-down establishment with no customers except our former Junior House Steward, Polodos. He sits slumped at a table in the empty main room with his head resting on his hands and a full mug of palm wine at his right elbow.

"The inn is closed," he says, still staring down at the table. Then he looks up and leaps to his feet. "Doma Jessamy! Thank the gods you have come."

I grab his arm, suddenly scared. "Has something happened to my mother?"

A drab curtain separates the front room where drink and food are served from the back where they are prepared. I smell bread grilling, but it is the familiar voices of my older and younger sisters rising behind the curtain that capture my attention.

"It's unfair I'm not even allowed to go to the night market!"

"To do what, Amaya? We don't have money to buy anything. If Lord Gargaron's stewards catch sight of you on the street, we'll be discovered."

"Lord Gargaron and his stewards only saw me once, Maraya. I know I have the sort of pleasingly beauteous face that attracts notice, but it strikes even me as implausible that important Patron men would remember." By the strength of Amaya's wheedling I can hear she has recovered from her near death by poisoned candied almonds in the tomb. "I can't breathe in here! It doesn't even have to be the night market. I'll hide my face beneath a shawl and walk down by the water and breathe fresh air and listen to the mellifluous cries of the wind-kissed birds who are allowed to fly free. *Unlike me.*"

"Do you have any idea how tedious you are, Amaya?"

"You have the heart of a fish! Cold and sluggish!" Amaya sobs as third-rate actresses do to show the depth and intensity of their scorned feelings. "This wretched compound might as well be my tomb if I can't ever leave its walls."

"Help me," whispers Polodos with a look of such desperation that I giggle.

An abrupt silence follows my betraying laugh.

The curtain twitches as a person on the other side hooks it open just enough to peek through. I would know those lovely eyes anywhere.

I say, "Amaya, if you cut off all your hair, smear mud on your face, and wear a dirty canvas sack with a hole cut for your head, then you can safely go to the market without being recognized."

With a shout of excitement, Amaya plunges into the room, flings herself upon me, and bursts into sobs while clutching me so tightly I have trouble breathing.

Maraya limps in, smiling. "Oh, Jes, I am so glad to see you! I was afraid it would be unsafe for you to visit us."

They look just as they did back when we all lived well protected at home, only without the fashionable clothing, perfectly beribboned hair in the most up-to-date style, and fragrant oils and perfumes to hide the smell of sweat. Had we grown up without a successful Patron father who acknowledged us, girls like us might have lived in a place like this, scrambling to make a living and able to afford only cast-off dresses and mended muslin shawls for wrappings.

"How is Mother?" I ask into Amaya's hair. When she hesitates I shove her to arm's length, gripping her shoulders so hard she winces. "What's wrong?"

"Jessamy? Is that you?" Mother appears at the curtain. She has to lean against the wall to hold herself up. She is as tall as I am, and the most beautiful person I know. But right now her dark brown complexion is sheeny with perspiration; her magnificent cloud of hair has been bound under a scarf; no earrings or jewelry ornament her, all the little gifts Father used to shower upon her. She coughs weakly. I rush over but Amaya bolts past me to reach her first.

"You shouldn't be walking yet, Mother! You are supposed to stay in bed until every trace of bleeding stops."

"What a scold you have become, Amaya," says Mother in her gentle voice as she takes my hands as if she needs to reassure *me*. Her grip is so frail that I fear I might squeeze hard enough to shatter her without meaning to. "I am so glad you have come back, Jessamy. Is Bettany with you?"

Anguish chokes my voice until it comes out as a leaky squeak. "You must go back to bed, Mother. You were so sick. Here, let us help you."

Amaya takes Mother's other arm.

She sinks down onto the nearest bench. "I would like to see other walls just for a little while. I have not been out of that tiny room since we came here."

Amaya and I sit on either side, snuggling close against her as we used to do when we were little. She has always been the warmth we relied on, but now her skin feels feverish. She's lost a lot of flesh too, and she who always smelled sweet smells sour. Yet her breathing steadies as she holds us against her. She was always at her happiest when the man she loved and the children she cherishes were gathered around her in the calm household she supervised in her benevolent way.

Lord Gargaron ripped out her heart and threw it into the street like trash. He walled her and my sisters up in a tomb so he could swear to my father that he had not killed them, and yet make sure they would never be found. All this so my father could marry Menoë and help raise her tattered status while his future military victories secure glory and prestige for Garon Palace.

We ran that trial, Gargaron and I, and I defeated him although he doesn't know it. This game won't end until I've made sure he can never again harm anyone in my family.

"Hush, Jessamy." Mother feels the harsh shift in my breathing. "Whatever troubles you, let it go. See how happy Maraya is."

Maraya rests a hand on Polodos's shoulder in an affectionate way that makes me smile despite the fierce anger I carry in my heart. Polodos is not a handsome man like Father or Kalliarkos. He has a gap between his front teeth, his ears are too big, his features are ordinary. But he is intelligent, cheerful, hardworking, and even-tempered, and most importantly he respects and admires Maraya so much that he overlooks her irregular parentage and the clubfoot for which any Patron man except my father would have smothered her at birth.

Suddenly I realize how right Lord Thynos and General Inarsis were to warn me against coming here. Now that I see Mother is not on the verge of dying, I know the risk outweighs my need for comfort.

"Let's help you back to bed, Mother," I say with a nod at Amaya.

Despite all her whining and wheedling and other annoying habits, Amaya has the strength of an ox and the stubbornness of a creeping fig vine that, once established, can never be eradicated. She and I guide Mother past the curtain. Behind lies a shabby courtyard lit by a single lantern. Cook stands over an open-air hearth, grilling flat rounds of bread. A lowborn Patron woman whom my mother rescued from abusive circumstances, Cook is so loyal she volunteered to be buried alive with my mother.

She squints, then recognizes me. "Doma Jessamy, I am sure you ought not to be visiting us."

At once Mother says, "You must not risk yourself, Jessamy. If there is danger for you, then you must leave."

"I'll just see you settled and I'll go," I reassure her. She who carried us all for so many years can barely shuffle now. Yet her first concern is *my* safety.

Amaya steers us into a room scarcely bigger than an alcove. There is no bed, only a ragged mat unrolled on the floor where any snake or scorpion might crawl upon my mother. The air carries the stench of dried blood, rank sweat, and urine. Two humble baskets hang from the low ceiling. As we lower Mother to the mat, one of the baskets gurgles, and is answered by a startled infant wail from the other basket.

Amaya pulls the wailing baby from its bed and shoves it into my arms. "Here, walk him around outside a moment. He's so fussy that he needs calming before he can nurse. He's like me: feels trapped in these walls and wants to fly!"

I resist looking down at the crying baby in my arms until I am outside within the glow of the single lamp. The infant boy Wenru looks a little like me if you go by hair and complexion, but I think he looks a lot more like Amaya based on the fact that his mouth is open and squalling and his face scrunched up in distress.

A person might wish to console a helpless little infant if she didn't know this baby had been stillborn. The baby Wenru died at birth. Who inhabits his body now I do not know.

"I'll take him," says Maraya with a fond smile but I whisk Wenru away to the end of the courtyard where the lamplight barely penetrates.

Here a gate lets onto an alley. I angle him so there is just enough light for him to see my face as I fix my stare on his infant eyes. His wail trembles and slackens as if he is suddenly unsure whether crying will get him what he wants. His rosebud mouth purses. He would be darling—so small and so sweet—if I weren't absolutely sure a false shadow and self and spark have lodged within this body, taken it over for themselves.

Every body is born with five animating souls: A vital spark, the breath, which separates the living from the dead. A shadow, which hugs us during the day and wanders out on its own at night. A self, which is the distinct personality each creature has, that makes one person different from any other. A name, which includes a person's lineage and grows over the years into a reputation the person builds through deeds and speech. A heart, which is the seat of wisdom, the flesh in which we live. The heart binds the five souls into one.

"Whoever you are, whatever souls reside within you now, I know you are not my brother Wenru because he is dead," I say in a low, singsong voice, so anyone listening will think I am trying to soothe him. His cry hiccups into silence. Those eyes lock on mine with an alert, anxious look no newborn ever had. "If you can understand me, blink your eyes three times."

I speak in Efean. The baby's gaze remains fixed on me as if he is trying to figure out what my words mean. After a pause I repeat myself in Saroese.

His little face wrinkles up as if in prelude to a squall.

Instead he blinks once, twice, then a third time.

My whole body tenses.

Whatever self bides inside this infant, it does not understand Efean, only Saroese.

I go on in Saroese.

"I understand you are confused. You now reside in the body of an infant boy. My mother is a good woman. Respect her, and she will care for you. Do otherwise, and I will throw you out on the street. Do you understand? You are tiny and helpless and cannot crawl or talk. If anyone besides me discovers you are an abomination, they will smother you. But I am giving you this chance to live because my mother's heart is already so weary and I do not want her to mourn her dead son all over again."

His arms and legs stir beneath the linen he is wrapped in. His tiny lips open as he says "Aaaa," and he mewls just as if he wants to speak but can't figure out how.

"You got him to quiet down quickly," says Maraya, coming up beside me and whisking him out of my arms. She brushes fingers over his downy head and smiles in an adoring way that almost makes me forget he is no infant. "He's usually so fussy, poor little flea."

"I am sure he'll be less fussy from now on," I say in Saroese as I press a finger against his cheek. He moves his head to look at me and, with a sigh, shifts his attention back to Maraya. "What do you know about magic, Merry?" I ask, using her pet name.

She's rocking him in her arms, not even looking at me, only at his sweet little face. "Only the Saroese priests are allowed to study magic."

"But we saw magic in the buried ruins beneath the City of the Dead. What were those sparks? The shadows? The pool that shimmered with a substance I can't explain?"

"The mineral phosphorous gleams in water. Shadows move when we shift lantern-light around them. As for the sparks, they might have been spark-bugs...."

"You don't believe that. You felt the magic."

The baby has gone quiet, as if listening, but she doesn't notice. With a frown furrowing her brow, she shakes her head at me.

"Even if it's true, what can we do about it, Jes?"

"I don't know. It just seems like you're the one to investigate it, the way you've studied so hard for the Archives exam. There must be some knowledge of magic buried in the Archives. I know you would love to search for it."

She looks away to hide her expression from me, but her flat tone gives her away. "With Father gone and us pretending to be dead, I have no hope of ever taking the Archives exam. It's going to be hard enough just to survive. Polodos spent most of the money Father gave us to buy this inn, sight unseen, and you see how run-down it is. We can't afford to stock drinks and food for customers. How will we eat once our money runs out?"

"I'll give you all my earnings, I promise you."

With a wry smile she turns back and pats my arm. Of the four of us girls she is the one who can never stay mad for long. "I know you will do everything you can, Jes. But meanwhile I'm here and you're not, and my first duty must be to care for Mother, the babies, and Polodos."

Amaya appears in the door with another bundle in her arms. "Here, Jes, I thought you would want to hold Safarenwe too."

I abandon Maraya and hurry over to gather my infant sister, Wenru's younger twin, into my arms. She is as precious as myrrh, born in a tomb and meant never to see the heavenly sky or the glimmering sea. Her perfect little mouth roots as for food, and she mewls hungrily.

Mother says, "Bring her to me, Jessamy."

I kneel and help position the baby as Mother lies on her side to nurse. Lying down, Mother looks less exhausted. She examines me with her usual quiet scrutiny.

By her steady gaze I can see that her five souls rest firmly in her body, no longer at risk of coming unmoored. She is weak, but all of her is here: Her spark. Her shadow. Her name. Her sense of her self that seems somehow doubled in strength even though the man to whom she devoted more than half her life abandoned her. Her capacious heart.

As the baby suckles, Mother rests dry fingers on my hand. Always her first thought is to comfort others.

"Your strength and determination are precious gifts, Jessamy. We wouldn't be here without you, for your sisters tell me you never faltered as you brought us all out of that terrible place."

"The oracle's tomb was terrible, it's true. But there was more to the journey than getting out of the tomb itself. How much do you remember?"

"I am sorry to say I do not recall much, only that I was carried through darkness for some way. At the end when I thought my body and heart had failed me I was touched by a presence that poured new strength into me. Was that you?"

"It wasn't me. But I can't explain what we saw. Hasn't Maraya said anything to you?"

"No." Her gentle smile is as heartening as an affectionate embrace. "You know how your sisters coddle me. What did we see?"

Maybe I shouldn't burden her with my questions, but Mother has always been the one person we can tell anything.

"The Patrons built their tombs on top of an ancient compound that reminded me a little of a huge Fives court. Do you know anything about that?"

"You know that I came to Saryenia from a distant village when I was sixteen, so I've always been a bit of an outsider in the city. I never heard any stories of a complex buried beneath the City of the Dead."

I lean closer, for although only she and I are in the room, I somehow fear the oracles and the priests will overhear the forbidden words I am about to speak. "What's buried ought to be lifeless, don't you think? But life stirs there with a still-beating heart. As we made our way through the ruins, sparks like tiny stars poured through us. Shadows with the shapes of animals tried to swallow us. And then you stopped breathing, Mother." My hand tightens on hers as the thought of how close we came to losing her chokes me, but we didn't lose her, so my heart opens and I can speak. "A light flowed out of a glowing pool and revived you. What can such things be if not magic?"

She shuts her eyes. Her lips move, words so faint that if I had not heard her speak them when she was delirious in the tomb I would not know them now.

"The land is the Mother of All. She gave birth to the five souls that bind us. The souls arise from the land."

"But the priests and the law condemn the old religion. Commoners can be imprisoned just for speaking of it. Even Father said the old traditions that ruled Efea before the Patrons came were nothing but superstitious nonsense better lost and forgotten."

A tear trickles down her face as she murmurs, "He is what his upbringing made him. Patrons have always looked upon the land they conquered with a certain contempt even as they claim to love and treasure it."

"Father was never contemptuous of you!" Yet I falter

as her gaze tracks to meet mine, a darkness there I've never before seen. How much do I really know about my parents? Tremulously I stammer, "W-was he?"

"He is a good man, Jessamy. Never doubt that. I would not have stayed with him otherwise." Her voice drifts, and I almost feel she is talking more to herself than to me. "You may think your father was overly strict with you, but when I consider the stories he told me about how girls and women had to behave in the town where he grew up, he was bold in how he encouraged each of you. He stayed loyal to us for far longer than another man of his birth would have. But when he was finally forced to choose, he could not shake loose from his heritage."

She squeezes shut her eyes, struggling not to weep, and I want to embrace her, to tell her it will be all right. But I can't lie: we both know it will never be the same for her again.

The baby sighs, letting loose of the breast, and at once Mother opens her eyes and indicates that I should burp Safarenwe and then return her to snuggle against Mother's chest. Through half-closed eyes she smiles tenderly at the tiny infant and then at me.

"Is a Fives stable the right place, Jessamy? Is it what you truly want?"

"Yes, it really is, Mother."

"Polodos says you won a trial at Esladas's victory games at the Royal Fives Court. Was your father there to see it?"

"Yes."

"He will have been proud of you, Jessamy. He always saw a great deal of himself in you."

I hitch closer and rest my head on her hip. Her smile deepens, and her eyes close more restfully this time. After a bit I think she has fallen asleep, but abruptly she whispers, "And Bettany? She is well too?"

"Of course."

The lie curdles in my stomach like rotted food. Her eyes open as she hears the catch in my voice. I have to think quickly before she starts to question me. Sitting up, I shake coins out of my bag.

"I'm sorry this is all I could bring you today of my winnings. Most of the money was placed into a holding account, and I can only withdraw a little at a time lest I make Lord Gargaron suspicious. My plan is to bring you some every week on Rest Day, and to pretend I've spent it on food and drink and the theater."

"How you fret about protecting us!" Her chuckle heartens me. "Take it to Maraya for now. She's managing things until I get stronger."

Amaya brings in Wenru. I kiss Mother and go outside to give the money to Maraya. For a while I lean silently against my older sister as I used to do when we were little, taking comfort from her presence. Finally I speak.

"Has Polodos been able to find any trace of Bett?"

The shadows fall heavily on her pallid face. "No. Lord Ottonor's death and debts were so public that people are still gossiping about the scandal. You would think they would remember a group of servants from Clan Tonor being sold into indenture, yet Polodos has asked at every market in the city where such transactions take place and found nothing. I would go myself but I'm afraid someone might recognize me. Don't tell Amaya I said this, but she's right. We can't live trapped inside this compound much longer. I don't know what to do, Jes."

"I heard that," says Amaya, appearing half in and half out of the doorway where she can keep an eye on Mother but also talk to me. "I never imagined I would say this, but I envy you and your Fives stable, Jes."

Maraya snorts, and I laugh. "You'll say that until the moment you have to pull yourself up the first climbing pole."

"I could surprise you!" Amaya's nose twitches, and her gaze flashes past me. "Oh! Can I have that bread, Cook? It smells so good!"

Of course Cook gives in to Amaya's blandishments, offering her bread fresh off the grill. I am surprised to see usually greedy Amaya tear the flatbread in two and offer half to Maraya.

"Is this coarse bread all the food you have to eat?" I ask.

"Good-quality flour is too expensive," says Maraya. "Prices for grain are going up with the war on. We couldn't afford to eat if General Inarsis hadn't brought flour."

"Inarsis is bringing you food?"

"He likes to have an excuse to visit." Amaya nudges me with her shoulder, her grin peeping mischievously in the way that makes me both love her and want to punch her. How she loves sharing gossip! "He has such a considering way of looking at Mother. I think he wants to marry her when she gets better."

"That's ridiculous. He doesn't even know her. He has to make sure you're secure, that's all," I protest, even as a worm of unease bites at my belly. "He and Lord Thynos risked their lives to help get you out of the tomb. If you're found, he'll be executed, so it's no wonder he's keeping an eye on you."

Maraya sighs. "You two! People are complicated, you know. From things General Inarsis says, I get the impression Mother became something of a legend among the Efean soldiers. They thought she must truly be a woman of exceptional valor and honesty for an ambitious Patron man to keep her beside him as if she were his wife. Like she was his talisman that kept him safe and gave him victory."

"Until he got handed a better talisman," mutters Cook, hammering down rounds of dough for the next batch of grilling.

"That's not fair. Father didn't give her up for ambition. He gave her up rather than see her dead."

"You always defend him!" snaps Amaya.

"Of course you would say so, Jes," adds Maraya sourly,

"but please, *please*, don't try to convince Mother of that when the hurt is still so raw."

"She's not the only one who has lost someone!" Amaya's chin trembles, her expression growing so distraught I think she is about to cry real tears. "Jes, have you heard anything about my friend Denya?"

I wince and glance away, because I know this will hurt her, but then take her hands and speak softly. "I'm sorry. Denya was taken to become Lord Gargaron's concubine."

Rather than shrieking in outrage as any normal person would, Amaya throws her arms around me with a cry of relief. "Oh, good! Then you can tell her where I am! She'll be so worried."

"I can't speak to her because I'm not allowed to walk within Garon Palace." I shake out of her grasp. "We can't risk telling her anyway. She might tell Lord Gargaron and then he'll know you escaped."

"Denya never would betray me!"

"Hush!" says Maraya abruptly.

From the other room we hear the creak of the outer door, the tramp of feet as men enter the inn. A wash of alarm races through my body.

Like the slap of thunder, Polodos speaks in such an exaggeratedly loud voice that I know he means us to hear and take warning. "Domon, with regret, I must inform you the inn is closed—" The scrape of a bench pushed back and the thud of it tipping over makes me jump. "My lord!"

He sounds scared.

Heart racing, I signal to my sisters that they should go hide with Mother. In the Fives a good adversary knows when to make the boldest leap, and that time is now. I hook a round of bread off the grill and flap it in the air to cool it as I stride down the courtyard, push past the curtain, and enter the front room while speaking in my most falsely sweet voice.

"Steward Polodos, I brought fresh bread for you...."

Lord Gargaron stands in the center of the room. He pulls his knotted whip out of his belt and taps it against his thigh.

"So, Jessamy, be assured I recognize this man as Polodos, formerly a steward in the service of your father. What possible reason could you have for being here with him, I wonder?"

7

I grope for any thought. Lord Gargaron smiles in anticipation.

Yet my visible agitation works in my favor. Think like a soldier, Father taught us. I can't win this skirmish, only deflect suspicion. So I say what I'm sure he expects to hear.

"You've caught me out, my lord. It's true I hoped to send a message to Lord Kalliarkos through my father. You will therefore be glad to hear that Steward Polodos has just informed me he cannot send any messages because he has left my father's service."

Like me, Gargaron can stand with perfect stillness while an entire trial's worth of strenuous feats of strength and agility races through his mind. His gaze flicks to Polodos, to me, and back to Polodos as he sorts through possibilities.

"In my comprehensive study of General Esladas back when he was Ottonor's captain, I ascertained he kept only competent men around him and was ruthless in releasing men who did not serve him with efficiency. He retained his entire staff upon his elevation to general. I allowed it because I see no reason to interfere with success. So why were you released, Steward Polodos?"

Whatever else caused Maraya to fall in love with Polodos, I learn a crucial aspect of her admiration for him when he doesn't even bat an eye at this dangerous question.

"I have poor eyesight, my lord. I am an effective household administrator but I cannot make out details at a distance. Therefore I would prove a liability on an army officer's field staff. General Esladas kindly gave me a seed fund with which to set up a new endeavor. I purchased this inn."

"I am surprised you thought it worthwhile to make the attempt with a dump like this." A flicker of displeasure disturbs Lord Gargaron's brow. He suspects something, that is clear, but he isn't sure what. "Jessamy, you will never set foot in this inn again."

I hold on to my soldier's obedient face but inside I am seething. "Yes, my lord."

"Attend me." At the door he looks sharply back because I have not moved.

Once my feet shift I will be cut off from my mother and sisters. I give a slight nod to Polodos. By his strained, unhappy expression he understands that I mean to figure out a way to stay in secret contact, and he nods back.

Gargaron laughs. "How like your father you are, Jessamy Garon. Do not ever think I do not notice how you silently give an order and he obeys. Your father trained you well. But I will keep this inn watched, and you will not return here. Now come along."

I have no choice. A carriage awaits, but as I take my place behind the rear wheels, expecting to walk as servants do, he gestures with the whip.

"No, no, you are a Challenger now, much too precious to waste your energy walking. You will sit in the carriage with me."

A horrible creeping sensation crawls over my skin like a swarm of insects, tiny legs prickling and tickling. I inhale to calm my racing heart, then mount the steps into the carriage. An embroidered cloth awning covers the two facing benches for shade during the daytime. He sits with his back to the horses and indicates I must sit on the opposite bench, facing him. When I do so, he taps my knee with the whip as if to hammer me into place. We are so close our knees almost touch, and I carefully shift so as to make sure my legs do not brush against his. There is a little of Kalliarkos in his face: Gargaron's uncle, Menos Garon, was Kal's grandfather, and I can see the resemblance, although I would prefer not to.

"In one way I was pleased to see Kalliarkos take up with you," he remarks as the carriage begins to move. "It was the first time he attempted to defy me and his grandmother or, indeed, anyone at all. But you see how quickly he acquiesced to his defeat. He hasn't the fire to compete. He has the character to be led, not to lead. What I am doing is the best thing for him. As for you…"

Again he taps the point of his whip on my knee.

With an effort I do not recoil, and his thin smile emerges because he senses my revulsion and he enjoys it.

"I have my eye on you, Jessamy."

I hate the way he keeps using my name as if he has the right to it, and of course he does.

"It's said that victory in the Fives is a mark of the gods' favor. With Thynos leaving for West Saro—"

Startled, I forget myself. "Lord Thynos is leaving?"

His eyebrows lift at the interruption.

I duck my head. "I beg your pardon, my lord. The news surprised me. No one at the stable has been informed."

He goes on. "With him departing, we need a new Illustrious to build renown for Garon Palace, and we expect you to become that champion."

He pauses, leaving space for me to speak.

My mind is whirling. The more important I become to Gargaron the better my chances to figure out a way to destroy him. So I nod to acknowledge his words even as I struggle not to reveal any trace of the crawling disgust I feel from the touch of his whip on my thigh.

"I run to win, my lord."

"You can reap manifold benefits from your victories. Kalliarkos is not the only handsome young fellow in Saryenia. If you succeed as I believe you can do, you will be able to choose from among Patron lords eager to parade themselves as the lover of a triumphant adversary of your skill and looks. Young women with your promise on the Fives court are a challenge to men. They see you and your ribbons as a valuable prize that many will try to claim for bragging rights. Guard your victor's ribbons carefully and you can do very well for yourself."

I am so repelled at the idea of bartering hard-earned victor's ribbons to lovers in exchange for attention and prestige that it takes a physical effort, a breath sucked in, for me not to blurt out a furious retort. But I know how to find the beating heart that anchors my four other souls. I settle into its rhythm and chart my course of feigned obedience. Even so my bitterness wafts like the sting of hot ash in the air.

"What happened with Kalliarkos was nothing I sought out or expected. Now he is gone I have no intention of repeating the experience." Speaking the truth makes my voice authoritative. In this one thing I can safely defy Gargaron to his face. "I do not dream of becoming an adversary addicted to the adulation of lovers. I want only to win."

A vile taste rises in the back of my throat as he presses the point of his whip into my flesh.

"Remember, Jessamy, I can *command* you to lavish your

victor's ribbons on certain lords of my acquaintance who might wish to boast of their ... association ... with a promising adversary like you. And I will, if I feel you are being insufficiently respectful."

He removes his whip from my leg and sinks back into the cushions on his bench. As we roll along he hums a melody I finally recognize as the whipping song from *The Cupbearer's Calamitous Contract*.

Night hides my angry, humiliated flush. With an effort I keep my gaze on the buildings passing by. The night looks so bleak, so dark, despite the beacons made by lanterns that light the main roadways. The rhythmic scrape of the wheels reminds me of the creaking rhythm of turning Rings, and I begin thinking through the ones spinning around me. I have to warn Inarsis so he doesn't go to the inn. With Thynos leaving, and Inarsis and me needing to stay away, my options for finding Bett and meanwhile keeping my family safe and fed are shrinking quickly.

Instead of taking the wide boulevard that leads up the King's Hill and thence around Garon Palace, we swing wide around the base of the royal hills and to my surprise head for the Grain Market on the lakeside of the city. Here, inside a large enclosure surrounded by a brick wall, grain, oil, papyrus, and other goods from the interior of Efea arrive in Saryenia by boat across Mist Lake. After the queen's clerks check the manifests and collect a tax on all goods, merchants take them away across the Three Seas to sell in foreign lands.

As we approach the gate I'm surprised to see guards wearing the royal sea-phoenix badge patrolling on the wall. I have walked down here in the past with Mother and never seen the Grain Market guarded like this, like the king is afraid of his own subjects. Of course Lord Gargaron's carriage passes through without question. Inside, rows of warehouses are connected to the Lakeport Harbor by a canal.

The royal warehouses are set apart behind a second enclosure, and to my surprise this area bustles with activity even though it is night. Workers load sacks of grain and amphorae heavy with oil onto wagons headed for the main harbors. Our carriage rolls to a halt in front of a warehouse close to the lake.

"Remain here."

"Yes, my lord."

Gargaron climbs out. As he approaches the warehouse, guards slide back its doors so he can enter its lamplit interior. Before they close the doors after him I see the tiny but sternly upright form of Princess Berenise seated on a couch examining gold bullion brought to her by stewards who strain under the weight of the ingots. Lady Menoë sits beside the elderly woman, dutifully filling out a manifest to her grandmother's dictation.

That glimpse of gold makes my head swim. Without gold, kings and queens cannot rule. In Efea the gold mines of the desert are owned and run entirely by the royal family, which means all the gold extracted from Efean mines belongs to King Kliatemnos the Fifth, Queen Serenissima the Fifth, their son Prince Temnos, their younger brother Prince Nikonos, their aunt Princess Berenise, and of course Berenise's royal grandchildren, Menoë and Kalliarkos. Gargaron has no access to gold except through his niece and nephew. No wonder he wants to make them king and queen.

A headache starts to throb between my eyes. What a fool I was to ever think Kal was meant for the likes of me! I can't even help my family, much less imagine what it must be like to have totting up such riches as one of my everyday duties.

The driver moves the horses around into the shadows, and I wonder if this is so casual passersby won't glimpse it and ask why Gargaron is here so late at night. Why does he want to hide this expedition?

When the carriage comes to rest at the side of the warehouse I lean out. The back of the warehouse faces the lake harbor, with a boathouse and a wharf attached. A barge is tied up to the wharf, and by the light of lamps strung along the wharf, men wearing Garon Palace livery prod shackled men with the shaved heads of criminals onto the barge that will convey them across Mist Lake and into the Efean interior. Condemned criminals are the property of the royal family, sent to work in the deadly mines.

That's when it hits me. Gargaron doesn't need to sell

Bettany and our other servants in the market. Garon Palace has its own agricultural estates that need workers. It's so obvious now. What if Bettany is right here, to be loaded after the criminals are shackled in place?

I jump down from the carriage.

"Hey! You're supposed to wait here with us, Spider," calls one of the grooms.

"I have to pee. You wouldn't want me to stain these expensive cushions."

The men laugh in a good-humored way. "There's a livestock pen on the other side of the boathouse. But hurry up or we'll all get in trouble."

"My thanks!" I call brightly, and give them the kiss-off salute, which makes them grin and laugh again, like I've honored them. This is the power success gives you: people want some of that victory shine to rub off on them, so they do you easy favors.

I slink around the corner of the boathouse, heart beating hard as my hopes begin to soar.

A high fence with a slatted roof wraps the far side of the boathouse to create a cagelike corral. Instead of livestock a small group of women and children sits with heads bowed in weariness. The smell of urine and feces hits hard as I peer in between the fence slats. A boy wriggles out of the group and with the impatience of youth paces the fence, running a hand along the slats as he sings a song under his breath.

With a thrill of excitement I recognize him: an Efean child my father called Monkey whose real name is Montu-en, a scamp of a boy who ran errands for Mother and got up to cheerful mischief. Father's trusted servants were part of his military household, Patron men chosen solely for competency, while Mother invariably rescued people from awful circumstances and gave them a safe haven, shelter, food, and a small wage in exchange for work.

The boy doesn't see me as he passes, so I thrust my hand between the slats and grab his arm.

"Shhh! Montu-en! Say nothing. It's Doma Jessamy."

He freezes, no sound except a huff of surprise.

"Get Doma Bettany. Tell no one else." I release him.

He bolts, and squeezes into the crowd of prisoners until I can no longer see him. From the wharf I hear the shuffle of feet as the loading of criminals continues. Soon they'll come for this group. I don't have much time.

The moment her shadowy form pushes out from the other women, I know her, as I will always know my twin. We came into the world together. Until this last week I have never known a day without her aggravating me, laughing with me, scolding me, scheming with me.

"Bett!" I stick my hand through the gap, desperate to touch her, to make sure she is real.

"Jes!" Her strong fingers clutch mine. Her skin is grimy with dirt, and she smells like she's not been allowed to wash for days in the heat of Efea. "How did you find me? What happened to—"

"Mother is fine. She's alive and well," I interrupt, because I don't know how long I have, and Bettany needs to know so she won't carve out her heart through worrying. "She gave birth to healthy twins, a boy and a girl."

"A boy!"

"Shh! I can't be seen talking to you. Lord Gargaron thinks you are all dead."

"Dead? What happened, Jes? After Father left and you were taken to the Fives stable, the Garon stewards came to escort Mother, Maraya, Amaya, and me away to sit the vigil in the tomb of Lord Ottonor. I switched places with our servant Coriander so I could help the servants and make sure they weren't mistreated. When Mother never came back I thought surely Father spirited them away to a safe place."

"It's complicated."

"But of course I should have known he wouldn't make sure they were safe," she sneers, "not when he was offered a general's rank and a highborn Patron bride!"

Her insulting tone grates on me, so I squeeze her fingers harder to shut her up. "What matters is that Mother and the rest are alive and well. You have to keep it a secret, though."

"Why? So no unkind words or proof of Father's shameful liaison with a Commoner lover will sully his polished reputation as a man of honor now that he is important? He abandoned them, and me, and even you, Jes!"

"He did no such thing. Lowborn men like Father can't say no to highborn lords like Gargaron. He did everything he could to help Mother!"

"I knew he would dump us the moment we became inconvenient."

"You can be such an ass sometimes, Bett! Half the time I think you just say these hateful things to prove you can! Now be quiet and listen. Do you know what they mean to do with you?"

She shakes her hand free of my grip and glances over her shoulder at the huddled prisoners, many of whom are looking toward us trying to hear what we are saying and figure out who I am. For the first time her voice quavers as she fights down a shudder of fear.

"We've been stuck in this cage for days with no shade and not enough water, and gruel once a day. Half of the women are suffering from sunstroke. I think they're just waiting for us to die."

"If Lord Gargaron wanted you dead, you'd not have been fed any gruel. Bodies who can work are too valuable to dispose of so carelessly. Like those criminals they're loading onto the barge right now. Do you know anything about them?"

"Every day they bring in a cartload, I guess people condemned at the Temple of Justice. They keep the criminals shackled inside the warehouse, away from us, thank the gods."

"Probably waiting for the barge to arrive. Has anyone said anything to you about what is going to happen?"

"You can be such an ass sometimes, Jes," she mocks. "Why would you imagine anyone ever talks to us? From things I've overheard I'm guessing we're being sent inland to work on one of the Garon Palace estates."

"Is there any kind of gap in the fence? To escape?"

"There's a small gap at the very top of the cage, enough to squeeze through, but I'd have to climb the fence and then go hand over hand up the top bars like on a Fives course."

"You can do that! Get out the top and lay low on the warehouse roof until the barge leaves. Then swim out to Mist Lake and you can walk back into the city and make your way to where Mother is staying—"

"I can't."

"Of course you can. You're strong enough."

"No, I mean I can't abandon the women and children who served in our household and are stuck here with me. Don't you think that's the first thing Mother would ask me? 'Are they safe, Bett?' I'd never be able to face her. I guess you could abandon them without a second thought because you're like Father."

Her scorn whips so hard it chokes me. I can't even manage a retort as she goes on.

"When I switched places with Coriander, it was so one of us girls could supervise the household while Mother was at the vigil. You didn't see Mother after you and Father left. She was so brokenhearted she couldn't stand. She could barely speak. The one thing she cared about was keeping everyone in the household safe. I promised her to protect the people she has always protected. I promised it on my five souls, Jes. I won't leave them behind. Either they escape with me, or I stay with them. Unless you want to crawl in and switch places with me."

I hesitate.

She laughs harshly. "I thought not. You could, though. The Patrons wouldn't be able to tell us apart."

"You and I don't look that much alike."

"We all look alike to them."

"Then they won't notice if you're gone!"

"Every one of us in here is listed on a manifest. If even one goes missing, they'll notice. So tell me how your beloved Fives skills can get all of us out of here without being caught and I'll come watch your next trial."

I snap back, "The money I earn running the Fives is what feeds our family now! Don't scold me! I'm doing my part! I rescued them from—"

A whistle interrupts me.

"*Shweet!* Spider! Where'd that girl go, curse it? His Lordship will whip us if she's not in the carriage waiting to go...."

Footsteps thump on the ground as two grooms lope around the corner of the warehouse.

Over at the wharf lamps swing, and a man calls out, "Load the women and children now. We want to get out on the lake before dawn."

I grab for her arm. "Climb, Bett! Quick!"

"I can't. I can't. I can't. Oh gods, I want to, Jes! I want to get out of here, but I can't do it, not when Mother gave me this task." A wild tide of fear swells in her rising voice, and she leans into the slats, doing her best to embrace me through the rough wooden bars that separate us. I feel her tears as she presses a cheek against mine. "Go! Hurry! Don't get caught if it means you'll get thrown in here with me."

"I'll find you!"

"Of course you will. Jes to the rescue!" She breaks away with a laugh that sounds more like a choked-down scream of hysterical fury, and staggers away as if she's been stunned by the slam of a hammer.

I'm so ashamed. I haven't done enough to help the people who rely on me.

At the wharf end of the corral a gate is opened, and a steward shouts at the prisoners to line up. When I try to take a step away my legs almost give out, as unsteady as if I'd been ill for days, and I sag against the bars, staring at my sister's back as she slides into the crowd of waiting prisoners. She doesn't look at me but surely that is only because she knows a look will give us away if anyone sees, if anyone guesses. Surely it isn't because she truly scorns me, as she has long claimed to scorn Father.

"Spider?" Two grooms hurry up.

"I ate too many pancakes, made me sick to my stomach on top of everything else." I wipe the back of a hand across my lips for good measure, hoping the awful smell from the cage will hide that I was no such thing.

They laugh. "Probably too much to drink. Not that you didn't earn it! Come on, Adversary. Let's beat the lord to the victory tower."

We get back to the carriage just in time, them grinning with excitement at the close call and me pretending that our race to get back without being seen is the same as a trial, and maybe it is. Lord Gargaron strides out of the warehouse and climbs in. At first he says nothing as we roll through the lamp-lit streets, passing from light into shadow into light again, and head up the King's Hill into the Palace District.

My hand feels crushed from Bettany's grip but it is the accusations she flung at me that hurt most. We love each other, we do, even if we fight. How can I manage to track her down and rescue her and the servants while also secretly funneling money to my family and training for the Fives? All without Lord Gargaron becoming suspicious?

"You have the oddest look on your face, Jessamy." Lord Gargaron's gaze bores into mine like he wants to use a pickax on my thoughts and hack out my secrets. "What are you thinking?"

Startled, I wait too long to reply.

His smile is a knife in my heart. "You can't hide your rebellious nature, can you? Your defiance is what makes you a good adversary. Don't ever believe I don't understand what you are, or that I don't know you would beat me to the victory tower if you could. Which you can't. I am the one adversary you can never defeat."

8

My friends are sitting up late under the thatched awning of the dining shelter, huddled around a single lamp and clutching mugs of beer. As my footsteps crunch across the courtyard they leap up.

"We thought for sure we'd lost you in the stampede," Mis cries, running over to hug me. "We saw the militia arresting people, looking for that poet."

"It took me a while to get free of the crowds." I'm fortunate they don't realize I'm the one who abandoned them, and that they never saw me talking to Ro. I have to compound my dishonesty by quickly coming up with a plausible way to encourage Mis to take pity on me, one that will pass muster if Gargaron hears that I mean to leave the stable again. "I guess I'll just have to spend Rest Day here. I had planned to go shopping in the Lantern Market tomorrow, but after that horrible incident I don't want to go back."

"I thought you would go home to visit your mother," Mis says. "Doesn't she live here in the city?"

I shrug, making a sad face that feels as false as my story. "My mother had to leave after my father's promotion. I don't have a home to go to anymore."

"Oh, Jes! That's awful. You're welcome to come with me to spend the day with my family."

"Truly? I'd like that. Thank you!"

Her smile is so warm that shame pricks me, because I am using her, she who has only ever offered me friendship. But I brush aside these feelings. In war a soldier must be ruthless in order to survive.

Yet when I go to bed, sleep does not come. Every slight noise jolts me, even a sigh as one woman turns over. I'm stretched so taut I think I hear the creep of moonlight across the roof. My thoughts skip from Bettany to Mother to Father, and spin over and over until I'm dizzyingly tumbled back to the way Kalliarkos held me close, the touch of his warm lips to mine, the way he looked into my eyes and said, "You're here with me because you want to be." Because I am the girl who chose him for himself, not a girl chosen for him by his interfering relatives.

I have to let him go.

I have to concentrate on those I'm responsible for, those I can help.

As gray lightens to pink, the cook and her assistants begin bustling around in the kitchen. Gira, Shorty, Mis, and I get up. We take a long, leisurely wash in the bathhouse, and Mis combs out and oils my hair before binding it under a scarf.

Then, hand in hand like Efean girls everywhere, she and I stroll down the King's Hill. We make our way along the straight streets of the Patron districts of the city, past the large compounds of the well-to-do and into the more modest streets where ordinary Patron folk live. Once I lived in an orderly neighborhood like this, in a tidy compound hidden from the street by walls and a gate. We pause at a tiny neighborhood vegetable market so I can buy flowers as a guest gift for the women of the household and a packet of honey candies for the household children.

The transition from the grid-plan Patron-built streets into the Warrens comes abruptly as we cross under an arch not even wide enough for wagons. On Patron-drawn maps of the city the streets don't change their straight appearance, but once inside, the lanes and alleys split off in random directions. They smash into sudden dead ends or circle in loops that bring you back to where you started, usually at one of the fountains where people gather to talk as they fill pots with water.

More than once we have to make way for men pushing carts stacked with raw linen from the weaving sheds and sheets of papyrus bound for West Harbor. Women file along with pots of water balanced on their heads and babies tucked in slings on their backs. Whenever a passing woman or girl greets Mis, she always introduces me. Among Commoners, not to exchange names is the same as an insult, like pretending not to see someone because they're too unimportant for you.

Mis's home resembles a mudbrick beehive with its series of interconnected small rooms, some roofed and some open to the air, some dug into the ground as storerooms and some three stories tall. The place reeks of scent because Mis's family distills perfumes in one section of the compound. My nose itches so much that, just as she brings me forward to present me to the women of the household, I sneeze loudly.

"Blessings on your five souls, child," says her grandmother, who as the eldest is the dame of the household and thus the ultimate authority.

I present the dame with the flowers. Everyone approves my choice of chrysanthemum and papyrus for their combination of lovely color and practical utility.

After I've washed my hands in a basin, the dame sends a child to fetch a warm bun sweetened with fig and honey, because it is the tradition of Efea to greet all guests with food. "Let you be welcome at our table."

After I have complimented the bun's delicious flavor and moist texture, Mis is given permission to take me to the kitchen and treat me like family. I'm set to chopping dates to bake into bread for the midday dinner, which is the main meal of the day. I like working in the kitchen in the company of her family.

Jostling about surrounded by women and children is what I'm used to, but even the camaraderie of Mis's friendly household cannot soothe the chafing burn deep in my heart as I wonder what my mother and sisters will have to eat today, and where Bettany is now, somewhere out on Mist Lake crossing toward a life of bitter servitude.

"Why so little bread today? Have grain prices gone up that much?" Mis asks one of her sisters, a strapping giant who kneads dough with powerful hands as she replies.

"Prices *have* gone up but the real problem is short supply. People are saying the king is exporting grain to raise money to pay the army."

"But the royal family controls the gold mines," I say. "Doesn't he pay the army with gold?"

The sister shrugs. "I don't know. All I know is there are lines to buy grain now. We hear rumors that Patron households are hoarding grain for fear they won't be able to buy more later. Poor people are starting to go hungry."

Midday dinner is a leisurely meal. Mis's family treats me with the greatest warmth, including me in their conversation about the Fives, my recent victory, current plays, what people are saying about the war on the Eastern Reach, and the growing market for Efean perfumes in the three kingdoms of old Saro across the sea. I haven't felt so relaxed since before Lord Gargaron ripped apart my family, but at the same time I calibrate the point where I can politely distribute the honey candies to the children and excuse myself on the pretext that I have to run errands.

By the time I leave, people are settling down for their afternoon nap, which suits me because it means so few folk walk the streets that I can make sure I'm not being followed, not that I have seen a single Patron high- or lowborn on these twisty lanes. If Gargaron had hired a Commoner spy to keep track of me it would be harder to tell, but there is nothing suspicious about a young adversary stopping at a tavern to drink a bowl of Efean-brewed beer.

I smile at a man leading a laden donkey. "Blessings of the day, Honored Sir. I'm from out of town. Can you tell me how to find the Heart Tavern?"

His eyebrows rise toward the heavens, then drop. "Ask at Cat Fountain, Honored Niece," he answers in the formal way.

Cat Fountain lies next to the Warrens' entry arch. Here I question a woman filling a jug with water, and she tells me to ask at Ibis Fountain. So onward, fountain by fountain, Elephant, Snake, Dog, Falcon, and I realize I am circling inward toward the center of the Warrens in the same order in which we adversaries pace out the menageries. At last I reach the center of the district, fetching up at an eight-spouted fountain in the heart of the Warrens. A tall man pretends to nap in the shade, but his suspicious gaze follows me as I approach.

"Blessings of the day, Honored Cousin. I'm looking for the Heart Tavern," I say.

"Blessings, Cousin. Sadly, I've never heard of such a place."

"I'm looking for the poet Ro-emnu. He said to speak the words *Efea will rise.*"

"Ah!" He leaps up and walks to a closed gate. As I follow he gives me a sidelong look-over. "You one of Ro's sweethearts?"

I snort. "Me? Why would I want to be his sweetheart?"

"Poets are irresistible to some people."

"And repellent to others!"

He grins. "Maybe so! The Mother of All gave him the poet's true gift, though. Everyone knows that."

He pushes open the gate and ushers me into a spacious courtyard shaded by arbors thick with flowering jasmine and hyacinth. Men and women face each other around circular tables crowded with mugs and pitchers of beer. Many seem to be debating in low voices, while others are trading verses from plays as if engaged in a contest to see who knows the most lines. Several are working in small groups, heads bent over papyrus, and in one shady corner a quartet works its way through the movements of a dance not unlike the graceful lines of the menageries.

Bit by bit they notice me, and piece by piece each conversation ceases as everyone looks my way. Self-conscious at their scrutiny, I look for Ro-emnu and finally spot him alone on a semicircular terrace of tiered stone seats that half surrounds a small raised stage. He's so engrossed in his work that he hasn't noticed the uneasy lull. His lips move in soundless speech as he rapidly sets words onto a scroll of papyrus clipped to a slate writing board set across his legs. As if my gaze is a spear that has wounded him, he looks up. When he recognizes me his lips press together in a gloating way that makes me stiffen. Not even a polite smile! So I don't offer one either as I approach.

He rises in greeting. Of course he does not speak first. No properly raised Efean man would ever address a woman before she spoke to him.

I'm so irritated by his air of superior restraint that I try to rattle him. "Blessings of the day, Honored Cousin. What does the phrase mean, *Efea will rise?*"

"Blessings of the day to you too, sullen schemer. If you don't know and can't guess, then I'm not about to enlighten you."

I can't keep irritation from my face as he calls me the mocking name his sister Coriander called me behind my back when she worked for our household. He smirks, delighted by my annoyance. Since I can see he means to needle me, I change the subject to one I am sure he can't resist. "Is this where you write your plays?"

"It is. Here in the Heart Tavern, where at the new moon the dames meet at council and with their wisdom and experience wrestle with the questions that plague us Efeans as we struggle to survive in our conquered land."

"Do you always spout this kind of poetic nonsense?"

"Why do you call it nonsense? Do you think Efeans have always been a conquered people?"

"Before the Saroese came, Efea was ruled by corrupt priests and selfish kings. Everyone knows that! However it happened, it was for the best."

"That Efeans had to be conquered for our own good is the story we've been told to convince us it is better to bow beneath the Patron lash. Of course it is the story you've been raised to believe. How could I forget that you count yourself a Patron even though no Patron will ever recognize you as one of them?"

I let the barb fly past and hold my ground. "Insult me all you wish. I'm here because you owe me a debt that I mean to collect."

"How do you mean to collect it? Will you accept a kiss?" A smile flashes, his face alive with the derision that makes me want to kick him.

"Do you think this is a joke?" I demand. "People's lives are at stake!"

"So they are. Excuse my poor manners. I've not greeted you with food in the proper tradition. Would you like a mug of beer?" Without waiting for my answer he signals to a passing man, then indicates I should sit.

Instead of sitting I tap my foot. "What *does* the phrase mean, *Efea will rise*?"

"Your relentlessness is impressive, Spider. The Heart Tavern is difficult for the censors to find since no Commoner will tell any Patron how to find it, or even that it exists. Despite your perfect Patron diction, Saroese manners, and honorable father I suppose you are not so very Patron after all, having made your way here like a good Commoner girl, however much you hate to admit it."

"I'm not ashamed of my mother!"

"Oh, but you are." His expression turns stony. With a wave of his hand he directs my gaze to the mural painted as a backdrop for the small stage below us.

In the painting a procession of tiny figures approaches a mountain from either side. On this mountain sits a gigantic woman with a dark face, hair in a hundred braids like the streaming channels of a delta, and arms extended with palms up in a gesture of bounty. Out of her arms flow fruits and date palms and golden pinpricks that might be bees or sparks. She is seated on a throne shaped like a caldera, which floats atop a lake of red fire.

"The land is the Mother of All, who gave birth to all that lives here," he says, echoing my mother's words at the inn. "Her heart dwells within the mountain of fire. But you have turned your back on Her, haven't you? Instead you worship the foreign gods brought to this land by the people who conquered us."

I sit down and answer in a low voice only the two of us can hear. "I'm surprised the authorities haven't arrested the owners of this tavern for allowing such an image in their establishment."

"I'm sure they would, if they ever saw it." He aims a

dazzling smile at me, even bats his eyelashes. "Are you going to tell them? Or is there something I can do to convince you to spare us now that you know the ugly truth?"

"You love to be provocative, don't you? I'm sure it impresses all your sweethearts." I make a show of looking around as if to identify a gaggle of waiting girlfriends, only to realize how many people are watching us with expressions of delighted interest. How humiliating! Ro chuckles in a way that makes me so furious that I have to count my breaths in and out to calm myself.

Footsteps pad up beside us as the waiter returns and hands me a bowl of the local brew, as thick and nutritious as gruel.

As I fumble in my pouch for a coin to pay him, Ro says, "We don't use Saroese coin here."

"She's that adversary Spider, isn't she?" says the waiter to Ro, an indirect way of speaking to me.

"I am Spider."

Given permission by my words, he grins at me with a sweet smile as genuine as Ro's are false. "A well-run trial, Spider. The beer is my gift, in appreciation."

Warmth creeps up my cheeks. "My thanks, Honored Sir."

He nods in acknowledgment and seems about to reply but has to hurry away as someone across the courtyard calls for him.

A grin untouched by mockery transforms Ro's face. "Was that a blush? You're not so untouchable and callous as you try to appear, are you?"

"Are you ever going to stop mocking me?"

"I don't mock at all. I believe you carry within yourself a power you don't comprehend." My back stiffens as he leans even closer. "Are you Patron or Commoner?"

"Why should I have to choose loyalty to one parent over the other? I love them both. I won't let anyone take that love and respect away from me!"

His lips part and he murmurs in a seductive voice that slides along my skin like silk. "Exactly. Don't you see the power you have, sullen schemer? You are both, and neither. Someone like you can fight for Efea in ways no Patron will ever see until it is too late."

I think of Gargaron, my interest piqued. "How? The Patron lords are unassailable. On the court of intrigue and politics they are the Illustrious with all the skill and training and the weight of power on their side while I am a mere fledgling with frail wings."

"Is that what you think you are? You've never watched yourself on the court, Spider. No one can look away from you. Not even me, and I don't even like you." He's laughing at me, and yet not only laughing as he teases words into new shapes with his tone. His eyes are like wells of precious midnight and all its secret pleasures waiting to be plumbed.

I flinch back from this sudden glimpse of the attractive man Amaya saw fit to flirt with in the tomb because she saw a different person from the obnoxious poet I see.

"Don't flirt with me. I'm not interested."

He lets go of the intensity and relaxes, taking a swig of beer from his half-empty bowl. "How is your pretty sister?" he says as if he can read my thoughts. "She wasn't too proud to admire a Commoner like me, was she? Yet why would you be interested in me when all your life you've been taught only Patron men matter? That only their looks are to be admired?"

"That's not what I meant! It's not because you're a Commoner that I'm not interested." Father would never have let a Commoner court one of his daughters, but I don't have to tell him that! I cough pointedly. "I'm not interested because you are rude and unpleasant."

He laughs. "That's a relief, for I admit I'm a bit vain of my looks."

Of course the words make me study him, as he intended: broad shoulders, a strong chin, and a dimple that flashes as he grins. Irritated that I fell for his cheap rhetorical trick, I push back. "Yes, you're not bad-looking, but you're not handsome like Lord Kalliarkos."

"How polite of you to say so." He sets chin on clasped hands in a casual way no Patron lord would ever be caught dead mimicking, yet his gaze drills into me with extraordinary force.

I glare back, not giving a single blink. "Speaking of Kalliarkos, he got you out of prison at great risk to his own honor and reputation. You owe him."

"I owe him, it's true, and my debt to him will be paid when he calls it in. As for you and me, schemer, your help getting me away from the theater last night cancels out the debt you owe me for my aid in getting your family out of the tomb."

"You still owe us for abandoning us in the ruins afterward. Also, you stole the oracle when you left us in the ruins with no light."

"The oracle never belonged to you. She was an accidental gift."

It's a fair point so I don't argue it. But I am curious. "What did you do with her?"

"The oracle is safe and well fed, and has a garden to wander in as the desire takes her, although that's not often, for the poor old woman is afraid of the open sky."

"Who is she really? Usually oracles are young, and they're never old women who have already had a husband and given birth to a child, however long ago that happened, as she said."

He shakes his head. "Ah, my darling and sullen schemer, I'm not giving up the secrets I've learned to the loyal daughter of General Esladas, a man originally from old Saro who faithfully serves our Saroese masters." His voice grows more passionate as he goes on. "It is Patron priests who condemn women to a living death in their foul tombs. It was the Saroese who destroyed our temples a hundred years ago and built their tombs on top of ours so no trace remains. It was the Saroese who stole our land from us. Why should I trust any of them, ever? Tell me one reason!"

His anger silences me. Not for the first time I wish Kalliarkos were here with his charm that won even Ro over, or so it seemed. All I can do is scrape roughly along, wondering whether to remind Ro that Patrons do not all think alike any more than all Commoners do. But I give way in favor of not antagonizing him. Someday I'll wipe the insolence off his face, but right now my family needs security more than I need to win. I remind myself of how Mother negotiated her difficult position all these years with generosity and dignity. She often made allies of women who at first didn't want to like her by asking them for a favor that made them feel powerful.

"I need your help." The quietness of my tone takes him aback.

"With what?" he asks in a normal voice, as if he and I are ordinary people having an ordinary conversation.

"I need someone to act as a go-between to deliver money to my family where they're hiding."

"Ah! Of course. You can't chance going yourself lest your master tracks you and discovers they're not still bricked into the tomb."

"That's exactly right. Lord Gargaron is having me followed and has already come close to finding them. You know what will happen if he discovers they are alive."

His expression softens into the appealing concern of a young man who has a sister of his own. "For the sake of the honored lady your mother and her newborn twins, I'll do it."

120

"Thank you." I hand a pouch of copper coins to him. "They're at the Least-Hill Inn."

He pokes through the coins with a skeptical frown. "Grain prices are going up. This won't buy much."

"I can't bring more than that or the Garon stewards will get suspicious. I daren't even come here every week lest they begin to see a pattern to my movements. Will you be here on Rest Day in two weeks?"

"I will be here unless a circumstance beyond my control stops me. But you can come anytime, you know, not only on Rest Day. Trust the dame who runs this tavern. Anything you leave with her she will deliver intact to me."

"Truly? That would make it easier to hide my movements."

"In this matter, Jessamy, I pledge on my five souls that I will honor our agreement."

It's odd to hear my name on his lips. He pronounces it differently than Father and Kalliarkos do, because he has an Efean lilt. He makes the name seem sweet and fragrant, like the jasmine flower I'm named for. Because I don't like the way the music of my name makes me feel, I drink down my bowl of beer so as not to insult the gift and take my leave as quickly as possible.

Even so, as I depart I pause to examine the mural depicting the Mother of All. The priests say the old Efean beliefs are superstitious nonsense. They say the old Efean goddess was a bloodthirsty monster who ripped the living souls out of Her victims to sate Her hunger. Yet this image reminds me of my own mother, giving generously of her heart and her strength to the people who process up on either side to ask for succor and mercy.

The mural strikes me as odd, though, a strange mix of Patron and Commoner, Saroese and Efean. To the right of the Mother of All stands a person wearing a mask of feathers and bearing a reed pen and a sheaf of papyrus as regalia. The mask and pen are symbols usually associated with Queen Serenissima in her role as chief accountant who oversees the honesty of all transactions. To the goddess's left stands a person wearing a helmet with wings and a mask with a lion's face. He—although I'm not entirely sure it is a man—stands in a chariot holding a bow drawn with its arrow ready to be loosed, exactly as King Kliatemnos is pictured on public murals as the chief soldier who protects the land.

The waiter, passing by, pauses. "May I help you, Honored Cousin? Have you something you need?"

"Just a question." I indicate the mural. "If Commoners hate the Patrons so much, then why has the artist who painted this borrowed the queen's mask and pen and the king's chariot and bow to depict two servants meant to be ancient Efeans?"

The waiter gives me a pitying gaze, like he's just realized I'm a mule and is sorry for it. "If you think their regalia is copied from the Saroese, you are mistaken. The invaders are the ones who copied the regalia worn by the Efean rulers of old.

Those two servants, as you call them, were the dignitaries who ruled us. They went by the titles *Custodian* and *Protector*."

"So *Custodian* and *Protector* is what the ancient Efeans called their queen and king," I say, in an effort to show I'm not as ignorant as the waiter's speech makes me feel.

"The words do not mean queen and king. It's the Saroese who thought they must, because the Saroese assumed the person wearing the custodian's mask must be a woman and the protector's a man. That's how Patrons see the world: they believe souls are rigid and singular instead of fluid and multiple. But it's not how we Efeans see things. You need to start looking with Efean eyes." When he smiles and turns his head to wink at me, I suddenly see a profile that, were the waiter dressed differently, I might call that of a woman, and now I wonder if I have always seen merely what I expect to see instead of what is really there.

The waiter's words chase me as I walk back through the late-afternoon heat, sweat slick on my skin. Father hired a tutor to teach us girls the regal history of the old empire of Saro. One hundred years ago, a fearful civil war caused it to break apart into the three kingdoms of West Saro, Saro-Urok, and East Saro. During this war Prince Kliatemnos fled with his sisters and army to the land of Efea, where he found refuge, overthrew the corrupt Efean rulers, and established a dynasty of his own. Everyone knows the king oversees the army and the administration while the queen oversees trade, merchants, and markets. But in old Saro kings rule alone, and their wives preside only over the private household, never over the public treasury.

Only in Efea do queens rule alongside kings. I never thought about why it might be different here. I never thought there might be another way of looking at how things used to be, much less another story for how things got to be the way they are now.

When I reach Garon Stable the grounds are still empty because people won't return until evening. Talon is seated in the dining shelter with a wax tablet and a child's copybook, laboriously copying letters onto the wax with the tip of a stylus and then erasing them with the little spatula on the other end. It surprises me to see her slow progress, as if she has just started learning even though she is at least as old as I am.

When Father taught my sisters and me to write he told us that, in old Saro, women rarely learn their letters and numbers. People think it would cause them to give birth to fewer sons. But here in Efea women and men both Patron and Commoner all learn writing and arithmetic.

Is that because the Saroese who came here changed, or because Efea changed them?

Sensing me, Talon glances up. Her gaze holds mine with a stare that isn't hostile but isn't welcoming either. Is she daring me to speak to her? Challenging me to keep my mouth shut, as if to remind me she is highborn and I am so obviously not? I try to think of something to say but words seem awkward as I realize I pity her.

The gate scrapes open. General Inarsis enters, carrying a leather pouch. I run to intercept him but before I can speak he confronts me, his words a slap to the face.

"I heard what happened at the inn last night. You can't be trusted to follow orders, Spider. This is not a Fives trial where you hurt only yourself if you fall."

"I know!"

"No, you don't know. In these Rings of politics and palace you are running above your skill level and you think you can keep up but you can't."

"But—"

"Still not ready! Do you want your honored mother to be discovered and killed?"

Surely my ears and tongue will steam off from the boiling words I want to shout out of sheer frustration and have to hold in. I can't let him have the last word, so I decide to throw him off his game. "Amaya thinks you are courting our mother with your daily visits and gifts of food. Are you?"

"Ah. An ambush." He examines me with a lift of an eyebrow, not one bit discomposed. "I think it a little early to discuss any such ventures, don't you?"

"Mother will never look at another man!"

"That's for her to decide, not you. But to reassure your sense of propriety, you can repay me for the money I've spent at a more appropriate and less dangerous time."

I consider telling him about the arrangement I've made

with Ro-emnu, and how I found and lost Bettany, and as quickly decide against it. For all his fine words, Inarsis serves Saroese masters. Maybe Ro-emnu isn't entirely wrong about whom to trust.

But there is one detail I've not forgotten that he can help me with.

"I know you and Lord Thynos are angry I sneaked into Garon Palace the night of the victory games. But I saw Prince Nikonos plotting with Lady Menoë in the garden."

Like a scorpion's strike, he grabs my arm. The iron grip of his hand reminds me that this is a man who killed a king in battle. "That's impossible."

"Of course it's not impossible. I heard them!"

"Ah! You heard but didn't see any faces, so you're just guessing and maybe trying to drive a wedge between your father and his new wife." He releases me to flick a piece of sawdust off his sweaty cheek. "I suspect you harbor an unrealistic hope that somehow, against all odds, your parents will be able to reconcile and live together again. They won't. General Esladas made his choice, and frankly I think he managed it in a cursed cruel way. There's no going back from what he did."

A pain like a blade of fire burns through my heart as I blink away hot tears. "That's not what I mean. I'm talking about Lord Gargaron's plot to put his niece and nephew on the throne. Which means deposing not just the king and queen but Prince Nikonos too, because he would become king if his older brother died. So if you were Prince Nikonos and were secretly plotting with Lady Menoë, you would need to get rid of Kalliarkos, and my father too, since he's been assigned to protect Kal. Father needs to be warned, just in case I'm right."

He considers me in silence. He's a big man, broad and strong, very powerful, too tall and heavyset to be successful on the Fives court but perfect for the smash and endurance of battle. After a moment he nods. "Very well. I'll send a courier in secret to the Eastern Reach."

"Nar? Is that you?" Tana One-Hand appears at the door of her room, rubbing her eyes as she wakes from the afternoon nap. "I thought you would be gone already."

"I just wanted to transfer this into your hands in person before I go." As she comes up, he hands her the pouch.

"Are you leaving?" I ask.

"I am. Naturally I wanted to make my farewells to my cousin before I depart."

"Tana is your cousin?"

"She is. It's the kind of thing Lord Kalliarkos would know within a day of meeting people. Just because you are a better adversary than him on a Fives court doesn't mean you would defeat him in every manner of trial." His crooked smile cuts me, as he means it to.

I look from Tana to him and back again. "Wait! Is this about Lord Thynos leaving for West Saro? Are you going with him? Why is he going?"

"The news will be out soon enough," he says. "Princess Berenise has arranged a diplomatic marriage for Thynos with a West Saroese princess in the hope of convincing the kingdom of West Saro to break its alliance with our enemies and make a treaty with us. He's not happy about it, but years ago in exchange for Berenise allowing him to run the Fives he promised to accept any betrothal if Berenise found it necessary."

Thynos gone, and Inarsis too! I feel more alone than ever with my family depending on what meager bits of prize money I can dole out to them without engaging Gargaron's suspicions. Without the help of people like Inarsis and Father who have a web of military contacts spread throughout Efea, I'll need a new plan to track down where Bettany and the others have been sent.

"By the way, Spider, I have news for you."

Tana's voice jerks me back to myself. She and Inarsis are both measuring me in a critical way that alters my posture: shoulders back, butt tucked, chin level. I have to stay sharp and not get distracted.

"I've been ordered by Lord Gargaron to enter you for a Challenger trial at the City Fives Court in one month. We need to follow up on your victory. People in the city are talking about you now but if we wait too long they'll forget. I'm just not sure you'll be ready."

"I'll be ready."

Tana walks all the way around me, noting my muscled

arms and my hair pulled back in a casual puff-tail. "You must decide how you mean to outfit yourself for the trials, Jes. Lord Gargaron will expect an elaborate costume, something flashy and bright that will declare you as running for a prestigious palace stable. You can even wear a stripe of gold to remind people of Princess Berenise's royal birth."

"I save my flash for my tricks."

"Don't think one victory makes you memorable." She raises her stump. The scar tissue gleams palely, lighter than her skin. "I aspired to become an Illustrious but I fell from the high Traps and crushed my hand. It became gangrenous and had to be cut off. A day will come, sooner rather than later, when *you* lose once too often, get too old, get too injured. How you dress is part of your strategy, don't you see? Do everything possible to get the crowd on your side. You want to encourage them to bet on you, cheer you on, sing your praises in the market. You want them to think you so dazzling they send you tokens of appreciation, all of which will fatten your bank account for your eventual retirement." She rests the stump on my shoulder and fixes me with a stare. "What you wear is part of the way you announce to the crowd that they must pay attention to this new Challenger called Spider. So what will it be?"

Ro-emnu's words from earlier still sting. And yet I see the truth in them.

Maybe I do talk and think like a Patron, maybe I was raised in a Patron household by a father I admire and love, maybe I won my first victory at the games held in honor of my father, the brilliant general whose name is on everyone's lips.

But I am also a daughter of Efea, loyal daughter to a mother I must pretend is dead, loyal sister to a twin marched onto a barge bound for an unknown servitude, and grandchild and niece and cousin to kinfolk I have never known. I'll run these trials for Garon Palace. Patrons will see whom they want to see, the girl who has no legal status because the law forbade her father and mother from marrying, the girl who triumphed anyway. The general's valiant daughter is a story they can cheer for.

But I can also send a message to the Commoners who will be watching, a message about a girl who lost her beloved family because a Patron lord ripped it apart to serve his own ambitious plans. A girl who isn't ashamed of who she is.

"Ordinary brown."

9

So it is that when I arrive at the City Fives Court a month later for my first trial as a Challenger I am wearing brown leggings, a brown tunic, and a brown mask. I'm not alone because Mis is making her first Novice run and Dusty is hoping for his first Novice victory.

We arrive in the Garon Palace procession, for naturally Lord Gargaron has decided to attend. The highborn are escorted away to the viewing terraces.

A Fives court is both the huge circular building with tiers of seating where trials are held, and the actual playing court in the center where five obstacles are set up. Tana escorts us to the adversary's gate, a staircase that leads down to the undercourt below. Crowds of people line the approach, silent as unknown

Novices arrive, and then cheering while tossing ribbons and rose petals under the feet of Illustrious who boast the colorful clothing Tana wanted me to wear.

Mis has chosen a glassy-white tunic and a splash of perfume on her feathered mask to go with her court name of Resin, a reminder of her family's perfume business. Dusty wears red. He stalks beside Tana in a way that makes me grin, because at the stable he's so funny, always joking and good-humored, and now he is putting on his court name of Wrath in the same way an actor puts on a mask to play a part.

The last time—the only other time—I entered the City Fives Court was for a trial I ran in secret in defiance of my father. That day no one took any notice of me, but now my dull clothes instantly draw attention because I am the only adversary not wearing brighter plumage.

"Spi-der! Spi-der!"

I descend into the undercourt as the chanting of my Fives name echoes after me. By the trickle of perspiration running down my spine I realize I am nervous.

The undercourt is a vast underground construction made up of two parts. The first is the area beneath the actual Fives court itself, sealed away from all people except the Fives administrators and engineers who devise a new version of the obstacles each week. The City Fives Court doesn't have the truly elaborate structures of the Royal Fives Court, but the Royal Court hosts trials only four times a year as well as the occasional

132

victory games. It can also be rebuilt each time, while the City Fives Court, where trials are held weekly, is rebuilt only once a year. No matter what variations the course architects create each week, the basic layout of the City Court will be the same for an entire year, which is an advantage for me because of my good memory for patterns.

The other part of the undercourt is the attiring hall, where adversaries with their attendants wait their turn to run. An adversary entered in the day's trials can *never* see the court before the bell rings. That would be cheating.

Mis can't stop pacing, so to help calm her I mirror her through a warm-up of menageries. My heartbeat slows. My mind steadies. When I clench my hands as part of bull I see how strong they are, ready for any challenge.

I can do this.

"Thanks, Jes," Mis whispers.

A bell rings. Deep within the structure the winches start grinding, pulling the canvas off the court. A roar goes up as this week's obstacles are revealed. Everyone sings the ritual opening song:

Shadows fall where pillars stand.
Traps spill sparks like grains of sand.
Seen atop the trees, you're known.
Rivers flow to seas and home.
Rings around them, rings inside,
The tower at the heart abides.

A custodian calls the names of the first group, Mis's among them.

I embrace her. "Keep your mind on the court. You'll be fine."

She hands over her entry chit and enters the ready cage with three other adversaries. I pace through another round of menageries with Dusty, staying warm and loose, and then he's called.

Tana taps my arm a while later. "All the Novice trials are complete. Are you ready?"

"Yes," I say. And I am.

My name is called for the first Challenger trial. I join my three competitors in the ready cage where we await the call to go to our respective start gates. It's always smart to study the adversaries you'll be running against. A lanky man with an aloof expression and the badge of a palace clan takes the green belt that means he'll start on Trees. He looks strong and sure. A petite woman binds on the blue belt for Rivers. She looks almost dainty, even harmless, but small women like her have an advantage because they have less length and weight to move around than I do. The last adversary is a stocky older man with a few streaks of gray in his hair and scars at his knees and elbows, like he has recovered from a brutally injuring fall. He has the red belt for Traps, while I bind on the brown belt for Pillars. I like starting at Pillars, whose maze gives me a chance to work my intelligence. Maybe they will underestimate me, as I am easily the youngest of us four.

The woman ignores me, lost in her own mental preparations, but the two men study me, and I see one shape the word "Spider" with his lips.

A bell rings, and we are handed over to individual attendants who escort us down separate corridors to our respective start gates at the four corners of the court.

My attendant and I reach the start ladder that leads up to Pillars. The gate-custodian posted there gives me a friendly nod. I become a spear, poised and ready.

The bell rings, the sound clear and sharp. I leap up the ladder, the polished rungs flashing past as I scramble out into the hot sun. Glare fills my eyes, and I blink to cool the blaze. All around the court rise the stone tiers of seating, a huge circle of people shouting and cheering as they wait for us to make our moves.

A carved slab of wood that swings on hinges faces me, painted with a design of overlapping right angles to indicate this as the entrance to Pillars.

Shadows fall where pillars stand.

I ring the obstacle bell and push through to find myself facing myself, a girl dressed all in brown, and her brown face masked with brown. The maze is lined with mirrors, and the mirrors are reflecting mirrors, making it easy to miss turnings.

Unless you look for how the shadows fall.

It's almost too easy.

I'm grinning as I climb up to the resting platform at the end of the obstacle. Sun drenches my face with heat. The grit of sawdust coats my lips. The crowd's gestures help me identify where the other adversaries are: two in Trees and one in Traps. One person is already ahead of me.

Right now I have to choose whether to go on to Rivers, which means I will then continue on through Trees and Traps before Rings, or head into Traps and go the other way around through Trees and then Rivers.

I clamber down and run through the narrow passage to Traps.

As soon as I enter, exhilaration fills me. This Traps has three levels. No Challenger will take the lowest level, a mere arm's length off the ground; that's for Novices. The lanky young man wearing the green belt is working through the middle level, whose ropes and beams run along at the height of my head: challenging but not likely to be fatal should an adversary fall. The "trap" here on the lower and middle levels is a pole swing, a jump from the end of one beam to the beginning of another with a pole staked between that you have to swing around: you get momentum to help cover the gap, but momentum can also make it easy to overshoot the narrow beam.

But there is one more level, the highest of all.

Even if I don't win, I have to make the best impression I

can to ensnare the crowd's affection by dazzling it. A murmuring buzz begins to build as I use my legs to power up a dangling rope, climbing past the middle level and straight to the top, three body heights off the ground. The wind teases across my face as I confront three challenges: a slack line, a beam split by a gap I'll have to leap, and a taut rope. At the lowest level this would be fledgling work, but up here it's possible for an adversary to fall to her death, adding spice to a trial.

Win, or die.

My father the baker's son didn't work his way up from his lowborn origins to become a general by not taking chances.

I cross the slack line with a series of tricks: a knees-up jump, a full turnaround spin, and an airborne somersault that lands me on the beam. The crowd roars its approval.

The beam is split into two parts with a gap between, and the flat top of the metal pole, the part you have to swing around on the lower levels, here functions as a stepping stone between the two halves of the beam. But I don't use the pole as a step to bridge the gap. I back up five long steps and run. With a twist and a tuck, I spin over the pole, across the gap, and land solidly on the other side.

No training has prepared me for the howl of excitement that lifts from the crowd. Remembering how I saluted my father at the victory games, I straighten my shoulders and tap my chest twice in acknowledgment, and they howl even louder.

Then I tune out everything except the taut rope. Never

look down to where death lies, far below. I breathe my racing thoughts into the calm pool of my innermost heart, and cross in ten swift steps.

Green Belt reaches the resting platform of Traps just after I do. I snap, "Kiss off, Adversary" before I vault down to the passage that leads to Trees. At the entry gate I shove open the door and step off to one side to study the obstacle, just in time, because my stocky red-belted opponent sprints past me to the first cluster of climbing posts.

The Fives song thrums in my head: *Seen atop the trees, you're known.*

"Kiss off, Adversary," Red Belt taunts before he swiftly finger-climbs up a set of boards to the top of the first feature. When I follow, the finger climb isn't too grueling; I've done ten in a row to that height in training. But when I reach the top I see I can't possibly beat Red Belt on this obstacle because it is nothing but strength-climbing up and down sets of posts arranged in various configurations between here and the resting platform above.

That's when I notice the posts themselves happen to be set into the ground close enough together that the tops of each could function as ascending stepping stones. Instead of climbing up and down each set of posts, a bold adversary could leap from the top of one to the top of the next in the same way a person might cross a stream one stone to the next. Anything that ascends counts as a climb, surely.

A slip means disaster—a broken leg or a broken neck. This route will take utter focus to ignore everything except speed, angle, forward propulsion, and balance, so I am just the person to try it.

Toes pushing, I dig deep, bending lower with each spring as my leg muscles thrust me up in a zigzag set of leaps, forward one two three four five six seven eight nine ten.... I'm slowing, and the gap between the last post and the final resting platform is too wide.

So I don't try for the platform. I leap into the wind as if I am the probing filament of a spider's thread cast into the air. I catch the edge of the resting platform with my hands, torquing my legs side to side to bring me to a halt.

For several breaths I hang, arms brushing my ears, body dangling.

Drifts of noise swell past like waves. Swinging up to the resting platform, I roll twice and jump to my feet. For once after completing Trees, my legs throb instead of my arms. Stocky is way behind me now. I flip him the kiss-off gesture to shouts of "Spider!"

I climb down and race along the next passage to Rivers. Quickly I negotiate the moving stones and then climb onto the nearest platform that gives entry into Rings, the final obstacle, at whose heart lies the victory tower.

In this configuration of Rings, short walkways and short stairsteps slowly rotate to produce a maze of brief connections that touch and vanish, creating both dead ends and open paths on the road to victory.

A foot scrapes the ladder as Red Belt climbs up, looking like he wants to punch me.

"You cheated," he says. "You didn't climb in Trees."

"I climbed the tops of the posts. Each one was higher than the last." My grin taunts him. "It's not your judgment to make, Adversary. Kiss off."

A jump takes me into Rings, and I ride each turning segment as it connects to another, choosing my path to carve the best route through. Blue Belt is already working her way through Rings and at first she is closer to the tower, but a wrong step takes her onto a path that pushes her on a detour while I make no misstep as I work my way in. I throw in a few flips for show.

In my first trial as a Challenger I climb the ladder and grab the victor's ribbon to the cheers—and a few intimidating boos—of the crowd. Facing the balcony where Garon Palace's winged and horned fire dog symbol flies, I pull off my mask to let them see my face.

Sunlight pours over me together with the surging clamor of the audience, as strong as wings lifting me. Grinning, I fling wide my arms to embrace the moment. The cheers, and boos, grow louder. Only then do I descend, victor's ribbon clutched in my hand.

Two of the adversaries await me by the ladder into the undercourt. Red Belt repeats his charge. "You cheated, and my

140

stable will file a protest." The small woman says, "That was bold, Spider. I liked what you did. But I'll beat you next time."

"Kiss off, Adversary," I say to her with a smile, and she flicks the kiss-off hand gesture back at me in amused reply.

I climb down into the retiring court, the section of the attiring hall reserved for adversaries who have already run. An attendant hands me a cup of royal nectar. Besides the royal family, only adversaries who have just completed a trial are allowed this drink. The sweetness hits so hard my eyes water.

I won.

With controlled breaths I quiet my dizzy heart, then look around as a Garon steward approaches me. "I am to escort you," she says.

I follow her through passages and stairs to the upper tiers. The steward shows a token to guards, who admit us into the area reserved for Patron lords. As I pass, sweaty and reeking, one mutters, "Well raced, Spider. No one saw that trick coming."

We walk into the rear of the Garon balcony. Masked servants bring platters of food to the highborn. Lord Gargaron and Lady Menoë sit in the front row. Behind them sit less exalted members of the household, men separate from women, all strangers to me.

My gaze catches on a very pretty young woman dressed in the beribboned glitter of one whose fortune is her looks. I know Denya because she and my sister Amaya were friends, and closer than friends to judge by things said in my hearing.

Denya's father, like mine, was a captain in service to Lord Ottonor before the lord died. When Gargaron paid off part of the debt of Ottonor's household in order to get my father, he took Denya as part of the payment owed him, to become his concubine.

A servant brushes past carrying a platter of spiced prawns sprinkled with paprika and kneels to offer these delicacies with a spry flourish to Denya. The servant wears a slim half-mask, a band of spangled fabric pulled across her eyes that does nothing to hide her lovely features and the luscious bow of her carmine-reddened lips.

My heart turns to stone. I open my mouth, then snap it shut as the servant turns her back on me to hide her very familiar face. Amaya can't possibly be stupid enough to have taken work in the household of our greatest enemy who must believe she is dead!

"Spider!"

A voice cracks over me. Stiffly I turn to face the front of the balcony, where two Fives administrators stand at attention before Lord Gargaron. Beads of perspiration seep down the back of my neck as I come to parade rest before the two administrators, one middle-aged and one white-haired but still hale and strong.

"Your victory has been declared forfeit, Spider." Oddly, Gargaron doesn't seem angry. He's not stroking his whip, and his fingers splay with utter relaxation on the armrests of his cushioned chair. "It has been explained to me that you did not complete Trees by climbing, as the rules demand. Therefore you will hand over your victor's ribbon to the lord engineer. Go on."

It is so hard to unclench my fingers from the prize, even if it is a slip of gold ribbon no longer than my forearm. My chest tightens with fear as I realize the danger I've put myself in. Being whipped by Gargaron would be a mercy compared to the other punishment that could be meted out: banishment from competition.

The middle-aged engineer yanks the ribbon from my grip.

Gargaron tilts his head to study me. "Had you a question or a comment, Spider?"

"I ascended the posts," I say, trying to hide my nervousness from my potential executioner.

"What? No excuse?" Gargaron taps fingers on the armrest.

"I wanted to win, my lord. After considering the options, it was clearly the fastest way up. Since each post was a bit higher than the one before, it seemed to fit the definition of Trees: that you have to climb."

Lady Menoë snaps open her fan and laughs behind it.

"What do you say, Lord Perikos?" Gargaron asks the older man, the lord administrator.

Lord Perikos's face is adorned with the smile of a person enjoying the theatricals. In fact, he barely restrains an outright laugh. "We will inform the engineers to do a better job in subsequent trials by not leaving openings that may be misinterpreted by bold adversaries intent on giving the crowd an exhilarating spectacle."

The lord engineer huffs like an offended bull. "We didn't imagine someone would have the temerity…the *audacity*… to risk themselves by leaping up along the tops of the posts."

I gesture toward the court, gaining courage from Lord Perikos's amusement. "From up here it looks exactly like a stairstep challenge. If the engineers didn't realize the posts could be used in the way I used them, then someone wasn't thinking things through."

The engineer sputters as Lord Perikos guffaws, then addresses Lord Gargaron. "Her sole penalty is to forfeit the victory. Henceforth she must follow the rules according to the regulations set down during the reign of Kliatemnos the Second. If she does not, she will be banned from the Fives."

After the two men depart, Lady Menoë lowers her fan. Cunningly drawn wings unfurl from the corners of her eyes in the current cosmetic fashion.

"I like your spirit, Spider. You showed them for the fusty, rule-bound old donkeys they are. You will attend me this coming Firstday when I go to the palace to visit Queen Serenissima."

"Yes, my lady."

The crowd breaks into a flurry of cheers melded with derisive boos as a herald announces the retraction of my victory.

Gargaron studies the teeming multitude. "Go stand at the railing, Spider. Let them see you."

I walk to the railing. With hands fixed behind my back I let the rush of sound wash over me as people see and acknowledge my presence. My father said that in battle, it is not just what you see but also what you hear that tells you the mood of your soldiers, of the enemy, of the day itself.

This is what I hear: A few might think me a cheater, but most people love what I did because I acted audaciously. If every adversary runs with caution then a stupor sets in. Tricks and impulsive chances give the Fives an intoxicating flavor. Skill matters, but daring and flair matter too.

I hope the Commoners in the crowd see a girl who outwitted the rules imposed by the Patron masters. That's how I will capture their approval.

My gaze strays to the trial under way. In Trees a man with excellent grip strength hangs at ease one-handed as he seeks his next hold. The fickle crowd forgets me and cheers him.

"That's enough, Jessamy. Go to the back and refresh yourself." Gargaron's sense of timing is impeccable, pulling me away from the railing as soon as he senses the crowd's disinterest. "Come back after you've washed. You will watch the rest of the trials from the corner of the balcony. Many of our acquaintances will wander by over the rest of the afternoon to get a closer look at you."

"Yes, my lord." I retreat without turning my back on him or Lady Menoë.

As I pass the benches where the women sit, Denya gestures commandingly to the servant holding the prawns. "Go on and see to her, but leave those on the table for us to finish."

A tent runs along the back of the balcony, divided by canvas walls into cubicles. The steward shows me to the farthest cubicle, where an old dog sleeps on a pillow, snoring. As soon as the steward leaves, Denya's servant enters carrying a pitcher of water, a basin, soap, and a towel. She has cropped hair as Patron-born servant women do to mark their lowborn rank, and a deeper golden sheen on her cheeks like she has gotten too much sun. The short hair changes the look of her face more than anything, making her chin seem sharper. But I know it's her. The moment she puts down the basin and pitcher, I grab her arm so hard she squeaks.

"What are you thinking?" I demand in a fierce whisper.

Amaya shakes off my grip. "Maybe the same thing you were thinking when you broke the rules in the trial you just ran. I know how to use cosmetics to hide what I am."

"Barely passing as a Patron won't protect you if Lord Gargaron recognizes you!"

"How would he? He only ever saw me *once*!"

Footsteps alert us. Amaya pours water into the basin. When a steward looks in to check on us, I am washing my face and hands.

"You are wanted on the balcony, Spider," says the steward, although her expression suggests she doubts my suitability to venture out there.

"I can tidy up her hair," says Amaya chirpily. "What a frightful mess it is!"

"Very well, Orchid. But hurry up." The steward departs.

"*Orchid?*" I mutter.

"You don't need to sneer at me like that."

"I'm not sneering. I'm trying not to laugh."

"I think 'Orchid' suits me! I always wondered why Father called our servants after plants and it turns out it's something all the highborn palaces do. He must have learned of the custom in the army." Her lips twitch. "It's better than the first thing the senior steward wanted to name me."

"Which was?"

"Jasmine, like you, Jessamy."

We both snicker, then clap hands over our mouths as the dog lifts its head, too blind to tell who we are. There is nowhere for me to sit so I kneel on the ground as she tidies my hair with her usual ruthless efficiency. The truth is, having her here yanking at my curls is comforting. She's the ally I've been missing, the one who knows everything that I can't tell anyone else.

"Does Mother know you're here?" I ask.

"I just told her I would get work, not where. Now that Polodos is saddled with the inn we need more money than what you sent to make a go of it."

"So Ro-emnu did bring the coin."

"Yes. The poet has quite fallen in love with Mother. I don't mean in a romantic way; I mean like people do, wanting to ask her advice about how to court a lover or how best to earn a living in the market. What fish is healthiest to eat. Which herbs are best to relieve which malady. He can talk to her for hours about her life in the village. He questions her endlessly about the customs they observed there when she was a girl."

"She barely told us about any of that!" It's not fair Ro-emnu gets to see her when I can't, that she'll tell him stories she never told me. "He's a dangerous man to have around, considering the king had him arrested once already for writing a play critical of the royal family."

"Maybe so, but he's helped Polodos and Maraya clean things up, and he brings friends to the inn to try to get a regular clientele started."

"What kind of friends? The last thing we need is his activities drawing attention to Mother!"

"Easy for you to say, with a fancy roof over your head and all the food you can eat! We can scarcely afford bread for ourselves, much less stock meals and beer for customers. So you see I had to get work to help with expenses."

"You didn't have to get work here."

"If you knew how unhappy Denya's situation is, you wouldn't criticize. At least with me as her personal servant, she has one person who cares about her in that awful place."

A knot twists in my chest as I think of Gargaron's whip. "Is he cruel to her?"

The hard tugs she gives as she tidies my hair betray her agitation. "He didn't extract her from the wreckage of Lord Ottonor's debts so they could discuss the latest philosophical tract from the Archives or who will win the horse races next week! I won't leave her, Jes. And you can't make me."

A reluctant grin tugs at my mouth. "I know I can't make you. You're the stubbornest person I've ever met." I chew on my lower lip. "It could actually be really useful for you to be in Garon Palace. As long as you aren't caught."

"You're the one who almost got caught because you have as much subtlety as a bull! I'm much better at disguise and play-acting than you are."

My mind is already spinning this new obstacle. "As Denya's handmaiden you're well placed to overhear gossip at parties and in the servants' quarters."

"Exactly! I've been waiting to tell you that I heard a group of women and children were sent north a month ago to one of the country estates to work, but I don't know which estate. It's possible Bettany is with them."

"She is with them," I say, and Amaya grabs my wrist in excitement, then releases me and steps quickly away as we hear someone approaching.

The steward enters. "Lord Gargaron wishes you to attend him *at once*."

What greets me on the balcony makes me want to run back to the privacy of the cubicle. The men chatting with Lord Gargaron trouble me with sly glances and leering smiles. Father would never have allowed us girls to be thrown into a situation like this one, where a Patron man would feel at ease sizing us up as if we were a platter of spicy prawns he is deciding if he is hungry enough to eat. Father's strictures annoyed me once, but now I see how hard he worked to make us safe in a land where we have no legal standing.

I pretend I am a pillar, smooth and polished and without expression.

One of the lords speaks to Gargaron although he keeps glancing at me. "Of course they had to strip her of her victor's ribbon, but I swear by all three gods she was astonishing to see, Gar. Some days the Fives are too dull to bear, but not with her here taking any kind of chance. I was sure she would fall and crack open her head!"

"I was sure she would not," says Gargaron.

My chin lifts at the praise, and then I remember who he is and what he has done.

Another man addresses me directly without any of the modest courtesy an Efean man would have shown. "They say you are General Esladas's mule daughter. You run like he fights, don't you?"

I look at Gargaron, for I dare not speak without his permission. He nods.

"If you mean that as a compliment to my father's ability to seek out an innovative solution in the heat of battle, my lord, then I thank you for the praise."

The men exclaim. "She speaks our language perfectly! Amazing!"

The man who was sure I would crack open my head whispers in Gargaron's ear, but Gargaron shakes his head and says, "Good Goat, man, show some patience. If she fulfills her promise there will be plenty of time to snatch her victor's ribbons."

A flush heats my cheeks. I don't want them to guess that they repulse me. Gargaron knows they do, and that is bad enough.

But he's playing a long game, just as I am.

Today the crowd will remember what I did, not who won. When I glance at Gargaron, I bind this thought tightly into my heart. However powerless I am, I am not nothing. He is not as safe from me as he thinks he is.

I remember what Ro-emnu said: *Someone like you can fight for Efea in ways no Patron will ever see until it is too late.*

10

On the next Firstday, Lady Menoë's party departs Garon Palace in a cavalcade of carriages, bound for the King's Garden outside the city walls where Queen Serenissima has retired to sit out a heat spell amid shady courtyards. Mounted guards ride ahead, resplendent in uniforms with calf-length tabards that flow and ripple, the Garon fire dog embroidered on flags fixed to the backs of the horses' saddles. Lady Menoë follows in the first carriage with her particular friends. A second carriage of Garon Palace wives follows, behind them the favored concubines and two carriages of servants, all Patron women concealed behind curtains.

Mis bounces up and down beside me as we stand at the gate to Garon Stable watching the procession go by. "Aren't you excited, Jes?"

"This dress is too tight."

A sheath gown of muted orange-brown silk hugs my body, the clingy fabric emphasizing my curves while its halter neck-tie exposes the brawny shoulders that Lady Menoë's friends exclaimed over. I have never in my life worn such costly fabric, which is embroidered with ivory beads and white thread to create a lacework meant to evoke a spider's web. Artisans must have stayed awake day and night to finish this in a mere three days. All I can think about is that I am going to rip something.

When the last carriage halts to pick me up, one of the guards calls, "You were robbed, Spider! They should have let you keep the victor's ribbon."

The rest of the rear guard murmurs in agreement as I carefully climb into the carriage, trying not to step on the hem of my dress. I sit alone, of course, for what Patron, even a servant, would sit with me? For me the curtains are tied back so people can see the adversary named Spider. I'm worth something to Garon Palace, otherwise they would not parade me through the city like this.

The royal city was named Saryenia in honor of Lord Saryenos, the father of the first Saroese king and queen, Kliatemnos the First and his sister Serenissima the First, who was his queen but not his wife. They built the king's palace atop the conical hill called the King's Hill and the queen's palace atop the Queen's Hill. Garon Palace lies high up on the King's Hill amid other palace compounds, and I stare across the city as we follow a road that twists back and forth down the slope. To the east the orderly streets of the newer part of the city turn into the jumble of the Warrens. To the south lies the Fire Sea, and from up here the wide waters shine like they've been polished.

Between the West and East Harbors lies the peninsula where the Saroese bury their dead and entomb the oracles through whom the gods speak to the living. I can't identify which is Clan Tonor's tomb, from which I freed my mother and sisters, but I gloat anyway.

The road turns inland, overlooking the reed-choked shoreline of Mist Lake. Boats crowd the lake harbor where I saw Bettany. Efea's fields and orchards and mines are so rich that our ports never sleep, transferring grain, oil, flax, cotton, natron, salt, and metals from the interior to the ocean fleets for export. No wonder our enemies wish to conquer us so they can bathe in the spoils.

Below the King's Hill we pass the wall that fences off the Grain Market. Long lines of people wait to buy grain, Patrons on the shade side and Commoners in the sun. As people look up to watch us pass it is remarkable how many recognize me.

"You were robbed, Spider!" a Patron man shouts.

"That was the best trick I've seen this year!"

"Don't let them kill your spirit with their stifling rules!"

When I look at the silent line of Commoners, many stare with hostility but some of the women press left hand to left breast in a gesture I have only ever seen Efean women make as a mark of respect, while some of the men hold up an open palm, five fingers spread. I don't know what it means.

Suddenly my carriage lurches to a stop. Shouts break out.

"The king is hoarding the grain!"

"We need bread!"

I lean out. Ahead, at the entrance to the Grain Market, the crowd has begun shoving, trying to get inside. On the wall the king's soldiers turn their crossbows on the crowd. If a riot breaks out, we are trapped here on the street.

To my surprise one of the Garon guards holds the curtain of the first carriage aside to reveal Lady Menoë. Her black hair is piled atop her head in a fantastical architecture of metallic ribbons and bows so bright they catch sunlight in their folds. The appearance of a highborn woman hushes the agitated crowd. For such an elegant person she has an astonishing voice that carries in the air without seeming shrill, the bold call of a commander in battle.

"I have heard the cries of folk who fear the grain supplies are running low. You fear the king sells grain to our enemies in order to finance his war. I can assure you as the granddaughter of the revered Princess Berenise that her ships will never transport grain to foreign ports as long as any household in Saryenia goes hungry. This very day I go to see the queen to beg that she make the same pledge on behalf of you, who are her children. Be patient, good citizens. I act as your champion!"

Ragged cheers applaud her stirring speech but an undercurrent of skeptical murmuring from the crowd makes me glance around to find an escape route if they swarm us. The fearsome glimmer of spider scouts appears, big metal creatures clanking up to the gate from inside the Grain Market. The arrival of the intimidating spiders causes the crowd to shrink back and quiet down.

We roll on and without further incident reach the city walls and the Royal Gate that leads to the King's Garden, carved with the sea-phoenix that is the emblem of the royal house. Not even Gargaron could have predicted that victory in the Fives would grant me entrance into a garden where only the king and queen, their household, and their invited guests may walk. It's an extraordinarily fortunate chance, especially if I'm able to discover proof that Prince Nikonos and Menoë are colluding.

Palm trees and shade trees fill the wide expanse. Sprawling bushes span the ground like clouds torn across the sky, their white blooms as bright as stars. We arrive at the famous Silk Pavilion. The ladies and their servants enter up a flight of steps to a portico hung with embroidered curtains depicting the ships on which Kliatemnos the First, Serenissima the First, and their sisters, soldiers, servants, and followers arrived in Efea.

Of course I'm not allowed to enter with them. My carriage travels on around the pavilion to a building in back where the kitchens are housed. Here I wait for an interminable time, hearing the clamor of people busy preparing a feast. The smell of cooking lamb and the heady aroma of cinnamon baked in pears makes my mouth water.

A Garon steward hurries up. "Lady Menoë wishes you to be presented to the queen. Come along, Spider."

We stride into the pavilion, which is made up of many ornately carved pillars from which awnings and curtains are hung to create tiny private sanctuaries or large gathering spots. A ripple of sweet-falling sound announces a gathering ahead. Servants bearing platters of food process into a courtyard shaded by gauzy awnings and surrounded by billowing fabric. Highborn women, Lady Menoë among them, sit on couches listening to a woman play a harp. The harpist wears a diadem of gold molded to look like sheaves of grain, and I realize this unremarkable-looking woman not much younger than my mother must be Queen Serenissima. To my surprise she plays with genuine skill.

The steward pauses at the edge of the courtyard as Menoë sees us and shakes her head to indicate it isn't time to bring me in yet. With a grimace the steward glances around for someplace to keep me out of view, and parts a curtain, waving me through. I find myself in a dim space made gloomy and stuffy by wool curtains tied down on all sides and a heavy canvas awning overhead. This area seems to be an empty buffer space, nothing stored here, no servants waiting.

The bark of a labored cough touches my ears. I tiptoe to the far curtains and peer out between a slit onto a second court-yard, this one shaded by an arbor whose vines sag with clusters of grapes. Under a purple silk canopy a man sits at a table stacked with books propped open with rods of gold. He's an ordinary-looking man, not handsome and not ugly, but very intent on what he's doing. He has a large book open in front of him and pauses to brush words into it before going back to reading a different book. A tray of honey cakes sits at his elbow, warm enough from the oven that their scent luxuriantly kisses my mouth. My heart staggers through erratic beats as I realize how close I am standing to the most powerful person in Efea.

A bell rings from behind a thick swag of curtains.

With the impatient frown of a man who is rarely inter-rupted, King Kliatemnos looks up and says, "Enter."

A resplendently dressed captain steps into view. "Your Gracious and Most Powerful and Enduring Lordship, a pigeon has arrived bearing a message from Prince Nikonos, with news of the army on the Eastern Reach."

"Bring it in at once, Captain."

A pair of soldiers carry in a birdcage in which rests a hooded pigeon banded with a gold collar. Whistling to calm the bird, the king slips a folded paper from the tiny pouch on its back and unfolds it. I chafe, wishing I could dart out and snatch it from his hand.

To my relief the king reads the message out loud. "'Gracious Brother, the gods have favored me with a victory at Pellucidar Lake.' 'Favored *me*,' Nikonos writes," Kliatemnos remarks in a tone of dour amusement. "Of course our brother gives himself credit for the victory but we are sure the credit belongs entirely to General Esladas. We are fortunate that in our time of peril such a competent commander is available." The king hands over the message. "Have a decree written up and announce the victory throughout Efea."

A victory! My whole body sags in relief, for I am sure if Father or Kalliarkos had been wounded or killed the message would have mentioned it. Yet I hadn't realized the enemy had already entered Efean territory, that they are fighting at Pellucidar Lake, where stands the easternmost fortress under Efean rule. Is the situation already so dire?

What makes it worse is that they still don't know Nikonos and Menoë are conspiring behind their backs, that they are in danger on both sides. Maybe Inarsis's courier has reached them with this news, but what if he hasn't and what if they don't believe it?

Another cough draws my attention to a frail-looking boy reclining on a couch off to one side in the shadow of a heavy canvas awning. He's ten or twelve years old and wearing a simple white keldi and linen vest. A handsome youth fans him with the bored expression of a person who knows he will be at this tedious chore for the rest of the day.

They aren't the only ones in this spacious courtyard. Under

159

a second arbor a stone's toss away, two men sit across from each other at a table, playing a Saroese game called Castle and Tower. The black tassels on their tall hats identify them as priests of Lord Judge Inkos who presides over the judgment of the dead and the afterlife.

As the captain, soldiers, and birdcage withdraw, an old man wearing a scholar's robe bustles into the courtyard. A tower of books teeters in his arms.

"What did you bring us, Thanises?" asks the king.

"The official texts of all the history plays produced in Saryenia in the last ten years, as you requested, Your Gracious Lordship. Although what you hope to find here I do not know."

The king breaks off a piece of honey cake and eats it absently as thunder brews in his eyes. "We want to find the reason why a Commoner poet stands in front of a crowd and proclaims our revered ancestress Serenissima the Third, the Benevolent, a murderer!"

I barely refrain from gasping out loud. The king knows about Ro-emnu!

"Of course the incident troubles you, Your Gracious Lordship. But it took place a month ago."

"And since then we have heard reports of graffiti scrawled on walls and insulting songs sung in taverns."

"Yes, yes, Your Lordship, but people will have their discontents. Let them bleed off their energy in harmless small acts."

"The poet will attack again, and more people will hear what he has to say. Why have our soldiers not tracked him down? Double their numbers. Triple them!"

The scholar scratches his forehead with a look of exasperation. "Your Gracious and Exalted Lordship, can you not tear your attention away from your hunt for this trifling poet to consider the pressing question of how to pay the troops with the gold reserves so low? Do you never wonder if there is a reason the gold supplies have begun to drop off in recent years, not just the vague assurances from Princess Berenise that the veins are giving out? Please let me counsel you, Your Lordship, that paying the troops is a far more serious issue than a poet's scurrilous accusations. It isn't as if his outrageous assertions are true."

The king pops a honey cake into his mouth and chews slowly. The hard look in his eyes is anything but reassuring.

"In our first year as king we personally supervised the destruction of all the Archival records from the year in which Kliatemnos the Third and Serenissima the Third, the Benevolent, ascended to the throne of Efea. The events cast such an unpleasant light on the royal family that we thought it better to eradicate all trace of what she did."

"The deified Serenissima the Benevolent murdered her own kinsmen?" Thanises tugs nervously on a sleeve.

"The flask she used for the wine with which she poisoned her father, her brother, and her brother's infant son sits at our bedside. She did what she did to save Efea, but people always misunderstand necessity. The poet must be arrested. Before he is executed we must discover how he found out, when we went to such trouble to conceal the entire history of her actions!"

Thanises presses fingers to his eyes and struggles for composure, then with a placating smile addresses the king. "I am pleased to inform you that this morning my investigators brought word that a poet answering to his description was spotted at a place called the Heart Tavern."

I find my hand on my throat before I realize I raised it. How can I possibly get out of here fast enough to warn Ro? What if, in tracking him down, the authorities discover Mother?

The boy on the couch suddenly begins gulping in wheezy gasps, rolling from side to side with spasms like a fish throttled by air.

The king leaps to his feet. "Thanises, you said it would be another year before his illness progressed this far again! I'll throttle you with my own hands if he dies!"

Thanises hurries to the child as the youth holding the fan backs out of the way. Alerted by the commotion, the priests leap up and rush over as well. At the scholar's touch the boy's movement ceases. I am so sure he has stopped breathing that I reflexively hold my breath as my fingers tighten on my own throat.

The king strides over, tapping a long knife against one thigh.

"Has he stopped breathing?"

With a strike as swift as a cobra's and all the more stunning for its precision, the king stabs the youth who is holding the fan.

The priests catch the lad and bind his mouth with a band of cloth before he screams. As he fights against their grasping hands, his squirming and choked attempts to cry out make my skin crawl as with a thousand spiders.

If I run out there they will kill me. A flash of heat like lightning courses through me. My vision hazes over as if filling up with blood.

The world is filling up with blood.

11

The priests trap the boy on the ground as blood pumps from the wound to soak his tunic. The younger priest waves a lit stick of incense beneath the youth's nose, making his eyes roll up while his struggle slows. The scent tickles my nose, causing my eyelids to droop and my legs to feel as heavy as logs.

The king watches without expression as the young priest presses a knee into the lad's chest and with a scalpel cuts into his throat, although not to slice through the blood vessel and let him bleed out: instead he cuts into the ridged tissue of the voice box to render him mute.

My heart has turned to stone. My hands no longer feel like my hands; my eyes belong to someone else. I have to pretend

I am standing in the back row of a theater watching actors about their work because otherwise I will scream and scream and scream.

They pull the cloth away from the youth's mouth. It stretches wide and desperate, but no sound comes out.

The younger priest pulls open the lad's arms, like spreading wings, while the elder slips on a pair of gloves and pulls a net of silver thread from inside his robe. He spreads the net over the lad's face and chest. Blood slides right over the fine gradient, not staining. The net glitters like a dew-moistened spider's web when morning sunlight catches on its threads.

Using his size and weight, the younger priest cracks the lad's chest. The sound assaults me, so resonant and so cruel that I can't control a violent flinch that stirs the curtains, but no one is looking this way.

Floating on the air like a mocking accompaniment, a glissade of notes from the harp cascades as sunlight might gleam through a rent in storm clouds. From behind the curtain, unaware of the terrible contrast their words make, women sing in clear, bright voices:

Let the Sun of Justice vanquish that which seeks to harm us!
Let the Blessed Lady heal our wounds and hurts. Let the Judge
grant us safe passage into the Underworld.

The older priest holds up an obsidian knife that seems to eat light out of the air, then deftly slices through skin and flesh.

Two fingers thrust between the gaps in the netting. He pries a pulsing organ—the lad's heart—out of the chest cavity until the netting wraps it.

A final rising tower of notes spills from the harp as the queen finishes playing, followed by a rush of applause from the ladies. The lad's heels drum against the earth in futile defiance. The king places a foot atop the youth's ankle to hold it down.

The lad exhales and does not inhale. The veined mass of his heart ceases beating.

Light cascades through the silvery netting. Brightness winks as brilliantly as a spark-bug caught in a cage. The priests have just killed a boy no older than I am and captured his spark in a net.

The old priest peels the net off the dead lad and, with the calm and practiced demeanor of a man who has performed this magic many times before, he spreads the netting over the face and chest of the prince.

The gleam in the netting fades as the spark caught in its threads seeps into the flesh of the prince.

My palms grow clammy. I want to scrub my skin over and over again with a stiff brush to scrape off the blood even though none touched me. With a sick sense of certainty it all comes clear: The prince has been living on borrowed sparks. People have died to keep him alive.

The prince gasps. His eyes flutter, and he sighs as if his sleep now curls through peaceful dreams. His color is already a healthy sheen instead of an ashy pallor. The spark of the dead youth is a strong one, filling the prince's flesh with vitality.

If this is the magic of Efea, then I want nothing to do with it.

The older priest peels the net off the prince. They bow and vanish behind a curtain, leaving the body behind.

Kliatemnos gazes on his son with a clouded expression no different from that of any worried father. "It is fortunate we had someone so close at hand, isn't it?"

In a low voice Thanises says, "My lord, the youth was the son of Lord Perikos, not a criminal."

"Yes, the lad's death does create a breach of courtesy."

I'm shocked that the king dares kill the son of a lord, and speak of it so calmly.

"I recommend you pay Lord Perikos ten talents of gold," the scholar says.

"As you reminded us before, we can't even pay our own troops, Thanises."

"Then transfer to Lord Perikos the deed to a good piece of property, my lord."

"Yes, yes." Seeing that the prince breathes with the vigor of any healthy child in a restful sleep, the king settles back at his desk and walks his fingers across the open pages of books as if looking for inspiration between the lines. "Ah! We shall transfer the deed to our vineyard on the slopes of Butterfly Pass over to the Ikos clan. Perikos visited us there and admired the view. In fact, it was on that visit when he pledged the youth to serve the prince at the palace. The boy is the son of a concubine, so he isn't an heir. A death hymn and the vineyard should content Perikos as a decent recompense for his loss. It's a shame. A good-looking and intelligent lad. Our son liked him."

Thanises studies the corpse with its terrible wounds. "May I recommend that Your Lordship inform Lord Perikos that the lad was attacked while carousing in the Lantern District? No, no, say he went outside the city to the horse races and got in a fight over a bet."

The king opens one of the books Thanises just brought. The dead youth has already ceased to interest him. "If the prince is apt to have seizures more frequently, we must keep a criminal on hand at all times. The last spark we gave him did not last long at all."

"The prince's disorder eats quickly at his life-force, my lord. Let us hope this youthful spark will carry the prince for many months."

"Mmmm." The king's attention fixes on the book. "Clean up quickly so he doesn't wake and see the body."

The priests return and with the scholar tidy up and cart off the body as the king remains engrossed in his reading. The air smells of myrrh and cinnamon burned to purify the ground but the stink of untimely, murderous death has stuck in my throat. Even to swallow makes me want to vomit.

Death—the moment when the spark leaves the flesh—is not a mystery nor need it be feared. When an elderly Commoner servant died in our household, Mother expected her daughters to help wash the corpse. What happened to Lord Perikos's son wasn't death but violence.

Belatedly I remember the conversation between the king and Thanises: Ro is in danger, and with him my entire family. Yet I'm trapped here until Menoë leaves.

With a relaxed yawn, the boy sits up and stretches. He picks up the big fan and glances around in confusion, looking for the missing youth. Swinging his legs off the couch, he stands, tests himself as an adversary might as she recovers from a fall, making sure her legs will hold her. He ventures over toward the king, who pats the lad on the arm and goes back to his books.

The prince wrinkles up his nose, sniffs audibly, and makes several funny little faces. Before I have the least warning, he trots to the curtain behind which I am hiding. He can hear the music too, of course. He knows where his mother is.

Too late I step away, meaning to escape down the servants' corridor. He sweeps the curtain aside. His eyes widen as he takes me in. If I bolt, it will look as if I have something to hide. A net of fear pins me to the ground.

"Gracious Father, I found a spider," he calls over his shoulder in a high, light voice.

The king, immersed in reading, does not react. Probably he hasn't heard. But if he finds me here he will have me killed.

I press two fingers to my lips. A smile lights the prince's face as if we are playing a game.

He grabs my hand and tugs me toward the women's courtyard. I'm so grateful to escape the king's notice that it doesn't occur to me until too late that the prince means to barge right in. His grip is frail; he's small for a boy of twelve. But I dare not break away as he leads me enthusiastically past the other curtain and straight into the center of the courtyard.

Seeing him, the four ladies who are singing falter. The queen looks around.

"Gracious Mother, look what I found," he says into the silence. "See how she is brown all over like a tomb spider! And she is wearing her web."

He traces the silvery threads on my dress to make sure everyone notices.

The worst part isn't the way they are all staring at me as if they will have to wash the sight of me off their hands the way a butcher cleans himself after he slaughters a beast. Queasiness twists in my gut as Lady Menoë rises, hands in fists and red lips flattened into a thin line that makes her resemble her uncle. Clearly I have arrived before she wanted me.

The queen extends both hands. "Why, little Temnos, you are looking well today!"

The prince releases my hand and crosses to his mother. She presses a kiss to his forehead. She is a dainty woman, short and plump with a round face and slightly bulging eyes that convey a vague sense of constant stupefaction.

"Where did the spider come from?" she asks, with a sharp glance toward the curtains. "Are you the king's new favorite?"

The ladies open their fans to hide their shocked expressions. I keep my posture rigid. Horribly, I can't figure out what to do.

Menoë glides forward. "Oh, Cousin! How can you think so? This is Garon Stable's new adversary. She's the one who defeated my dear Kal at the victory games last month."

"Why did you bring her here?" Queen Serenissima's mildly foolish countenance doesn't look so foolish when she examines me.

"I thought you would find it amusing to see her tricks close up."

The prince has begun stuffing spiced prawns into his mouth in the manner of a child who hasn't eaten in a week, oil oozing down his fingers. His gaze flicks from Menoë to his mother and then to me. The measuring intelligence in his eyes isn't reflected in his childish speech. "I want to see her tricks! Please, Gracious Mother, I want her to be my special adversary and run for me in the palace."

Lady Menoë flutters her fan so hard I am surprised the

171

curtains don't fly right away. "Prince Temnos, my dear cousin, how is the spider to train as an adversary if you keep her caged up for your own amusement?"

"Are you going to call her Spider just like I said she was?" His vapid grin makes him look about six. He extends a hand, inviting her to take it.

"Of course, little Cousin." She ignores the proffered hand.

"Can you show me some tricks right now, Spider?"

"Not wearing this dress, Your Lordship," I say.

The ladies tap each other with their fans with as much surprise as they might if a crow spoke instead of cawed. "How well she speaks Saroese!"

Menoë can calculate opportunity as well as the next person. "With your gracious mother's permission, Prince Temnos, I can arrange for a small Fives court to be built at the queen's palace, and then I can bring your spider over to show you her tricks whenever you wish."

"It needs to be built properly," I blurt out, irritated by how ignorantly they risk my body and skill. "The greatest risk to adversaries is obstacles so shoddily built that they give way or don't work properly. That's how most adversaries get injured."

Pressing my lips shut over the rest of my rant, I brace for a flood of abuse from highborn ladies offended that I dared to speak up.

But they have already gone back to talking with each other about an Illustrious two of them have enjoyed as a lover, and whether to attend the City Fives Court next week instead of the horse races. A wave of servants moves through with fresh trays of food. Amaya is enjoying herself hugely, wandering amid the queen's court just as if she belongs there, and she does in a way I never can.

Envy claws at my breast, and for a moment I hate her. Then her gaze flicks to me and she gives me a half wink to remind me we are in this together. And we are. She can learn things I can't. She's the only one here I can fully trust.

An older servingwoman brings a tray of cups and a pitcher of decanted wine to a table beside the queen. Each cup is filled with wine, and then the queen sips from each before handing them out. The first goes to Lady Menoë, and thence down the line of importance.

The prince seizes my hand with his greasy one and pulls me toward the curtains. In an altered and much older tone he whispers, "That is how my gracious mother shows her visiting friends the wine isn't poisoned. Never drink anything here unless it's been tasted first. Come along. I'm going to show you to my gracious father so he'll know you are my new friend."

His new friend with a knife up under her ribs should he have a mortal attack of his disorder while I am close enough to be slaughtered.

Yet it isn't his fault he lives on the sparks of murdered men.

"Call me Temnos," the boy adds. He takes two steps to every one of mine.

"Your Lordship, I am too lowborn to be allowed such familiarity."

"I command you to do so! When you call me Temnos then I know we are friends."

As Temnos leads me through the curtains into the king's courtyard, both Thanises and the king look up in surprise.

"Gracious Father! I have found a spider. She is an adversary who is going to come every week to show me how to train for the Fives. But she doesn't speak a word of Saroese. May I be allowed to learn to speak Efean so she and I can talk?"

He grinds his weight onto my toes as he speaks.

"What is Serenissima thinking to let the boy overexert himself?" the king mutters.

"Can I have a Fives court of my very own, Gracious Father? A properly built one, I mean, nothing shoddy."

Thanises murmurs, "Exercise would do the prince good, Your Lordship. A strong spark burns within him now. A gentle regimen will help him gain strength."

"If you are sure...There is no need to learn the crude tongue of the Efeans, Temnos. We can have an interpreter brought in. Where did you get the adversary?"

The boy's fingers loosen and tighten with the quicksilver working of his mind. This child is not as innocent as he pretends to be.

"Cousin Menoë brought her, Gracious Father."

"Is Menoë here? I don't like her visiting your mother. She's a bad influence." The king's forehead wrinkles as his gaze darkens, and I'm surprised by his lapse in calling himself *I* instead of *we*, as if Menoë's presence genuinely agitates him.

"I will just take the adversary back to Cousin Menoë now. I wanted to show you so you aren't surprised when you see her next time."

The prince tugs me back into the buffer space. The gap between the king's and the queen's courtyards signifies something about their relationship but I can't guess what. How I wish Kalliarkos were here so I could ask him to explain it, or if he knows how the priests are keeping Temnos alive. What will happen to Temnos if Gargaron's plans to put Kal and Menoë on the throne succeed?

"Spider!" The prince pulls so insistently on my hand that I bend over. His mouth presses against my ear. "You must never, ever, ever let on that you were left to stand behind the curtains next to the king's private courtyard. If the king guesses you might have overheard, as I am sure you did, he will kill you. I don't want you to be killed, Spider. I like you."

"My thanks, Your Lordship."

"You're to call me Temnos."

"Temnos, how can you know if you like me when we are strangers?"

"Just do as I say and you won't get hurt," he commands in the same imperious tone as the king.

Dread eats into my heart. The obstacles of the Fives court

seem so clean and pure compared to this pit. No wonder Kalliarkos wanted nothing to do with it.

The far end of the curtains surrounding the queen's courtyard ripples, and a servant enters. I would recognize anywhere the way Amaya used to parade up and down our courtyard at home pretending to be a lady-in-waiting in the queen's court. How we mocked her! Now I'm just grateful she's so good at it.

"Forgive my thunderous intrusion, Your Gracious Lordship Prince Temnos," she says softly. Her voice has all the musicality my blunt speech lacks, and it is also so ridiculous I want to laugh. "Lady Menoë has instructed my humble self to guide your spider adversary to the kitchens where by the generous and gracious order of your gracious mother the queen, the royal servants may deign to sweeten the adversary's lips with leftovers from the supper table. May I have your permission, Your Gracious Lordship? For as it says in the play, 'Let no one enter or exit the palace without the benevolent oversight of our royal parents.'"

"Do you attend the theater?" he asks a little breathlessly.

Amaya sweeps through an elaborate genuflection, and I hide a smile behind a hand. "I do, Your Lordship. It is my chiefest pleasure in life. Do you attend the theater?"

"No, I'm not allowed to go anywhere outside the royal grounds." A sigh heaves his frail shoulders.

"Then you and I shall devise a means by which you can convince them to allow you to walk into the city, Your Lordship."

She steps into a vein of light shining through a gap between curtains. The way the rays illuminate her face is striking.

"Oh! You are very pretty!"

She frames her face between upturned palms and flutters her eyelashes. "You flatter me, Your Lordship."

Choking down a laugh, I end up snorting, but the prince is too enchanted to notice.

"If you serve Lady Menoë, then you can come along when my spider comes. Maybe the two of you can be friends." He tilts his head to one side, examining her as she lowers her hands and then studying me. A squint creases his forehead. "You look a little alike. Isn't that odd?"

A jolt of adrenaline slams through me, but Amaya gives a twitch of her chin to signal me to keep my mouth shut.

"The gods have a strange sense of humor, do they not, Your Lordship?" she says with her most amiable smile. "I laugh and laugh all the time. Do you laugh?"

Infatuation glimmers in his gaze, the mark of a boy beginning to have a man's interests. "I will laugh more when you are here to entertain me. What is your name?"

"I am called Orchid, Your Lordship."

"Orchid," he murmurs, as if awash in the heady scents of a flower garden. "I like that name."

He reaches into a pocket and gives me and then Amaya each a gold coin. Gold! A cold flash of uneasiness shivers through me. I've never held anything worth so much in my life.

"A prince is meant to be generous to his followers. You will come next week to teach me the Fives, Spider. Now you're my trainer."

"Of course, my lord." When I glance at Amaya, she is still staring, mouth popped open, at the gold coin in her hand.

"Now I'm going to go look for my friend Perikos the Younger. He was fanning me before but I can't find him. Did you see him?"

All I manage is a shrug. He vanishes back through the curtains, secure in knowing that whatever he hears his father say, he will not be murdered for it. As Amaya pulls me into the servants' corridor, she blinks at me like a mirror sending signals across a battlefield.

I murmur, "Do you have something in your eye, Doma?"

"You're so irritating! Tuck that coin away before someone takes it from you." She walks a step ahead of me, slanting whispered words back over her shoulder. "We only have a few moments to talk. The ladies are distracted by Lady Menoë tantalizing them with hints about what happened to Prince Stratios."

"The husband everyone thinks she murdered?"

"Exactly."

"Did she murder him?"

"I don't know, but I can believe she's capable of sticking a knife into a man's heart. Now listen! Lord Gargaron will be leaving soon to conduct his annual tour of the Garon estates.

At my urging Denya has convinced Gargaron to take her along on his trip, and thus me. That way I can look for Bettany at the estates we visit. Now who is the brilliant one?"

"It's a good plan," I mutter, wishing I had thought of it.

"It's a fantastic plan, and you know it, Jes. You just hate admitting I'm smarter than you are."

"Except you can't move among Commoners the way I can. Efeans won't trust you." I suddenly remember the Efean I need to talk to. "I have an urgent problem. I have to warn Ro immediately that the king knows where he's hiding, but I can't leave until Lady Menoë goes."

She laces a loose ribbon through her fingers. "That *is* bad."

"If he's arrested, they might trace his movements and find Mother."

"If I can get you out of here now, can you get to Ro-emnu right away?"

"Yes. But won't you and I get in trouble if I leave without Menoë's permission?"

"I'll tell her you became ill from the rich food. Clutch your stomach and don't say anything. Follow me."

Amaya minces through the antechamber, brandishing the ribbon, which is braided with the gold and purple reserved for the royal family. It's so odd to see Patrons—even just stewards and servants—step aside to let us pass. Once we are outside Amaya accosts the driver waiting by the carriage I arrived in. I press my hands to my stomach and look at the ground.

Her words have the sparkling diction of the highborn, for she can mimic any manner of speech. "I am ordered by the Most Pure and Elevated Lady Menoë to see that this adversary returns to Garon Stable at once. Be about this charge quickly!"

I climb into the carriage as Amaya gives me a nod, the only way we can communicate in front of others. I nod back.

As the carriage rolls away I whisper, "I pray you, holy one, let me reach Ro-emnu in time."

But I'm not really sure to whom I'm praying.

12

To my utter disgust I find Ro-emnu at his ease in the Heart Tavern reciting poetry to an audience made up of simpering young women and a handful of young men probably hoping to console the girls who don't catch Ro's eye. As I stride up he breaks off.

"You have such a look on your face, schemer! More frantic than sullen."

"I need to talk to you."

"I would never have guessed." He stands, kisses three of the girls, and leads me over to an isolated table in a shady corner. Neither of us sits.

He studies me for longer than is comfortable. "I didn't expect you to visit me again so soon. Is all well?"

"You have to get out of the city. The king is searching for you."

He shrugs. "Weak sauce, Spider. I already know that."

"No, you don't know. His investigators learned the name of the Heart Tavern just this morning. It's only by chance I was able to get here as quickly as I have." After returning to the stable I took only enough time to change out of the impossible dress before coming here, although I was careful to take a roundabout path through the Ribbon Market in case I was being followed. "His soldiers could be here at any moment!"

He leans so close I have to grit my teeth to stop from taking a step backward. It isn't that he scares me. It's that I feel the heat of his presence like a dare, as if I'm just one of the girls who want to cluster around him. "It's so sweet that you care about me."

With three fingers I press into his chest hard enough to get him to move back. "I don't care about you. I care about my mother. She's in danger because I asked you to take money to her. I've just discovered the king is more obsessed with finding you than he is with fighting the armies of old Saro. I can't chance him tracing your movements to my family."

I can tell he wants to grab my wrist and shove my hand on his chest away but instead he leans into me so I have to brace myself to take some of his weight. "You shouldn't worry, schemer. I'm a very careful person."

"Didn't you hear what I said? The king's soldiers are on their way here right now!"

He laughs and with a flourish steps back and holds up both hands. "No, they aren't. Do you think we are fools? We fed false information to the king's agents. They will be led to several establishments that have nothing to do with this one."

"How can you be sure?"

He gestures toward the young men and women he was lounging with when I came in. "Look. Here comes one now."

"One what?"

A young Commoner woman walks briskly in. She's got a basket balanced on her head and a line of sweat staining her dress down the length of her spine, as if she's been walking a long way in the heat. When she reaches the cluster of young people she sets down the basket, gulps a drink, and speaks to them, glancing several times at Ro. After she's finished a different girl grabs the basket and she and two of the young men depart.

"We have people all over the city who are shadowing the movements of the soldiers and bringing us reports. That's how we know where they are and why they don't know where we are."

"But you were caught once, that time in the Ribbon Market."

"Yes, when you and I first met. How could I ever forget that day, when a spider scout crushed a tiny child and kept walking?"

I look away, remembering the dead baby and its screaming mother, how the scouts and the soldiers ignored the devastation they left behind as they cornered and arrested Ro.

He goes on. "They caught me because they knew where my father worked. Since then I've arranged for him to leave Saryenia for a safe haven where he can't be found."

My voice trembles as I think of how weak my mother was when I last saw her, how insecure the Least-Hill Inn is, how easily Gargaron followed me there. "Is there truly such a haven?"

He shrugs, his expression more serious than before, his voice a little gruff as if he's suppressing powerful feelings. "As safe as any place can be in a country where foreigners rule us without our consent. I sent my sister there too, if that means anything to you."

The pulse of risk-taking quickens my heart. If I'm wrong about him, I will have made a horrible mistake.

"I'll make a bargain with you. Leave Saryenia and take my mother and family and the oracle to this safe haven. Just until the king's interest in you dies down."

"It's a prudent idea I've already considered, schemer, but you forget one thing. I'm a poor man from a poor family. It took all my poet's earnings to get my father and sister out of town. How am I to afford such an expensive venture as your whole family, the oracle, and me with no hope of earning any more money to support us all?"

I set the gold coin from Temnos on the table between us.

He thumps onto the bench like he's been felled by an ax.

If I weren't so wound up I would laugh as he pokes at the coin with a finger as if he fears it will dissolve.

"A little subtlety might be prudent," he says.

"Never attempt subtlety when everyone is already looking at you." I give a jaunty wave to his friends, who wave back cheerfully.

"Is this from your victory game winnings?"

"No." I sit across from him. "Prince Temnos gave it to me. Lady Menoë took me with her to the King's Garden today. That's where I overheard the king speaking of you. Eavesdropped, really. I'd be dead if he knew I'd heard."

He sets his elbows on the table. "You're a quick study, aren't you? A gold coin from the prince! You've already learned how to grease the wheels of gift-giving with unctuous compliments and oily lies."

"He's just a lonely boy who craves friendship."

"A lonely boy who will inherit a kingdom built on Efean backs. Once he's grown out of his innocent, ignorant charm he will crush our lives and dreams as cruelly as his forebears have done. Rather like Lord Kalliarkos, don't you think?"

My entire body tenses and I come up off the bench, hands in fists. But I'm better than this. I won't be provoked. I sit back down. His mouth quirks, but he says nothing.

"I didn't ask for money from the prince. He has no idea of its value. He handed it out like candy. But you and I both know this gold coin is more than enough to pay for a year's lodging and food for an entire household in an isolated village where Patrons never go."

He weighs the coin in his hand. "I'm amazed and indeed honored that you would trust your mother to me."

"That you know of a safe haven and clearly have a network of accomplices makes you a reasonable ally in this situation."

His eyebrows lift as he thinks for a moment. "A fair point. But why the oracle too? What does she matter to you?"

"How did you know that Serenissima the Third, the Benevolent, murdered her father, her brother, and her brother's infant son in order to make her uncle king and herself his queen?"

"You do listen to my poetry! I'm so flattered."

"You have a loud voice when you're onstage; I could hardly have missed it."

He chuckles, so genuinely amused by my retort that I feel he's given me an intimate compliment. But I stifle the thought and get back to this game we have to win right now. "I heard King Kliatemnos say he personally destroyed all the records of those years. So maybe you made a wild guess. Maybe you found a cache of missing documents. Or maybe you coaxed the story out of the oracle."

His bright gaze drills into mine. "I'll let you know what she told me in exchange for a kiss from your sullen lips."

My gaze touches his mouth and for an instant—no longer

than it takes me to suck in an outraged breath—my mind flashes an image of his lips brushing mine. Then I shake it off like a hard fall when I have to get back up and running. "Is bribery the only way you can convince people to kiss you?"

"Ah!" He slaps a hand to his chest. "The spider's venom stabs deep!"

"Not deep enough. Here's what I think. The way the oracle behaved in the tomb suggests she is highborn. So if you spin everything together, it's likely she has ties to the palace or even to the royal family—"

"You're amazing," he breaks in. "You have everything. Presence, skill, flair, and intelligence. You draw the eye. You make people want you to win. You make people want you to—"

"Stop flirting with me!" Do all poets craft a sensuous voice like his, one that curls through the air to wrap clarity and beauty and warmth around their listeners? "Even if I wanted to kiss you, which I don't, kisses are no way to make an agreement, not in a life-and-death situation like this one."

"Alas, you argue with a ruthless logic that appeals to my mind while it torments my heart."

I roll my eyes. Kalliarkos never exaggerates like Ro. "Get out of Saryenia before the king captures you, and take my family with you. Do it to keep innocent people out of the hands of the conquerors you claim to hate. Do it for the Efea you claim to love."

He palms the gold coin but never takes his eyes off me.

"I'll get your mother to a safe haven, but I do it for you, sullen schemer. Thus putting you in my debt."

I can't get away from his mocking smile fast enough.

⬲

Waiting is agony, I reflect weeks later in the garden of the queen's palace as I watch Temnos balance on a low beam, arms held out to either side and a smile like flame on his face. His cheeks now have a ruddy color instead of an invalid's pallor. "Look at me, Spider! I am a fledgling adversary, aren't I!"

"Of course you are," I lie, the words dripping like fat over a fire. It's impossible to concentrate while I wait for news. I wonder how Kal is, and if he and Father get along, and if he ever thinks of me.

Glancing at me, Temnos wobbles. I catch him under the elbow.

"Don't speak false flattery, Spider," he scolds. "I command you to tell me the truth."

"Like any fledgling you are making basic mistakes," I go on more sternly, letting a little of my frustration leak out. "Don't look down. Feel out the beam with your toes before you put your weight on your foot."

Ecstatic at being corrected, he grins triumphantly and insists I spot him forward and backward along the beam. It's not his fault I'm forced to attend on him, taking precious time away from the training I desperately need. After two more passes he hops down from the beam because unlike me he can start and stop whenever he wishes.

"We'll take a rest now, Spider."

He strikes like a bee to honey to where Amaya sits on a narrow bench embroidering a festival mask. She shifts so he can squeeze in beside her, sitting the way we sisters often did as little girls, smashed together like puppies. Of course I have to stay standing.

"Orchid, is that the mask you're making for me so I can be like Spider?"

"Why, it surely is, my lord," she says, displaying it with a prim, pretty smile. "You can wear it when you come to the City Fives Court with Lady Menoë to see a trial."

Under the shade of a grape arbor the queen and Menoë have been whispering together on a couch. At Amaya's words, Serenissima looks up.

"Temnos!" The queen calls him over. She studies him with a frown as she sniffs delicately. "You have a smell of sweat about you. Your feet are dirty, and there is a smudge on your face. Go inside and wash."

"Yes, Gracious Mother." Temnos casts a smile in my direction before he goes indoors.

Ladies gather to await the carriages as servants tidy up. I retreat to the Fives court to check all the joints and fastenings on the obstacles, a trainer's duty every night and every dawn.

Amaya's path leads her close to me and, under the pretext of bending over to pick up a ribbon she has deliberately dropped, she whispers, "Jes, have you heard yet if Mother and the rest are safe? I'm so worried."

"Yes. The contact Ro gave me at the Heart Tavern told me last Rest Day that Mother and all of them are safe."

"Do you believe it?"

I remember Ro's face as he spoke of honor. "Yes, I do."

Amaya presses a hand to her heart and for once the gesture does not look theatrical but heartfelt. "It's been so hard, not knowing. You're right that Commoners will never confide in me, even when I speak Efean to them. I just wish..." She glances around. There is no one in sight as dusk layers the garden in shadows. "Now that I know Mother is safe, I wish you and I could search together for Bettany. I would feel more secure if you were close by while we are touring the Garon estates."

"Are you afraid of someone in Garon Palace?" I ask sharply.

"I'm afraid for *you*, trapped in this pit of nasty people with no skills to fend them off—" She breaks off, grabs my hand, and tugs me sideways so hard I stumble after her into the maze. Beyond the canvas walls, feet scrape along the ground.

"Dearest Cousin, your visits have worked magic on my son. I confess I have long feared he would die untimely but now I can hope he will live to adulthood."

"I am surprised you never had another son if you were afraid this one might not survive."

"It is not so simple. I fear him. He has a wicked temper."

"You fear the king?"

"No." The queen's tone drops as into a chasm. "I fear my brother Nikonos."

Menoë murmurs in the voice of a woman luring a wounded dog within reach of her hands, "Nikonos? What can you mean, Serenissima?"

"Nikonos said I mustn't get pregnant again or he would murder Temnos and any newborn I might give birth to. Now Kliatemnos believes I prefer and trust Nikonos over him, and he despises me for it although I love only him. I don't know what to do."

Menoë's silence drags on just a little too long. Either she is truly shocked, or she is calculating. I know which I'm betting on, because when two women want to be queen, one has to lose.

She goes on in an altered tone that sounds like cold lies disguised as ardent truth. "I also know what it means to be helpless against a man who wished me harm. My husband Prince Stratios was all smiles in public, but he debased me when we were alone. No one believed my attempts to beg for help, for all in the East Saro court loved him. My grandmother was sent false reports of my situation while I was locked away in a suite of rooms. And then...then..."

Menoë breaks into soft weeping whose emotion wrings my heart even though I have no reason to feel sympathy for her or even trust that this story she spins is not a false tale concocted to gain Serenissima's sympathy. Amaya's hand fastens on my wrist, tightening like she's angry.

"And then what?" the queen asks breathlessly.

A new voice breaks in. "My lady Menoë! The carriages are here! But we can't find Orchid."

I drag Amaya through the obstacles to come out far enough away from the maze that I hope no one suspects. But I need not have worried. Oblivious to me, the ladies chatter among themselves as they climb into the waiting carriages. Menoë's trilling laugh rises as bright as birdsong among them as if she weren't just weeping plaintively moments before. Amaya swirls into their company with a last fierce look at me.

Afraid for me? She's the one living in the palace amid all the vipers! But she's right: now that Mother is safe, she and I are free to work together to find Bettany. In a different Efea, I could have left Saryenia and started a search for Bettany weeks ago; I wouldn't have been trapped here because I belong to Garon Palace while Bett suffers somewhere far from us. In a different Efea, Bettany would never have been herded onto that barge at all.

Alone in my carriage, I have plenty of time to think about what Ro said.

In this Efea, Commoners have no say in a land that once belonged to them.

⊙⫷⫸⊙

I stand atop the high beam in Traps and, from this vantage, see the small woman I raced against last month cutting her way through Rings well ahead of me. It's my second City Fives Court trial as a Challenger, and if I'm not going to win I need the crowd to love me anyway. So I give them the dangerous tricks they want, a somersault and pike twist along the high beam toward an obstacle known as "the sapling forest." I've planned my last trick to coincide with the leader's reaching the victory tower so every eye will fix on me instead of her.

I leap for a rope swing meant to loft me over the cluster of poles, and at the height of the swing I let go as if I've slipped. The crowd shrieks, expecting to see me fall broken and bloody, but I tuck into a tight spin and extend to snag the nearest pole with outstretched arms. The polished wood squeaks beneath my palms as I slow my momentum by flinging myself in wide sweeps from pole to pole, each time dropping lower.

The winning adversary grabs the victor's ribbon just as I drop safely to the ground. Blood trickles from a scrape on my left palm but I don't feel the sting yet. I'm grinning, my heart wide open, because while half the crowd is chanting the name of the woman who won, the other half shouts, "Spider! Spider!"

When I reach the Garon balcony Lord Gargaron is meticulously choosing from a platter of tiny coriander breads shaped to look like the animals of the menageries. Instead it is Menoë who calls me over. She studies my brown clothing, which, by her orders, has been sewn across the back with silver thread in the shape of a spider's web.

"We shall have to try something else because the pattern wasn't visible from up here. Maybe beads."

I imagine beads scraping off and slipping under my feet, ruining my trial, but I keep my mouth shut.

"Menoë, go to the railing with the adversary," says Gargaron from his chair.

I walk like an obedient puppet behind her. Dyed a pale green, her long sheath gown is embellished in the pattern of a spider's web with sun-colored beads that glitter as we step out of the shade into the direct sunlight. A brimmed hat shades her face while the sun hits me full on, not that she notices.

In the interval between the end of my trial and the beginning of the next one, vendors trawl through the crowds selling roasted nuts and chickpeas and dried strips of fish. Usually they would also be selling freshly grilled flatbread, but the price of flour has risen so high it's hard to get bread at all. Yet to my surprise a stream of men and women carrying trays laden with tiny loaves pours down into the cheap seats. Those who receive the free bread cheer. As individuals and then in groups and whole sections they look toward the Garon Palace balcony where Menoë and I stand in full view, and the crowd offers the adversary kiss as if to a victor.

Gargaron himself brings a platter crowned with bread to Menoë, an act meant to remind the crowd that she has royal blood while he does not.

"Eat so the crowd will see the royal princess and the fresh new Challenger sharing their bread," he says, stepping back so all eyes will be on us.

The little loaves are cunningly shaped: a braided scorpion's stinger, a bull's horn like a cornucopia, an hourglass wasp. Menoë chooses a simple round roll of bread stamped with an eight-legged figure representing a spider. She breaks the roll in half and, to my astonishment, hands half to me in sight of every person looking our way.

The bread is still warm, the crust crisp and the inside melting on my tongue with the most delicate of textures. I savor it while Menoë basks in the crowd's approbation.

"That was clever of you to pretend to fall from the swing when you saw you were losing," she says.

She has given me an opening. "Far be it from me to complain, my lady, but these Challengers have run many more Novice trials than I have. I cannot regret the honor of becoming a Challenger so quickly, but my career as an adversary would have been better served if I could have ascended through the Novice ranks in the ordinary way. I fear the crowd will grow tired of me too soon if I don't perform well enough."

She glances at her uncle. "Spider fears she is not good enough to win a victory as a Challenger."

"That is not what I said!" I blurt out, my pride stung. Then I wince. Such presumption will get me whipped.

Gargaron hands off the platter to a servant, then moves up beside me. He places a ringed hand on the balustrade, boxing me in between them. A white scar arcs over one of his knuckles, like he parried a knife blade with a fist.

"Then what did you mean, Jessamy?"

I see the path and take it, for they will account my words as competitiveness and never guess I have an ulterior motive. "My inexperience hurts me. Never doubt that I will work my way up in time, for I intend to gain the rank of Illustrious. But meanwhile all the glory that shines on me now will fade." A hunk of bread still warms my fingers. "The bread that rises too fast may collapse. Sudden fame is not always a boon, my lord."

"True. I know your mind is working all the time, Jessamy. Do you have some idea you wish to share with me?"

Amaya could manage this with more subtlety. I decide to bull my way through, because that is what he expects. I just have to hope he grabs for the bait.

"The skill of Challengers here in Saryenia is much higher than that of the provinces. I don't fear the competition. Not at all. But if I lose too many times I'll lose the favor of the crowd."

The emotion that grips my throat like the heady taste of ambition is no lie, no theater. It is real. "If you send me to run in the provinces I could gain valuable experience against opponents of a more comparable skill level, and thus have a better chance of more victories."

"It speaks well of you that you hate to lose, Spider. There may be a solution that will meet all our needs."

"What is that, Uncle?" asks Menoë, startled and suspicious.

But my hopes rise, and I have to battle to keep my expression blank.

"Nothing to do with you, Menoë. My tour to check up on the finances of our far-flung estates begins next month. Bringing a few adversaries with me to hone their skills on the provincial circuit will heighten awareness of Garon Palace and our royal connections throughout the land, which also serves our greater purpose."

I clamp down on a rush of triumph, but a grin escapes anyway, a big smile that I have to force off my face by coughing.

He doesn't even notice as he plucks a sculpture of bread off the platter now held by a patient servant. It has a narrow neck and stubby wings, meant to resemble the firebird who rises from the ashes of defeat, the symbol my father always uses to identify himself. Ripping off the firebird's head, Gargaron chews and swallows while he contemplates.

"This will do very well. Menoë, make sure you hire poets

to gabble about Spider's provincial tour. News of her victories must be trumpeted about here in Saryenia."

A frown withers her pretty features. "But with Spider's help I have been making such good progress on working my way into the confidence of Serenissima and the boy, Uncle. He dotes on Spider. He'll be distressed if she leaves."

"With your lovely face, polished manners, and sharp wit I am sure you can flatter this monstrous prince into falling in love with you instead."

A startling glimpse of enmity surfaces from below the false serenity of her face. "Exactly the words you said to me on the day I left for East Saro on the happy occasion of my first marriage, Uncle. We all know what came of that."

Gargaron slips the whip from his belt and lays it athwart the railing. "Let us not raise the ghost of unpleasant gossip and the imprudence of your indelicate actions."

A mask of fury turns Menoë's beauty into stone, but my excitement drives her ugly past out of my head. Tears prick at my eyes from sheer, brutal joy. Gargaron has no idea of the chance he's given me.

Amaya and I are going to find Bettany and bring her home to Mother.

13

$\backsim$⚊⚊⚊⚊$\backsim$

Lord **Gargaron and** his entourage leave Saryenia in a cavalcade of carriages and supply wagons. Tana, Mis, Dusty, and I travel in the last carriage. It takes most of the day to swing around the vast expanse of Mist Lake, but by midafternoon we reach the fields of a Garon estate, strung along irrigation channels that link it to the water. Laborers dot the fields. Many are molding bricks and setting them out in rows to dry while others plant wheat.

"Let's get out and run the rest of the way," I suggest. "We need to keep up our training."

"Go ahead."

Given Tana's permission, we three adversaries trace a winding path through the fields. I get a decent look at the workers, who pause to stare as we race past. Many of the men have the posture of former soldiers, and the familiarity of the stance, so like my father's, fools me into thinking there is someone I know here. But I didn't really expect to find Bettany or anyone from our old household so close to the city. I just want to set a precedent, to get the guards used to us ranging off on our own, because that gives me a chance to search.

We pause to catch our breath at the ruins of an abandoned building. Standing atop its tumbled brick walls, we gaze over the lake. It's too far to see the south shore or any trace of Saryenia. There's nothing but a distant sail seeming to float in the haze. Here, away from the city's incessant voice, the ancient heart of the earth speaks through the feel of the wind on my face and the pressure of heat on my eyes and the scent of earth and vegetation and rot, that which is born, grows, and dies.

"I've never been so far from home," I say in a low voice, a little shaken by the view. "The land seems so wide out here, like it could go on forever."

"You haven't seen 'forever' until you've seen the desert," says Dusty with a laugh. "This is nothing compared to the endless wilderness that lies beyond the fields of my village. Let's go. I'm thirsty. The best beer in Efea is village beer."

We arrive at the gate of the main estate compound at the same time as the carriages. As Denya and Amaya alight from the third carriage, Amaya flashes an "all's well" hand sign at me that Father taught us girls. I allow myself to relax as a steward shows us to the stable. It's an actual stable where animals are housed, where we are given a stall with hay for our beds and a single flimsy cot, presumably for Tana.

"You can get your wash water from the horse trough," the steward says. "At the back door of the kitchen you can get food."

My mouth drops open, and yet I can't think of anything to say.

As soon as the steward leaves, Mis prods the cot with a toe. "This is insulting."

With his usual good-natured grin, Dusty tosses his gear down. "I've slept and washed in worse places. At least it's well kept!"

"Pick your gear back up, my lad." With the blandest expression on her always-calm face, Tana uses a foot to flip over the cot. "We'll sleep in the guesthouse in the village. And eat there and bathe there too."

"Will they welcome us like people do in the city?" I ask.

"Of course they will," says Tana. "Anyway, I grew up here. Now come along."

The village lies a short walk from the main compound down a path lined by fig and pomegranate trees. Children spot us and run ahead to give warning. The dames greet us with food. It's a prosperous village with many houses linked by walkways and a complete, if simple, Fives court at the center. By the time Tana has raced us through our paces on the court it is dusk, and most of the village has gathered to cheer us on. Afterward we bathe with the fieldworkers in a stone-lined pool.

It's easy to strike up conversations. They're a sunnier group than I would have guessed village laborers to be, happy to ask about goings-on in Saryenia, a place many visit only once a year. When I carefully remark about a barge full of prisoners that left the city three months ago they scoff; criminals aren't welcome on an estate like this, they tell me. As law-abiding people, they have a contract with Princess Berenise.

"You're paid for your labor?" I ask, trying to hide my astonishment for fear of insulting them.

"We are allowed to keep a third of the harvest, very generous terms."

A third doesn't seem generous to me, but Tana explains that on other estates the entire harvest belongs to the Patron lord and the workers get nothing except a daily ration.

The eldest dame speaks up. "Princess Berenise sponsored an entire regiment of men from this region into the Royal Army, including my son, Inarsis, whom you may have met at your stable."

Startled, I look more closely at the old woman with her silver hair and wrinkled face, but I don't see a resemblance. "I have met him. I suppose she must have gained some profit by placing Commoners in the army?"

"People are complicated, Jes," says Tana as if my frown reveals my thoughts. "When Princess Berenise saw what a promising adversary I was, she paid for my training in Saryenia. She saw profit in me, of course, but that's not all there is to her."

"Good fortune for you," I say politely, knowing the truth: they may think highly of the old princess, but she sat in that warehouse counting her gold while women and children were penned up outside in the hot sun before being dragged away into servitude.

⚭

Weeks later I stand atop a victory tower overlooking a town called Akheres Oasis. Beyond the town wall stretch fields of wheat and stands of date palms. The vegetation is irrigated by canals dug out from two shallow lakes whose shores are choked by reeds. Birds swarm the waters. The smell and richness of the oasis contrast with the stony red dirt and high ridges of the desert that surround this dazzling spot of green.

The court's terraced seats are packed and the crowd unusually appreciative, the air thick with whistles and cheers. Victor's ribbon tied to my vest, I descend the ladder. As is the custom in the provinces, the losing adversaries gather at the foot of the ladder to salute the victor with the kiss-off sign and to share a cup of honey mead. No one drinks nectar this far from the royal palace.

"Big crowd today," says one of my opponents, a cheerful Challenger named Henta who in Saryenia would still be running at Novice level. Outside Saryenia it is odd how few Efeans have bothered to learn the language of the ruling Saroese. In the city any Efean who wants to get ahead has to learn it. "People are excited to see adversaries from outside Akheres Oasis. You minded to have a drink with us later? We meet at a tavern called the Adversary Kiss."

"My thanks. I'd like that." I would enjoy her company, I'm sure, and the chance to pump her for information, since this is our last stop. After this we return by an arduous route south across the desert to the sea and thence by ship to Saryenia. "But I'll have to get permission."

The younger of the two male adversaries blurts, "Are you a slave? I hear that in Saryenia the Saroese have turned all Efeans into slaves, not like out here where we can still work for ourselves."

Mortification heats my cheeks.

Henta says, "For shame, Khamu. Apologize at once."

"It's all right." I'm not used to Efean manners, whereby women may chide men in public without repercussion. "It's not that simple. But it is true that if not for my skill at the Fives I might have ended up laboring in the mines. That's supposed to be dreadful work. There is a royal gold mine near here, isn't there?"

I launch a smile at Khamu, hoping he'll speak more freely if I charm him. The woman chokes down a laugh, probably because my attempt at flirting is so clumsy.

He stands straighter to impress the city girl who just beat him, although to be honest his big ears and round face don't attract me. "Yes, the royal gold mine, north of town. It's the richest vein of gold in Efea," he brags, as if he is personally responsible.

"Who works the mine? I thought it was only criminals." I decide against fluttering my eyelashes as Amaya would because I am sure it would merely look as if I had gotten something caught in my eye.

He is eager to enlighten me. "Skilled workmen are needed for many of the jobs. My uncle is a miner and makes a good living, though it is always dangerous. But the worst of the dirty, backbreaking work is all done by shackled criminals."

"Where do the prisoners come from?"

"A group from Saryenia came in about three months ago, not long after that foreign doctor showed up."

I want to ask if there were women and children but I don't know how without being awkward. "Do people from around here go to the mine often to visit their relatives? Is it far? I wonder if we will go to see it."

Henta takes the empty cup from my hand. "Your master's already been. He rode out at dawn to inspect the workings when he heard there'd been a collapse in one of the shafts. I believe he returned in time to watch you run, though."

"Did men die?"

"Yes. They often do. As Khamu said, it's dangerous work."

She hesitates, then mutters, "It's shameful when they send women and children there, like in this most recent group. We saw them marched past. No one deserves such a punishment."

As she speaks, a terrible image of Bettany lying broken beneath rocks fills my mind's eye. I can't be sure she's here, yet where else could she be? We've visited every other Garon estate.

Just as I decide that Henta's dislike of children's being punished and Khamu's comment about slaves mean I can risk a more direct question, a steward appears and beckons to me. Mis and Dusty have already raced and gone upstairs. I stump along, my thoughts as heavy as my leaden footfalls. How did I miss Gargaron's morning expedition to the mine? What if Bettany and the others are there, where they most need rescuing, and we've lost our chance to find them?

The balconies reserved for nobles are little more than coarse stone terraces with railings made of rope, not wood. Gargaron travels with sponsored men, ambitious fellows given the opportunity to rise with the aid of his riches and influence. Men like my father. As wind rakes along a canvas awning strung up to give shade and dust gets into every possible crevice, they strive not to look disgruntled and uncomfortable.

Gargaron is entertaining a stranger, a foreign man neither Saroese nor Efean whose youth, good looks, and strangely pale hair draw the eye. Gargaron is so caught up in their conversation about the injuries suffered in the mineshaft collapse that he doesn't notice me enter and even forgets to gesture me forward to the railing as he always does when I win. So I stride up to the rope and come to parade rest in view of the crowd. The four Challengers running the final trial are a stolid lot, their choices so boring that the crowd soon notices me and begins to cheer, "Spider! Spider!"

I extend my arms to each side in the theatrical manner I've taken on, as if I would make a sail of myself if only I had wings woven of spider silk. On the court an adversary slips from the high beam and barely catches himself, and immediately the crowd's interest shifts to this near disaster. Mis and Dusty sidle over as I lower my arms.

"How did you do?" I whisper.

Dusty grins what I call his victory grin, while Mis waggles a hand to show she did neither well nor poorly.

"Spider, come here! Lord Agalar wishes to inspect you."

Dusty lifts his chin with a side-eye glance, as if in warning, but I don't know what he means, and anyway I have to go. As I walk over to where the two highborn men sit together, Lord Agalar stands. His hair is so light that it doesn't look real, but it is his supercilious expression that instantly makes me dislike him. He points to a spot and, in perfect if oddly accented Saroese, says, "Place yourself there and do not move."

I look at Gargaron, who nods. By now everyone on our balcony is watching because my barely concealed consternation is much more interesting than the dull trial below. Once I take the position, Lord Agalar paces slowly around me, studying me from all angles. A flush heats my face as I suddenly fear that a man has finally offered so much money for my favors that even Gargaron can't refuse.

Without asking permission Agalar grasps my wrists. It takes all my self-control not to pull away. He turns my hands over to look at my palms, then cups his own palms over my shoulders to measure them, and finally tilts my chin back with a finger to examine my neck. His gaze isn't amorous. It's far more unsettling, like he means to strip skin and flesh away, flaying me down to the bone.

"Your ability to target your landings on your spins is remarkable, especially at that height when the slightest miscalculation would result in severe injury or death. What mix of parts gives you that skill?"

"Practice and boldness," I say into his arrogant face.

Gargaron laughs.

"I advocate practice and boldness myself," Agalar replies with a nod, oblivious to my tone. He releases me and sits down. "Very interesting, Lord Gargaron. Mules often display an endurance, intelligence, and vigor that their sires and dams lack. I have it in mind to more fully investigate this phenomenon with studies and experiments in my medical practice. Can I buy her from you?"

My heart goes cold.

"Alas, no," says Gargaron so genially that I wonder if he is a little drunk to be so mellow. "Spider is far too valuable on the Fives court. She's nowhere near her peak yet."

"What about the other mule?" Agalar asks.

"Dusty, come over here," says Gargaron as Mis stiffens, her fingers brushing Dusty's arm as if she wants to cling to him but then dropping away.

Agalar isn't looking at Dusty. He's looking into a shaded corner of the balcony where Denya sits on a cushioned bench as far from Gargaron as possible. Denya is always required to accompany Gargaron in public so she may entertain any ladies who arrive with their lords, but today no one attends Denya except Amaya. They share a platter heaped with chopped dates packed inside apricot halves, a delicacy they often share as if it has a special meaning to them. Their giggling, whispering intimacy makes them appear exactly like lovers flirting in a theatrical comedy, but Gargaron never takes any notice unless he wants Denya's attention.

"That one," says Agalar, and I can't help myself: my hand lifts to my throat as he indicates Amaya. "She's a mule too."

Gargaron's gaze sharpens as Denya and Amaya, belatedly sensing a threat, look up together. Denya blanches and, with a gasp, clutches Amaya's hand, but Amaya's expression remains blandly pleasant for I am sure no shock oversets my little sister unless she wants it to.

"Orchid, come here," orders Gargaron, and she releases

Denya's hand, rises gracefully, and glides forward as if onto a proscenium for a performance. "Are you a mule? You don't look like one."

Agalar speaks before Amaya can. "She's powdering her skin to lighten it. I suspect she irons her hair to get any bit of curl out of it. And her brows are wide, more Efean than Saroese. Small things, but visible to a discerning gaze."

I lower my hand, hoping no one has caught my frightened gesture. Amaya shows no sign of distress as they examine her. She even turns her head to display her profile to best advantage. Her show of cool confidence would make me want to laugh if I weren't so terrified for us both.

With a frown Gargaron says, "You've been in Garon Palace long enough to know by now that we never employ people with Commoner ancestry. What do you have to say to this accusation?"

Amaya opens her hands to show they are empty, not hiding anything. With eyes cast down in the manner required of Patron girls, she speaks in her prettiest voice with not a hint of anger. "I beg your pardon, my lord, but I must protest most indignantly any suggestion that my mother is common or indeed anything but what she always professed herself to be. As for my father, he is gone, so any secrets he might have hidden I cannot know, but never in my hearing did he speak of Commoner ancestry among his foremothers."

Denya is the quietest girl I've ever met but she speaks up

now, her voice so soft I barely hear it. "If I have pleased you, my lord, please do not separate me from an accomplished and competent servant who takes care of all my needs."

"Lord Agalar, I think you are stretching too far for this one." Gargaron dismisses Amaya with a wave. "The girl was obviously raised in a proper Patron manner. Furthermore, Denya has soldiered through this difficult journey without complaint and without losing her polish, so I am inclined to let her have her way in this. You may understand that I must protect my own comfort."

A flash of annoyance curls Agalar's lips like that of a man unaccustomed to having anything denied him. "I understand some men value comfort over learning, Lord Gargaron. I am not among them. I have traveled the length of the Three Seas in pursuit of medical knowledge without regard to my comfort. Why would I have traveled into the desert if not because there is nowhere else I can so productively study how mining injuries are exacerbated by heat and dust?"

"A good question," remarks Gargaron in a way that makes my neck prickle, as if he sees something here that I don't. "Yet it's true the supervisors at the mine report that you have saved many valuable workers who would otherwise have died. In fact I have many more questions to ask regarding your expertise. Would you consider joining me for a midday feast in the much cooler and more pleasant garden of our house? I can offer date wine, fresh bread, and spiced fish."

"I accept with pleasure, Lord Gargaron."

We adversaries wait for the highborn to leave first. Amaya hangs back to place the food in baskets, and scratches her right ear in the signal we've arranged. I walk over to the table as if to snatch a handful of candied balls of diced dates and walnuts, then pretend to drop one. We both kneel at the same time.

She whispers, "Have you heard anything about the mine accident? We've been to every Garon estate. This is the last place we could hope to find her. What if she and the others were among the victims?"

"I wondered the same thing."

My expression must be as bleak as my heart, because she blinks away a tear and adds, "I hear there is a hospital in town with a basement where they store corpses. Maybe we can find a way to view the bodies."

"Orchid!" a steward calls. "The carriage is waiting!"

"Did she say something to you?" Dusty asks breathlessly as we three adversaries follow the rest of our party out of the court.

"Yes. She scolded me for being so clumsy!" I would laugh at his crestfallen expression if I weren't all twisted up with dread. Amaya is right. If Bettany's not here, then she's dead, or she's lost beyond our ability to find her.

As we cross the dusty plaza to the carriage reserved for us, I watch Lord Agalar stride up to his own vehicle, a sturdy traveling carriage, which to my surprise is hitched to mules, not horses. He pauses with a foot on the steps leading to the interior.

"Beauty! Come!" he commands, as if calling a dog, then climbs in.

A young woman carrying a scribe's box—a hard rectangular surface with compartments beneath for writing paraphernalia—hurries forward out of his entourage. She hands the box in to him and jumps up after to sit beside him.

I jolt up short, and Dusty slams into my back.

Mis grabs my arm to steady me. "Jes? Are you all right?"

Agalar's carriage rumbles away, leaving me out of breath and trembling. Surely I'm mistaken and yet I know I am not, that I could never be mistaken.

The beautiful girl with the scribe's box is Bettany.

14

The short journey to the Garon Palace compound at the outskirts of town seems to take forever.

"Are you all right, Jes?" Mis asks as I shift for the hundredth time on the bench. I just can't keep still for trying to figure out how I can possibly find a way to talk to Bettany. Why is she with Lord Agalar? Where are our household servants? Is she all right?

Dusty says, "That foreigner was very rude. Imagine saying such a thing about Orchid! Anyone looking at a beautiful girl like her can see she is Patron through and through."

"Ah la la," sings Mis in a tone with a hint of spite, "Dusty is in lo-o-ove."

Tana taps Dusty's chest with her stump. "Keep your hands

out of the palace, Dusty. Even if a Patron girl was within your reach, which even a servant is not, the last thing any adversary wants is to get caught in the dealings that go on inside those walls. The choices Jes will have to make if a lord wishes to parade her about as his lover won't be easy ones, and there may come a time when she can't say no. Like with Lord Kalliarkos."

"I could have said no!" I snap. "He didn't force me to anything."

Tana grasps my wrist and squeezes until I wince. "I do not doubt you thought yourself in love with him. He's a handsome lad, and a charming young man, and a prince besides. Hard to resist on any count. I was glad to train him for he never showed anyone in Garon Stable the least disrespect. But you walk a delicate rope now. I don't know what this foreign doctor wants but he seems interested in you in a way I cannot like and that I'm surprised Lord Gargaron tolerates considering his plans for you."

"His plans for me?" I echo.

"To become an Illustrious," says Tana with a chuckle. "You're distracted today. Don't tell me you've taken a liking to that foreigner and his peculiar looks?"

"No, no, it's just so hot and dry here and I didn't drink enough," I babble as we enter the gates. I lean out, hoping to see Bett, but our carriage splits away from the others. They go on to the main house while we head directly for the stable, where we four Efeans eat and sleep.

Yet no sooner do we adversaries reach the dormitory than the captain of Gargaron's troop of soldiers shows up to tell Dusty and me to report to the dining pavilion just as we are, still in our sweaty Fives gear.

"I'll come along, with your permission, Captain," says Tana protectively. "I don't often see you running errands that a steward could as easily manage. Is Lord Gargaron worried that this Lord Agalar means to steal our Spider?"

"I couldn't say, Tana." Captain Neartos treats her with the easy respect all the soldiers show us adversaries. Besides liking the money they win by betting on us, on this journey they've been training with us to stay fit, and we beat them more often than not. "But a lord is wise who vigilantly guards his most valuable assets."

As he leads us toward the main house down a path lined with ranks of sycamore, palm, and fig trees, he gives me a nod. He's at least thirty, loyal, calm, and good at what he does, just as Gargaron demands all the men be who seek advancement in Garon Palace. Dusty elbows me like he thinks Neartos is flirting, and I elbow him back so sharply that he gasps.

"This isn't a joke," I whisper.

We enter a lovely garden with a bathing pool, three altars heaped with flower wreaths in front of statues of the gods, and a pavilion shaded beneath an arbor of thick-flowering jasmine. Gargaron and Agalar are seated beneath the arbor, being served by Denya rather than any of the servants. The graceful way she pours wine and decoratively arranges helpings of food on their plates is exquisite, revealing her as a girl raised with meticulous observance of Patron customs. But every time a servant appears bearing another platter of food she flinches nervously, then settles when she sees it isn't Amaya. She's afraid for her around Agalar, just like I am.

Neartos has Tana, Dusty, and me stand in the shade at a corner of the arbor and takes up a station behind, exactly as if he is guarding us. I don't see Bettany or indeed any of Lord Agalar's entourage, and it's incredibly frustrating that I can't go looking for her.

"So, you hail from the Shipwright territories, is that correct?" Gargaron is asking as he picks at the delicacies on his plate. "Shipwrights are infamous as mercenaries. Some are said to hire themselves out as pirates and thieves."

Agalar offers his cup to Denya to refill. "I can't answer for the life and work of others. For my part, as I said, I am traveling the Three Seas to gain experience in treating different categories of disease and injury."

"Thus your interest in our gold mine?" Gargaron says with a lift of the eyebrows that makes me smile despite myself, because he's so good at the sardonic stare.

"Mining injuries hold a particular interest for me." Apparently Agalar has all the sensitivity of a rock because he doesn't seem to notice Gargaron's skepticism. "Why does most air give us life while noxious air trapped beneath rock may choke life or even burst and explode when it meets fire? What happens to the lungs of men who breathe in dust for years?"

"There are mines in other lands you might have visited with far less trouble."

"The desert conditions, the type of rock here, and the mining technique unique to this area all create special complications that can't be found elsewhere. If you would like to come along later this afternoon to the Akheres Town hospital I would be happy to have you watch as I perform a surgical technique I invented that should save the leg of an injured man. One of your skilled mine workers, mind you. You will not witness another doctor as proficient as I am."

Gargaron laughs outright. "You are young to say so."

"Youth is a condition that will correct itself with time. I cannot say the same for incompetence." He looks around. "Ah! Here are the 'adversaries,' as you call them."

"Yes. I'm curious why you are so interested in them."

"The human body interests me, Lord Gargaron. How do we breathe? Why do some run fast and others slowly? What mix of traits allows adversaries to excel in your game of Fives while this lovely young woman, Doma Denya, can pour wine without spilling a drop and yet would struggle to

218

complete a single obstacle? Are you certain you won't sell the mules to me?"

"I'm certain, but if Captain Neartos will call in a few of his soldiers, I will have them run through a menageries together and you can compare the soldiers to the adversaries."

"That would be delightful!" says Agalar, but a flicker of displeasure mars the words, and I think he is lying; he isn't delighted at all.

Nor are we delighted, given that we are the ones forced to pace through a full round of menageries in the glare of the hot sun. But fortune favors me, for once we are finished, overheated and thirsty, Gargaron dismisses us to the kitchen to get drink and food. Tana returns to the dormitory and makes sure Mis joins us.

The kitchen is another pavilion, open on all sides, and includes a dining shelter like that in Garon Stable for the servants. Here I find Amaya flirting masterfully with the men and women of Agalar's entourage, Bettany among them. Trust Amaya to find a way to get close to her! Agalar's people are as mixed in their looks as sailors, as if the doctor has been collecting specimens from every shore of the Three Seas. In all the weeks we have traveled with Gargaron we Commoners have never been allowed to sit and eat at a table with Patrons, even lowborn ones, but Agalar's people wave us over without the slightest hesitation. A young woman with the same straw-colored hair as Lord Agalar starts flirting with Dusty, Mis grins as several young men address her with the brash manners of foreigners, and two older people begin grilling Tana in broken Saroese about the ins and outs of the Fives.

Several speak to me, but it's hard to concentrate when I have to force myself not to stare at Bettany. She sits at another table with the scribe's box in front of her as she writes on a roll of papyrus. She doesn't even look up from her work, nor does Amaya have any excuse to venture past her because a full mug of beer and a full bowl of lentil stew sit untouched at her side.

After I hastily drink two cups of cool well water and eat a bowl of stew I excuse myself more loudly than I need to and walk out of the kitchen courtyard. Once I reach the path that rings the outer garden, I step behind the massive trunk of an ancient sycamore to wait.

The moment Bettany comes out of the kitchen gate and onto the path, alone, I make a dove's soft coo. She pauses, I coo again, and she figures out where I'm hiding and hurries over. The silent heat of the afternoon pours over us as we embrace, two people bound together for longer than either of us can remember.

"I thought I'd lost you," I whisper.

For a moment we cling to each other but, so quickly it startles me, she pushes me away.

"I can't take long or someone will come looking."

Her frown falls like the weight of a tempest about to break

over me. There's always been something wild and impossible about her, the part Father could never comprehend because it went against everything he himself is and everything he thought girls were meant to be. The rest of us found our own ways to relate to him; Bett never tried—she just raged and stormed in an undisciplined way that never accomplished anything. I brace myself now as she shakes her head in her usual infuriating manner.

"I didn't think I'd find you with Lord Gargaron. And Amaya too! I suppose she couldn't bear to be separated from Denya."

"You knew about her and Denya?" I ask, distracted from the urgency of our situation by this glimpse of our old life.

"Everyone but you and Father knew about Denya, Jes. You because you're oblivious to everything except the Fives and him...well, never mind *him*. He's nothing to do with us anymore." She grabs my arm and shakes me. "Listen! I convinced Agalar to buy you and Amaya from Gargaron."

"That's not going to happen."

"You have to come with me."

"I'm an adversary now."

She pulls back. "It's always the Fives with you, isn't it?"

"There's nothing wrong with me wanting to be an adversary."

"Except that you are running for a Patron master."

"I could ask the same of you! Why are you with Lord Agalar? Where are the household servants? Are they condemned to the mines?"

"Even I didn't think a group of innocent women and children would be marched with criminals all the way to the mines. But we were. It was an awful journey."

I press a hand over hers where she is still holding on to my arm. Whether fighting or laughing, Bett and I have always relied on each other, held each other up, listened. "Did anyone die?"

Her body goes as taut as a tightly strung rope. "We all survived the trip, if that's what you mean. Do you know what they use women and children for at the mines?"

Suddenly I don't want to hear. "Hauling rock?"

"Yes, hauling baskets of debris out of places too narrow for men to get into, but also as rewards for the prisoners to get them to work harder."

"Oh gods, Bett…" Words choke in my throat and a wave of horrified dizziness makes me stagger. I catch myself on the tree trunk.

Yet her expression lightens, and her chin lifts in triumph. "We were spared that because of Agalar."

The relief that washes through me leaves me unable to speak. Wind rustles in the trees and, in the distance, I hear the buzz of laughter and chatter from the kitchen, a reminder that Bettany is traveling with a group of foreigners whose languages we can't even understand.

"What do you mean?" I ask when I've got my voice back.

She glances around to make sure no one is on the path or wandering the outer garden. "He was already at the mining village, studying injuries, as you must have heard. When we arrived the supervisor asked him to inspect all the prisoners to see who would be best fitted for which work. I knew what kind of work I was intended for. So when I was brought to him and saw he was a foreigner, I begged him to save me and the others. And he agreed."

"Why would he agree? Did he want you for himself? He called you Beauty. Like a dog."

"He gives all his people nicknames. It's just his way." But she looks away to hide her expression from me.

"What aren't you saying?" I demand.

She chews on her lower lip, her face in profile. Bettany's beauty is that of fierceness melded with perfection of feature: eyes, chin, cheekbones, brows, and lips all so fine and proportional that sculptors and artists sometimes came up to her on the street to beg that she might model for them, although of course Father would never allow it. Her frame is tall and voluptuous but I can't help but notice that she's thinner now than when I last saw her.

"I was desperate, so I tried to impress him. I said he

should choose a girl like me to be his assistant, that I knew a great deal about herbs and medical care and also that I could take care of household tasks for him...." Her hesitation makes my skin crawl with disgust at how vulnerable she was and still is. "I said I would do whatever he wanted if he would save the people I came with. It seemed better than the alternative."

"I'm so sorry," I murmur. "It's not your fault, Bett. It was really courageous of you. What did he say?"

Her smile, like Father's, comes rarely, and it shines now. "He asked me what seemed like a hundred questions about plants and their efficacy, about wounds and diseases. I couldn't answer most of them! I thought I knew something about healing but I really don't, not compared to him."

"Yes, he seems to think a great deal of his own knowledge," I mutter, for I have never heard Bettany speak with such enthusiasm of our own parents; she only ever criticizes them.

"But he was satisfied with my performance because then he insisted I accompany him on his afternoon rounds. He treated me as if I was his assistant and observed how well I was able to complete the tasks he gave me, whether I flinched at blood, and if I could manage a neat stitch sewing up a gash in a man's leg."

"You were always good at helping Mother with sick people."

She isn't listening; she's caught in her memory, a little glassy-eyed. "After that he told the mine supervisor he was impressed by my intelligence and calm—"

"You? *Calm?*"

"Shut up!" But she grins and elbows me. "I can be calm when I'm doing something important, like trying to save a person's life. My hands never shake. He took me on as an assistant. Of course they all thought he meant he was taking me as a lover but it isn't like that, Jes. It isn't."

I want to grab her chin and force her to look me in the eye and repeat it, but I know her too well—she'd rather kick than cooperate. "Then what is it like?"

"Beauty?" an unfamiliar female voice calls from the kitchen gate, in accented Saroese. "Are you out here?"

She grabs my shoulder and whispers, "When the collapse in the mine happened and so many people were injured and killed, we took advantage of the disorder and got all of Mother's people put on the wagons for the injured and dead. They are at the hospital here in town, pretending to be dead."

My mouth drops open. "You saved them!"

"Them and myself. Are you angry I stole your chance to rescue us?"

"Of course not! Why would you even say that?"

"Beauty?" the unknown woman repeats, as if she's heard our voices. "We're leaving."

Bett pulls me close. "I was joking! Anyway I haven't saved them yet. They could still be discovered at the hospital."

"Where do they take the dead?"

"There are tombs outside of town, in the desert. But without water and food they'll die, and this oasis is so isolated they can't possibly walk anywhere without help. I have no reason to think anyone here would assist us. Agalar only knows the Patrons who run things, the mine supervisor and those sorts of people. Of course they'd just turn them back over to Gargaron."

Ro isn't the only Efean angry at the Saroese who rule us. "I have an idea, but I don't know if it will work. Will you be going to the hospital later?"

"Yes. He has surgeries to do."

"Go." I step back from her. "If I can manage to get help I'll find a way to come to the hospital tonight. Have our people ready." I kiss her good-bye.

She smiles with her typical blend of mocking me while still being proud of me. "I'll be impressed if you can actually pull something off. Why won't you and Amaya run away and come with me, so we can all be together?"

"That's sweet of you, Bett. But Amaya and I have things to do here."

"But Jes—" She pulls a hand over her head: her hair has been shorn short in the fashion of prisoners, giving her a stark look as she breaks off and changes her mind about whatever it was she was going to say. "Never mind."

226

"Beauty? I know you are out here. Come along! You know he hates to be kept waiting."

I shove her. She slaps me on the shoulder the way she's always done, then lopes off.

As soon as I hear the sound of carriages rolling away I head back inside.

If is a slender word to hang a rescue on, but right now it's the only one I've got.

15

~~~~

I walk into the kitchen to find all of Agalar's people already gone. Dusty, Mis, and Tana are standing awkwardly to one side of the dining shelter since it's now clear the Garon servants would very much prefer we Efeans had never come into their eating area at all, but we haven't been dismissed by Gargaron and so can't leave. Amaya's distinctive laugh rises from within the inner house.

Captain Neartos strides in as if looking for someone and stops short, as surprised to see us in the Patron kitchen as the kitchen staff is unhappy we are there. "Are you still here? You may return to the stable."

"With your permission, Captain, I need to speak to Lord Gargaron," I say as Tana gives me a stern look. "May I ask when we are leaving Akheres Oasis?"

"Tomorrow, after all the cargo has been loaded, inspected, and sealed." He doesn't need to say the main cargo is gold bullion. We all know it. "We'll make a dawn journey to the tombs, then travel at night along the desert road with the waxing moon to light our way. Why do you wish to speak to His Lordship? He's gone to take his afternoon rest."

I repress a shudder, thinking of Denya and then of the fate Bettany has, I hope, narrowly escaped. But I plunge onward, for I must move quickly. "After my victory today the adversaries I defeated invited me to join them for a drink as a gesture of goodwill. Didn't I come here to build my reputation and make a memorable impression on behalf of Garon Palace?" I give a half-smile to remind him of our greater purpose, for any captain in Gargaron's household must be aware of the plot to elevate Kalliarkos and Menoë to the throne.

"No need to bother His Lordship. Such a scheme fits our purpose exactly. I give you permission on his behalf, and you can take the carriage so you needn't walk. Let all of you adversaries go."

Just as we start to leave Amaya minces into the kitchen. "Wine for His Lordship and Doma Denya, if you please," she says with a sweet smile for the cook, who pats her kindly on the arm. Of course all the servants love her.

Captain Neartos speaks as abruptly as if he's been waiting here hoping she would appear. "May I carry the tray for you, Orchid?"

"Oh, no need, Captain. But my thanks for the offer." She casts him a coquettish smile that actually causes him to blush, and I shudder to a stop, wondering if I will need to defend her too. But then I recall with what incredible self-possession she faced down Agalar's dangerous accusation, and I realize that maybe there are some things my baby sister can do better than me. Her gaze flicks my way, and I dip my chin in the hope she'll understand I spoke to Bettany and will communicate with her later.

Tana says, "Dusty, come along!" as Mis rolls her eyes at him.

As we walk back to the stable through the heat, Tana adds, "Dusty, don't stare at that girl. She's not for you."

He sighs. "Yes, Honored Lady."

When Tana turns to me I'm afraid she's going to scold me for looking at Amaya also. "My thanks for that brilliant piece of management, Jes. I've a hankering for some of the special date wine brewed here in the oasis, and just between you and me, I'm happy to have a chance to socialize with people who won't look down on us. For that matter, you need it too."

"What do you mean?"

"The trial today is over. You can relax now and again."

"I can never relax," I mutter.

The driver sets us down in a dusty square surrounded by a warren of streets too narrow for vehicles. Tana beckons to a pack of giggling children and gives them each a copper coin to lead us to the Adversary Kiss. Mis grabs Dusty's hand and hauls him after the children. I think Mis is infatuated with him even though it is blindingly obvious that he mopes after my unobtainable sister, to whom he has never even spoken.

Drowsy Akheres Town comes to life at the end of the day. Vendors sell grilled whitefish caught from the oasis lakes. Shops display brass lamps, decorated leather footstools, and glass beads. Gates into elegant wine gardens and raucous beer taverns stand graciously open. In one garden people dance side by side, not touching and yet deeply in contact with each other. I have never seen dancing like this in Saryenia. The slow curl of arms and the sway of bodies are enthralling. It makes me think of how it felt to kiss Kalliarkos. It makes me think of how happy Amaya and Denya always look when they are together, how they didn't let impossible circumstances keep them apart.

But I let the thought go just as I let him go. It's over. I made the choice to protect my family, and now for Mother's sake I have to make sure the next time I see her I can tell her that her daughters worked together to rescue the people she herself rescued from difficult situations and gave a haven in our household. We girls can't do less than she did many times over.

The Adversary Kiss is a wine garden catering to the Fives crowd. Tana makes a show of our entrance, and so many people compete to buy us drinks that it's flattering. Women come right up to us in the direct way Efean women have, but it soon becomes clear some have been drafted by male friends or relatives to open the way for men to talk to us.

In a way I am excited at the attention. The chatter is lively, the wine quenches my thirst, and Mis and Dusty are immediately surrounded by admirers. I settle beside Tana, who is seated with older people who train adversaries in Akheres. We discuss strategies for a little while, until I spot Henta entering through the main gate. I excuse myself and go straight to her.

"Spider!" She grins as she introduces me to her companions. I make small talk for as long as I can stand, then hook fingers over her elbow and draw her aside.

"Listen, I have something to say to you in private, Henta. It's a risky matter, and if you want nothing to do with it please forget what I'm about to say."

"All right," she says with a slow nod, but I can tell she's curious as we make our way to a quiet corner.

"What if I told you there is an opportunity, tonight, to rescue the most recent group of women and children who were brought to the mine? Eleven in all." Twelve if I can convince Bettany to escape with them, but I don't say that.

She shakes her head with a regretful sigh. "Do you suppose

we who live here in Akheres haven't thought of plots and plans? That we don't hate what we see? The punishment for runaways and anyone caught helping them is death. More than that, on the last occasion a prisoner escaped the mine, the Saroese who run this town chose by lot one of our own innocent young people to take the place of the criminal who vanished. I'm sorry. I hate this as much as anyone. But it's too dangerous, and eleven people is far too many."

"What if I told you the mine supervisor believes they are all dead?"

She crosses her arms. "Are you certain of this?"

"Yes."

I see in the tightening of her jaw the moment she makes the decision. "Come with me. There's someone at the Rasp and File I will introduce you to."

The Rasp and File is a much fancier wine garden a few streets over. Servers carry trays of food in to private parties screened in small, separate courtyards. It's the kind of place that in Saryenia would be a Patron establishment where a well-to-do captain like my father might take his family to dine once a year. That's why it seems strange that every single person at the Rasp and File is Efean, and that they are all speaking Efean. On a far wall, beneath lamplight, I see a mural depicting the Mother of All that reminds me of the one in the Heart Tavern, right out in the open.

Henta greets the elderly dame seated by the gate, whispers to her, then escorts me to a tiny courtyard near the back with a single table and two cushioned chairs. She sits; I'm restless, so I stand at parade rest, hands clasped behind my back and my heart racing.

An older Efean man comes in. Having grown up with a father who is a soldier makes it easy for me to identify the squared shoulders and honed movements of men who have military training. He also has a mangled hand, badly scarred and healed, perhaps a legacy of battle. He looks at me, then at Henta. Of course he does not speak first.

"This is Emsu," she says, rising. "I'll wait just outside, Spider."

He clasps his hands behind his back in echo of my own parade rest, but he's as tense as a man who is thinking of reaching for his knife.

I know this moment well: in the Fives, when I'm in the air having rejected one landing spot, just before I reach out to grab for a new one. I have one chance to gain his trust.

So I say, "Efea will rise."

A genuine smile of comradeship lights his face. In fact it staggers me how quickly he accepts me. He nods emphatically. "Efea will rise. But you are an adversary with Garon Palace. What brings you to me with that phrase on your lips?"

"Often we do not have a choice in what path we walk, Honored Sir. That is why I run as an adversary for Patron masters. But that is not all I am."

234

"As I see by your looks."

"Excuse me for being blunt, Honored Sir, but the matter is urgent. In the recent terrible accident in the mine, eleven women and children were claimed to be dead by the foreign doctor, Lord Agalar. They have been taken to the hospital basement with the corpses and can be smuggled out right from under the nose of the Saroese."

"And taken where?"

"I need help to cart them out of the hospital, and if possible get them out of the desert and to a poet named Ro-emnu, who will see that they reach a safe haven."

To my utter astonishment he murmurs, " 'This is your ugly history. The truth you've buried beneath the tombs of your dead. Hear my words! Heed my call!' "

" 'Efea will rise,' " I finish. "You know of Ro-emnu?"

"Of course we know of him. He is our voice. But what's in it for you, Spider? You're climbing the ladder of the Fives, and if you're implicated, you'll be executed."

The path opens. It's a huge risk, and I could fall to my death, but I make the leap anyway.

"I am General Esladas's daughter."

His laugh startles me. "Ah, yes, we know of him here. He gained his captaincy in the spider scouts who guard the chain of desert forts on the road south of this oasis."

I'm pleased Father is so famous, and not really surprised, given what he's accomplished. "Then perhaps you also have heard that my mother is an Efean woman he kept faith with for many years. Until the lord I now serve tried to kill her and sent her household here so their labor would enrich his treasury. Over the years my mother had rescued all those people from the streets of Saryenia. As her daughter I am obligated to rescue them again."

He examines me. The silence weighs like pressure on my shoulders. Father taught us girls to always have a backup plan, but I've made my one gamble.

"Yes, I can arrange it," he says.

Elation hits so hard I want to sit down and cry but there isn't time.

He adds, "The man in charge of carting corpses from the hospital to the tombs outside town is a cousin of mine. We Efeans who live here in Akheres don't take our dead to that place, but prisoners whether Saroese or Efean who die in the mine are taken there because they have lived and died under Saroese gods and Saroese laws."

I'm stunned that this really could happen, and even better, that Gargaron will have no idea we're stealing back the freedom he stole from them. "It will cost money to feed and clothe them, to help them travel to safety. I don't have much but I can give you my victor's earnings—"

"No need, Honored Niece." It is the first time he has addressed me in the Efean way, a sign of respect I never knew I could desire so much. "To rescue those who have been wrongfully punished by Patrons is a responsibility all Efeans take upon themselves. We need nothing from you but this chance you have given us to act. But you must come with me to the hospital."

"Of course. I'll have to introduce you to the girl"—I don't want to say Bettany's name; it seems safest to pretend we aren't related—"who is in charge so she knows to trust you."

As we step out of the tiny courtyard Henta lifts her eyebrows in a question. I nod, and Emsu says, "We will be gone for a bit."

"I'll pretend I'm sharing a private meal with the adversary," she says.

He takes me out the back through an alley. In the east a three-quarter moon rises with a glory that dims the nearby stars. The world seems ablaze with hope.

"Did you serve in the army?" I ask.

"I served with General Inarsis. Many of us left the army with him, when it became clear we would not be given positions of responsibility even though we won a battle on behalf of our Saroese king." He glances at me. "But of course you may know him, for he is employed by Garon Palace."

"I do know him, and I've often wondered why an Efean man who left the army for the reasons he did would turn around and work for a noble Patron household."

"Ah," he says, and afterward there is a long silence as we walk through the dark streets. Wind scrapes across the nearby roofs.

"You don't trust me, do you?" I say. "Why take this risk, then?"

"I happen to have heard that an unusual number of people were killed in the mine accident, so while it is possible you mean to betray me for some manner of reward, a spy sent to uncover disloyal subjects, it's as likely that your request is an honest one, in which case I am obligated to act."

"Thank you, Honored Sir. I won't betray your trust."

The hospital's warehouse-like stone building stands by the southern gate, set against the town wall. At the far end of the building wait six mule-drawn wagons marked with the white death flag.

"Good thing you came when you did," Emsu says. "They're ready to load the bodies. Where is your contact?"

"She'll be with Lord Agalar. Is that the main entrance?" I point to a portico and gate halfway down the building, lit by oil lamps. A carriage is pulled up out front, grooms and driver tending the horses, and I recognize the servants with a stab of fear. "Oh no," I whisper.

"What's wrong?" He catches my arm in his to restrain me. He's very strong.

"Those are Lord Gargaron's people." For a blinding,

horrible moment I wonder if somehow Bettany has turned traitor on me, but then I remember. "Lord Agalar invited him to observe a surgery this afternoon. They must be here still. What if he takes a tour of the facility?"

I'm shaking, and Emsu's fingers tighten on my arm as he touches the hilt of the knife tucked in his belt.

"It isn't a trap," I say, for only bald honesty will work now. Desperation makes my voice hoarse. "I swear on the gods of my father's people, and by the Mother of All. I just want revenge on Lord Gargaron for what he did to my family. If I can free our household servants then that is a small victory. Please believe me, Honored Sir."

He takes in a breath and lets it out, then releases my arm. "Come this way."

We go in a side entrance to a staging area. To my left a ramp slopes down into an underground chamber I can't see, while to my right doors open to a large room lit by many lamps. Agalar's penetrating voice echoes through the entry hall.

"Amputation is the usual treatment in such cases. But I have been experimenting with a means of salvaging the limb. If you'll look here, you'll see how I have stitched together the blood vessels and packed the injury with natron as a healing barrier."

I take several steps until I can peek in. The surgery room is furnished with tables rigged with straps for tying people down and benches lining the walls for spectators, as if it's common for a doctor like Agalar to perform in front of an audience. A shroud covers a body on one table. Bettany appears with a basket, which she sets down by the door so casually that it takes me a moment to realize the basket contains a severed foot all crushed and bloody and a mangled arm cut off just above the elbow. Sweat breaks down my back as my skin goes hot and then clammy cold. She looks up and our gazes meet.

She gestures me closer and points to the basket.

I choke but make myself move toward her.

Agalar is droning on about clamps and arteries and gangrene. With slumped shoulders and bent head to hide my height, I cross the open area and slide in at a crouch on the other side of the basket. A stench of sickly sweet rot wafts up, making me heave. Bettany reaches over the basket and squeezes my arm as my eyes water and I slap a hand over my nose and mouth.

"They are in the underground chamber. I told them you would be coming and not to go with anyone unless you were there to say it is safe," she whispers. "Have you found someone to help?"

"Yes," I whisper into my hand, indicating Emsu with a lift of my chin.

"Everything I have seen here has impressed me," says Gargaron, his voice suddenly much closer than before.

He and Agalar have moved around the room and now

240

stand in plain sight of me. He hasn't seen me only because his back is turned to the door as he studies the unconscious patient lying on a table. Agalar, standing opposite, notes Bettany, and me in her shadow.

"That is because it is impressive work, as you'll see if you look here," Agalar says in his usual arrogant way, drawing Gargaron's attention to him. Trying not to throw up, I grab the basket and hurry across the entryway to where Emsu waits by the ramp. "Any other doctor would simply have cut off this limb, but I have saved it. This man will work productively again."

"If you have ever considered traveling with an army and testing your skills on battlefield medicine, I hope you may consider an offer to travel with me. My general is a competent and well-organized man. I would be happy to pay you handsomely to spend as many months as you desire studying the peculiarities of wounds received in battle and teaching our field doctors your innovative techniques."

"I've worked with soldiers but not during an actual war. I'm intrigued by the prospect of seeing so many varieties of wounds, and in such numbers. Beauty!"

I thrust the basket into Emsu's hands. If I hold it any longer I might heave up all over the horrible remains jostling inside. Bettany pauses in the door and, with a glance in my direction, touches fingers to her chest, heart to heart. I tap my chest in answer.

"Beauty! I need you to sew up this patient's flesh at once."

She scurries into the room.

Gargaron says, "You trust such delicate work to a Commoner and a woman?"

"Women have a precise and steady touch that makes them skilled seamstresses and surgeons. I also find women more amenable to instruction, less likely to argue, and more adept at learning. Now, if you'll come over here, I will show how I successfully amputated a foot and an arm, and then I will give you a tour of the rest of the hospital."

Emsu has already started down the ramp, carrying the basket with the tenacity of a man who has seen worse mutilation in battle. I follow, hand over my mouth as I take in shallow breaths and slowly swallow the urge to vomit.

We descend into a long, low chamber dug into the earth and supported by such a dense grove of brick pillars that it feels as if I am in a gloomy orchard. Only a few lamps burn, a row of shrouded bodies lost in shadow. It's so much cooler down here that I shiver. Two men roll a body onto a stretcher, keeping the shroud in place, and carry it past us.

"Greetings, Emsu, what brings you here?" asks one. They glance at me but, when I say nothing to them, don't acknowledge me.

"Where's Tefu? I need to speak to him."

The fellow whistles, the sound echoing strangely through the crypt, and he and the other continue up the ramp with the disciplined steps of former soldiers used to marching in unison. An Efean man limps out of the darkness with a smaller figure creeping behind his back like a shadow.

Emsu makes a sign with his hand. "This is Spider. I vouch for her. She's asked for our help securing that one group of corpses from the mine."

"I wondered what we were going to do with them," says Tefu. His age allows him to address me before I speak to him. "Greetings of the night, Honored Niece."

"Greetings, Honored Sir. My thanks for your help. I know what you risk."

"Doma Jessamy!" The small figure bounces out from behind Tefu.

The old man startles and exclaims, "Rascal! Did you follow me?"

With his head shaved and his face and body so thin, it takes me a moment to recognize Montu-en. For his age and height he might be the twin of Prince Temnos except that Temnos is a Patron lord and Montu-en a Commoner boy. "Are you here to rescue us, like Doma Bettany promised?" he says eagerly.

"Yes." I pat him on the shoulder before addressing Tefu. "I see you have an old injury, Honored Sir. Are many of you soldiers who served with General Inarsis? Akheres Oasis seems so far from Saryenia."

"Our net is widely spread. When we left the army we

243

returned to our homes across Efea bringing the lessons we learned."

"What lessons were those?"

"That the Saroese who rule us will always give with one hand and take away with the other. But now we know how to fight, and we have a general to lead us. Efea will rise."

If lightning had struck I could not be more jolted. What does General Inarsis have to do with Ro's poetic phrase and the whispered discontents of Commoners? Doesn't he serve Princess Berenise? Isn't he friends with Lord Thynos?

"Are you saying that—?"

"Shhh!" warns Emsu.

From above we hear Lord Agalar. "We store corpses in the basement because it is cooler. Even so they must be moved immediately to the tombs south of town because of how quickly they rot in the heat. Ah, I see the many casualties from the recent collapse are already being loaded into the death wagons."

Footsteps approach down the ramp as Emsu glances back in alarm.

"Honored Sir," I say to Tefu, "let the boy and me lie down with the others."

"I don't like lying under the shroud, Doma. It makes me feel like I'm dead."

I grasp his hands, remembering what Temnos found appealing. "Think of it as a daring adventure."

He brightens.

"I know where to go," he whispers excitedly.

Hand in mine, he leads me into the back of the crypt, where the light barely reaches, and the bodies lie as shadowy lumps under cloth. I lie down on the hard stone floor and pull a shroud over me just as lamplight lances through the pillars, cutting shadows into angles. Montu-en rolls in beside me, his body tucked against mine. I put an arm around his shoulders. By the tiny shifts of his body I can tell he is trying not to squirm. I squeeze his shoulder and he quiets.

"The collapse was bad enough," says Agalar, his voice so close that my heart seems to knock out of my chest with fear. "But the real reason so many people died is that the fall released a pocket of noxious air that strangled all who breathed it. I often wonder if this poisonous air remains in their lungs and can contaminate others, which is why I ordered these victims to be placed in the back. Do you wish to investigate more closely?"

"No, I've seen enough."

I want to laugh at how easily Agalar has manipulated Gargaron, but of course beneath the coarse linen shroud that is all that separates me from disaster, I don't.

"I am leaving Akheres tomorrow."

"Tomorrow!" exclaims Agalar, for the first time sounding surprised. "So soon?"

"Yes, if you wish to travel with me, you will have to decide quickly. Perhaps your household cannot be ready."

"I'm accustomed to packing up in haste. Which route do you intend to take, Lord Gargaron?"

"South. I always stop on the way out at the tomb of my uncle, Lord Menos, to make the appropriate offerings. Then the eight- to ten-day desert crossing to the sea."

"I can meet you at the tombs, if that's agreeable to you."

Their voices fade as they leave the crypt.

I get up and twitch the shrouds back to see the blessedly familiar faces of women I grew up with: our two laundresses and three cleaning women, Cook's assistant and the water and scullery girls, all rescued by Mother from abusive circumstances. The two other boys who, like Montu-en, she saved from the streets. Those she could not help to make new lives elsewhere remained with us for as long as they needed to. However much Bettany stayed with them for Mother's sake, she'll never acknowledge that these people were able to live in our household because Father allowed it, either because he agreed that they deserved shelter or because he knew if he tried to forbid it Mother would leave him. There's so much about my parents I never thought of until now, and may never understand.

"Doma Jessamy," they whisper, touching me to convince themselves I am real.

"You can go with these men. It's safe. It will be a long journey but in the end you will return to Doma Kiya. I have to go now before I'm found missing, but I wanted to reassure you."

They kiss me in the Efean way, on the cheek, a gesture they never would have dared make when we lived under Father's roof, and it makes my chest grow tight with longing for what we have lost and what we never had.

16

We leave before dawn, while it's still cool, in an impressive column of twenty-four cargo wagons carrying dates, natron, and gold, eight supply wagons for our own needs, four carriages, and the troop of Garon soldiers under the command of Captain Neartos. Where the road climbs steeply out of the oasis our pace slows to such a crawl that I swing down to walk alongside, then stop to look back the way we came. Moonlight bathes Akheres Lake in a sheen like pearls ground into gauze and cast over its waters. All lies eerily still except for pinpricks of lamps on the town walls.

I can almost hear the land breathe as a brush of wind stirs dust on the road like a mirror of my own restlessness. Am I both Patron and Commoner, or am I neither? I no longer know. Maybe a mule is a creature with no home, only a long road ahead and a doubled burden to haul.

"Jes?" Mis trots toward me out of the shadows. The lantern hanging from the back of the last wagon in the line sways, its light receding up toward the high desert plateau above us. "Are you coming? Ugh, I drank too much."

She bends over, hands on knees, and coughs up bile. I try not to laugh but I do anyway as I slap her on the butt.

"Don't you know better by now?"

She moans, spitting one last time, then falls in beside me as we stride after the wagons. "Where did you go last night, anyway? You have the most peculiar habit of running off and then not coming back for the longest time."

An awkward silence between us grinds as harshly as the wheels on the road. I have an answer prepared but I'm so tired of lying to the people I should trust. Yet I can't endanger her by telling her the truth, just as I can't risk that she might accidentally blurt out the truth at the wrong time. "It turns out that the adversary Henta has an uncle who had met my father years ago when he was stationed in the desert. It was a chance for me to hear a few stories."

I wait, wondering if she'll bite. Her silence drags on so long I don't dare glance at her.

"Do you miss him?" she asks, one of the perceptive questions I've come to expect from her.

"Yes."

"I hope you don't mind my saying so, Jes. Please don't take offense. But it's just so odd, knowing a Patron man like him acknowledged you and raised you."

"He did the best he knew how," I say, remembering Mother's words. "And I'm not offended."

As our feet crunch on the surface of the road and dust spits into our faces, I feel a peculiar sort of peace. For all that I struggle with who I am and where I belong, my parents did their best to make a space for us girls in the world. They wanted me, and my sisters, and maybe it is only now that I can recognize how much that means.

We reach the top of the incline. The corpse wagons, empty and headed back to Akheres Town, are waiting to the side of the road until Gargaron's cavalcade is all up so they can start down. White-haired Tefu sits on the driver's bench of the first wagon. Seeing me, he holds out a hand, five fingers spread, and although I don't exactly know what the gesture means, I can guess what it signifies: victory.

I bask in a thrill of triumph, knowing I've bested Gargaron again. It doesn't matter that he'll never know. It matters that we've won.

All that's left is to get Bettany free of Lord Agalar. To manage that I'll need Amaya's help.

Mis and I run forward, passing the slow-moving wagons. Toward the front of the line, Denya has the shutters of her carriage open. Captain Neartos rides alongside, and Amaya leans out to speak to him as she raps him flirtatiously on the arm with her closed fan.

"I wish Dusty would give up on wanting what he can't have when what he can have is right in front of him," murmurs Mis.

"He's an idiot."

She sighs. "She is really pretty. And she doesn't sneer at us like the other servants do."

Amaya catches sight of me, and I take the opportunity to tap my chest twice with a fist, guessing she'll know it means the household is safe. She snaps her fan shut and touches it to her right ear with a smile for Neartos as if she's inviting his conversation, but I know the signal is meant for me. She'll make a way for us to meet at the tombs. I drop back, and Mis and I swing up into our own carriage.

Soon after dawn we turn aside from the main road to follow a gully. Barren cliffs hem us in like fortress walls. The gully opens into an almost perfectly circular depression, a hidden oasis ringed by cliffs pitted with numerous cave openings. Date palms and sycamores grow everywhere amid mounds of flowers. At the center, a jumble of long-abandoned buildings surrounds a large circular pond. Water lilies bloom like stars around a monumental statue rising at the center of the pool, whose curves and pose reveal this as an image of Lady Hayi-yin, Mistress of the Sea.

The tombs for the dead are built into the cliff walls, taking advantage of the caves. Lord Menos's tomb is easy to spot on the far side because a stone ramp leads to a ledge decorated with marble pillars and a gleaming marble wall built across a cave mouth. Behind that wall an oracle lived out her life in darkness, breathing stale air and never again seeing the sun.

Our procession approaches a gleaming temple dedicated to Lord Judge Inkos, whose priests live here year-round as caretakers. Of course we Commoners are not allowed to enter the temple area. For us an awning has been strung up in the ruins of an old building well away from the holy grounds. Mis is still feeling hungover, and Dusty has a cough from all the dust we've eaten by traveling at the end of the line, so they stretch out on our cots and promptly go to sleep because we won't be leaving again until dusk. We've been warned to sleep during the day in preparation for moving at night under the waxing moon.

Tana keeps daily notes in a bound book. As she writes I sit next to her, wondering how long it will take Amaya to get away so we can discuss our next move. I sip water and think about how filthy I'll be by the time we reach Port Selene, since on the harsh desert crossing we can't carry enough water to wash.

"Why are we stopping at Lord Menos's tomb?" I ask.

She keeps writing, not looking up. "Lord Gargaron always makes an offering on the way south, for good fortune. For years he would also ask a question of the holy oracle, while she lived, poor creature." Belatedly she glances at me in alarm. "Meaning no disrespect," she adds in a placating tone I hate to hear from a woman I respect so much.

No Commoner—no *Efean*—can be heard to criticize Patron ways. That will earn us a whipping. But does she think I would be the one to report her?

"To become an oracle seems a frightful fate to me too," I say, to reassure her. "How long ago did Lord Menos die? Why is he buried out here?"

"When Princess Berenise was younger she made the journey to the mines and the tour of the estates. Lord Menos always accompanied her. He died in a mine accident here."

"Why was he buried with an oracle? I thought only kings and lords who are head of their clan or palace did that."

"Lord Menos *was* head of Clan Garon at that time. When he died, the title passed to his and Princess Berenise's son. That son died in battle, and the title would have passed to his son, Lord Kalliarkos, but Kalliarkos was only two years old at the time. Menos's younger brother—Lord Gargaron's father—was dead by then too, so Lord Gargaron took over as head of the household."

"Does that mean Lord Kalliarkos is the rightful successor to be head of Garon Palace when he comes of age?"

"I never thought about it," she says, surprised. "Gargaron has always been lord since I've been part of Garon Stable."

She finishes her notes and lies down. As soon as she is asleep I grab a waterskin and leave our shelter. The ruins make it easy for me to sneak up to a spot where I can overlook the servants' gate into the temple. A din of wheels announces the arrival of three carriages and two supply wagons, all pulled by mules. Lord Agalar has arrived, just as he promised. He steps down from his carriage and strides to the back of the line, where two armed men mounted on sturdy desert ponies are bringing up the rear. One is a dark, bearded man with a dreadful scar that has seamed shut an eye; the other is fair-haired like Agalar and even resembles him a little. The scarred man leans down as Agalar speaks, then gives a gesture of assent, like a salute, and the two men turn and ride back the way we all came in. Agalar enters the temple with his retinue through the servants' gate, as Gargaron would never do.

Soon after, Denya emerges from the gate, holding a parasol over her head and with Amaya carrying a basket behind her.

"It's a shame women aren't allowed to walk in the temple garden, Doma Denya," says Amaya in the voice actors use to make their words carry without sounding like they are shouting. "Perhaps we can find shade by that lovely pond for our picnic, where I am sure no one will be rude enough to bother us. I forgot a blanket to sit on. Just a moment."

That's all I need.

I work my way in toward the center of the ruins through a maze of half-fallen walls and dead ends. Finally I stumble onto a clear path down a string of stone-lined pools of different shapes and sizes. It brings me through a partially collapsed tunnel that doubles back twice through a thick wall before opening onto a circular plaza that forms a rim all the way around the perfect circle of the tiny lake. The statue of the goddess, twice life-size, rises on a plinth at the center of the waters. Footsteps crunch. Denya and Amaya approach, having found their way here by a different route.

"Bettany is here," I say breathlessly.

"I know. Gargaron told Denya earlier that we would have Lord Agalar's company on the desert crossing. When I went back inside just now I managed to pass word to Bett to meet us here as soon as she can. Search out a private place for us to talk. Denya can keep watch and warn us if someone comes."

I seek out the highest remnant of wall and scramble up. Amaya and Denya laugh and chat as they lay out a blanket and little baskets of food in plain sight. They look radiant together, embraced by blossoms and lake and sky. Beyond them lies a tangle of overgrown salt cedar, perfect for hiding.

I shade my eyes and turn a careful circle to make sure no one is sneaking up on us. Even though I can always say I am practicing for the Fives by climbing walls, I can't be caught with Amaya.

The morning light softens the shapes and edges of the ruins but it's still instantly obvious this was once a circular complex separated into four distinct building styles. A maze of tiny passageways and tinier rooms might be likened to Pillars, and a cluster of slender towers, many still intact, resembles an orchard of stone trees. The Inkos temple stabs right through two of the sections, all right angles and strong lines.

A plink grabs my attention as a fragment of stone strikes the wall I'm standing on. I drop to a crouch. Bettany stands below me, where the maze of alleys dead-ends into the wall that encircles the lake. She climbs up, and we scoot down to a lower section, out of sight of the temple, and sit together, legs dangling.

A breeze swirls around us, bathing us in the scent of flowers.

She takes my hand just as she used to when we were little girls, before she started hating everything in our lives. Her presence at my side is the most familiar thing in the world, like we are tucked back in the womb together, not that I have any memory of that time. A part of me that I hadn't known hurt quite this badly finally relaxes into memories of a happier time before this storm broke over us.

"I've been so worried about you, Bett," I say in a low voice.

"How did you manage the rescue?" she asks. "Are you sure you can trust the people who took them away?"

"Yes." I start to explain, but stop. "I don't want to say more until you're free of Lord Agalar."

"What makes you think I want to be free of Agalar?"

"I am not climbing up there, not in this dress!" Amaya's voice interrupts my reply. She stands at the lakeside base of the wall, staring up at us. "If you haven't found a better place, Jes, we can go talk in the cover of the salt cedar without being seen."

"Bossy as ever," remarks Bettany.

In the old days, Amaya would have poked back, unable to help herself because she felt we older girls picked on her. Instead she gives a shrug, like she can't be bothered, and walks toward the feathery shrubs.

"The way you and Amaya used to squabble seems so pointless now," I say.

Her face looks drawn and worried as she watches Amaya vanish into the foliage. "Jes, I—never mind. I'll say it to both of you."

I follow her down the wall. We push through branches to find Amaya in a tiny clearing, seated on an ancient stone bench placed right at the edge of the pool. She leaps up and hugs Bettany.

"Oh, Bett, I was afraid we had lost you." Releasing her, she wipes tears from her eyes. "But what about the rest of the household? They're safe, right?"

I break in. "I haven't had opportunity to tell you yet, Amaya. They're free."

Amaya's shriek is followed by more tears, and she grabs both Bettany and me by the wrist, drawing us close. "If only Maraya were here to see how we got the better of that awful man. How did you manage it?"

"Bettany and Lord Agalar got them to pretend to be dead, killed in the collapse at the mine."

"Oh, that is brilliant!"

"It was Agalar's idea," says Bettany in a tone that makes Amaya pause and look more closely at her.

I go on. "I found Efean men willing to smuggle them out of Akheres. They've promised to convey them to Mother."

"Do you trust these strangers?" Amaya asks.

"I do. They're associates of the poet."

Amaya's mouth quirks. "He likes you, you know. Even if you don't want to see it."

I clench my jaw, feeling a blush crawl up my cheeks.

"Where *is* Mother?" Bett asks sharply.

I'm grateful for her question, because I don't want to think too closely about why I feel embarrassed at the thought of Ro. "I don't know precisely *where* she is, but I know she is with Efeans we can trust because they do not love our Saroese masters."

Bettany laughs with her usual spark of derision. "So you are Efean now, Jes? No longer Father's good little Patron daughter?"

Amaya pinches the skin of Bett's arm hard enough for her to exclaim as she flinches back. "Stop it, Bett! At home you always acted like you were better than the rest of us because you played the rebel who made a show of rejecting everything Father stood for while still benefiting from it. You just enjoyed the attention you got from being angry all the time!"

258

"Why shouldn't I have been angry all the time? I wasn't lying to myself like the rest of you were. Father abandoned us the instant we weren't convenient for him anymore. Mother knew the day would come and yet loyally served him like the cow she is."

"That's not fair!" Amaya and I cry together.

"Maraya drinking down the lies they tell in the Archives, hoping her Patron looks will get her a pass where Jes and I could never hope to walk. Fine for her, isn't it? And then of course doting over the first Patron man who spoke to her kindly—"

"Polodos is a good man!" objects Amaya.

"Yes, and dull as wash water." She waves dismissively in the direction of the picnic. "I suppose you think the attention of a pretty Patron friend makes you not a mule while meanwhile all the other Garon servants are whispering that you're on the catch for that captain."

"You don't understand me at all." The way the sunlight cuts through the salt cedar, pouring across her, gives Amaya's shadow the look of a cat's, arching and hissing like she is about to scratch.

"You always wanted to be a captain's wife," retorts Bettany.

"Of course, before Father abandoned us, a marriage with an army captain was my best hope of getting a household of my own and a husband who was gone for months or years at a time to the wars. But now I don't have to." Through a gap in the foliage we can see Denya in the distance, bent intently over

259

a bright red silk ribbon she embroiders with expert stitches. "Denya is saving up all the gifts and money Lord Gargaron confers on her. I have my gold from Prince Temnos. When Lord Gargaron settles his attention on a new concubine, as men always do—"

"Father didn't!" I object.

"Oh, leave off defending Father." Bettany laughs humorlessly. "For once I'm honestly interested in what Amaya has to say."

As Amaya relaxes her position shifts and the feathery leaves fragment her shadow into an ordinary patch of shade. "Efean women live in households headed by women. Why can't we? Denya and I are thinking of selling masks and ribbons in the market. We plan to earn enough money to support our own household as well as our destitute mothers. Her mother also suffered when Clan Tonor fell."

Bettany's lips twist like she is about to say something mocking, yet after a pause she relents and gives Amaya a sisterly peck on the cheek. "That will certainly be shocking, to see the daughter of General Esladas selling masks and ribbons in the market."

"It's odd," muses Amaya. "When Father left us to die in a tomb it freed me from thinking I had to do things the way he thought proper."

"He had no choice! And he didn't know about the tomb!"

"You always make excuses for him," Bettany sneers.

But Amaya squeezes my hand, and she replies in a calm but determined voice. "You weren't the one bricked up, Jes. But when the lives we had before were torn apart, I finally saw that I had other paths I could take. Like the way you can see multiple paths through spinning Rings."

"Like the way Jes used to arrange her food on her platter to simulate a Fives court until Father caught her doing it?"

We all laugh, and my heart feels light as air, floating on the shared memory.

The water lies as still as a mirror. Bending over, we see our faces side by side. Bett looks the most Efean of us four girls, as dark and beautiful as Mother, just as Amaya looks more like Father with straighter hair and the golden skin of the Saroese. I'm the one who looks most like both our parents, Efean and Saroese parts shared out equally to make up my whole. Anyone looking at me knows exactly what I am, whereas Bett and Amaya can slide into one half of what they are. Studying my reflection, I think again of Ro's words, about how I can use this to my advantage. I'm not one or the other; I'm both and neither, just as the land of Efea itself can never be as Saroese as old Saro and yet is no longer the Efea it was before the Saroese came.

Towering above the water, the goddess watches her daughters with benevolent concern. Her arms are filled with bounty and her curly hair is fashioned as ropy strings. I suddenly realize that she does not resemble in any way Hayiyin, Mistress of the Sea, who has prim lips, Saroese eyes, and straight hair flowing down her back all the way to her feet.

Amaya's gaze has also drifted up to the statue. "She looks a little like Mother, doesn't she?"

My thoughts run back to Ro-emnu sitting in the Heart Tavern. To the words the waiter said to me. "She reminds me of a painting I once saw. What if..." The thought is so staggering, going against everything I've been taught, that it's hard to force through my lips. "What if this statue was carved and erected before the Saroese came? What if Hayiyin was copied after the Mother of All? What if the Patrons stole Her from *us*?"

Bettany waves an airy hand in a disparaging way that really irritates me. "No, it is Hayiyin. Agalar explained to me that all representations of the Efean Mother of All are copies of Hayiyin. They look similar because they are made by a conquered people who wish to identify their old beliefs as being as strong as those of the people who conquered them."

"How would he know? He doesn't even live in Efea."

"He knows more than any person I've ever met, besides being a brilliant doctor."

"Yes, and he seems quite satisfied to tell everyone how brilliant he is too. After all your complaints about Mother giving up everything to stay with Father all those years, I never thought I'd find you like a bridled mare following docilely along behind that arrogant doctor—"

262

"Don't call him arrogant! He has the right to be treated as the scholar he is."

"It's so sweet to see you crawling on behalf of a lord who calls you Beauty instead of your name. One who orders you around like a dog!"

"You're more of a dog than I am. Running as an adversary in a lord's stable! Garon owns all five of your souls. Agalar paid my indenture fee and hired me as his assistant. He says I am as promising an apprentice as any young man. In the Shipwright territories, there's nothing unusual about a woman being a scholar or a doctor. He says I have a healing gift."

"Is that what he says?"

"If you'd seen him pull people back from the brink of death, if you'd watched him sew up a man's crushed leg, you'd not mock. He can teach me things no one else can. You're just jealous it was his idea that made it so easy to rescue our household. You think he stole the glory you wanted!"

Her ingratitude hits like a punch to the face. "Amaya and I searched all over Efea for you. And it *was* me who found allies in Akheres to help us after you didn't know what to do next!"

"I think you're just afraid Agalar is smarter than you. It must be hard not having Father around to make you feel like the best of us all the time."

"I never said I was the best of anything!"

"You never had to say it. Once you became obsessed with the Fives all you wanted us for was to cover your tracks."

Amaya steps between us. "Would you two stop fighting? We're supposed to be celebrating, not arguing! Bett, I know you resent how the Fives took Jes's attention, but there's no point holding a grudge now that our old life is gone—"

"You resented the Fives?" I slump down on the bench and stare at her. "All your silences? All your screaming? That was about the Fives?"

"Oh, Jes! Please! It's not always about you. Yes, I was jealous you had so little time for me, but that's only part of it. Don't you see? While Maraya was studying for the Archives and you sneaked out in secret to your Fives and Amaya wrote poetry and plotted an advantageous marriage, I watched you all lie to yourselves about who we really are."

Amaya crosses her arms and taps a foot impatiently. "We don't have much time, and I'm not interested in listening to you lecture us, Bett."

I stand, because I can't think sitting down, and grab Bettany's hand. "Amaya's right. We don't have much time, so let's not argue about our old life. Bett, listen to us. I know this doctor dazzled you and that you feel obligated to him because he saved you. But you don't really know anything about him. You'll be completely at his mercy if you leave with him."

She opens her mouth but I speak before she can.

"Hear me out! Amaya can smuggle you a waterskin and some food and you can walk back to Akheres to the people I met there, join the household servants, and return with them to Mother."

"What makes you think I want to return to Mother?"

I blink, too stunned to reply.

"You and Amaya are the ones who should escape with me," she adds with an intensity that startles me.

"I'm not leaving Denya!"

"I can't go," I object. "I'm an adversary now. How can you not want to return to Mother?"

"I could ask the same of you that you ask of me! Both of you should run away from what is nothing more than servitude to a Patron master. I can't even imagine how dangerous it must be for you, Amaya. A concubine's servant has no protection. What if this Captain Neartos decides he wants you for himself?"

"Believe me, I know every trick to keep out of the way of the men in this household. As long as Denya pleases Lord Gargaron, I'm safe."

"You said yourself the favor he shows her won't last forever." Now it's Bett's turn to grab Amaya's hands, an affectionate gesture she rarely made at home. "You have to get out. Both of you!"

"Why?" says Amaya. "We'll be back in Saryenia soon enough. Once we're there we'll send a message to the poet, and he'll tell us where Mother is."

"It's a dangerous eight- or ten-day journey through empty desert with wagons full of gold. Aren't you afraid of bandits?"

I snort. "Lord Gargaron has done this run many times,

always with soldiers as escort. I think he understands the danger. Anyway, Father used to be in charge of the northern desert frontier. He scoured the land clean of bandits years ago with his spider scout patrols."

Her caustic laugh rakes like nails scratching on my skin. "Do you ever listen to how you worship Father when he never did anything to deserve it, Jes?"

Amaya steps on my foot to remind me not to start the argument again so I take in a breath and let it out, shifting course.

"Bettany, Mother is so worried about you. Do you think she can rest if she doesn't know what's happened to you? What is Agalar to you that you care more about him than Mother's peace of mind?"

"I'll tell you what he is. He's not Saroese and he's not Efean. I despise the Saroese as the greedy conquerors they are. Meanwhile your Efean allies think by rescuing a few hapless prisoners they prove they haven't rolled over for the Patrons, but all Efeans have ever done is roll over. I want no part of any of this. I've made a choice. *My* choice. I'm going to sail the Three Seas. I'm going to see the world. That's something that never occurred to either of you, is it? You're too trapped by your stupid dreams. The day I wash the dirt of Efea from my feet is the day I'll finally be happy."

It's fortunate we are too far away from the temple and caravan for anyone to hear her words, which evaporate on

266

the wind like the cawing of crows. Tears trail down Amaya's cheeks but she doesn't utter a single word. The dry air has sapped all moisture from me.

"Why won't you escape now when I am giving you the chance?" Bettany cries.

"Because this is *my* choice," says Amaya quietly with a glance toward Denya, who has paused in her embroidering to look in our direction with an expression of concern on her face.

I'm too angry to be reasonable. "Why do you suddenly care so much? It isn't as if you cared before."

Bett wipes what I am sure is a tear from her eye. "No, never mind. There's nothing I can do. I tried my best but you're both trapped. I love you, but it doesn't matter, does it?"

It almost seems she is talking to herself. She gives us each a perfunctory hug, then shakes herself and pushes away through the foliage. She's leaving us.

As I take a step after her Amaya grabs my hand.

"Let her stew, Jes. You know how her rages come in a fury of battering wind and rain before vanishing utterly. We'll find another way to talk to her on the desert crossing."

"Yes, that's right. I can coax her into a place of calm and then she'll listen and give up this infatuation with Lord Aga-lar. In Port Selene we'll find a way to get her out of his hands and back to Saryenia. Don't you find it odd the way he calls her Beauty? The way she acts around him?"

Amaya squeezes my fingers, but it is her weary gaze that

startles me. "Yes, there's something frightening about it all that I don't understand. Now let Denya and me go before Captain Neartos comes to fetch us. I'm not in the mood to fend him off graciously today. And don't follow until you're sure no one will catch us together. We can't risk this kind of meeting again."

Yet I'm too agitated to return to our shelter. The sight of Bett's back turned to me slaps at my thoughts like regrets. Why did I never take seriously how much she hated our life? She said so all the time! I just never believed her.

Amaya and I will find a way to change her mind. I have to, because something about her situation stinks to my nose. She's not right about everything, not like she thinks she is. If only she could have met Kal, who is nothing like Agalar. He isn't arrogant, and he never ordered me around like a servant. I didn't hang on his every word.

Did I?

Do I really know Kalliarkos, or am I just seeing what I want to see in him?

The question troubles me. Like a dog with a bone, I can't stop gnawing on it. I ramble aimlessly through the ruins, following a path dictated by moving away from the temple, away from the Patron life that once ruled my every action.

Ro-emnu was right. I'll never be a Patron even though Father pretended we were. Father was lying to himself as much as to us. Maybe Bettany is right that he deserves nothing but scorn, but I can't hate him as she does. I can't hate Mother for the choices she made.

I don't want to hate. Now that my family and household are safe I can earn my place as an Illustrious without feeling I have sacrificed them to win.

At length my wandering feet lead me past the corralled mules and the cargo wagons pulled under awnings and into sight of the ramp leading up to the sealed mouth of Lord Menos's tomb. A murmur of voices alerts me to movement at the base of the ramp, where a small opening that's little more than a crack cuts into the cliff beneath Menos's tomb. A pile of bricks sits heaped to one side, a sealed opening recently broken. A splash of color brightens the pile: a bouquet of fresh flowers set on top.

Captain Neartos stands guard over a file of twelve shackled Efean men, each bearing a criminal's scar on his cheek. They carry the small but heavy chests marked with the royal seal of gold bullion. The harsh sun washes across the slumped backs of the clearly exhausted men as they shuffle into the crack and thus out of my sight. Neartos draws his sword and follows them inside.

For a long while the world seems to stand still. Then, so faintly it might just be my fervid thoughts pretending to sounds that aren't there, I hear a surprised grunt, a scream and a shout, a scrape and a pleading cry. I can't stop myself from imagining the captain coming up behind each shackled man, slitting each throat as they are helpless to resist. My whole body feels on fire, then goes cold as Lord Gargaron appears at the tunnel's mouth, as neatly turned out as if he has just come from a palace supper. He stands in the shade with hands clasped behind his back, utterly relaxed and at peace, eyes half closed.

I ease down to my knees—no sudden movements, nothing that would draw his attention—and roll under the nearest wagon. A bird flutters past. A gust of wind swirls dust along the ground, and I cover my mouth and nose to stop from sneezing.

Captain Neartos appears with a lantern in one hand and a bloody sword in the other.

"They are all dead?" Gargaron asks.

"Yes, my lord."

I breathe my shock into the dust of the earth, my throat thick with rage and my heart sickened. Gargaron picks up the flowers and climbs the ramp to leave this propitious offering at the walled-up entrance to his dead uncle's tomb. After he departs, Neartos carries over a bucket of mortar to the pile of bricks and picks up a trowel.

I'm too afraid to move so I lie there as he seals up the crack until it looks like just another closed-off minor tomb.

"Please, O holy one, grant peace to my troubled heart," I pray in silent words to the goddess Hayiyin, Mistress of the Sea, but in my mind's eye her features transform to become the face of the Mother of All seated on a mountain surrounded by the hotly flowing blood of Efea. The blood of my mother's people, soaking into the earth.

I lie there with the heat baking my bones until he finishes, until he leaves, until a hawk swoops down from the sky to poke amid the disturbed earth.

Lord Menos's oracle is long dead. I don't need to ask her any questions to know what I've seen.

Gargaron is stealing the royal bullion that legally belongs to the king and queen. He's keeping it secret by killing those involved, all except Captain Neartos. It's brilliant, really. If he hides the gold, then the king and queen can't pay their troops, and they can't pacify Saryenia's restless population with bread. If I were plotting to take over the throne, it's what I would do. Besides weakening the current king and queen, he is also amassing gold that will help pay for the soldiers and allies necessary to support Kalliarkos and Menoë's bid for the throne.

I never saw it so clearly as now.

I don't want to watch these Rings open.

I don't want to be part of his plot. But I'm already in it neck-deep by pretending to be friends with Prince Temnos as part of the plan to lull Queen Serenissima into trusting Menoë, by parading my victories in front of the crowd so they will learn to love and support Garon Palace.

If Gargaron is caught, if the king and queen figure out

what is going on while they still have the power to act, they'll kill him. And they'll kill Kalliarkos and Father too.

I can't let them die. Which means Lord Gargaron has to win, and I have to help him.

Bettany is right. Whatever she is now, I'm trapped in a way she isn't.

17

Sound carries in the cold desert air: the creak of wheels and the tremor of hooves. The tombs lie two nights' travel behind us. Dusty, Mis, and I walk rather than endure the rattling and jouncing of the carriage.

Bettany sits beside the driver of one of Lord Agalar's carriages, a pale, stocky Soldian woman whom Agalar treats exactly as he treats the men in his employ. All amiability, Bett chats with her like they are old friends, and except for a single glance our way she ignores me. Failure twists in my gut, and I quicken my stride.

"Let's run," I say to Mis and Dusty.

We move up to the soldiers riding at the front of the line and I call to Captain Neartos, "Just taking a training run. We'll let you know what the scenery looks like up ahead."

He laughs and waves us on, oblivious to the frown on Dusty's face.

We take a sip of water before settling into a steady, ground-eating run, the sort we adversaries take outside the city walls several times a week to build endurance. Mis and Dusty pound easily along beside me. We so often run together during training that their presence pours through me as strength.

The desert spreads out around us. Everything is flat except the spikes and ditches of my thoughts. The almost full moon has passed its zenith and begun to descend to the west, its light strong enough to wash the nearby stars into invisibility.

I say, "Dusty, Orchid's not going to fall in love with you."

"You don't know that," he mutters. "She smiled at me seven times."

Frustration at the hopelessness of his infatuation grinds against my lungs, and I have to settle myself back into the flow or I will get out of breath from choking on the things I can't talk about.

"A Patron-born girl like that won't look at you unless you're a rich Illustrious, Dusty," says Mis.

I change the subject. "Is that your ambition, Mis? To become a rich Illustrious?"

"I don't know." She shrugs with a half-cocked grin on her good-natured face. "After this trip I'm not sure that being an adversary is what I want anymore."

"How can you not want to be an adversary, Mis? You're good."

"Yes, I'm good, but I'm not relentless like you are. I enjoy running the Fives, I really do. I love training. Running these trials out here in the provinces has been exciting and fun. But I just can't be what you are, Jes."

"Sour and no fun?"

She and Dusty laugh.

Mis elbows me without breaking stride. "You're not sour. You just never ever stop running trials in your head. I can't live like that."

"What about you, Dusty?" I ask. "Haven't you always dreamed of being an adversary?"

"No."

The blunt answer throws me off my stride. They get ahead and I have to put on a burst of speed to settle in beside them.

Dusty usually seems easygoing but a harder piece of him surfaces as he talks. "I grew up a mule in an Efean village where no one had a good word to say about Patrons. The other kids would beat me up on the street if they caught me, which is why I'm a fast runner. The only respect I got was on the Fives court. So I assumed being an adversary was the only way a person like me could belong. The truth is, when I was little I wanted to be a soldier like my father. I used to dream I might actually meet him until I came to Saryenia and realized that even if we did meet, no Patron man would acknowledge me as his son. Then I met you, Jes. Your father treated you like his own child."

"I am his child."

Dusty goes on eagerly. "I saw you salute your father from the victory tower at the Royal Fives Court and how he saluted you back, the day you beat Lord Kalliarkos. Everyone saw an honored Patron general acknowledge a daughter like you. Don't you realize how amazing that was for every person who witnessed it?"

"I never thought of it that way."

"If your father isn't ashamed to acknowledge you, maybe I can find my father and he will be proud of me."

"I hope so, Dusty," I say, even though I'm sure it will never happen.

His comment spins like Rings through my head. Is this what Ro-emnu meant? Is this why Commoners respect me, and Patrons take notice? Not because I'm a successful Challenger but because I'm a successful general's acknowledged daughter?

Our steady pace, the slap of our footsteps, and the scrutiny of the stars become the whole of my world. Saryenia breathes, and talks, and stinks, the crush of people and the constant activity an incessant hum both day and night. Out here under the desert sky, the emptiness makes us seem like the tiniest creatures in the world, no more significant than bugs. In a way it feels freeing.

The dry air has sucked all moisture from my mouth, and I'm wondering if we should pause for water when I see a strange movement on the horizon like a kick of dust and a lurching, fluttering tree.

"Did you see that?"

"See what?" Mis asks.

Wind rakes along the earth, throwing dust up into our faces, then sighs and goes quiet. Probably the movement I saw on the horizon was just an eddy of wind spinning coils of dirt. Yet I can't lift this uneasiness from my shoulders. Father taught us to listen to what itched at us.

"There!" shrieks Mis so loudly that I jump.

Four white scorpions scuttle across the road a stone's toss ahead.

We all freeze. They vanish into the rocky verge.

"I hate scorpions," mutters Mis. "I got stung in the foot once."

Dusty shrugs. "Scorpions only sting humans if they feel threatened. In my village we used to milk their venom."

Mis shudders. "That is so disgusting."

Nothing moves as we wait to see if there are more scorpions. Silence embraces us until its smothering blanket makes me sneeze.

"Blessings on you," says Dusty hastily.

I inhale quickly because of the old superstition that a sneeze can expel your souls. No one wants to dislodge any part of their five souls, especially at night, when untethered shadows roam and may devour souls knocked loose from their moorings in our bodies. So my heart is pounding as I scan the road in front and behind. The angle of moonlight catches in hoofprints left in the sand blown over the road.

"A large party is riding the road ahead of us. Don't you find that strange?" Again a flash of movement against the horizon catches my eye, then vanishes so quickly I can't be sure I've seen it. "Let's go back. We can't see the carriages."

We run back. I fall in beside Neartos.

"Hey, Spider." Like the rest of the soldiers he has come to see me as an amulet of good fortune. My victories bring them luck and winnings. "Have a good run?"

I may not like the way he looks at Amaya but that's not going to stop me from letting him do his job. "I thought I saw something, although maybe it was just the wind kicking up dust. Hoofprints too. A company of riders not too far ahead."

"Easy to see bandits everywhere when you're carrying the royal gold," he agrees genially. "There haven't been problems with bandits for years along this road, not since your father cleared them out when he was in charge of the spider scouts. But we'll keep our eyes open. Also, we're coming up on the Bone Escarpment and Crags Fort. Sometimes people mistake the rock pillars around Crags Fort for men."

"My thanks, Captain."

Before dawn the flat plateau starts crumpling like the gods took a giant rake and cut into the soil. Still too nervous to rest, I walk alongside as the road winds between towering pillars of rock. The sound of our passage echoes strangely until I realize I am hearing a steady thumping woven into the noise of our wheels.

Two spider scouts clank out to inspect us. The stolid mules merely flick their ears, but the nervous horses have to be reined aside as the spiders approach. Each as tall as two men, the eight-legged metal constructions stamp heavily over the ground, able to brace themselves on four or six or eight legs as needed. Four of the legs end in clawed metal feet for stability, and the other four end in pincers or blades. A brass carapace protects the soldier tucked into the belly of the spider. Although the soldier guides the legs with levers, what powers the metal creature is magic. The priests have learned how to pour a life spark into metal.

Their thudding walk reminds me of the day in the Ribbon Market when a spider scout captured Ro and inadvertently killed a child. I would have been taken too, if Kalliarkos hadn't intervened. I run to our carriage and jump in to get out of their way.

Mis grabs my hand as a spider clumps down the line of wagons, its soldier surveying each vehicle. "I hate them. Don't you?"

"No. My father started in the army as a spider scout. He

showed us girls how to control one. The hardest part is feeling the constant sting of the spark that buzzes inside it. It's like a wasp vibrating against your skin."

She shudders. "They say the spiders are given life by cutting the sparks out of living men. Don't you think that's awful?"

I wince, remembering how the king coldly killed an innocent lad to save Temnos. "My father used to tell us they got their sparks from desert spiders."

The sun breaches the eastern horizon as we reach Crags Fort, which is built on the upper rim of the Bone Escarpment, a vast cliff wall named for the bones of unknown creatures that fall from it when rare cloudbursts of rain wash away at its edges. I walk to the brink to take in the view, trailed by a scolding crow.

From one horizon to the other no break mars the escarpment except here, at Crags Fort, where a scar like the cut of an ax has chopped out a wedge in the cliff. The fort stands at the top of this steep canyon down which we must travel to reach the coastal plain. The trail down is too narrow for wagons, so people, horses, and mules will descend via the trail while our cargo will be winched down and loaded into a new set of wagons at Canyon Fort below.

Half of our contingent of Garon Palace soldiers are already riding down the narrow trail to secure our cargo. Up here a giant mechanism of ropes and pulleys is being readied as chests and baskets are transferred into wheelless carts with copper bottoms that will scrape down the incline, controlled by the ropes.

But as amazing as this feat of engineering is, that's not what I'm looking at. From this height and through the clear desert air I think I see against the southern horizon not sky but the far-distant glimmer of the sea still many days' journey away.

The crow takes wing as footsteps crunch up behind me.

"Are you the adversary called Spider?" The speaker is a sun-weathered Patron man wearing a sergeant's tunic. He has short hair, a scar on his chin and another on his left forearm, and a limp.

"I am," I answer cautiously.

He studies my face in a way that makes me uncomfortable. "I see him in you."

"See whom in me?" I reply, careful to use my most educated Patron speech.

"Esladas. I'm Sergeant Oras. I was your father's most junior recruit when he was Sergeant Esladas of the spider scouts. He was promoted out of the Desert Command after being elevated to captain. We heard one of his daughters was traveling with Lord Gargaron as an adversary." He nods in a way that brings tears to my eyes and I don't even understand why. "You must be Jessamy."

I want to ask him a hundred questions but I don't know where to start. "How do you know I'm Jessamy?"

"I met your family once. You couldn't have been more than five. I had leave and wanted to tour the sights of Saryenia but had no money for such a luxury. Your father kindly allowed me to sleep and eat at your family's home. Your mother treated me very graciously although I fear I said ungracious things in her hearing that I much regret now. I was ignorant, and she was very beautiful, and I envied your father but pretended to despise him for acting like an Efean woman was his wife."

I don't know what to say. It's as if he is asking me to forgive him for an act I have no memory of and that wasn't directed at me.

"My apologies," Oras goes on. "Regrets are a burden we carry our whole lives. I hope your mother is well."

I can't chance the truth. "I'm sure she understood your struggle."

"I hope so. Funny to hear that you are running the trials as an adversary. No reason a strong girl like you couldn't scout as well as many of these scatterbrained lads I have to train. You were the one your father said he wished could follow him into soldiering, as a son would have."

I hastily wipe away a tear but he's already seen it and has drawn his own conclusions.

"Do you want to meet the particular spider he fought in?"

My mouth drops open, and he smiles as if I've given him a gift. I wish I could share it with Amaya and Bettany but of course I can't.

"This way."

We enter Crags Fort through its single outer gate. The interior is split into two courtyards: the outer courtyard with barracks, stables, workshop, cookhouse, and wheelhouse, and the inner citadel, the stronghold where the thirty-six men stationed at this fort can hold out against a larger force as long as their supplies of food and water last. The outer courtyard is crowded with wagons waiting their turn to be unloaded and Garon Palace soldiers watering the animals. The lords and their retinues have already entered the inner gate to the citadel, where they will surely relish the chance to lie on padded couches in a cool, dark chamber before a jolting ride down a hot, dusty, precipitous trail.

The dim interior of the spider stable smells of oil and has a disconcerting taste that buzzes on my tongue like salt. The thick mudbrick walls make the inside cooler than the outside. There are twelve stalls but only four spiders, legs folded down and carapaces tipped forward, like animals at rest.

Sergeant Oras stops at the last stall. As my eyes adjust I see a sheen chase like captured lightning over the brass surface of the spider. It gleams enough that I can make out all the joints and curves. Even folded down at rest it is as tall as I am, pitted with wear and amazingly beautiful.

"Can I touch it?"

"You can."

I press a palm to the metal. A buzz like the murmuring of

wasps vibrates up my arm, and with a nervous laugh I snatch my hand back.

"Where do the sparks come from?" I ask boldly.

He tenses. "That's a question for the priests, not for the likes of me to discuss. See here." He picks up a copper rod and taps a pronounced dent at the forward rim of the carapace, over the harness where the soldier fits in. "If the carapace hadn't caught that blow, your father would have taken it right in the face. We could have hammered out the dent, but those of us who still recall how we almost died that day because of a cursed idiot of an officer keep it to remind ourselves."

"Remind yourselves of what?"

He glances down the length of the stable but we are alone. "That sometimes you have to take drastic measures to win."

"You mean my father *did* kill the captain in charge in order to take command and save Efea from invaders?"

"We don't tell the story quite like that. Do you know how to harness in?"

"Yes, Father taught me. Who scouts in this spider now?"

"A young fellow named Cestas. He's our newest recruit."

"Where are the other spiders? Out on patrol?"

"Six are on patrol. Cestas is on fort duty. As sergeant in charge I always oversee the pulley when a big shipment comes through."

"Because of the gold?"

"*Gold* is a word I would not speak aloud, my girl. But you're well protected. We just had a company of soldiers from the Akheres Garrison ride through ahead of you to make sure the road is clear."

That explains the hoofprints, although now that I think about it, Neartos never mentioned an extra company of soldiers.

Oras goes on without noticing my silence. "As for those two spiders, their sparks extinguished just in the last month. Bad fortune for two to go at once! We've had no sparks to revive them, not that we are complaining about that."

It strikes me as a strange thing to say, since surely soldiers in a fort like this would want all their spiders in working order. I walk down to the sparkless machines. Their brass breathes no stinging aroma; they don't gleam. When I set a hand on the metal, I feel only brass finely pitted by a thousand thousand grains of blown desert sand over the years that this mechanical creature has patrolled the frontier.

"Jes!" Tana calls from outside.

"That's my trainer," I say. "I have to go."

"My thanks for allowing me to share my memories with you, Jessamy. Your father was a good man and an even better sergeant."

"My thanks, Sergeant Oras," I answer awkwardly.

Shading my eyes, I hurry out into the sunlight. Tana is standing at the gate.

285

"What were you doing in there?" she asks.

"Looking at the spiders. My father served here. At this very fort." I'm grinning so hard I can't stop.

"Best you not walk around alone among Patron soldiers, Jes."

"No one has shown me any discourtesy!"

"It only takes one. It will take most of the day to lower and secure all the cargo and supplies. We won't follow until late afternoon. Lord Agalar asked if he and his retinue could watch me put you three through a training session. He seemed very curious to know how you 'acquire your skills,' as he put it." She snorts. "He's kind of an ass, isn't he? No offense to donkeys."

I laugh, and I seethe, but I wonder if Bettany put him up to watching me run a trial as an excuse to have a chance to talk to me.

Tana leads me outside the fort toward what looks like a corral with high mudbrick walls and climbing posts tall enough to be seen over them. Agalar and his retinue are sitting expectantly on a shaded viewing terrace while Mis and Dusty stand in the doorway of a ready room built into the enclosure's wall. They are drinking cups of chicken broth. I change into my practice gear and take a cup as well. Just as we are finishing, a young Patron man barely older than us dashes in, glances at Agalar's party, then runs over to us.

"I'm Cestas!" he says to Tana, bouncing on his toes with so much excitement that it's charming. By the way he talks I can tell he is Efean-born of Saroese ancestry, not an immigrant from old Saro like my father. He's wiry, tall, and enthusiastic. "Sergeant Oras said you needed a fourth for a trial. It's an honor to run against the famous Sergeant Esladas's daughter!"

Mis snorts audibly. Dusty pretends to bow to me as if I am a highborn lady.

"Very well, Cestas," says Tana with her best unimpressed face. "Start with a warm-up round of menageries."

Heat pours over me although the sun is not yet a handbreadth above the horizon. My muscles warm as we pace from cat to wasp to tomb spider. My awareness of Agalar's incisive gaze and Bettany's silent presence at his side falls away as my thoughts focus on the stamp of my feet on the ground, the movement of my arms, the jump and turn into a crouch, the stretch into a forward bend.

Just as we finish warming up, an unexpected final audience member arrives. The fort's priest is an older man with broad shoulders and an intent gaze made disturbing by the fact that he has no eyes, just empty sockets not even covered by patches. A crow sits on either shoulder, and I suddenly wonder if one is the crow that watched me at the cliff's edge. To my surprise the priest flashes us four adversaries the kiss-off sign as a gesture of respect just as if he can see us.

I get the draw to start on Rivers and take my place. The court is clearly hand-built by the men themselves over years, a standard beginner's course, but its level of sophistication doesn't matter to me. I want to show Bettany I haven't been selfish, that the things I've worked for mean something, that she should be proud of me and not leave us and the only home we've ever known. That Efea means something. That we can make it mean something through our actions.

The start bell chimes.

Lacking water for Rivers, the soldiers have constructed rocking benches and circles of wood resting on wobbly bases to run across, made more difficult by varying balance points so the center is not always the best spot to place the foot. I make it across but Cestas knows the court well, giving him a considerable advantage. I decide to go to Trees next to grab a panoramic look over Traps and Pillars.

So it is that when I climb the highest post in Trees I pause longer than I normally would to examine my surroundings. Mis balances easily on a slack rope in Traps. I don't see Dusty. Cestas enters Trees behind me.

Something seems off. I pause a moment longer, instincts tingling.

All along, the regular thumping grind of the pulleys being turned as a cargo bin is lowered down the incline has sung as a rhythmic background, like drumming to build tension in a play. My gaze drifts over the fort walls to the wheelhouse shelter just as I realize I'm holding my breath waiting for the next thump, which never comes.

Over by the pulley Sergeant Oras staggers into view with an arrow jiggling in his neck. As I stare in speechless astonishment, hardly able to believe I am not sitting in the high seats at the theater, he folds over like an actor bowing at the end of a scene and falls to the ground.

18

I stick two fingers in my mouth and whistle the three-tone pattern Father taught us girls, which he called "the desert alert." In a flash of wings one crow takes off from the priest's shoulder. A moment later the sentry in the watchtower sounds a trumpet blast. Soldiers bolt for the inner gate to take refuge in the citadel, just as another two men stagger from the wheelhouse with arrows sticking out of them, like dolls stuck with pins. Armed men holding shields over their heads swarm out of the wheelhouse. These new soldiers wear the uniforms of the Royal Army of Efea, and that confuses the Garon soldiers and the fort's defenders for an instant too long. Their hesitation allows the attackers to pick off several of the sentries on the wall as well as cut down men who are trying to shove the cargo wagons into the citadel.

The priest turns to Agalar. "Get to the citadel."

"Wait!" I call down from my post. "If we go into the fort we'll run straight into the line of attack. The enemy is already inside the outer courtyard. What about the spiders in the fort?"

"Curse it," says Cestas. "Do you see any attackers outside the walls?"

I scan but see nothing except an eerie landscape filled with places an enemy can hide. Even the spider scouts from earlier are missing. A fierce misgiving flares in my heart. This can't be random. Inside the fort the fighting breaks into clusters amid the wagons. The priest scrambles down the terrace with the confidence of a man who knows exactly where everything is as he and all the adversaries converge on my post in Trees.

"We must get in by the roof, Cestas," says the priest. "If we climb in through the roof trap before they suspect what we mean to do, you and I might get two spiders out."

Someone has shut the citadel gate, leaving the men in the outer courtyard to a cruel fate. From up here I see Sergeant Oras roll up to his feet as he snaps the arrow's shaft in two. Blood is splattered down his shoulder like red paint, but although the point pierced the skin of his neck it appears to have hit nothing vital. He staggers for the spider stable and, vanishing inside, slams the door shut.

"Sergeant Oras has gotten inside!" I call down.

"We must free the trapped spiders!" says the priest.

He and Cestas bolt. As Agalar and his people begin

climbing down the terrace, I descend the climbing post so fast I get a splinter in my palm. The sting focuses my mind but before I can say anything Bettany trots up, looking more cool and collected than she ought.

"Hey!" she calls to me. "Just stay in the Fives court, don't get involved, and I promise you it will be all right."

"People are already dead! We have to go!"

"Will you *listen* to me, Jes? You won't be in danger if you stay out of sight. They're only after the gold—"

"That's what worries me! What will they do when they find out the gold they're looking for isn't there because Lord Gargaron—" I break off as I remember the hidden gold is a secret I must keep. As I realize Bettany shouldn't be so calm, as if she knew an attack was coming.

Agalar steps into view like a wolf that has finally cornered its victim. "Where is the gold, if not in the cargo wagons?"

He draws his sword, and Bettany does nothing to defend me. She just stands there.

She can't be in on it.

She can't be.

She'd never do this to me. To Amaya.

Where is Amaya?

Tana nudges me from behind with a wordless message, then steps forward to place herself between Agalar and me.

I run, Mis and Dusty right behind me.

From behind, Agalar shouts, "Get after them! Kill the priest and destroy the spiders. Move!"

We grab the gate and shove it closed.

Dusty shouts, "Jes, go after the priest to warn him. We'll find a way to fix the latch to keep them penned and then follow."

I don't even acknowledge them as I race after Cestas and the priest, whom I chase around the outer wall of the fort. Off in the distance I spot riders approaching, and I still don't see any spider scouts coming to save the day. The sentries on the wall either are casualties or have gone down to join the fray, so when I catch up with Cestas and the priest no one has yet noticed us.

Where a crude stick figure of a spider has been carved at the base of the wall, Cestas starts climbing, finding invisible handholds and finger's-width ledges with the skill of a person who has made this ascent many times. I suddenly remember one of Father's stories about a secret entrance he built into the spider stable as an emergency way in. He said people forget that spiders can climb.

"What are you doing here? Go hide!" The priest's back is to me but the crow on his shoulder, facing me, bobs its head aggressively.

"We've walked into a trap! Lord Agalar is working with an enemy to steal the gold. The riders who got here ahead of us are part of it. They want to kill you and destroy the spiders."

I flex my hands, marking each hold Cestas used, then start up after. The priest follows. Desperation gives me wings, hones my instinct so fine it seems my fingers find each hand-hold without my even thinking of it. Just as I reach the top of the wall an arrow sings past, a whistle of death an arm's length from my head. I duck, roll past a downed sentry, and slam into Cestas, who is lying prone on the roof of the spider stable. A half-open gap in the roof shows where he was pushing away a trapdoor cut into the roof.

When I shake him, he gurgles and rolls over.

He has an arrow in his eye.

The whole world goes cold and dark. My vision blurs out. I can't see but my hearing sharpens. Each crash of sword against sword, the grunt of a man hit and falling, even Cestas's pulse as his blood leaks out of the dreadful wound: all hammer like thunder, a noise that drowns out the rest of existence.

Until an arrow thunks into the roof next to me and a slap on my back jolts me.

I've been hit.

The priest scuttles past me. "Move! Help me open this."

He's the one who slapped me. I haven't been hit at all.

Together we shove the trapdoor aside, then he grapples Cestas's legs and shoves him into the opening. The young man falls, and hits with a sickening thud. A crow flaps past me into the interior. The priest swings down inside. As another arrow hits beside me I follow, hanging by my hands and then dropping.

The moment I hit the ground a blade taps my head from behind.

"Stand down!" says Sergeant Oras.

"It's me! Jessamy."

The sword drops away. "Curse it, we can't rescue you, stupid girl."

"Grab the boy's ankles," says the priest.

In the windowless stable a strange glow glimmers into being as the priest, now wearing gloves, shakes out a lacelike netting exactly as the other priests did that day in the King's Garden. He's kneeling by one of the sparkless spiders.

"Hurry! We need to get his spark into the spider before it's too late."

Cestas croaks out words. "Give me the honor of serving even after death."

Blood smears his lips.

I can't move.

Sergeant Oras looms in front of me. "Assist me!"

I grab the young soldier's ankles and with Oras haul him over to the priest. Cestas groans. I feel his life leaching away through my fingers.

"Blessed be the gods that I can serve as a soldier even after..." His hand gropes at air, and Sergeant Oras grasps his fingers tightly.

"You will serve the army with honor, Cestas."

I look away, shuddering, so I don't see when the priest casts the netting over the dying soldier, cracks the breastbone, and cuts out his heart. The brilliance of Cestas's spark turns the netting into a light so bright I see Oras's blood-streaked face and a linen cloth tied around his neck glimmering with moist blood. I see the spiders in their stalls, and hear the clamor of battle outside and a distant trumpet. I see the empty hollows of the priest's eyes.

Oras says, "We have to break free and save these spiders. Jessamy, hide in one of the empty stalls. Stay out of sight and pray they don't find you."

Where are Amaya, Tana, Mis, and Dusty? If I think about it I'll start screaming so I channel all my fury and raw grief into my stance as I face down Oras.

"I am General Esladas's daughter. This is my fight too."

I run to Cestas's spider. My father's spider.

I always wanted to please my father more than anything except for running the Fives. Back in Saryenia when he showed us girls how to harness into a spider, Maraya was interested only in the details of the spider's construction, Amaya wove spider masks out of netting and silver ribbons, and Bettany fought with him until he stopped asking her to try. But I practiced over and over so I could show him how well I had learned. So he would be proud of me.

Tip up the carapace.

Step into the seat, fix the straps, and pull down the leather shield that protects my front. Slide feet and hands through brass rings that allow the scout to control the eight legs with all four limbs.

The buzz of the spider's spark courses through me, as uncomfortable as if I have fallen into a nest of wasps whose bodies pulsate against mine. When I put pressure on my palm, the splinter hurts so badly I gasp in a choked burst.

I lift my right knee and the spider unfolds forward onto its four bracing legs.

Sergeant Oras slings a heavy pouch onto hooks bolted to the inside of the carapace. "Go."

If I were a real scout I'd be wearing a helmet but there's no time for that. The movements come awkwardly as my spider stomps out of the stall. I slam twice into the walls as I angle myself under the roof. An object slams into the top of my carapace. A javelin skitters over and falls past my face. With my right hand I guide the spider's right fore blade in a punch straight up to the trapdoor.

An impact shudders through the spider's metal frame. A man screams, although I can't see him. With pincers and claws to brace on walls and clutch the roof, I clamber out with so much speed that I almost hurtle over the outer wall, teetering on its edge as arrows slam one two three into my carapace. The sun blasts my eyes. Dust swirls in the wake of the riders closing in on the fort.

The distance from the top of the wall to the ground outside is only the height of three men but it seems like an impossibly long drop. Yet I have spun tricks at this height more times than I can count. I will do this.

I hook two metal legs on a battlement and lever myself over, then drop the rest of the way, hitting with a thud that throbs through me like I've been shaken by a giant's hand. I stagger four steps one way, two back, before steadying myself on six legs as I swivel around to scan for threats.

A spider slams into the ground beside me, absorbing the impact into bent legs.

"Move!" shouts Sergeant Oras and then he is moving west away from the wall.

I stride after, using six legs to walk, holding my fore blade and fore pincer ready even though I have no experience fighting in a spider. I shrug my carapace back so instead of being tilted to look down at the ground I'm upright, looking forward into the wild desert landscape. A third spider moves up alongside me: the one brought to life by Cestas's spark, the priest working the levers with the skill of an experienced soldier. A crow sits on his shoulder.

By tapping my shoulder to the left I swing the carapace around just enough to glance behind.

The sea-phoenix banner of Efea still flies atop the citadel tower as enemy riders approach the outer wall. Bettany runs out from the Fives court to meet them with Agalar and his retinue behind her. I don't see Mis or Dusty or Tana.

Oh gods. Oh gods.

Another group of soldiers races out from the fort, waving the hawk banner of the kingdom of East Saro. They must be the ones who attacked up through the wheelhouse from below. When Agalar greets them like long-lost friends I'm sure the pair of soldiers at the front—one fair and one dark—are the two men he spoke to in the desert ruins.

When Bettany reaches the riders, she gestures in my direction.

Horsemen start in pursuit.

My steps falter. I wrench my spider to a halt.

Bettany has betrayed Efea. She's betrayed Father and Mother and everything they gave us girls. She's betrayed her sisters.

She's betrayed *me*.

"Face forward, Spider!" shouts Sergeant Oras. "Follow me. Move!"

The enemy riders are cutting the distance between us. Two crows flap past me, the last creatures capable of fleeing the attack. Too choked to speak, I slam around and stamp after Oras and the priest.

19

Oras leads us straight to the edge of the Bone Escarpment and clambers over without slowing down. The cliff isn't sheer but it's terrifyingly steep, and I spot anchor bolts and carved-out ledges that create a path for spiders. Oras descends with the speed of a man who has practiced many times on this slope. The priest goes after him. They'll leave me behind if I can't keep up, sacrificing one spider to save two.

I have to think of this as just another obstacle. I fix the route they're taking into my mind as I go over the brink. At once I begin sliding.

I slam my fore blade into the rock to try to halt myself, grab at a passing bolt with a hooking claw too late to secure myself, and in a rush I realize I've lost control and all I can do is keep my legs moving so I don't crash as I race headlong down the precipitous incline. I almost sideswipe the priest, and Sergeant Oras scuttles out of my way as my legs hammer too fast for me to register the shocks through my body.

The steep slope tapers, I skid on rubble, turn all the way around without tumbling, and stagger like a drunk onto level ground, where I jolt to a halt. My breath comes in bursts, like my chest is about to blow outward. I taste blood; I've bitten my tongue but I don't know when I did it. I begin to laugh, and lift an arm to wipe my running nose. Blood spots my elbow.

Oras stumps up next to me.

"Good Goat!" He too is laughing with what Father would have called battlefield humor. "I thought for sure you'd break your neck. I guess you're well named, Spider."

He keeps moving. The priest passes without a word of encouragement although one of the crows alights on the shoulder of my fore-blade leg and examines me with the bright interest of a curious bird. Yet in its shiny gaze I sense the disapproval of the priest, as if his is the intelligence seeing out of its eyes.

The crow flies away.

I clump after them, still shaking, still exhilarated, and yet sickened by fear for my friends and nauseated by the thought of Bettany. Back at the tombs she was trying to pull information out of me about the gold. I see that now. Meanwhile the others—even Amaya—may all be dead. It's like the tomb all over again: people I care for marched into a living death while I stand outside.

The desert landscape is a rippling wasteland of bone-dry gulches, and little ridges and hills. If I weren't following Oras I would be lost in a heartbeat. When I swivel around to look behind I see the escarpment running east and west but I can't see either the upper or lower fort from this angle. Faintly I hear a trumpet's call, but I can't tell what direction it comes from.

I keep walking on and on and on through the appalling heat. Sweat beads on my forehead and evaporates as quickly. My mouth is coated with grit, the splinter blazes like fire in my flesh, and my tongue stings. The spark that powers the spider hums in my bones. Odd flashes of sound throb in and out of my head: a man's soft voice saying, *Give me the honor of serving even after death.*

Vision swims. I rock to a halt, awkwardly turn an entire circle, and realize I am standing in a barren gully and I am alone.

A crow calls, and I see it shifting impatiently from foot to foot where the gully makes a bend. I stump over there and as I come around I almost slam into Sergeant Oras, who has turned back.

"Spider! You're falling behind."

The heat is obliterating with the sun striking right onto my face.

"Hey!" He studies my face. "Why haven't you wrapped your face to keep out the dust? Did you drink anything?"

My voice sounds like dry rags turned stiff. "What... where...?"

"Curse it." He reaches past me, unhooks the leather pouch he gave me, squirts warm water into my mouth until I've swallowed several times. Afterward he makes me eat two dates. Their sweetness bursts like color in my mouth. "A quarter turn allows you to grab the water with your left hand. Don't take frequent sips. Take longer deeper drinks, and never go too long without water or the desert will suck you dry and you'll die. There are dates, salted fish, dried figs, and raisins in the pouch. Do you understand?"

I'm already starting to feel better. "Yes."

He digs into the pouch and pulls out a finely woven indigo scarf. "Wrap this tightly to cover all of your head except your eyes. Your crossbow and bolts are hooked here on the other side but don't use them unless you have training. I've got a spare short sword in my kit you can have in case we get into a hand-to-hand fight. Can you manage that?"

"I know how to shoot a crossbow and hold a sword. But I've never actually fought."

"That'll have to do. Now get down and I'll show you how to rig the canvas over the carapace to keep the sun from cooking you."

We shake out two lengths of cloth and Oras shows me the

clever way wooden rods and rope string an inner black cloth beneath an outer white cloth to make an awning over the spider's brass carapace.

"What happened with Cestas?"

His grim expression makes me wish I hadn't spoken. "When we sign on we swear an oath to fight as spider scouts while living and to give our last spark in death to keep fighting."

The priest stumps over, his head and face completely covered by a scarf, all except the eye sockets, a sight so disturbing I look away.

"Sergeant! We must hasten. There's a double patrol of spider scouts advancing toward Canyon Fort from the southeast."

"Our scouts?"

"I believe so."

"Are they approaching along the road from Port Selene?"

"No, Sergeant, they are coming out of the east, through the desert."

I break in. "I'll bet they're coming from the Eastern Reach, from the Royal Army. Maybe General Esladas sent them. How can you see them from here?"

One of the crows hops, and I realize what a stupid question it is as the priest addresses the sergeant, ignoring me as if I hadn't spoken. "They are flying the sea-phoenix of Efea."

"It could be a mask to hide the enemy," says Oras.

"The enemy has no spiders. Only we priests in Efea know

this magic. My concern is that this patrol will walk straight into the enemy at Canyon Fort and be ambushed as we were ambushed if we don't warn them."

"We'll hurry to catch them," agrees Oras. "Jessamy, if you get separated from us, do your best to find the road and make your way to the coast and Port Selene."

"It isn't fitting for women to act as soldiers," says the priest to Oras.

"She saved a spider, Your Holiness."

"The spider will have to be purified before a man can safely inhabit it again."

Oras glances away but not before I catch him rolling his eyes.

My mouth twitches, but instead of insulting a holy priest I snag a strip of salted fish from the provisions pouch and let it soften in my mouth to dissolve the words I'd like to say.

We emerge from the gully into a broad valley. The beat of legs striking the ground creates a soothing rhythm, and after a while I begin to rely on what I hear and how my own body moves with the flow of the spider legs rather than watching the legs before I move them.

Ahead a raised line cuts across the plain. We have reached the road that leads from Akheres Oasis to Port Selene. The Bone Escarpment rises to the north, now far enough behind us that I can see the ragged outline of the craggy ridge but not the walls of Crags Fort. Instead of turning south onto the road, toward the sea, the priest leads us across it. If he is seeing through the eyes of his crows, I'm impressed with his coordination. A crow swoops past and speeds away east. We stride across a rocky landscape of conical hills and sandy hollows whose wind-rippled surfaces we avoid.

Spiders are not built for speed. They are built for toughness and agility, like me.

Once my father must have spent days and nights on patrol out in this wasteland, and yet in all my life I never remember hearing him complain. The scarf shielding my nose and mouth makes breathing easier but my eyes burn and my palm throbs and my feet feel hot and swollen and my friends are dead or worse, but I will say nothing. I will do my duty, as he would have done.

A whistled alert grabs my attention. Exhaustion sloughs off me as a spike of excitement drives through my flesh. I swivel around until I see puffs of dust off to the north, in the direction of the escarpment, the telltale sign of large creatures on the move. The chance to save someone from the fate dropped on Amaya, Mis, Dusty, and Tana gives me purpose and energy.

We stride up a long, gentle slope and come around a weirdly twisted pillar of rock. Below us, in a bowl of a valley, what looks like the final act of a tragedy is playing out.

Spiders circle in with the inexorable patience of vultures as ten bloodied, battered soldiers flying the hawk banner of East Saro's army make a barrier of foundered horses. They kneel behind the poor beasts, whose flanks heave with exhaustion. The men look little better than their dying horses but Father always said men can fight long beyond the point when they should give way.

From the spider ranks, crossbow bolts flash through the air. Most tear into the flesh of the poor horses, who scream in agony, a sound that burns my ears. One bolt topples a soldier, sunk into an eye. The rest of the bolts kick up dust as they skitter away over the ground.

In answer an arrow sings out from amid the cornered men, but it thunks pointlessly against a carapace as the scouts turn their brass backs. Javelins and arrows cannot pierce a spider's metal body, merely dent it. The spiders settle into a waiting stance, encircling the enemy position. The canvas that shields them is tattered and ripped but still effective to give a little relief from the sun, which the riders do not have. The heat will destroy the enemy's exhausted ranks while the spider scouts loose arrows at their leisure onto the trapped men.

A spider detaches from the main group and clumps up to investigate our arrival. Oras signals to me to stay put while he moves forward to meet his counterpart, an equally grizzled veteran. As they exchange information, a burst of movement catches my eye from below.

The last enemy soldiers leap over the downed horses to rush at the spiders with swords and spears. My heart seizes. I can't look but I have to, because I know what is coming and I can't bear to see it, and yet I must witness. There is more honor in being struck down by a blade than in being struck down by the uncaring sun.

The spider scouts wield their cruel bladed legs with such precision it is beautiful. A downward cut splits open the head of a helmet-less soldier. A sweep takes off the leg of another. A pincer crushes the torso of a struggling man.

One by one the enemy dies, and in silence their blood pools on the ground as the sun soaks it up.

I am become hollow, empty of feeling.

When Oras signals that we should follow him down to meet up with the others, I obey with no thought, only movement, a puppet on strings. My eyes take in the way the spiders are severing the head of each corpse to make sure every man is thoroughly, utterly, irreversibly dead.

Three scouts settle their spiders into resting stance and drop out of their harnesses to walk over to inspect the downed horses. They are dressed in the loose black clothing typical of desert troops, heads and faces concealed by indigo scarves like the one I'm wearing. One wears the short cape of a captain's uniform.

I blink sand from my tired eyes as I stare at the back of the captain.

I know that walk, those shoulders.

Just as the three men reach the horses, a man rises up from where he's been hidden between two horses. Like Cestas before him, he's not yet quite dead from a bolt in the eye. He throws himself at the captain, and his weight sweeps the other man off his feet. Together they hit the ground with a smack that echoes against the hills, the captain caught beneath the enemy and thus absorbing the worst of the shock.

Maybe I scream in anguish as I race toward them. The pound of my spider legs jolts through me but I am too late....

One of the on-foot scouts grabs the enemy and flings him off just as the other scout raises a javelin and stabs it down to where the enemy was lying atop the captain, but the enemy isn't there anymore, only the captain's unprotected back.

I flash out my spider's bladed foreleg without any thought, just reaction, and catch the javelin an eyeblink before it drives into the back of the prone captain. My fore blade sweeps the javelin away, rips it out of the hand of the soldier, and I freeze the leg out there as my hands fumble at the harness and shove open the shield.

Leaping out of the spider, I jar my knee but the pain barely registers. Nothing registers except the body lying facedown in the dirt. As I dash up a scout shouts in warning and grabs for me, but I dodge him and drop to the earth.

I take hold of the captain's shoulder and ease him over,

praying under my breath that I am wrong as I pull down the scarf to uncover his face.

But I am not wrong.

I could never be wrong, not about him.

Kalliarkos lies unmoving on the ground, eyes closed, not breathing.

20

〰️

You! Get the priest immediately!" I use Father's command voice. "You! Make sure the enemy isn't dead yet. Don't kill him. We need his spark. Lord Kalliarkos is not breathing."

Both scouts obey, hurrying off.

I run a hand down Kal's clothes, trying to find a stab wound, but his chest is all hard muscle. Gently I turn his head to see if he has cracked his skull open, but except for a trickle of blood at his ear he's untouched. Either the enemy smote him with a terrible magic or the impact from the tackle killed him.

It's taking too long for the others to act.

I trawl through my mind, seeking any scrap of hope.

Mother taught her daughters certain humble healing skills but I was always too impatient to sit still and memorize such details when I could be up and moving around instead. Bettany was the one who kept asking Mother question after question. I remember that now as I stare into his lifeless face.

Breath is life.

I press my dry lips to his mouth and I breathe my breath into his body, only to feel my own breath puff against my cheek from his nostrils. Clear the mouth of obstructions, then pinch the nostrils closed. That's what Mother taught us.

He does not stir as I swipe a finger through his mouth, then pinch his nose shut, then set my mouth to his in a kiss that has all of desire in it: not the desire for love but the fierce need to save him. My lips to his, I breathe the force of my stubborn determination into him, once, twice, three times.

I will save him.

I will.

My chest brushes his, and just as I realize his chest has risen to touch mine, his eyes flutter and open. As I tilt my head back his gaze fixes on me. With a puzzled wrinkling of his brow, he shapes my name—"Jes"—and yet no sound comes out.

His eyes roll up, and close.

Hands grab me and drag me away. When I kick, fighting them, the meaty impact of my fist into flesh gives me pleasure.

"Spider! Leave off! Step back!" Oras's bark of command seizes me like a spider's pincer legs. All the air sags out of me as I'm hauled away from the men clustering around Kalliarkos. The priest rises from beside the body of the enemy soldier.

Misty ghosts like the dregs of shadows drift in the sockets of his empty eyes. The glittering net hangs from his hands, light whispering through its threads.

The scouts scuttle aside like a cloud of locusts.

When the priest kneels beside Kal I can't see him, only hear the intake of many breaths as the soldiers wait.

Breath is life.

"Is he alive?" I whisper.

Sergeant Oras guides me back to my spider, which I have left precariously balanced on three legs, such was my haste to get to Kal.

"That was a breach of protocol, Spider. Don't do it again."

"But—"

"Next time you'll get whipped if you're fortunate and executed if you're not. You do not approach a lord captain in that reckless, careless way."

"I was trying to save his life."

"Just get in your spider and obey orders."

"Where are we going?"

"We'll have to regroup and make a new plan," says Oras.

"Where will we regroup in this wasteland?" I demand.

"The desert is no wasteland for those who know it. We spiders have carefully built nests, camps hidden away supplied with food and water for our long-ranging patrols."

I get into my spider and shift position until I can see Kalliarkos. He's still lying on the ground but his eyes are open and he is rubbing his head. The priest stands over him like a parent over a child who needs to be scolded for trying to do too much after an illness. A crow hops up Kal's torso and peers intently into his face.

The scouts efficiently loot the enemy gear. Several bring out long knives and begin butchering the horses. In the desert you never leave food behind, only corpses.

When Kal is up and back in his own spider, we march out, Sergeant Oras in the lead, heading south toward the coast although we don't return to the road. Conical hills turn into rocky ridges whose southern slopes are heaped with sand blown by the winds out of the south. We clank in our file down a narrowing canyon, sticking to a patch of blessed afternoon shade. Oras leads us into a roughhewn cave mouth that turns into a short tunnel, which brings us into a tiny valley. It's baking hot and waterless, but there are shelters built of rocks, covered cisterns, brick hearths erected at the openings of overhangs, and even a clay bread oven.

After I come to a halt I sit in the harness, too dull to think about anything except that Kal is alive. Kal is alive. Kal is alive. My mind veers away from the uglier truths that press down on my shattered heart.

"Hey! Soldier!" Sergeant Oras wavers in front of my blurry vision.

He talks me out of the harness and with a hand under my elbow guides me over to a shelter and forces me to drink a

314

repulsively salty brew and eat two figs. Afterward I lie down, head pillowed on my scarf, and close my eyes.

In the haze of my thoughts my last vision of Bettany vanishes into a puddle of blood. She's dead.

She's dead to us. A traitor.

I fall into a restless sleep.

When I wake, night has come. The smell of sizzling fat and sage-smoked meat makes me sit bolt upright. There's a covered bowl next to me filled with tepid water, and I gulp it down like it is royal nectar.

The stars and moon bathe the valley in a light that casts a shimmering web over the many spiders tucked up at rest. The Great River of Light that Efeans call Our Mother's Milk splashes its way across the sky. According to the Saroese, the universe is a celestial sphere that embraces the humble earth; stars abide in the immortal heavens while mortal creatures live and die below. But Mother once told us that stars are souls, each a luminary that shines for the space of its celestial life and then, like all living things, dies.

We will all die, if not now, then later. It's time to face the truth.

I test my feet and, finding myself steady, stand. All the hearths are lit, men cooking meat over them while others sleep, covered by blankets against the cool night air. At the entrance to this overhang Oras sits with three men I don't know, turning spits over a smoldering fire.

I walk over, and the three strangers stare as if I have two heads.

Oras hands me strips of hot meat. "Horse," he says.

It's the best thing I've ever tasted, and I lick my fingers as he talks on in the genial tone of a man accustomed to death and heat and close calls.

"These three fellows are one of Crags Fort's missing patrols. They followed a crow here. But four of our scouts are missing." A strip of linen caked with dried blood wraps his neck but he doesn't seem to notice.

As the food and water settle, I test my voice. "Where is Lord Kalliarkos?"

His frown hits like a blow. "Good Goat, girl, you can't just walk up to a highborn lord like that. What were you thinking?"

"I thought he was dead."

"You did act quickly," he admits grudgingly. "That one last enemy soldier still had a spark in him. Saved the lord's life, the priest did."

"But he wasn't dead."

"That's right. Thanks to your quick thinking, the priest saved the lord captain."

No. Kal's eyes opened. I'm sure he saw me before the priest came. He had started breathing again. Either the priest didn't see it or he didn't want to believe I could have saved him.

I clench my hands, feeling dizzy. My head aches, I am aware all over again that a cursed splinter is dug into the flesh of my palm, and that I left my friends and maybe Amaya to die. A great gaping maw of dread and pain opens a hole in my heart for those I left behind. For Bettany's betrayal.

And yet Kalliarkos is alive.

I stand there in mute anguish, torn between grief and joy.

A bearded man comes into the firelight. I recognize him as the one who almost stabbed Kalliarkos with a javelin. Alone among the scouts he has a true beard, not the stubbly growth of a man who hasn't had time to shave.

"Sergeant Oras, Lord Captain Kalliarkos wishes to speak to you."

"Very good, Sergeant Demos." He glances at me. "Stay here, Spider. Don't go wandering around. Don't forget that scorpions hunt at night."

As soon as he and the sergeant depart, I try out one of Amaya's poor-kitten faces on the three scouts, who are staring at me like they are afraid I am going to sprout a third head.

"Is there a place I can...you know."

Their embarrassment almost makes me laugh.

The bravest one attempts to answer, speaking in the slow, slightly overloud Saroese many Patrons use around Commoners, even though I have just addressed them in Saroese. "The latrine, yes? The latrine next to the tunnel mouth. Be careful of scorpions." He gestures with a hand, trying to replicate the scuttling walk and stabbing sting of a scorpion, as if he fears I still can't understand.

"My thanks," I say in my most polite tone.

Of course I do not seek out the latrine. I use the darkness to follow the two sergeants to another overhang illuminated by a hearth fire where five men stand and three men sit. Besides the crow priest there is another, younger priest, a man who also has both eyes cut away and an escort of crows. The third seated man is the lord captain.

From the shadows I examine Kalliarkos's face. He's thinner, and his usually clean face is smeared with grit and prickly with the stubble of days-old beard growth. A hard resolve has chased away the soft charm that used to light his gaze. I can't stop staring at him.

"We will march to relieve the citadel at Crags Fort," he is saying to the assembled sergeants. "My patrol was sent out from the Royal Army in pursuit of a company of East Saroese light cavalry that marched northwest into the desert. General Esladas feels the likeliest scenario is that they are attempting to cut off the road from Akheres Oasis to Port Selene."

"It appears he was right," agrees Sergeant Oras, "since an enemy force has attacked Canyon Fort and Crags Fort."

Kal nods decisively. "I'll need your knowledge of the terrain to plan a strategy to retake the forts, especially since we are outnumbered."

"The forces inside the two citadels will support us once we arrive," says Oras. "If we can coordinate an attack with them, the enemy will be caught in the forts between hammer and anvil."

"You think the two citadels can hold out?"

"Oh, yes. The forts were designed specifically to sustain a siege. The inner citadels are built to survive six months because all the stores and water are kept there. Meanwhile the attackers will only be able to scavenge water and supplies from Lord Gargaron's supply wagons, which won't sustain their numbers for more than a week—"

Taking a step forward I break in. "They aren't after the road or the desert forts. They're after the gold."

Kalliarkos's head snaps back, eyes going wide as if the sound of my voice has shot through him like burning sparks. His gaze catches on my form where I stand in the shadows behind the others.

Sergeant Oras turns. "Spider, get out!"

"My lord," I add, belatedly remembering my place.

"Jes!" Kal slaps a hand on the stone bench, mutters under his breath, then speaks too loudly, like he's trying to convince the men he just said anything other than my name. "Just! It's *just* that there are good strategic reasons to believe the old Saro alliance is after the forts."

The crow priest's sightless eye sockets halt on me. "My lord, this creature should not have addressed you. I will have it taken away at once."

"Of course you won't! This is war, not a temple with its elaborate code of purity. In war any person with potentially useful information must be heard, especially in such desperate circumstances as our army is in now."

Kal looks at each man in turn, a trick I've seen my father use to assert his authority. I study his face, his eyes, a healed cut on his chin, and the square stubborn set of his shoulders. He was willing to let those enemy men die from sunstroke by waiting them out. Only a few months have passed since I last saw him and yet there's an intangible aura about his presence that feels utterly different. Harder. More ruthless.

"Come forward, soldier."

I obediently walk forward, the men moving aside to let me through.

"Why do you believe the attack on the forts is directed at gold, not at any strategic goal?"

"Because I heard one of the leaders of the attack say so. Everyone knows the king and queen of Efea sit atop a mountain of treasure."

He glances away as I repeat words he once spoke to me, and I falter, remembering that night and how we kissed like the whole world had offered us its promise. But the Fives has taught me well. I can't afford distraction.

"Gold is a strategic goal, my lord. Gold pays armies and buys grain to distribute in a hungry city ripe for rebellion.

Gold can lure discontented mercenaries who haven't been paid into switching sides and fighting for old Saro instead of Efea."

"That's true. But you are underestimating the importance of the chain of desert forts as a line of protection to hold the enemy on the Eastern Reach. If the old Saro alliance takes control of the desert forts and road, then they can move a force safely through the desert and hit our army from the north when it reaches Port Selene."

"But the Efean army isn't at Port Selene," I object. "It's on the Eastern Reach, at Pellucidar Lake."

"We've lost the Eastern Reach," says Kalliarkos. "The Efean army is in retreat."

There's a sudden silence as Oras and I are struck dumb by these unexpected words.

Kal goes on. "In fact, Sergeant Oras, I don't understand why your forces weren't on high alert. General Esladas specifically gave orders to send word up the chain of desert forts about the defeat at Pellucidar Lake and the need to protect ourselves from an attack through the desert."

"But we heard the battle at Pellucidar Lake was a victory, my lord," says Oras.

"A victory for our enemy!" exclaims Kalliarkos. "Only the brilliant tactics of General Esladas saved us from utter annihilation. It's due to him the army is still intact and able to retreat along the coast at all."

"But King Kliatemnos made a proclamation of victory," I say.

"Why would Kliatemnos lie about such a thing?" Kal mutters.

"He thought it was the truth. He got the news by messenger pigeon."

At last he looks at me. I stiffen, because I can't interpret the meaning of his regard. "And you know this...how?"

"Your sister, the gracious Lady Menoë, took me to the palace with her to meet the queen and Prince Temnos." I'm irritated enough by his suspicious gaze that I can't help the sarcastic drawl of my tone, rather as if I'm speaking to Ro. "I am a famous young Challenger, as you know."

His voice comes out clipped. "Oh yes, I am well aware of that."

"The message claimed to come from Prince Nikonos," I add, hoping he'll see the warning in my eyes. If Nikonos truly is plotting against Kal and my father, then any of the men surrounding us may be traitors. "Perhaps there is an enemy spy in the ranks of the messenger service who managed to send false information to the king."

Kal rubs a finger along a fresh scar on his chin as if reminding himself of how he got it. "Prince General Nikonos is in charge of communications and the messenger pigeons. Explain why you're so sure this attack on the forts was specifically after gold."

"A foreign doctor named Agalar came to Akheres a few

months ago, purportedly to study how to treat mining injuries. But he is actually working with the enemy soldiers who attacked the two forts. With my own eyes I saw the attackers fly the hawk banner of East Saro. So isn't it likely that the plan to steal the gold was in place some months ago? After the battle at Pellucidar Lake a second plan could have been put in place to take the forts for strategic advantage, once our army was in retreat. The two could be coordinated. If the citadels are set to withstand a siege, then I think we need to warn General Esladas before we do anything else."

The crow priest rises and points an accusatory finger at me. "It is an affront to the gods for a woman to speak counsel to men."

Kal raises a hand and, to my surprise, the crow priest gives a heaving sigh of disgust and sits down. "Defeat and dishonor are affronts to the gods. As are lies."

"I'm not lying!" I snap, and then, "My lord."

"No, alas, I do not think you are lying," he murmurs with a flash of annoyance.

"My thanks." The words lie heavy between us, and Oras glances from Kalliarkos to me and back again as if he is beginning to suspect there is more to our exchange than there should be.

"Although I advise against believing you understand the undercurrents awash in the palace when you did not grow up there."

"I thank you for the advice, my lord," I retort, irritated by his scolding, he who now sits wielding the whip of command when he once swore to me that the last thing he wanted was to serve in the army. I lower my voice. "If I were you, I would give orders to put a heavy guard on your grandfather Lord Menos's tomb."

His hard, measuring gaze fixes on mine. After a moment his eyes widen slightly, and he nods. Finally he addresses his men.

"It's most important to alert General Esladas about what we've seen and learned. The citadels can hold out for now. Sergeant Oras, you will take your scouts to Akheres Oasis to give warning. We must assume the men besieged in Crags Fort citadel have sent a message by pigeon to Akheres Town, asking for help from the garrison there. You should bring up a relief force to drive the attackers away. Akheres Garrison must reinforce the desert forts and make ready for a possible invasion from the east through the desert."

"Yes, my lord."

"Your Holiness," he says to the crow priest, "you will accompany Sergeant Oras. I charge you in particular with making sure the holy Akheres tombs are properly guarded from any impiety."

The crows bob their heads.

"The rest of us will march south to Port Selene. We leave as soon as every spider and scout has been inspected for repair and injury."

He taps his fist twice to his chest, just as my father does to pass on an order. As one, all of us, even the priests, respond with the same salute. The two crows on the priest's shoulders open their wings and furl them again. From far away comes an answering *caw* from a third crow.

"Spider, come along!" commands Sergeant Oras. In his voice I hear the anger that will scald me once we are alone because I disobeyed his direct order not to follow him.

"Sergeant Oras, sit down and let me inspect your wound," says Kalliarkos.

The sergeant turns, surprised.

Kal goes on in a lighter tone and with a wry smile that makes my heart twist with longing. "I have made it my practice to examine all injuries sustained by the men under my command, to determine whether they are fit to fight. General Esladas taught me that he used to do the same when he commanded a small enough company of scouts that he could see to every soldier in it. Even now he tours the army hospital every day."

"Of course, my lord captain." Sergeant Oras sits gingerly next to Kalliarkos.

Kalliarkos beckons to an officer lingering in the shadows in the manner of a military aide-de-camp. "Bring me my medical pouch, Captain Helias. I'll need lint, grease, and honey."

I can't bring myself to walk away from him, not when we've been reunited so unexpectedly, so I stay, watching how deftly his hands unbind the crude linen bandage from Oras's neck wound, how he precisely moistens the driest spots of the cloth so as not to cause more damage as he peels cloth away from the skin to expose the injury. Flakes of dried blood drift through the aura of lamplight. The wound shines ghastly, two holes gashed through the neck, oozing fluid out of raw pink flesh.

Maybe I blanch, because Oras cracks a smile even though he is clearly in pain. "Can't stand the sight of blood, eh, Spider? General Esladas was exactly the same."

"He was?" I croak.

"He always threw up at the sight of blood. That's why he taught himself to treat injuries. He refused to look away from what made him uneasy."

Kalliarkos smiles in a way that makes me catch in a breath, but he isn't paying attention to me. He's concentrating on smearing grease and then honey on the wound with a tiny brass ladle, each movement precise and delicate. "He still throws up after every tour of the army hospital. He just makes sure to do it out of sight of the wounded."

How can it be that after only a few months with my father Kalliarkos knows things about him that I was utterly ignorant of? Mother dealt with the sick and injured at our house, never Father. We just thought it was something mothers did.

"Don't speak or move, Sergeant. I'm going to bind it up so the gashes can knit back together. Here, take this."

He holds out the ladle, clearly meaning any extra pair of hands to take it from him. The aide holds the lamp, so I reach for the tool. As I grab it, Kal's fingers brush mine. He winces. The ladle presses against my palm right where the splinter is lodged, and I grunt from the pain. He glances up at me, and for an instant I think he thinks I'm repelled by the contact, but then his gaze drops to my hand and his eyes narrow.

When he finishes sewing up Sergeant Oras he says, "Let me look at that hand."

"It's nothing, my lord."

"Don't say it is nothing when something is clearly paining you."

You are paining me, I want to say, but instead I answer, "It's just a splinter, my lord."

"My lord captain, I can take care of it," says Oras, rising quickly to hustle me away.

The crow priest says, "It is not fitting that you touch one such as—"

"I did not ask for comment or counsel. Sit down!"

I sit.

"Your hand!"

I hold out my hand, palm up.

This close, I see how he puffs out a little breath in resolve as his eyelids flutter from thoughts he isn't speaking. After a pause, he firmly takes hold of my fingers and studies the reddened palm. I study him. His face is leaner. A scar cuts a white line just below his lower lip. His hair is as short as ever, the only practical way to wear it on campaign as my father always says. The dry air and sandy grime make the strands stand up every which way. Probably we both reek, and yet all I sense is the warm press of his fingers on my skin as he gently probes closer and closer to the entry point.

"Ouch!" I jump.

His mouth twitches like he wants to laugh.

"Tweezers," he says in a cool voice, and the aide, Captain Helias, hands him tiny brass tweezers perfect for prying out splinters or stingers.

He tests the entry to see if he can get hold of the end of the splinter. Pain flashes up my hand and I blink back tears.

"Does it hurt?" Satisfaction edges his tone.

"More than I can say," I reply in a low voice, then grit my teeth as he teases apart the skin.

"General Esladas says that pain is the measure of a man, that we can let it defeat us or we can teach ourselves to live with the pain we have no control over."

"General Esladas is a wise man."

He looks me full in the face. We are so close I could lean forward and kiss him on his dry lips, and I see by the flare of his eyes that he is having the same thought. But under the scrutiny of the men standing around us, I do not let even the merest attempt at a propitiatory smile touch my lips.

He doesn't smile. If anything his expression grows more stony and distant.

"General Esladas is the most honorable man I have ever met. He has made it clear what he expects of me, and I would never do anything to lose his good opinion of me, now that I have it."

He bends over my palm, neatly inserts the tweezers to capture the end of the splinter, and slowly pulls.

I hiss at the pain, and then it's out. He holds up a sliver of wood.

"Where did you get this?"

"On a Fives court."

He stiffens, releases my hand, and stands.

I jump up at once, for no Commoner or lowborn Patron may sit where the highborn stand.

He busies himself with the medical pouch. "I thought I was dreaming when I came to, out there, and saw a face I certainly never expected to see in such circumstances."

"It will not happen again, my lord," says the crow priest.

"The fault is mine, my lord captain," says Oras, "but the girl did save a spider we'd otherwise have lost."

Even though I know I should not speak and must not ask, I say, "Were you going to let sunstroke and dehydration kill those soldiers rather than allowing them a noble death in battle?"

This is not the Kalliarkos I knew in Saryenia. He looks at me with bleak, brutal calculation. "Our battered army is retreating along the coast hoping to reach Port Selene before the combined armies and navies of the three kingdoms of old Saro can cut us off, surround us, and obliterate us. This isn't a Fives court, or a play in which nobility is a fine costume an actor can take on or off. This is war, and we are fighting for our lives. We are fighting for Efea itself."

21

At the end of the first long march we take a break in the last cool shadows of night with dawn a rosy promise in the east. I do my best to copy the others, settling my spider in formation. I use the shelter of the spider to pee, then come out from under and stretch.

"What is this braying mule who hauls alongside us?" Four soldiers circle in.

They look as filthy and exhausted as I feel but that's no comfort. My hand fixes around the hilt of the short sword Oras left me, but I can't outfight them with a blade. That's not my skill.

"I'm one of Lord Gargaron's adversaries. A Challenger, if any of you want to take me on at the nearest Fives court, not that you can beat me."

The one with the biggest sneer and the meanest eyes steps

in on me, pressing me back against a spider's leg. "There's more than one way to beat mouthy girls, sweetheart."

"Muster!" cries Captain Helias.

The four men give me the kiss-off sign in the most obscene way possible and hurry away to form up. I cautiously follow, keeping to the back of the pack. Kalliarkos hops up on a rock and brandishes his captain's whip.

"We have wiped out the enemy cavalry! You have displayed your determination, skill, honor, and courage."

They cheer. I cross my arms, glad I'm standing at the back because I know he's not talking to me and I wish he were. He has a voice that catches at the heart and makes people want to like him.

He extends the whip, pointing south. "We've a four-day march to the coast on short rations and short of sleep, but we bring news of a victory to an army that will be cheered."

They nod, liking his upbeat tone.

He pauses long enough to look each man in the eye and get an acknowledgment in return, marking each man, studying his mood. When he goes on his voice is more serious, quiet enough that we all lean forward to make sure we don't miss a word.

"We bring something more important even than this. We will bring General Esladas and Prince General Nikonos the crucial news that King Kliatemnos in Saryenia was sent false intelligence about the defeat at Pellucidar Lake. Do you know what this means?"

He waits. The silence draws out so long I can't bear it.

"There is a traitor in the Royal Army," I say. "Someone with access to the royal messenger pigeons."

"The cursed mule can't stop braying," mutters one of the men who accosted me earlier.

"Mules will kick," adds his companion, and many of the men laugh in a mocking way that may as well be them spitting in my face.

Kalliarkos slashes the whip through the air three times so fast its whistling shuts them up. "Yet it is this Efean woman who risked her life to save a precious spider from the attack on Crags Fort even though she has had no training as a scout. Did any other run into the battle not knowing if he would live or die and yet bring out a spider? Are you the sort of men who cast dishonor on an act of courage?"

They shuffle their feet, glancing at each other.

"This adversary offered us the crucial confirmation that the message delivered to the king and indeed to all the garrisons in Efea was a lie. This adversary uncovered the enemy plot to steal the royal gold! Are these not acts worthy of our respect?"

They scratch their heads. A few glance at me.

"I call us fortunate!" He cracks his famous grin, and his

men begin to relax. "What other spider patrol can boast of its own kicking mule, I ask you? None but ours."

That easily he hooks them, even as I hide a flinch because I know better than to let them see my pain. And of course his speech works, for he will be listened to when others would be shouted down. A few of the scouts nod at me like we are chance-met drinking companions and they are inviting me to sit down at the table.

"Inspect your spiders, drink, and eat. We won't rest again until the afternoon. At each rest stage our mule will lead us through the menageries to keep our bodies supple and strong. At ease!"

As we break ranks I have more friendly comrades than I can manage, men wanting to show me how to oil the joints of my spider, share food, ask if I really am a Challenger. They line up behind me when I lead menageries, and my skill at the forms and the flips impresses them.

Lord Captain Kalliarkos does not speak to me. He's merely done his job: smoothed out a source of potential conflict within his unit.

He called me a mule to my face. The humiliation stings more than blown sand, even while I understand why he uses language they can hear and will respond to. Even though I understand why he won't talk to me or show me the least measure of preference, the slightest hint that we already know each other, it still hurts. It really hurts.

I don't have anyone to talk to about Amaya, Mis, Dusty, and Tana, and the grief grinds with every step, with every passing day. Bettany's betrayal stabs at my every breath, but I've no one to pour my troubles into. I miss Mother so much.

⟲ᨏᨏᨏ⟳

Four days later we finally march into sight of Port Selene. The road winds down a long slope with the shoreline laid out below.

The sea shimmers beneath the afternoon heat, ships floating offshore like so much flotsam tossed onto the waves. Orchards and fields spread on either side of the road in narrow strips of cultivated land along the sea, fed by wells and cisterns. It seems so peaceful, except for the massive army camp boiling like a nest of termites set up outside the city walls. That the Royal Army has been forced to retreat this far into Efean territory, fleeing the enemy invasion, means things really are much worse than I realized.

The military encampment is huge and neatly laid out in four quarters, tidy and organized just as my father likes things. As he once said, discipline is even more important in retreat. The command compound sits at the center, the official tents flying circular banners that spin in the sea breeze like Rings on a Fives court. Our spider camp sits at the farthest remove from the cavalry quarter, since horses generally fear the clanking spiders.

A surprising number of people rush out to greet our company, flocking around Kalliarkos as if he is an Illustrious sauntering through the Lantern District to the accolades of the crowd. We leave the spiders to the care of support staff who will oil and repair them. A woman with Saroese features works on a spider alongside a white Soldian man, her small hands easily getting inside the tightest crevices of the articulated joints. A sleeping baby is tucked up in a sling on her back. She glances at me as I walk past and offers a smile, woman to woman, and I am suddenly sure she is from old Saro because no Efean-born Patron woman would smile in such a friendly way at a person like me. Like my father, she has traveled far to make a different life for herself.

A two-wheeled carriage is brought, drawn by two horses and attended by twelve cavalrymen as a mark of respect for Kalliarkos's rank. He takes the reins from the driver and then, to my surprise, calls me up to sit on the passenger bench beside him.

The encampment is so large it's no wonder Kalliarkos prefers to drive rather than walk. Each unit has a separate compound fenced off with canvas walls and marked with its badge, giving the camp the feeling of a town.

"I appreciate what you did to get the soldiers off my back," I say in a low voice.

He does not look at me as he expertly guides us through the foot and wagon traffic. "My apologies, Jessamy Garon."

"For what?"

"For calling you a mule. It was a hurtful thing to say, and I'm sorry for it."

I can't think of a reply because I'm so gratified at his apology that my chest feels tight with emotion, even as the insult still stings.

He frowns, glances at me, then goes on. "I did not mean to humiliate you, but it was the only way I knew to quickly make the soldiers accept you."

Yet instead of making me feel better, his explanation grates. "Was that really the only way? If they respect my father so much, why didn't you just tell them who my father is?"

"Because it's one thing to know a man has kept loyal company with an Efean woman and another to actually see his child walking around acting like she is Saroese."

"I am as much Saroese as I am Efean," I say recklessly.

"But that's not how they see you." His rigid back does not relax. "They just see you as a mule with too much kick."

"They treated me like their pet," I mutter, watching his shoulders brace with embarrassment. I can tell so much about him by the way he holds his shoulders. "And you let them."

His expression turns tight even as his hands stay light on the reins. "We've had a grueling and exceedingly bitter few months. These men have served with loyalty and courage. It seemed better to turn their hostility into camaraderie rather than punish men already pushed to the end of their rope. I know it came at your expense, and I truly am sorry for making you endure what must seem hateful to you. But I considered my options and made the best choice, just as you do on Rings."

"It's true it would have been much worse for me if you hadn't intervened." I pause. I'm torn, not sure how to react, so I settle on changing the subject. "You're good at command, my lord."

"How fortunate I'm good at something, considering my lack of skill on the Fives court."

But his shoulders don't seem as angry as they should be, given his words. He has relaxed, as if getting the apology out was the part that scared him the most. As if he was afraid I would reject him. And here I sit, close enough to touch him after I thought I would never speak to him again. A big grin creeps onto my lips however desperately I try to hold it back. How Amaya would laugh if she could see me!

"You know how to talk to people," I say, and allow myself a teasing thrust. "Except maybe to me."

"Please remember that I am taking you to your father. He made it clear that any particular attention I show to you will hurt you, not help you."

"I don't care."

"You have to care. I'm trying to protect you, Jes."

He glances at me again, but this time his expression has opened and the warmth I've been hoping for gleams in the vehemence of his gaze. He still cares. Before I can answer, a cheer rises from soldiers along the road as they recognize him.

"All hail Lord Captain Kalliarkos, hero of Pellucidar Lake!"

The shout is taken up by soldiers streaming out of their compounds to cheer as we pass. Many of these are mercenary companies hired for the duration of the war, and I wonder what Kalliarkos has done to make men who fight for pay hail him as a hero in a battle that was a disastrous defeat for our forces.

When I glance inside the mercenary compounds I see, amid tents and cook-fires, soldiers polishing weapons and repairing their kit, women sewing up tunics and cooking, and big children hauling water while little children run about at play amid the guide ropes that brace the tents. The people in these mercenary companies are not just Saroese but people from all around the Three Seas: straw-haired Soldians, Amarans with their hair concealed by turbans, bowlegged cavalrymen from the plains of Dey, and the island-dwelling Tandi whose women carry weapons exactly like the men. A few wear the complicated braids famous among the Shipwrights, and I think of Agalar, and then Bettany.

Kalliarkos says, "What's wrong?"

But I can't utter her name. I still haven't figured out what I'm going to tell Father, and now I don't have any more time. We pull up before the entrance of the central command compound.

The guard captain makes a salute. "Lord Captain! The general awaits you."

Grooms take the horses as Kalliarkos climbs down from the carriage. I hang back, three paces behind. This is not a Fives court where I want the crowd's attention. My palms start to sweat. What will Father say when he sees me?

At the center of the command compound stands a tent flying the gold banner belonging to Prince General Nikonos. As we pass I recognize Sergeant Demos slipping in a back entrance. I know it is him because I've been marveling at that beard for days, wondering how any man can endure the bugs and grit that must get caught in it.

Kalliarkos has already reached the entrance to a huge tent flying a firebird banner beside the winged fire dog flag of Garon Palace. The guards salute with hand to chest when they see him. He walks in without waiting to be announced, me hurrying after so I don't get trapped outside. The tent is so large it is divided into multiple interior rooms by curtains. In the outermost area seven officers stand around a table on which a map has been unrolled. His back to the entrance, Father is addressing his subordinates.

"By luring the enemy into a pitched battle here, in the ravines east of Port Selene, we will force them to narrow their front line." He points to a spot on the map with his command whip. "That way they cannot bring their greater numbers to bear on our smaller ones. Also, the rocky terrain will slow them down when they try to spread out and wrap around us."

He turns, hearing our arrival. "Lord Captain Kalliarkos. A runner brought the welcome word that you and your scouts have arrived safely back with no losses—"

He chokes on his next word as he recognizes me. But Father is a man famous for never letting any battlefield disaster rattle him, so he coughs as if it were just a tickle in his throat. "Your report, Lord Captain?"

"A drink and some food would not go amiss," drawls Kalliarkos. "I am parched, General. We made a forced march."

When he pulls his scarf off his head, sand spatters everywhere. Dirt makes his short hair stand on end, and his skin is so coated with dust that his complexion has taken on the reddish-brown cast of the desert soil. I see an unspoken communication pass between the two men, as if in a mere four months they have learned to know and trust each other well enough to become confidants. Father pretends not to notice me although the officers give me curious looks.

"Dismissed," he says to the officers. "We'll meet again at dawn when I will have Lord Captain Kalliarkos's full report."

The moment we are alone Father fixes on me a gaze so harsh it melts my feet into the ground. I couldn't move even if I thought it wise to bolt.

"I can explain why she is with me," says Kalliarkos hastily, looking much less the bold captain and much more a sheepish youth.

"I expect a thorough explanation," says Father. "Haredas!"

His senior steward steps forward. He too is giving me a disapproving look, as if I have done something wrong!

"Bring tea and bread. Have Lord Kalliarkos's steward draw bathwater. And for this one—"

He doesn't even say my name!

"—she will need a bath and respectable clothing. Bring Ganea to assist her."

"Yes, General." Haredas brings us a tray of drinks and a platter of bread. Then he goes out, and we three are alone.

"Now, your report, my lord," says Father.

I'm impressed with the efficiency of Kalliarkos's report although it is hard to keep my full attention on his story as I gulp down mint tea sweetened with honey. With as much self-control and dainty good manners as I can muster, I devour two entire rounds of warm, delicious flatbread by ripping them into small pieces between drafts of tea.

Father asks only a few clarifying questions before turning to me.

"So. Jessamy." That bland voice is the rock that hides a scorpion's sting. "It is no exaggeration to say I am surprised to see you. And by no means pleased to see you in the company of Lord Kalliarkos after you were expressly forbidden from speaking to him ever again."

My gaze strays to Kal just as he glances at me. We both look away. My cheeks get hot.

"*Well?* What do you have to tell me?"

He never stands with anything except perfect posture, at a soldier's readiness, but by the flexing of his hands I can tell he is anxious about far more than my misadventures. All my life it's always been the first thing he wants to know: if Mother is well since his last news of her. But he has sworn to never again speak of her, and anyway here he stands next to his wife's brother.

I meet Father's gaze and nod once, firmly: a silent message to let him know Mother is alive and well. He nods in reply, understanding my message, and allows himself to relax just a little.

"May I have your whip, Father?" I ask.

He opens his lips to question me, then hands it over. We three are alone in this part of the tent but I am well aware of how sound carries through cloth walls. I make a circuit of the curtained chamber, poking his whip along the cloth to make sure no spies hide behind to listen.

I give him back the whip and in a low voice I tell him— and Kalliarkos—about Menoë and Nikonos plotting in the garden of Garon Palace, the grain shortages in Saryenia, Menoë taking her ladies to visit the queen, the spark that saved Prince Temnos, the king getting false news of a victory at Pellucidar Lake, the gold bullion hidden in Lord Menos's tomb and how they can never mention it to Gargaron because Gargaron doesn't know I know.

"I think it likely Lord Agalar has guessed that the missing gold is somewhere in the tombs, so we must assume the enemy has already returned there and found it. There's another thing. It may just be coincidence, but in the final skirmish with the East Saroese cavalry, Sergeant Demos almost stabbed Lord Kalliarkos in the back. It could have been a mistake in the heat of the moment but just now I saw him enter Prince Nikonos's tent."

"You are suggesting that Prince Nikonos sent a deliberately false message to the king," says Father.

"Maybe it wasn't false. He just said it was a victory, for him. He didn't say it was a victory for the king, or for Efea."

"That implies he is colluding with the enemy. This would be treason."

"Lord Gargaron's plans to overthrow the king and queen and place his niece and nephew on the throne are treason too, are they not? Who knows how long Garon Palace has been altering the manifests and stealing the royal gold?"

"Good Goat," mutters my father. "Lord Kalliarkos, did you know about this?"

"I did not. Garon Palace is rich, and my grandmother already gets a cut of the royal bullion. Why steal more?"

It seems so obvious to me! "So the king and queen don't have it. If the king and queen can't supply hungry people with bread and can't pay their troops, but Garon Palace can, that will make the populace look kindly on Lady Menoë and her brother, won't it?"

"Lady Menoë said nothing to me about hidden gold," muses Father.

"Why would she confide in you?" To think of her and my father conversing as wife and husband boils my blood.

Kalliarkos is quick to pick up on my agitation. "My uncle didn't tell me, so maybe he didn't tell her either. She blurts out the most outrageous and angry things. Uncle Gar might not have trusted her with such a secret."

Father shakes his head. "Lady Menoë and Lord Gargaron are both deep in this conspiracy. She is a good strategist, my lord. Do not underestimate your sister because she speaks sharply out of impatience. Intelligence may chafe when it wishes to gallop and is being held to a walk."

To hear him praise the woman he abandoned my mother for makes my tongue burn. "She said such disrespectful things about you to Prince Nikonos, Father!"

"Of course she did. She told him what he expected to hear."

"Are you *excusing* her? She *murdered* her first husband! You'll be next when she decides she doesn't need you anymore."

"That is enough, Jessamy!" His tone cracks down over me, and I flinch.

Kalliarkos makes a business of rubbing sand off his chin.

He and I are both still filthy, and the crust of sand distracts. "I've heard enough about Menoë, I pray you. Run these Rings for me, Spider. Why would Nikonos bribe Sergeant Demos to kill me?"

"He wants you dead so he can rule as king with Menoë as his queen."

Kal shakes his head. "No, Menoë won't betray me."

"So you believe." What fools they both are! Menoë is poison all the way through, a blade aimed at both Father's and Kalliarkos's hearts.

"Especially not in favor of Nikonos," Kal adds.

"Even if she wouldn't, which remains to be seen," I say, "that doesn't mean Prince Nikonos doesn't want you dead. I would say he has good strategic reasons to kill you."

Kal's charming grin staggers me. "This is why you're so good on Rings, Jes. You see every possible path."

Father clears his throat, and we both look away. "We are done for the moment, my lord. You and I will attend a feast in Prince Nikonos's tent this evening. Notables from Port Selene are joining us, including several shipowners whose goodwill we must cultivate because we need to ship our wounded back to Saryenia and I haven't the gold to pay them. Indeed, I am sorry if we have lost the most recent gold shipment, for the royal pay-chest is quite empty. Mercenaries who can't be paid are likely to join the other side." He gives us each a searing look, then adds, "You did well, Lord Kalliarkos. You surprised me at Pellucidar Lake by the calm way you took charge when the lord captain of the spider scouts was killed in battle."

"I did what any officer would have done to rally the scouts and cut off the enemy attack."

"I have seen many officers, my lord, and I must respectfully disagree. You acted with composure where another man might have panicked. You display a capacity for leadership that will serve Efea well."

Kalliarkos's chin lifts. If a man could burn with two sparks giving him the greatest intensity of light and being, he would glow like this: shining with praise, and yet humble enough to take it without gloating. Then he looks at me to make sure I heard my father's complimentary words.

I feel the old warmth leap the distance between us and catch in my own heart.

While my father watches.

Too late I drop my gaze and pinch down my hopeful smile.

"Lord Kalliarkos, I believe you and I have had in full the conversation about your relationship with my daughter."

Kalliarkos snaps to attention like the lowliest soldier. "Yes, General."

"That is all." He claps his hands. Haredas and another steward appear. Thus dismissed, Kalliarkos follows the steward into another part of the tent.

"You keep Lord Kalliarkos close by, do you not, Father?" I ask.

"As is my duty, to keep him alive." He twists the whip in his hand. "As your father, Jessamy, I have words to say to you on this matter, which evidently is not yet concluded. He is a member of the royal family. Do not reach for what you can't have."

"Do you mean to scold me for having the same ambitions you have yourself? After what Lord Gargaron tried to do to our family, you still affiliate yourself with him to pull yourself higher. You support his bid for power."

"I serve Efea."

"Yes, how grandly you serve Efea! You began life as a humble baker's son in a provincial town in the old country and now you command the Royal Army of all Efea and are married, besides, to a woman of the same royal blood I am told I can't reach for. But I'm just a mule, aren't I? Even to you!"

"I have heard enough rude talk from you, Jessamy! Now you sound like Bettany, scolding me for injustice without any understanding of the complicated nature of our lives."

I bite my lip and say nothing. Even after all this, I'm not ready to tell him about Bettany. It's still too raw. I just can't bear to hear what he will say.

He goes on without seeming to notice my grimace. "We are at war, and yet we are ruled by a king who spends his days reading plays from seventy years ago and who arrests poets for writing unkind words about his ancestors. You wonder if Prince Nikonos is a traitor, but at least Nikonos is fighting. I find it far more likely that King Kliatemnos received news of our defeat and ordered it to be announced as a victory."

"Why would he do that?"

"Because he is a weak, selfish king who cares only about the story people tell about him. Did you read the message yourself to know what it said?"

"No. But the scholar Thanises did."

"The king pays for Thanises's house, food, servants, and books. Of course Thanises will say whatever he thinks the king wants to hear. We need leadership, not honey cakes. Our army is retreating because the king would not heed his generals' requests for better training. He and the queen have not wisely managed their resources, leaving us without the means to enroll more recruits. We are fighting against a stronger enemy, and *we are losing.*"

He pauses to let the dreadful truth sink in, then goes on.

"I fight to save Efea, which is why I serve Lord Gargaron, and why you must as well. Do you understand, Jessamy?"

Angry tears seep down my cheeks as I nod.

"Haredas! Take her away and get her cleaned up."

"This way, Doma Jessamy."

Haredas leads me past a curtain into a small space furnished with a camp bed, a traveling chest, and a folding table on which incidentals are laid out: my father's humble sleeping space. He gathers up the shaving gear and a folded uniform trimmed with gold braid.

"Are we really losing the war, Steward Haredas?"

He does not look at me. "Yes, Doma. We are horribly outnumbered. But our situation would be far worse if your father was not in command. I do not think any other commander could have held the army together for a controlled retreat as he has done."

"What about Prince Nikonos? Isn't he in command?"

"He is wise enough to leave strategy to the general. His royal presence gives heart to the men. But it isn't enough. King Kliatemnos should have taken the field himself, a king facing other kings, not sent his younger brother and his young cousin. Is there anything else you need?"

"No."

"Very good, Doma." He leaves.

An elegantly dressed Saroese woman enters.

"I am Doma Ganea, and you are Doma Jessamy, the daughter of General Esladas," she says in a Saroese accent that marks her as being from the old country. "What a striking girl you are! Your mother is the Efean woman?"

Good Goat! Has my father been keeping a concubine while he's been off at the wars, none of us the wiser?

She gives me an acute look-over, as if she guesses my thoughts, and keeps on talking as servants carry in a tub and fill it with warm water. "Haredas always said General Esladas would not subject his woman to the rigors and insults of camp life."

350

"Are you my father's—"

"No, I am not. Yours is not a dainty constitution, that I can tell by looking at you, so I will speak bluntly. I have been Haredas's lover for over ten years, traveling with the army. We call ourselves camp-wives, Doma. Women who follow the army. The soldiers become our lovers. Some become our husbands. Some of us bear children. We share the risks and rewards of war."

"I didn't think soldiers took their families with them."

"When soldiers march for many years away from home it is natural they will wish for the comfort and trust a family brings. A pleasant bath like this one, for example."

The clean water does look tempting. Now that she and I are alone I strip out of my Fives gear, shedding sand everywhere. The glorious water embraces me, moistening and cooling my dry, hot skin.

"Ah! This feels so good. My thanks, Doma."

"I will have the laundresses wash your clothing. Here is soap, Doma. I have brought several garments you may wish to try, although I will have to adjust the shoulders to fit you."

Cautiously I say, "Does my father have a camp-wife?"

Her fingers brush her lips to cover a smile. "General Esladas? No, Doma. That is why his loyalty to the Efean woman was legendary."

She takes care of everything, just as Mother always did for Father's comfort. In old Saro women wear layers of clothing quite unlike the light sheath dresses of Efea, and I like the feel of a loose inner shift beneath a bright blue wrapped jacket that reaches my knees, and a skirt with plenty of room to kick. As my hair dries she wraps it back behind my head in a sun-yellow scarf and pins a blue ribbon woven into the shape of a five-petaled star-flower behind my right ear.

"To show you are an unmarried girl," she says. "It's the custom in the place where I grew up. Go out. I'll be along in a moment."

By now it is dusk, and lamps hang from the tent poles in the outer chamber where Father waits for me. He has shaved and changed into court clothes, a long formal keldi and a gold-trimmed jacket with a general's epaulets. He regards me a moment so very critically, like a general surveying his troops in the hope of finding them battle-ready. Then his mouth softens and he nods.

"You look well, Jessamy. Doma Ganea will take charge of you for the evening until I return from the feast."

"Doma Ganea says many soldiers march with their families. Why couldn't we have gone with you, Father?"

"I would not have made your mother endure it."

"Being apart from you for months and years at a time was better? This doesn't look so bad!"

"Jessamy, the women who march with the army are tough and brave."

"Mother is tough and brave!"

"If a man dies in battle, especially in a foreign land, then the woman and the possessions he leaves behind are vulnerable." His stern expression extinguishes my indignation. His tone makes me feel so naïve. "She may be forced to attach herself to a man she likes less in order to protect herself from predatory men. I would never have subjected your mother to such a life. Especially because she is Efean and thus some men would not feel any need to ask her permission for that which they might wish to take from her. Girls like you and your sisters are particularly vulnerable. You have yourself seen fit to remind me that you are seen as lesser than the Saroese, while many Efeans regard you with suspicion. This is what I have protected you from your whole life, Jessamy."

I think of Dusty and his stories of being beaten up in his village. I think of the soldiers threatening me and how Kalliarkos got them to see me as a sign of good fortune instead.

"Yes, Father," I whisper.

Father's voice drops so low I can barely catch his words. "No one who conversed with your mother could come away doubting her intelligence and her dignity. She is more of a queen than any woman who parades in finery and jewels. You are her daughters, and my daughters, and I will allow no one to treat you with disrespect. While you are in this camp you will sleep in a camp bed in my tent attended by Doma Ganea, you will walk outside only with an escort appropriate to the status of a general's daughter and attended by Doma Ganea, you will dine with me or with Doma Ganea. And. You. Will. Obey. Me. Is that clear, Jessamy?"

Before I can answer Haredas hurries in. "The delegation from Port Selene has arrived at Prince Nikonos's tent, General."

"Very good." Father gives me a last long warning look, and I am about to say something placating, to assure him that I do understand the world is more complicated than the quiet life we lived for so long, when Kal walks in bathed and dressed like a prince in a gold keldi tied and pleated in the front and wearing an embroidered gold jacket with his captain's cape flowing down behind. His short hair sets off his fine features but it is his eyes I notice because they halt on me and grow wide.

No one could mistake the blush that reddens his cheeks.

Father taps his command whip against his leg. "Jessamy will take supper here with Doma Ganea."

"Isn't she coming with us?" says Kalliarkos.

"Of course she is not!"

"But why not, General?" Kal's amiable smile pokes like a stick into a nest of ants. "You are General Esladas, commander of the Royal Army of Efea. Why would you not bring your daughter to a supper to be introduced to the local notables?"

"Kal," I mutter, but he has his stubborn face on.

"Surely you are not ashamed of her?" Kal adds slyly.

"Of course I am not, but she is Efean—"

"She is as much Saroese as she is Efean," interrupts Kal. "Everyone knows that General Esladas has four mule daughters—"

Father stiffens. "I pray you, my lord, do not use that term."

"Yet if the commander of the army refuses to bring his daughter to a supper he is himself invited to, then isn't he as good as admitting that he thinks of her as a mule? If you will not invite her, then I will. And you cannot say no to me if I insist."

Silence follows this threat. I should say I don't want to go. But when Kal looks at me with that warm and admiring gaze, I can't.

A veteran soldier knows when to retreat. "Very well, my lord. Jessamy, you will speak only when spoken to and you will sit beside me."

With stewards and guards in attendance we process to the sprawling tent of Prince Nikonos, which is lit by a hundred lamps, an expensive waste of oil. In a curtained chamber the distinguished visitors are all standing because Prince Nikonos has not yet arrived. To my relief the introductions go smoothly as Father makes me known to Lords Bucestos and Rokomon, and to Ladies Petreia and Ranise, both of whom have the sleek, confident look of successful businesswomen although Lady Petreia has the complexion of a woman who gets a lot of sun. All I have to do is answer with polite phrases and not glance too often at Kal, who has a smug little smile on his face as, with his polished court manners, he sets the visitors at ease. He's so much more confident here than on the Fives court.

Once we have all arrived, Prince Nikonos sweeps in. He's tall and good-looking in the Patron style, and he has the air of a man who expects everyone to bend their backs so he can walk on them.

"Cousin, I am relieved to see you returned safely from your perilous expedition," he says, acknowledging Kalliarkos with an unctuous smile that makes me want to grind his face into the sawdust of a Fives court. "General Esladas…"

The prince trails off, eyebrows rising as he sees me. "Good Goat, General, have you replaced the old concubine with a fresh young one? I cannot imagine your honored wife, Lady Menoë, will be pleased to hear that you invited your Efean mistress to your table and not just to your bed."

"Jessamy is my daughter," says Father in a voice so quelling that any other man would shut up.

Nikonos gives me an exaggerated double take. "So it is! The brawny adversary once linked to you, Kal. Everyone was laughing about how first she seduced you and afterward crushed you on the Fives court like the veriest fledgling. Has the general brought her here for your comfort? As a little bribe to help you find your courage? I hadn't thought the honorable General Esladas would reel out his daughters as bait—"

It happens so fast that even my stony-faced father doesn't anticipate it.

Kalliarkos springs past two of the visitors and slugs his royal cousin right in the mouth.

22

Nikonos staggers back, hand clapped to his mouth. Fists raised, Kalliarkos stalks after him.

"Lord Captain Kalliarkos, I pray you, stand down." Father's right eye is twitching, a sure sign of anger, but his voice remains calm. "Prince General Nikonos meant nothing by his jest."

Kal opens and closes the hand he punched Nikonos with, then glances at me. Heat creeps up my cheeks but I can't look away. He wants to know if I want him to punch Nikonos again.

I give a very slight shake of my head, but it is all I can do not to break out into a stupid, stupid grin.

"Lord Kalliarkos, if you will be seated we can begin." Father's boot presses on my sandaled foot to keep me standing next to him rather than running over to Kal, as if I would be so foolish!

Nikonos pats blood from his lip with a handkerchief. "You have become so impulsive, Cousin, but I forgive it by reason of your exhausting patrol. General Esladas, I do not care to be seated at the table with a mule."

All my glee vanishes. If only I could disappear as everyone turns to look at me, and then at Father, waiting for his response. He hesitates.

Surprising everyone, Lady Petreia steps away from the table. "Shall I depart then, Your Excellency?"

Nikonos lowers the cloth. "Why should you depart, Lady Petreia? Are you also averse?"

Lady Petreia's smile glints more brightly than a blade's edge. "Why, then I could never sit with myself, could I, Prince Nikonos?"

He shakes his head. "You have as distinguished a lineage as any person in Port Selene, Lady Petreia."

"Yes, I do. My great-grandfather arrived in the fleet of Kliatemnos the First. He was an honored lord who helped the royal family escape old Saro. At that time he married a rich Efean lady from this very region, and their descendants have flourished here ever since. Can it have escaped your observation that I am darker than most Saroese women? You made no complaint when you visited my intimate chambers for a late supper last night. So it seems odd of you to object to General Esladas's daughter when her origins are at root no different from my own, even if my Efean ancestress is several generations removed."

She meets my eye and offers such a kindly smile that I put a hand to my chest because of the weight of emotion her words press into me. I can't grasp that a highborn woman like her would under any circumstances claim a connection to a girl like me.

She turns back to Nikonos with a faint tone of mockery. "Unless it is the general's lowborn origins you object to, which are well known to all of us and yet were seen as no impediment when King Kliatemnos appointed him as commander of the army of all Efea and Princess Berenise agreed that he marry her granddaughter."

"We do many things in the field we would not tolerate at home," remarks Nikonos, but by the surly look in his eye I sense a storm coming.

"Oh dear." Lady Petreia coughs meaningfully, and the other locals smile as if they are used to and approve of her pointed wit. "I know you city folk believe that all of us who live outside of Saryenia are provincial, but we have developed our own ways of doing things and over the years they have served us well enough. Now, Prince Nikonos, I pray you, the urgent business of war presses anxiously on all our minds. Old Saro is our shared enemy. I hope we may be seated so General Esladas can tell us how many wounded need transportation by ship to Saryenia. Perhaps you mean to evacuate the entire army, General?"

"No," says Father, his gaze on Prince Nikonos as he speaks, "we must fight on Efean soil so the old Saro alliance can march no farther into Efean territory."

Nikonos hands the bloody linen to a steward. "What brings your daughter here to the army, General? You are famous for having kept your household matters far apart from military matters over the course of your career."

"I had nothing to do with her arrival, my lord. For that you must apply to my lady wife's uncle, Lord Gargaron, at whose behest my daughter travels as an adversary."

Lady Petreia smiles graciously. "Perhaps tomorrow we can arrange a Fives trial at our lovely Fives court. Lord Bucestos is administrator and has recently refurbished the undercourt to allow for more complicated obstacles."

"By all means, it would be most entertaining to see General Esladas's daughter run the Fives," says Nikonos. "My cousin Kal can be one of the adversaries running against her. Would that not amuse us all?"

Nikonos isn't even looking at me. I am nothing to him. His barbs all fall upon Kalliarkos.

"I'm surprised you even suggest it, Cousin," says Kalliarkos with an airy wave of a hand that cannot disguise the tense set of his shoulders. "It would scarcely be a contest, since we all know Doma Jessamy is destined for greatness at the Fives while I serve the king and queen as a humble captain of spider scouts. I wonder you can even consider such a trivial matter when our enemy marches along the coast not two days behind us."

"Quite right, Lord Kalliarkos," says Lady Petreia with an approving nod. "I should not have suggested a Fives trial at all. Now, Prince Nikonos, I beg you, may we not eat?"

With the precise manners of people accustomed to burying past grievances under polite smiles, we take our places, mine being the part of the general's dutiful daughter.

"Is this your first time on campaign, Doma Jessamy?" says old Lord Bucestos with the slightly raised voice of the hard of hearing.

I glance at Father and he nods his permission that I may answer. "Yes, my lord. I have grown up quietly in Saryenia."

"Did someone mention you are an adversary?"

"Yes, my lord. I am a Challenger."

"Quite a success for one so young! I ran the Fives when I was your age, before I had more pressing duties—"

"Not just an adversary," breaks in Nikonos, who, being seated at the head of the table, is far enough away that he ought to be attending to the people beside him and not to me. His tone mocks. "I hear she marched with the spider scouts. The general's valiant daughter! Just like the famous play although not, we pray, with the same tragic outcome. How does it go? A cautionary tale about the shame of pretending to be something you are not."

I sit with rigid control, ashamed of what must come next, remembering how Father kept us carefully sequestered. He never allowed our rare presence at social events to bother any Patrons who found our origins disturbing. Always before he would make excuses and beat a strategic retreat.

But not this time.

The man who started life as a humble baker's youngest son in a provincial town now boldly looks the prince in the eye. His voice is firm, and his gaze steady. "Jessamy is a credit to her parents, Prince Nikonos, a daughter any father can be proud of."

Heat flushes my cheeks. I blink back tears.

Silence falls, disturbed only by the hiss of burning oil and the drum of hurried footfalls outside. Everyone looks at Prince Nikonos. But he is like an adversary standing before Rings whose pattern he can't untangle. It clearly puzzles him that a Patron man would unflinchingly defend the dignity and honor of a girl like me, and so Nikonos hesitates, stymied by an action beyond his comprehension.

Lady Petreia leaps into the game. "General Esladas, I hope when you come to my town house tomorrow morning to discuss how many ships you need that you will bring your lovely daughter to meet my own girls."

"You honor us, my lady," says Father in a hoarse voice I scarcely recognize. Beneath the table his hand squeezes mine as he smiles without looking at me, and my heart opens as I see him, the man whom no fierce attack can rattle, taken aback by this gentle act of kindness and respect.

A royal steward appears.

"My lord prince, Lord Gargaron has arrived."

"My dear friend Gar!" Nikonos laughs as at the merriest joke. "Send him in at once!"

Father stands, as the lowborn must when a lord enters any chamber where they are seated. I hastily rise beside him, although in my shock I have to steady myself against the table. Nikonos doesn't look one bit surprised as Gargaron strides in wearing the exhausted and travel-stained look of a man who has journeyed too far too fast. He stops short, sketches a cursory and almost insulting obeisance to Prince Nikonos, and looks at me for an unpleasant interlude in which several disturbing expressions flash across his face.

"Lord Gargaron," says Father. "Did the scouts under the command of Sergeant Oras find you?"

"We met them on the road. I am filthy and starving. May I wash my hands and face before I sit down to partake in this delightful repast? As you can imagine, under the circumstances I have traveled at speed with a very small group. General Esladas, I wonder if you could go and settle my soldiers and household in. I will seat myself in your place."

"I'll come with you, Father," I say in a low voice for now I am imagining the disaster that is Father discovering Amaya after I have gone to such trouble not to mention her situation to him, not to mention Bettany.

Gargaron begins washing his hands at a basin brought by a steward. "No, no, Spider, you will stay and entertain us with the tale I have heard of how you saved a spider from the attack at Crags Fort and then marched here in the company of veteran scouts, keeping up just as I would expect from an adversary of your skill and determination. Why, Kalliarkos, here you are. I have heard some trifling praise of you as well, I am glad to note."

"Jessamy," Father whispers, like a question.

"It's fine. I can manage."

Because I *can* manage. Gargaron thinks he knows me, and maybe he does know the part of me that is a little like him. With a last warning look Father departs, as he must, and when Lord Gargaron sits beside me, shedding sand and smelling of days on the road, I put on my game face. Father is right. We choose our allies as we must.

Gargaron regales the table with the story of the attack on Crags Fort and how the attackers grabbed the supplies and departed immediately.

"Across the desert?" Kalliarkos asks in disbelief.

"We heard some shouted argument before they rode off," says Gargaron. "Evidently they were to rendezvous with a cavalry company that never arrived."

"We dealt with that group," says Kalliarkos with a glint of satisfaction.

Gargaron sets hands flat on the table. "They killed thirteen of my guards and my best Fives trainer. Bastards."

"Tana?" My vision goes white. I lose all sensation in my limbs.

The next thing I know Kalliarkos is holding my shoulders and offering me a drink of wine while Gargaron studies the two of us with a thoughtful expression I cannot like.

"Yes, I fear that everyone caught outside the citadel was killed except for the spiders who escaped."

It takes me three tries to get out words. "Mis and Dusty..."

He looks puzzled. He doesn't know their names.

"...the other two adversaries..."

"Take a sip," says Kal, his hands firm on my arms.

I can't drink. I'm shaking so hard, sobs that I can't release caught in my chest. I had hoped by some chance they might have survived. I didn't really believe it. But I had hoped.

"Ah, yes. The attackers took the lad with them. I suppose they saw a strong youth like him as a good mule to carry their burdens and do work around camp, but they cut down Tana because of her missing hand. What a cursed waste of an excellent trainer! The girl adversary is small enough that she was able to squeeze inside one of the traps on the Fives court and escape detection. She is with the rest of the household. We rode at a bruising pace since we could not assure ourselves that we might not be attacked again." He raises a hand to beckon to a steward. "Bring me more of the beef."

I choke down a sob.

"Uncle, let me take her back to General Esladas's tent, I pray you," says Kalliarkos. "You can see she is overset by this news."

"Yes, these adversaries form tight bonds, do they not? I'll come when I'm finished."

With all eyes on us, Kalliarkos leads me out. When the night air hits my face I sway, the world spinning Rings around me, and he sweeps me up into his arms and carries me.

Tana is dead. Dusty taken. Bettany betrayed us. She is in part responsible for the death of people I cared for. My own sister, my twin.

I sob into his shoulder.

Kalliarkos carries me straight through the outer chamber of Father's tent and into the space where Father sleeps. He sets me down on Father's camp bed and kneels beside me. I am woozy with grief.

"Jes?"

"It was my idea. I made the other adversaries come because I was so sure I could find and rescue Bettany. I got cocky, just like they warned me against. Now it's too late."

"You're not the one who attacked."

I try to rise but my head swims and the world tilts, and he eases me back down.

"Lie here and don't move. I'm going to find Doma Ganea."

He kisses me on the lips so briefly that, after he is gone and I lie in darkness, I am sure I dreamed it.

I close my eyes. Grief and exhaustion overwhelm me. I fall asleep, or maybe I pass out.

When I wake Amaya is shaking me, whispering in my ear.

"Jes? Jes, wake up! Help me! Father is furious and you can't believe what he's done."

I swing my legs over the edge of the camp bed. My clothes are rumpled and my head is clear. A streak of pale light shines along the bottom of the tent: I've been left to sleep all night, and dawn has come.

She shakes my arm so hard I think she is going to shake it right off.

"Ouch! Stop it!" At once I'm sorry I yelled at her, and my voice trembles. "Amaya, I have to tell you about Bettany."

"Bettany! As if I care about Bettany. She stood right next to Lord Agalar as he tried to negotiate with those of us trapped in the citadel, and then when Lord Gargaron told him to go soak his head in a vat of piss, she rode off with those foul murderers and thieves like they were now her best friends. She chose her own path, Jes, and I spit on her. I'm just glad you survived."

"Did you tell Father about her?"

"Of course I didn't tell Father, and you shouldn't either!"

"Then what else could possibly have gone wrong...oh no! Has Lord Gargaron figured out who you are?"

"Oh indeed, no! No! Father saw to that, didn't he? He wants only to torment me."

"What are you talking about?"

"Lord Gargaron and his guard are leaving to return in haste to Saryenia."

"They are?" Where is Mis? I should have sought out Mis, trapped alone among people who care nothing for her. I rise.

Amaya grabs my arm again and proceeds to attempt to yank it off. "Father said that rather than have Doma Denya endure another grueling march, he would take her as a camp-wife!"

"Denya?" I can't even make sense of her statement.

"Oh, he doesn't care about Denya. He doesn't want *her*. He's just doing this to ruin *my* life. He is furious at *me*."

"As he should be!"

"But Jes—!"

We hear Father's voice. "No, Haredas. Let Lord Gargaron believe I am keeping both girls with me. They must wear disguises and be placed on the ship with the wounded. Let no one know."

Sweeping the curtain aside, he enters. Amaya and I bolt upright to attention.

He is literally shaking with anger as he fixes an accusing

gaze on me. "How comes it you were traveling all this time with your sister and did not see fit to warn me, Jessamy? If Gargaron had recognized her and realized your mother is alive...!"

He is too stricken to finish the thought.

"Amaya can explain herself," I say.

Amaya pinches me.

"Ow!" I step on her foot.

"Enough!" Father's voice whips down over us, and we both straighten. "Is there anything else you are keeping from me, Jessamy?"

Amaya nudges me with a knee.

"No. Nothing else. Am I to sail to Saryenia with Amaya and Doma Denya as well?"

"That would be my preference but unfortunately by express command of Lord Gargaron, you will be riding with his guard. Doma Ganea has left your clean clothing on the side table. You were sleeping so soundly I told her not to wake you." He shakes his head. "My girls...my own girls...have I taught you nothing that you defy me like this? Have you no respect for your father? No thought for your precious mother's safety and that of your sisters and of the infants your mother has safely borne beyond all chance and hope?"

Amaya and I clasp hands in solidarity. His anger is so rare and so forbidding.

370

Never in my life did I think I would welcome the sound of Lord Gargaron's thin voice raised from the tent's entrance.

"General Esladas? Are you here? Where is my adversary?"

"Just making ready now, my lord, with the aid of Doma Denya's maidservant."

Cursed if Lord Gargaron does not push the curtain aside and walk right into this intimate space as if he has every right to, which he does. Amaya drops immediately to her knees and makes herself busy unfolding my gear. He glances at her short cap of hair and the back of her slender neck, which is all he can see.

"I have promised the maidservant to Captain Neartos as a reward for his loyal service, General."

A spasm of pure fury passes across Father's normally controlled expression. Amaya ducks her head, digging into the clothes as if to hide in them.

"Yes, indeed," says Father in a tight voice that may fool Gargaron but does not fool me, "and when Doma Denya has found and trained a new maidservant to her satisfaction, I shall have this one sent along to you."

"I am surprised you have taken a liking to Denya. She's a pretty morsel and has more spine than I expected, but that's nothing you can't find in a hundred women in this camp."

Amaya's hands wring the fabric of my tunic like she is wringing the neck of a chicken.

"Her father was my rival captain in Lord Ottonor's retinue and often made light of my low birth."

"Ah! Now you will have the last laugh, will you not?"

"So I will," murmurs Father as I stare firmly at my hands and Amaya keeps her head bowed.

But as Amaya knew all along, there was never any reason for Gargaron to remember her face. We are trivial compared to the danger Efea is now in.

"Can you defeat the old Saro alliance, General Esladas?"

"I can slow down their advance, but to defeat them, my lord, I need more troops."

"I and my guard will ride at speed to Saryenia. We may need to take drastic measures sooner than expected if Kliatemnos refuses to fund new soldiers."

"Take Kalliarkos with you, my lord."

"Is he so hopeless that you rid yourself of him?"

"Not at all, my lord. Quite the opposite. He is a promising commander, cool-headed in action and with a rare instinct for how to keep up the morale of his troops. But our situation here is precarious. I advise you not to risk him."

"You're afraid we are going to lose."

"If we can win against such odds, we'll win whether he is fighting with us or gone with you. But if he is dead, we cannot win."

"I understand. I will take him with me in case I need to

act precipitously against the king and queen upon arrival in Saryenia."

"Do not underestimate him, my lord. He is a stronger weapon than you may believe. Now, with your permission, may I have a moment alone with my daughter?"

"One moment only, General. The horses are being saddled as we speak."

Gargaron goes out.

I embrace Amaya, hold her close, wish her well. She kisses my cheek and lets me go. At least she will be safe on a ship.

We do not speak of Bettany.

Father examines me. He wears his military uniform because he must be ready to defend Efea, because he is always ready to defend the country he made his home, yet in his gaze I do not see the stalwart, brave commander but just my father struggling to make sense of the people his daughters have become.

"Act boldly when you need to, and be cautious when you must," he says.

I want to tell him that Kalliarkos kissed me, that he's wrong about us, but this isn't the time. Yet maybe Father understands because he takes my hand and Amaya's, his grip strong and comforting.

"Run your Fives, Jessamy. Whatever comes, do not fear to climb the victory tower."

He kisses my forehead in the familiar way, and he lets me go.

23

After fifteen brutal days and nights of travel, our three carriages and ten guards—survivors from the attack at Crags Fort—reach the gates of Saryenia at dusk.

I lean out the open window of the third carriage, where Mis and I sit crammed in with the traveling chests and provisions. The main avenues should be bustling this time of day as people make their way home, finish their errands, or get ready for an evening's revelry, but the streets feel oddly empty. It's almost like we've entered a foreign country, not our familiar and beloved hometown.

A militia patrol halts us. "Do you have a pass?" its captain demands of Captain Neartos.

"A pass for what?" asks Neartos with a look of genuine confusion.

"No one is allowed out after nightfall without a special pass stamped with the king's seal. If you have no pass, I must arrest you."

Gargaron climbs down from the front carriage, while Kalliarkos stays out of sight. "I am Lord Gargaron, head of Garon Palace. I have just traveled at courier speed from the Eastern Reach with news of the war that the king needs to hear immediately. You may either escort me to the king's palace or move out of our way."

The sergeant hesitates, measuring the carriages, our grim-faced guards, and his patrol of eight men.

Then he sees me looking out of the last carriage and takes several steps closer.

"Is that Spider, the adversary? They say you marched a spider right out from under the nose of the enemy and saved the life of Lord Kalliarkos during an enemy raid."

"Ah, so the news out of Crags Fort has reached Saryenia before us?" Gargaron asks with his thin smile.

"Everyone has heard the rumors. You know how Commoners can hear every whisper on the wind. There's even a song about it—fantastically entertaining! Well, we wouldn't want to delay the arrival of this noted Challenger, would we?" He and his soldiers salute me with an adversary kiss, then start to sing as our party rolls on.

The general's valiant daughter will fight for Efea,
She'll fight for Efea, and win!

For days Mis has sat passively, wept quietly, and barely spoken, but now she peers out the window as we make our way up the Avenue of Triumphs to the King's Hill. Patrols move along the streets in force.

"How odd they know your story already, Jes," says Mis with an edge in her voice that makes me feel I walked right over a secret without seeing it. "Just like someone flew it here by messenger pigeon on purpose, to sweeten our arrival for their own gain."

"You think Lord Gargaron arranged it?"

She just looks at me, saying nothing, and I feel ashamed.

We two adversaries are set down at Garon Stable, where we are greeted with a stunned surprise by our stablemates. Rejoicing turns to tears as we tell our stories. Afterward we wash and we eat. Mis leaves the table before I'm done and when I follow her I find her in her cubicle packing her belongings into a small storage chest.

"What are you doing?" I ask.

"I'm quitting the stable. I'm going home." A lamp casts light on her determined face.

"How can you just quit?"

"Why do we run the Fives to enrich Patron treasuries and enhance their prestige? There was room in the front carriage for you to sit. You who leaped from Novice to Challenger at her first trial! The hero of Crags Fort! Now subject of a popular song! But even so the daughter of the great hero General

Esladas is still crammed in with the baggage because her mother is Efean."

I open my mouth to reply, then shut it.

"The enemy slaughtered Tana because we Efeans weren't allowed into the citadel when we first arrived. Had we been inside, she'd be alive. And then the enemy took Dusty because he is young and strong enough to bear their burdens, and Efean enough to be discarded when they no longer need him."

"He'll survive. I'm sure of it."

She straightens to look me in the eye. "Don't pretend that things turn out all right for people like Dusty, Jes. Don't insult him in that way."

"But you escaped, Mis. It happens sometimes." Her expression closes its claws around my throat, and I know I am just saying so because I don't want to face the truth. "You care for him, don't you? More than just as a friend."

"Much good it did me! He only had eyes for a Patron girl, like I'm nothing."

"Mis..."

"Do you know why I escaped?"

"Because Tana sacrificed herself to save you, me, and Dusty."

"Yes, she did, but that's not why I survived. After you ran off to warn the priest, the doctor and his servants broke open the gate, caught Dusty and me, and handed us over to the East Saro soldiers. They were to send me with the captured wagons as a beast of burden, like they did Dusty, but the doctor's Efean concubine convinced him to leave me behind. I think she didn't want me to suffer what she suffers."

My body sags, and I brace myself against the wall. Bettany saved Efean women and children, including Mis. I see now that she tried to get Amaya and me out of the way, but no matter how I turn it, once she realized we wouldn't leave she let us ride into an ambush knowing we could die.

"You saw the empty streets, Jes. Soldiers on patrol. A curfew in place. When we left Saryenia, grain prices were already so high people stood in line to get a ration of bread. Imagine what it is like now for hungry people. For poor people."

"That's why we have to fight for Efea. As the army does."

"The Royal Army fights for the power of the king and queen, for the lords, for the Patrons, not for us! Never for us."

She breaks off as we hear footsteps in the corridor. Talon pads past without even glancing in to see what we're doing.

"I've been here a year and she's never spoken to me because she's too proud to speak to someone like me," Mis whispers. "Don't you understand? I'm going to find a way to fight for Efea. For Efeans. Not for them." She grasps my hands. Her grip, like mine, is strong and true. "Come with me, Jes. My family will hide you. You deserve better than this, running trials so they can win."

"Jes!" Darios calls from the entry of the women's barracks, for it's not proper for an unrelated man to step inside

378

a dormitory where unmarried women sleep. "There's a steward from Garon Palace here. You've been summoned by Lord Kalliarkos."

Mis shakes her head in a pitying way, kisses me on the cheek, and releases my hands. "At least I can leave. You're the one who is trapped."

The steward escorts me through the servants' entrance into Garon Palace. He guides me down servants' pathways, out of sight of the residents, and up to a rooftop terrace that looks across the city. Princess Berenise sits in a cushioned chair, hands in her lap. I look around for Kalliarkos, but she and I are alone except for her attendants. I am brought before her and allowed to kneel. Age has bent her body but her gaze is fierce.

"Ah. Spider. Here you are."

"Your Highness." Mis's anger still throbs in my ears, so I speak imprudently and perhaps a bit tartly. "Does this mean Lord Kalliarkos is not the one who summoned me?"

"You must show patience." Her voice has a clarity that impresses me, each word so distinct I feel I could pluck it out of the air. "I can bring about many things, if I so choose."

"Yes, Your Highness." I wait as a servant hands her a cup. She sips, and the servant takes the cup and stands to one side, ready to offer it again.

"I recommend you listen closely. In the few months you have been gone from Saryenia, Menoë has begun a tradition of passing out bread to the populace at the weekly Fives trials.

It keeps the Fives court packed, and of course it has made the citizens of Saryenia sing her praises."

"A cunning plan, Your Highness, but I don't see what it has to do with me."

She lifts a hand. "Patience. Menoë has become the confidant of Queen Serenissima, who is weak but no fool. The queen sees the restlessness of the population but she only knows how to control people through force. It is Serenissima who pushed through the curfew to keep the streets quiet at night. She sees how detached Kliatemnos has become, sunk in his Archives as he hunts for this Efean poet who he is sure has a secret about our ancestors hidden away."

I think of the oracle we rescued from Lord Ottonor's tomb.

Expecting no reply, Princess Berenise goes on. "Menoë has a persuasive manner—"

Certainly Menoë seems to have persuaded my father of her keen strategic mind and her innocence in any plotting with Nikonos! But I can't say that aloud until I understand where Berenise stands.

"—and has convinced the queen to allow Prince Temnos to make carefully supervised trips outside of the royal grounds. He attends the Fives trials every week now. The crowd loves him because of his delicate constitution and because he presides with Menoë over the weekly distribution of bread."

A smile touches my lips. Temnos must love the adoration of the crowd as well as the chance to watch the Fives. I wonder if anyone has been training him or if they even really care about him except as a tool to use in their plotting.

"Prince Temnos took a strong liking to you, Spider. As it happens, tomorrow is Fivesday, and as a special surprise for the prince, who will be attending, you will run a trial so he can see you."

"But Your Highness, I haven't done more than pace through a daily menageries to stay limber and practice a few tricks, not since Akheres Oasis. I'm not ready."

"An adversary is always ready, Spider. Do you understand me?"

The words fall as a threat so I suck in my anger and reply in a cool voice. "Yes, Your Highness."

"I am sure you do not," she remarks with the asperity of the old who can easily perceive when the young are lying. "You are no more of a fool than your father is, Jessamy."

That she uses my name makes me very nervous. It's so hard not to jump up and pace around but I hold still.

"You may believe I am a weak old woman in thrall to Gargaron's ambition to rule in Efea through my beloved grandchildren, whom he believes he can control. But you would be mistaken. Let me tell you a story."

My whole body tenses, for I am sure there is nothing worse than being told a secret that might kill you. But of course I remain silent. As Mis said, as Bettany said, I'm trapped.

"As the younger sister of a king and queen I was naturally

sent away to marry an ally, who at that time happened to be Sokorios, the king of Saro-Urok. When he was killed by a rival, I barely escaped with my life and my tongue. I was saved by the timely intervention of Menos Garon, whom I married even though his rank was below my own. Menos and I did well enough together. I respected him, and he respected me enough to leave the administrative reins of the household in my hands."

"Menos was head of the Garon household, and Lord Gargaron's father was his younger brother," I say, remembering what Tana told me.

"Indeed." Her nod is like a golden star of approval whose radiance makes me shine. "I have always believed that my husband, and later our son, Kalliarkos's father, were assassinated. But their deaths were covered up with the explanations of a mining accident and a battle. Because of the nature of their deaths I've never had proof, only suspicion."

Her gaze has years of weight. She can crush me as easily as she can breathe, and a conjecture that I have in some manner mistaken the genesis of this plot becomes visible on the map in my mind. So I leap.

"Their deaths allowed Lord Gargaron to become head of the household when otherwise he would have remained a lesser member of the clan."

Her smile is no smile. It is a knife, put away into its sheath as she decides not to slit my throat. "Yes, you comprehend the situation. A man willing to murder his own kinsmen in order to take what belongs to them, merely because he covets it for himself, is a dangerous man. There is enough for all, but he is not a person willing to share. Aware of my vulnerability, I have lived a quiet life, built up my treasury, and bided my time for my grandchildren to come of age. Do you understand?"

"I believe so, Your Highness. If I were in your place I would hope to see my grandchildren become king and queen and leave Garon Palace to the dangerous man who craves it most."

"Among the Saroese, women play their role from 'behind the curtains,' as the poet wrote. We learn to negotiate through misdirection and trade." Her face is unreadable, for she is a woman who has survived many decades by never displaying her true feelings. "I made the offer to Gargaron: put my grandchildren on the throne and I will not push Kal's rightful position as head of Garon Palace."

"It was *your* idea? You had the Fives court built for Kalliarkos without ever meaning for him to become a real adversary?"

"He is a prince, with a claim to the throne of Efea through me and to the throne of our enemies in Saro-Urok, thanks to his mother's lineage. The Fives is nothing but a game."

I clamp my lips together. The Fives is more than a game if you are playing it for bigger stakes in the world. But I'm not going to disagree with her to her face. "So it was a piece of misdirection to let Kalliarkos train when all along you meant him for the throne."

"Yes. You came along at a perfect time. When Gargaron was investigating your father to see if he was the military man we needed for our plan to work, he discovered you and had you followed and studied. Together we determined you might be the vehicle that could put an end to Kal's senseless daydream."

A sick anger twists inside me and I can't speak. To speak is to die. They murdered Lord Ottonor and condemned his entire household to penury and disgrace. They threw away my mother and sisters and all the people to whom Mother gave refuge under her roof. They treated Kal's dreams with contempt. All for an ambition that benefits their own selfish desire for power.

But after all I'm too angry not to speak, because too many lives are on the line to let the most important question go unanswered.

"Your Highness, how can you trust Lord Gargaron if you think he murdered your husband and son?"

"I don't trust him. But he has no blood relationship to the lineage of the first Kliatemnos and Serenissima. He has no possible claim to the throne. Therefore, once my grandchildren become king and queen, it will serve him to keep them there."

I have to tell her. If for nothing else, to protect Kal. "Menoë is in league with Nikonos. I heard them plotting that night in the garden when I followed Kal into the pavilion. She means to betray you all." The words hiss on my tongue, so bitter, and tears sting in my eyes, and I realize I am crying for Bettany— my own sibling betrayer.

"Certainly not." Her tone brooks no disagreement.

Menoë has fooled them all, and there is no way I can convince them.

"You do not understand the full nature of the situation, Jessamy, daughter of Esladas. Imagine Menoë as queen. Once she gives birth to a boy, that boy—your father's child—will be formally and publicly announced as the son of Kalliarkos and named as heir to the throne of Efea."

"What will happen to my father?"

"Why should anything happen to your father? He's too lowborn to make a claim to the throne, and Efea needs his military skill now more than ever. The king and queen are understood to be father and mother over Efea, so any child the queen gives birth to belongs to the king, and of course the ignorant populace will believe it is truly Kalliarkos's child."

"Does that mean Temnos isn't really Kliatemnos's son?"

"No. He is the king's son in every way. Kliatemnos and Serenissima chose to bind the power more tightly into the family by both marrying and breeding inside it. We will keep our bloodline pure through Menoë. Don't you hear what I'm saying? In due time, your half brother will be king of Efea."

My hands go slack. My shoulders sag. Her words fall like nonsense because they are impossible. As my thoughts hit this unfathomable wall I lose all my strength. I just kneel there as she continues speaking. This is the ordinary way people go about murdering and bribing to gain and hold on to power.

And now I am truly part of it.

I know every piece of their plan, one that requires the deaths of Kliatemnos, Serenissima, and Nikonos to succeed, and if I do not go immediately to the king and queen, I am complicit, a traitor. Princess Berenise has made sure of that.

"Your part in this task, as I was beginning to say, is to capture and keep Prince Temnos's loyalty."

"What will happen to Prince Temnos?" I whisper hoarsely, for I fear to hear the answer.

"Nothing will happen to him. He's an invalid, a weak boy who suffers seizures. No one expects him to survive to adulthood. As a rising Challenger, you will work to win the crowd so thoroughly to your side that, when we make our play for the throne, the populace will support us without hesitation, as I believe Gargaron has already made clear. Your reward for your successful part in our endeavor will be to receive all that you desire."

She pauses.

I murmur, with the obedience I have no choice but to show, "Yes, Your Highness."

"Very good. Now, I am going inside. You may remain here. Please, go over to the railing and enjoy the view."

It is such a peculiar order that I puzzle over it for exactly as long as it takes for her attendants to help her away, removing all but one of the lanterns, and for the breathless arrival of a person who runs up the steps to the roof.

"Grandmama, my apologies for being late. I just got word you had summoned me...."

He sees me standing at the railing in the outer aura of lamplight and stops dead, then looks around as if unable to believe there is no one else up here, that we are alone.

That Princess Berenise knows we are alone.

My hands tighten on the railing. I should reject being used like this, but I can't take my eyes off him: his dark eyes, the strong curve of his shoulders, the parting of his lips as he takes in a resolute breath.

He walks over and stands next to me, careful to remain an arm's length away. His presence feels like a fire illuminating my five souls, the heart of me: I have wanted him from the moment he spoke to me as an equal, adversary to adversary.

The garden, laid out below, magnifies our silence because there is no wind to rustle its leaves. Under curfew the city rests uneasily, as if holding its breath. Lamps mark the wharves of Saryenia's famous harbors.

A trumpet sounds the hour, the sound rising so suddenly that I jump. When the horn fades he speaks.

"How are you come to stand here in Garon Palace, on the roof of my grandmother's pavilion, Jes?"

"I was told you had summoned me, but when I got here it was Princess Berenise who was waiting."

"I did not summon you. But it seems Grandmama knows you are here."

"Yes, she does."

"She summoned me, as she often does. She likes to eat an evening supper here atop the roof."

"I know nothing of that, my lord."

"You're right to be suspicious of me. I said things I regret after the victory games, because I felt humiliated and I wanted you to feel hurt too. What I've seen in battle has made me see how selfish I was, how small the world I lived in before, how little I could see of what really goes on beyond the palace walls."

"My lord—"

"Please let me finish. I've chewed over these words for days. When we met up again in the desert I wanted to tell you that I'd gotten over my anger, but I couldn't speak to you when we were with the scouts. At camp your father was so adamant that you and I never be alone, and I was not about to confide in you with him present! And then on the journey here Uncle Gar was with me day and night."

"I do not expect you to say anything, my lord. Your anger is understandable. You could have said much worse after the Fives trial. I'm sorry."

"You're not sorry you defeated me!"

"No, I'm not."

"Of course you wouldn't be. I knew you would say that." He laughs curtly, and I can hear that for all his fine words, losing his dream—*his senseless daydream*—still hurts.

"I'm sorry for what it meant to you," I say.

"What it meant that day, and what it means now, are two different things." He shifts impatiently, rubs his eyes. "I'm not an adversary any longer. I can't be an adversary, or at least not in the Fives. I see that now."

"You are heir to two thrones, my lord. Your grandmother just told me so."

He is so fiercely not looking at me that I flush self-consciously. As he inhales I tense in the way a good adversary does right before she leaps into Rings.

"What did she tell you?" he asks.

And so I tell him, because I have to see for myself how he reacts, where he nods because he already knew and where he winces because he's as appalled and disgusted at their plans as I am. When to my utter relief he nods and winces in all the right places, and I finish, I bow my head and wait.

He takes in a slow breath and lets it out. I don't rush him although I feel his presence beside me as I would feel the promise of a brilliant fire on a cold desert night.

Finally he moves, and I startle, but he's just pointing into the night.

"Look at the lights on the water."

The sea spreads as a mantle of darkness, broken at the horizon where stars pour upward into the vault of the heavens. Distant spark-bugs float between sea and sky: the prow and stern lamps on ships far out on the water.

When he lowers his arm he places a hand on the railing so close to mine I could exhale into him. The temptation to lean sideways and brush my shoulder against his washes so strongly over me that before I realize it my shoulder touches his. He starts. At once I straighten to attention as if Father stands behind us, watching to see that a gap is fixed between his daughter and the lord she must not desire.

"We could run away," he whispers. "We could join a mercenary company and leave and never come back."

Oh how it hurts to hear those golden words.

Oh how it hurts to answer.

"I can't leave my mother and siblings. I just can't." *I can't— I won't—be Bettany.*

An unexpectedly sweet smile paints his lips. "I knew you would say that."

"I'm sorry, Kal."

"Kal?"

How that name crept out I cannot imagine. "My apologies, my lord."

"Oh no, no, now you've said it and I can't unhear it." He rests a hand over my hand and turns to face me so that courtesy impels me to turn to face him, and thus we stand with the heady aroma of jasmine drifting up from the garden and the vast dome of the heavens our starry crown.

"Jes," he whispers.

It is the easiest thing in all of creation to kiss him.

I test his lips to mine as our hands clasp and our fingers intertwine.

"They're using us," he whispers.

"I know."

"They're letting us know they won't stand in our way, as long as we do what they want."

"I know."

"Jes—"

"I know."

And then we don't speak until I am so breathless that I am the one who has to break it off.

I stare at him because in all my dreams over and over I imagined this moment, that he would still care, and now that it is here it feels like it couldn't possibly be happening.

A man coughs.

I spin to face the intruder, but Kal grabs my shoulder. He catches my eye, and with a look settles my pounding heart. I am not alone. He is with me. We are together.

In a more dignified manner, we face the single lamp and the man standing beneath it.

Lord Gargaron studies us with that thin smile on his thin face.

Defiantly I grasp Kal's hand.

He says, coolly and sardonically, "Uncle Gar, how unexpected to find you invited to come up to take the view from Grandmama's private roof."

"Do not pretend you aren't both perfectly aware of what this means, and the reward you will receive if you both play your part."

Somewhere in Garon Palace a woman laughs, and I wonder: Is it Gargaron's wife, pleased to hear he has passed Denya on to another man? Kalliarkos's mother, rejoicing that her son has come home safely from the war? Lady Menoë, exulting in the unfolding of her cunning plan to smile to their faces and then stab them in the back?

"Why change your mind, Uncle? Why throw us together now when you did everything to keep us apart before?"

"What makes you think this wasn't part of the plan all along? When I sent you to the Eastern Reach, Kal, I knew it would either make a man of you or break you so you would cease attempting to defy me. All I needed was for you to give up your naïve dream of being an adversary on the Fives court and accept that you are an adversary in the only game that matters."

"Heir to two thrones," murmurs Kal. "My inescapable fate."

"Until your corpse walks to its tomb, you will never be free from the responsibilities laid on you by your birth. Now,

Spider, you have a trial tomorrow. A steward will escort you back to the stable. Study this."

He holds out a scroll.

Kalliarkos snatches it out of my hand before I can unroll it. "What is this, Uncle?"

"It is for the adversary, Kal. Not for you."

Kalliarkos pulls it open enough to reveal a schematic that I instantly recognize as an engineer's design for the configuration of a Fives court.

"It is the configuration of the Fives you'll be running tomorrow," Gargaron says to me as Kal slaps it closed. "Memorize it, and then burn it."

"But that's cheating!" I cry. "I don't want to win by cheating."

"You can't demand an adversary cheat," says Kal. "Besides the dishonor—"

"As if anything matters besides the dishonor!" I interrupt.

"Truly," he agrees, "but besides that, cheating will get her barred from the game for life."

"Cheating! Is that what you young people call it these days?" Gargaron's brow wrinkles as a measure of his disdain. "You are so sheltered, both of you. Have you not noticed we are at war? Threatened by the armies of old Saro, all three kingdoms allied against us? Our own Royal Army is in retreat, and the king cannot give them the resources they need to fight. Do you think Kliatemnos is able to lead Efea through this calamitous time? *Do you?*"

Kal holds out the scroll to his uncle. "The Fives has nothing to do with this war."

"Of course it does. Nothing we do is separate from the times we live in. It is your ancestor Kliatemnos the Second who codified the rules that adversaries follow. It is gold that builds a Fives court, and money and prestige that honor the winners. We win or we die, Kal. If Kliatemnos and Serenissima rule, Efea falls. Do you not see it? They cannot win, just as you could not win against Jessamy. That is why she defeated you, and why we must defeat them. To save Efea."

He grabs the scroll from Kal, unrolls it, and holds it open so lamplight glows on the papyrus. I mean to look away but my gaze follows the lines like bees follow the scent of blooms to flowers: I don't look because I want to win by cheating; I look because it is a Fives court and I have trained for years to study everything about the Fives.

"How did you get this?" I ask. "The administrators and engineers are meant to be irreproachable, on pain of death."

"The administrator Lord Perikos had a favored son, the child of a concubine I grant you, but you of all people should know how a man can favor his concubine and her children above all proper sense and reason, Jessamy."

I shut my eyes, because I don't want to see, but it just makes the vision clearer: the prince spasming; the king stabbing the youth; the spark....

"The boy died under mysterious circumstances in the service of Prince Temnos. Lord Perikos was not satisfied with the king's explanation. Thus Perikos has become a willing accomplice in our plan to strengthen Efea by ridding ourselves of a dangerously ineffective king."

Kal steps between me and the scroll. "Jes, you don't have to do this."

But his frown mirrors the bitter stain of complicity spreading across my heart.

24

I **stand atop the** victory tower clutching the victor's ribbon in my hand, and I hate myself as the crowd roars approval. Spider has returned a hero. They don't know she has cheated to win.

But I know.

When I climb down the ladder into the undercourt I don't want to look the other adversaries in the eye but I do it because I must. If shame could turn my heart to dust I would already be a walking corpse. Near to weeping, I drink the royal nectar even though I don't deserve it.

I am trapped, and for once in my life I see no path through these Rings.

Four Garon stewards wait in the undercourt to escort me to the Garon Palace balcony.

"Spider! Spider!" call the people as we pass along the wide corridors. Some among the crowd wear a lacework web on their garments instead of ribbons, in my honor. I glimpse a face, a bearded man who looks my way, surprised to see me, and quickly ducks out of view.

What is Sergeant Demos of the spider scouts doing here in Saryenia when he should be with the Royal Army?

As we enter the Garon balcony I keep looking for Tana but it is Darios who comes forward.

"You ran well," he says. "You were conservative on Traps but I think that was wise given the weeks you've been traveling. You were a little unsteady on your landings."

Nothing in his serious and grief-stricken expression suggests he suspects the trial was rigged. Tana's death, Dusty's kidnapping, and Mis's abrupt departure have distracted everyone in the stable. I haven't even had time to ask if anyone knows where Inarsis went, since he didn't go overseas with Lord Thynos, or if there's been news of Thynos's marriage.

Lord Gargaron rises from his chair. Menoë and Kalliarkos are seated on either side of him: I recognize the towering ribbon-laced architecture of her hair. Even though Kal stares resolutely straight ahead, I know he knows I've just walked in because I can sense him as acutely as if we are touching. A bitter smile brushes his lips, mirror to my own feelings. My heart still pounds from the exertion of the trial and yet this victory tastes so poisonous.

"Ah, Spider." Gargaron beckons. "There is someone here who wishes you to greet him."

"Spider! I knew you would win!" Prince Temnos pops up from the fourth chair. His delighted smile breaks like sunlight through clouds, tugging a smile out of me.

"My lord." I drop to one knee before him.

He wears a long court jacket made of brown silk, embroidered with shimmering silver threads in the shape of a spider's web. "Come, come! I'm going to show you off!"

He yanks me forward to the railing. His head doesn't even reach my shoulder and so there we stand, the brawny adversary and the frail prince. Seeing us, the crowd begins to sing:

The general's valiant daughter will fight for Efea,
She'll fight for Efea, and win!

Many wave brown banners sewn with a spider's web as they shout, "Spider! Spider!" and "Long life to the prince!"

"My gracious mother allows me to attend the Fives every week with Cousin Menoë and my companions! She says it is good for the people to see me and know I am a generous prince."

I glance around to see his gaggle of highborn comrades wriggling like eager puppies, waiting for Temnos to give them permission to come forward and greet me.

He tugs on my arm to pull my attention back to him. "Is Orchid back too? She is my favorite. She tells me the best jokes and feeds me sweets whenever I want them!"

A heavenward glance is my only outlet. Of course Amaya is his favorite.

He chatters on, oblivious to my silence. "I have been practicing since you have been gone, Spider! I'm very good now. I defeat all my companions. You have to come run a trial against me and I wager I will defeat you!" He giggles, but at the same moment gives me a canny sidelong glance to gauge my reaction, and I realize he too is wearing a mask, pretending to innocence and ignorance.

I squeeze his hand daringly, and he squeezes back as his lips turn up in a secret smile that acknowledges us as conspirators.

Menoë glides forward to stand on the other side of Prince Temnos. "Cousin, would you like to announce the distribution of bread? The people await your generosity."

He raises both arms. The noise of the crowd bursts, then quiets with an uneasy anticipation that presses on my senses more as tension than as excitement. The air itself seems ready to explode but whether into ecstatic celebration or riot I cannot tell.

Below, four Challengers race through a trial but no one is looking at them. The people in the crowd have turned to eye the stairs. I am impressed by their discipline, hungry people remaining in their places as vendors begin to walk along the aisles passing out loaves of bread.

"Kalliarkos, go forward," says Gargaron. "Join your sister at the railing."

"Yes, yes!" cries Temnos, bouncing on his toes. "Cousin Kalliarkos, you can stand with us now you are back. Everyone says you are a hero too! Even if you aren't a very good adversary."

Ouch. There is a dagger in the boy, isn't there? Or maybe he's just been taking lessons from Menoë.

I take a step back as Kalliarkos walks forward. His gaze meets mine, the slightest upward tilt of his glance like he is rolling his eyes at Temnos's comment. I give the barest nod as I make way for him, acknowledging our shared promise that whatever comes we will not doubt each other. It's all I have to cling to at this moment with the filthy cheat a bone in my throat. I will not let their machinations sour my feelings for him. We did not ask for this. We will not be destroyed by it.

As he takes his place I know that just as the crowd sees him and his sister standing on either side of their cousin, reminding everyone they are royal cousins, the crowd also sees me within arm's reach of the young lord rumored to be my lover.

Guard your victor's ribbons carefully and you can do very well for yourself, Gargaron told me.

As the crowd tears into its bread the cheering breaks out again, banners waving, shouts and cries hailing Lady Menoë, Prince Temnos, Kalliarkos the hero of Pellucidar Lake, and even me, the spider, standing in my ordinary brown behind the blazing colors of the highborn.

"Do you like the spider-web banners, Kal?" Menoë says over the head of Temnos. "We had our own people infiltrate the audience and wave the first ones. Then the fashion took off. But our little Prince Temnos here made the fashion for clothing sewn with webs popular by appearing in them every week. What a clever boy he is!"

"I don't like it when you speak over me in that tone, Cousin Menoë," the boy objects. "You sound very condescending. I don't really think you like me. I don't think you like my gracious mother either, even though you pretend you do. Where did Spider go? Now she is back I want her to stand next to me, not you."

Menoë whips her fan so fast back and forth in front of her face that it blurs. "Why is it all the men in my life want nothing more than to talk about you, Spider? But if it keeps Kal happy then I suppose it doesn't matter."

I flush.

"What does Cousin Kalliarkos have to do with it?" asks Temnos sharply. "Isn't he going back to the army?"

"Of course he is!" Menoë's bright smile is such a lie I am amazed it doesn't strangle her.

No wonder Garon Palace has taken the little prince under its wing. Invalid he may be, but he is a threat to their plans, the only other obvious heir. Everything nags at me like a threat, after days and days of waiting for an attack. That's why I can't help but notice a subtle shift along the outer aisles of the Fives court as men with the bearing of soldiers move into view, walking in twos and threes like casual Fives-goers, but really more like they are infiltrating the crowd.

Probably I'm just imagining things, but I take a step up behind Kal, and nudge his leg with my knee.

"Are those men moving along the aisles off-duty soldiers hired by Garon Palace to make sure there are no riots as the bread is distributed?" I murmur.

He follows my gaze along the terraces of seats that surround the court. His brows tighten as he examines the men filtering in through the crowd. They are all Patrons, of course, and I realize many have long hair and beards, which are rare in Efea.

I whisper urgently, "I saw Sergeant Demos when I was walking here after my trial. Since he didn't travel with us, why has a spider scout abandoned his spider and come here?"

"Something isn't right." In the intense focus of his eyes and the readiness of his shoulders he looks like an adversary studying Rings as he decides which path to take. He doesn't hesitate at all. "Step up to the railing, Jes."

As we swap places he retreats to where Gargaron sits and bends to speak to his uncle, whose smile of approval at the crowd's cheers turns to a frown whose contours send a shudder through my flesh. Gargaron shades his face with a hand as he scans the seats.

Kal returns to the railing. "Jes, we are making a tactical

retreat. Menoë, you and Jes will escort Prince Temnos out of here as quickly and quietly as possible. I'll leave by a different route. Uncle Gar will remain here to keep attention on the balcony for as long as possible."

At once he leaves the railing and heads for the back.

Temnos's eyes grow wide with enthusiasm. "Are we having a dangerous adventure?"

"Yes, Your Highness," I say as I take his hand. "We are, and you must obey me without question, just as you do when I am training you to become an adversary. We have to practice sneaking out of the Fives court without anyone noticing."

"Oh, that's easy! My gracious father taught me how to do that long ago because he said someone might try to assassinate me. I will just change clothes with my dear companion Lord Elotas and he will pretend to be me and I will pretend to be a servant."

His blithe mention of assassination really stuns me, as if that was ordinary supper table conversation between him and his father, and probably it was.

I smile with false cheer. "That is supremely clever, Your Highness. We shall implement your tactics at once."

"You are a supremely adept flatterer, Spider," mutters Menoë. "No wonder Kal can't resist you."

"In fact," I add as inspiration strikes, "Lady Menoë should escort Lord Elotas, because everyone will expect her and you to leave together. Then you and I will make our way to Garon Palace on foot. Can you walk that far, Your Highness?"

"Of course I can!" he says stoutly, although I have my doubts. But he's so thin I can carry him, and no one will remark on a Commoner girl carrying a Patron boy on her back.

"Oh, very well," says Menoë with a spiteful look. "It's not as bad a plan as it could be. Just make sure you bring him to the servants' gate, Spider. Don't try to enter through the main gate as if you belong there."

"Of course, my lady." My obedient smile annoys her, just as I hoped it would.

"Jessamy." Gargaron calls me over. He sits in his chair surveying the court—one of the adversaries is spinning through Rings and will soon reach the victory tower—with the same matchless arrogance he displays when he knows he holds all the power in his hands. "I fear these men you've noticed may be soldiers encircling the Fives court to prevent us from leaving. It would be just like Kliatemnos to cut our feet out from under us by arresting my niece and nephew and charging them with treason."

"Do you think the king suspects?"

"He's a suspicious sort of man. It is of crucial importance that you keep Prince Temnos away from both king and queen if we wish to succeed, and if you wish to keep Kalliarkos alive. Do you understand?"

"Do you not fear you may be a target by staying behind, my lord? You have only a few guardsmen to protect you."

"I have the gods' righteous judgment on my side. Anyway, to show fear to an anxious dog will make it bite. Kliatemnos has no proof of any conspiracy and thus cannot prosecute me."

"Couldn't he just kill you, my lord? For it seems to me that the highborn have the means to rid themselves of inconvenient rivals. Accidents happen."

His hard gaze examines my expression just a little too long, a provocation I can't look away from even though I should have kept my mouth shut. Then he relaxes into the thin smile that makes me stiffen before I remember I must never challenge him openly. He knows it too.

"It is not so easy to kill a palace lord as it is to dispose of less noble but equally inconvenient rivals. Remember that, Jessamy, for I am certain you do not think kindly of me when you lie down at night to sleep. I would think less of you if I thought you did. Now take Prince Temnos to Princess Berenise. We need him in our custody in order to succeed. Go!"

The curtained shelters at the back of the balcony offer a convenient place to change. By the time I strip out of my Fives gear, pull on a simple linen sheath dress, and cover my hair with a scarf, Menoë and the false Temnos with the rest of the prince's companions have already departed.

I look around for Kal and find him now dressed in a

groom's uniform, while the man whose clothing he's taken wears Kal's rich clothing. Strip the silk and gold away from Kalliarkos and I still can't stop looking at him, because it isn't his rank and riches that make him so striking.

"Where are you going?" I ask in a low voice. My hand drifts near his but in this public place I dare not be the first to make contact.

"I'm going to scout. We can't know anything until we see what is really going on in the streets."

"How will you get around safely? With the city in such tumult a man alone on the street will be vulnerable."

"If a man has allies, then he is never alone." The charming smile that his uncle and sister have long dismissed as lightweight looks like strength now, a means to reach out and connect with people instead of grinding them under his heel as the others do. "Do you remember the poet Ro-emnu?"

Despite the circumstances a heat blushes my cheeks, but of course he's too focused on our dire situation to notice.

"Ro owes me for getting him out of prison. Once I get word to him, he will raise a network of Efeans who can move through the city without being noticed. Then I have to secure Garon Palace and make sure Grandmama and all our people are safe."

He raises my hand to his mouth and kisses my knuckles. I close my eyes as the world falls away and all that remains is the precise pressure of his lips on my skin.

"Jes?"

I open my eyes. His gaze holds me as if I am precious, and in that moment I know I am.

"Don't go to Garon Palace," he says. "If this really is Kli-atemnos going after us, then Garon Palace is the first place that will be searched."

"I'll take Prince Temnos to the Heart Tavern in the Warrens."

"Yes, good, that's where Ro took me after I got him out of prison and where I intend to bring anyone from our household who has escaped. I'll meet you there."

Without hesitation he leans in and kisses me, right in front of everyone. As we part, my heart turns over and then slams around in my chest a hundred times. I don't want to leave him, but soldiers and adversaries do what needs to be done, and my duty right now is to get Temnos to safety. So I let him go, and with a last look at me he strides to the balcony exit and vanishes from my sight.

"Spider! Psst! Spider! We need to hurry!"

A very rude masked servant boy tugs at my arm, then tips up his mask to show his face. "Come on!"

"My lord Temnos, is that you?" I whisper, pretending surprise.

"This is the most exciting thing I have ever done!"

"My lord, you must not speak. Every word out of your mouth betrays that you belong to the palace."

"It does? Why is that?"

"Highborn Patrons speak Saroese a bit differently than other people do, my lord. I will stop calling you 'my lord.' Do I have your permission?"

"Yes! Yes! Call me Temnos." He grabs my hand. "Let's go! We don't want to get left behind!"

We've stayed too long already. I look to the front of the balcony where Gargaron sits as relaxed as if it is any routine day at the Fives.

"Keep your servant's mask on." I snag a discarded mask for myself and pull it down over my face, then grab a tray of half-eaten food and a full waste bucket.

The boy recoils. "That stinks!"

"I'll carry the waste bucket, but you must carry the tray just as if you are really a servant."

"No, no! I'll carry the waste bucket. No one will ever suspect Prince Temnos would do that, will they?" His grin heartens me.

We hurry past the main aisle to the servants' passage along the back wall of the court. I hear the tramp of feet, men approaching from the right.

"We'd better go to the left," Temnos whispers.

"No, wiser to do the opposite of what they expect. Keep walking as if you have no idea what is going on. Keep your shoulders slumped."

He's a good soldier and makes no complaint. We head toward the sound. Around the curve of the outer wall marches a file of men who absolutely must be soldiers dressed in civilian dress that, up close, cannot hide the bulky armor they wear under humble linen jackets and loose cloth tunics. Just as they start eyeing us too closely, Temnos lets a little urine slop from the bucket.

"It's so heavy," he whines.

A covered bucket reeking of urine and feces is the perfect disguise.

"Cursed clumsy brat!" yells one of the men.

"Shut up and keep your mind on the job," snaps their commander. "Move! Our target should be just ahead."

They are headed for the Garon balcony.

In a strange and entirely unwanted flash of feeling, I realize I admire Gargaron's courage in staying behind while the rest of us escape.

Temnos and I scurry on as shouts break out behind us. I have to keep reminding myself to walk at a brisk but not panicked pace. We make our way down from the high terrace by stairs that lead to an area outside the court reserved for a kitchen that serves only the highborn. I've not been back here before so we stumble around a bit, getting in people's way, although I do manage to dump the tray of shrimp. Servants are still cooking in the kitchen while others are peering out at the square where carriages wait.

"What's going on? Look there! Isn't that Prince Temnos's carriage? Is he leaving already, before the last trial?"

A harried woman steps in my path. "Get that stinking bucket out of the kitchen. The latrines are that way!"

Several male servants stumble in from the court. One has a purpling bruise on his right eye from a punch. "There's a disturbance up in the highborn terraces. I hear a rumor foreign soldiers are loose in the city, maybe some kind of uprising."

I nudge Temnos along.

Going out the back brings us into an open space with latrines dug on one side and a wall separating this area from the square. With a grunt, Temnos sets down the bucket, shaking from the effort of carrying it all this way.

"Now what, Spider?"

"Hush."

"What's going on?"

"Quiet! Get down!"

He's not quite tall enough to see over the wall but I am.

And I wish I were not.

The square has become a scene of chaotic confusion, people scattering everywhere as men run after the prince's gaily decorated carriage, surround it, and force its driver to halt. The servants attending the carriages of other lords cower or hide.

The assailants wrench back the curtains. Amid screams, the youth dressed in the prince's golden jacket and keldi is

410

dragged out of the carriage. His companions leap after him. Unarmed, they throw themselves over his body to protect him. Some are stabbed while others are yanked out of the way as the attackers step in to cut down the helpless Lord Elotas in a flurry of blades.

25

Lady Menoë appears, fighting against a man attempting to pull her out of her carriage. As I brace myself to see her murdered beside the boy, Sergeant Demos appears. He signals orders to the men, and they lower their weapons and push her back inside. The bloody corpse of the dead boy is slung into the carriage while his dead companions are thrown into a second carriage where Menoë's women cower. The two carriages are driven away in the direction of the King's Hill, surrounded by armed men.

I don't have time to feel anything. I have to act.

By now spectators are beginning to rush from the court like folk fleeing fire.

"Temnos, we are going to take off our masks and join

the crowd. You have to stick right with me, hold my hand the whole time so I don't lose you."

"What happened, Spider? Your face is like ash. You look like you swallowed a bug."

"Don't call me Spider, Temnos. Say Jes if you must." I take his hand and we hasten past the latrines and out a back gate where worried guards ask, "Do you know what's going on?"

"No," I say, slipping past, "but if I were you I would clear everyone out and hurry home."

"What do you mean?" they call after me, but Temnos and I slide easily into the streaming channels of people. We're jostled and shoved. Someone steps hard on my foot. Temnos yelps in outrage as he is elbowed.

"Keep moving," I say, my fingers clamped over his frail wrist.

"Where are we going?" he asks in a preternaturally calm voice, the tone of a person who has finally stripped off his mask to reveal the real face beneath. "Are you trying to save me or hurt me, Spider?"

The accusation stings, and yet how can I fault him? "I promise you, I'm trying to save you. But if you prefer I will let you go on your own way, alone."

He considers in silence as we stride along. He really thinks it over, the poor boy. What considerations whirl through his head I cannot fathom, and yet to him these are normal concerns

413

that he has been taught by his father to evaluate: Who may wish to kill me? Whom can I trust?

After a bit he shakes his head. "I'll stay with you. I don't know how to get around the city by myself."

As we weave in and out of the masses of people headed out of the Fives court square and down into the city, I consider the paths that are unfolding. This can't be the king's attack on Garon Palace: Why would Kliatemnos and Serenissima try to kill the son they have been keeping alive with magic? It doesn't make sense.

What if this is a cunning plan by Gargaron to rid the king of his heir and blame it on interlopers? But that path is a dead end. As Princess Berenise said, Temnos will likely be out of their way due to his illness once no priests are ordered to revive him with sparks stolen from other people. This isn't worth the risk.

The presence of Sergeant Demos tells me everything I need to know. No one else saw it coming because they don't want to believe it.

Menoë and Nikonos have made their move.

I should have insisted Kal stay with me and never let him go off so confidently by himself into the maelstrom, still believing he can trust his sister.

As the crowd masses into a boiling, buzzing, frightened swarm trying to get out of the square, we are slammed from behind by the crush. Temnos stumbles and goes down onto his knees. He's almost trampled but I manage to hoist him up on my back. He scarcely weighs anything; I've trained with heavier sacks of sand over my shoulders. I batter a way out of the bottleneck and down a street, then follow a lesser trickle of citizens into the relative quiet of the Lantern Market.

Vendors are folding down their awnings and closing up their stalls, covering up stacks of mouth-watering melon and jars of sweet-smelling date wine. News travels fast. People are quick to crawl into the nearest refuge where they can hope to weather the storm.

We pause under the portico of one of the theaters to catch our breath. All the theaters are closed on Fivesday, when the city trials are run, so no one pays us any mind as they hurry past.

Temnos clings to me, arms wrapped around my waist. He isn't crying but his face is so pale, trembling as he presses his cheek against my arm.

"You're doing very well," I say to encourage him.

"I know. I'm very scared."

"I'm scared too," I say even as I pack my terror as into a jar and seal it away. Nothing can be allowed to trouble my concentration, not now. "Temnos, we need to find your father and mother. They are the only ones I trust to make sure you are safe. Your father made a very clever plan to protect you by switching clothes with Lord Elotas. Did he perhaps choose a rendezvous site should some disaster overtake the city? Some-place away from the royal palaces?"

415

"Oh, yes! I should have told you before this. If ever disaster overtakes me, I'm supposed to meet my gracious father at the Playwrights' Pavilion in the Archives. I know a secret way in. I'm thirsty, Spider."

"Can you make it a ways farther? I don't have any money so I can't buy you anything."

"Can't we just take whatever we want?" he asks with a bewildered expression. "I am the prince!"

"Shhh! But you are acting the role of a servant, remember?"

"That's right!" He slaps the mask back over his face, but even so he forgets to speak as a servant would. His voice is bold, thoughtless, and so sure. "Masks are how we know who is a servant and who is a master. That's what my gracious father says. He says that back when my honored ancestors first came to this land, the Efean rulers wore masks as a sign of honor and authority. So by making our servants wear masks we remind ourselves that we Saroese now rule and Efeans serve us. Just like you serve me, Spider."

My hand twitches as I suck down the urge to slap him. He's only repeating the world he sees around him. He's just a child. Yet his comment claws at me as we stride through the Lantern District because it reminds me of the painting I saw in the Heart Tavern. It reminds me of Ro-emnu's righteous anger.

It reminds me that Efea and Efeans once ruled themselves.

The streets are slowly emptying out as news of the

disturbance spreads, although I spy no foreign soldiers searching for us. Temnos is starting to lag, so as soon as we cross under the West Gate of the Lantern District I kneel and again have him crawl onto my back. I am a mule, after all. The word has never felt more caustic as I carry an invalid prince through the streets to save his life when I have come to doubt it would ever occur to him to take any action to save mine.

Everything changes once we reach the Avenue of Triumphs. It swarms with uniformed men wearing the bird tabards of the Saroese kingdoms. From partway up the slope of the King's Hill we can see across the city the ships that fly the flags of our enemies anchored in the twin harbors: the hawk of East Saro and the peacock of Saro-Urok.

"We are being invaded," Temnos whispers into my ear as his spindly arms cling around my neck, almost choking me. "Where is the Royal Fleet? Where is the Royal Army, Spider?"

"Maybe the invasion on the Eastern Reach was a decoy all along," I say, because there is no use in trying to hide the ugly truth from him. Like Kalliarkos, he is already in the viper's pit. "If so, it worked perfectly to draw the main army away from Saryenia and the royal palaces so this invasion by sea could happen with less resistance."

"Will the invaders kill me?" He doesn't sound frightened, more resigned, and that is saddest of all: that he knows his part in this precarious game. He's just a child. I'm sorry for the hateful thoughts I've had about him.

"I am sure the king has a plan in place to get you out of the city."

The Archives aren't far, and he and I are so very unimportant-looking that we rate not a second glance. When we reach the monumental entrance of the huge library we find no foreign soldiers on the prowl, nor any guards at all, which troubles me as I set him down and study the entrance with its wide marble steps and high portico. But we've already chosen our path through this obstacle, so I decide to keep going.

"I've never been inside, so you'll have to lead the way, Temnos."

He takes my hand. "Come along, Spider. I know exactly where we are going."

The Archives are a place of learning, founded at the order of Serenissima the First during the tenth year of her joint reign with her brother Kliatemnos the First. Here all the books and scrolls containing all the knowledge of the world have been collected, and Archivists study and write about every endeavor of human life and unravel the mysteries of the world as well. According to royal decree the Archives are freely available to all. In reality Commoners are welcome here only as servants.

Temnos limps, drooping. He's exhausted but gamely courageous, a true adversary. Under the vast stone entryway we creep like mice into a storehouse of grain. Statues of the royal couples who have ruled Efea in the past one hundred years stare down upon us from high plinths: Kliatemnos and Serenissima the First, known as the Saviors, who safely guided refugees over the Fire Sea to a safe landing in Efea; Kliatemnos and Serenissima the Second, known as patrons of the arts; Kliatemnos the Third and his niece and queen, Serenissima the Benevolent; their son and daughter who married and reigned together as Kliatemnos and Serenissima, the fourth of the name. These last two are the elder brother and sister of Princess Berenise, and parents of the current reigning king and queen.

Past the entry lies a great courtyard whose marble pavement is carved with the words of the ancient sages. We tread upon their wisdom as Prince Temnos guides me to the first of several pavilions, built as a series of meeting rooms situated around a central open area.

"This way," says Temnos. "The warden of this pavilion is a particular friend of Scholar Thanises. My gracious father comes here sometimes in secret to argue about which playwrights are the best and which are rated too highly. The warden has a private office in the back, with a secret door...."

A crack like a board snapping startles me.

"Hurry," I say, for now I hear the deadly tread of footsteps coming closer and I fear being trapped inside the pavilion with no way out.

He lets go of my hand, runs along the portico to the back

corner where a door stands open, and dodges inside. Just as I reach the door I glance back to see a phalanx of soldiers enter. No civilian clothes disguise their armor; they wear the hawk of East Saro.

Praying that I have not escorted the prince into a trap, I walk straight into a sticky pool of drying blood.

Temnos stands with arms lax at his sides and a slack expression as he stares down at the corpse of King Kliatemnos. The king's torso is a mosaic of red wounds. Thanises is bent back over a chair with his throat cut. A drop of blood rolls off the scholar's pale hand and spatters on the marble floor. A man wearing an Archivist badge lies sprawled under a table that's piled with open books and a scatter of scrolls.

The chamber is large, with couches, chairs, and several more tables all piled with books and scrolls and scraps of paper someone has been piecing together. Statues of famous playwrights line the walls. It has no obvious outlet other than the door we came through, and windows set into the thick walls higher than my head.

I grab Temnos's shoulder. "Do you know where the secret door is?"

He doesn't answer. His gaze has the slightly wild look of someone about to collapse.

"We'll find a place to hide. They must have killed the king and now they're searching."

420

"They're searching for me," he whispers. "They're going to kill me."

"I should have done what Kal told me," I murmur. "We'd be safe at the Heart Tavern by now, whatever Gargaron and Berenise have planned. Oh gods I should never have brought you here. Temnos, we've got to get out of the Archives. I know a safe place. A truly safe place."

"The secret door is by the statue of Serenissima the Scribbler. Here." Temnos pokes at a tapestry. The fabric gives way. I yank it aside to find a narrow passage built into the wall.

"This isn't a secret door," I say.

"It is if you don't know it's there!"

Footsteps tramp closer. I have no choice except to shove him into the passage and let the tapestry fall over the gap.

"Where does this go?"

A musty smell gets up in my nose. I can barely see my hands, much less the prince, who has already taken several steps away from me down the black passage.

"It runs along the outer wall all the way to the Head Archivist's office in the Hall of Scrolls. There's a secret door like this one letting into the warden's office of each pavilion. It's so the wardens can bring scrolls in and out to visitors without going through the courtyard and exposing the paper to sun or rain."

"Good Goat!" exclaims a man's thunderously loud voice as

421

a group of people clomps into the chamber we've just left. "Did that dry, dull stick Kliatemnos really have that much blood in him?"

"You can let go of my arm now," says a sneering, haughty voice I recognize as Lady Menoë's. "I won't faint."

"Oh, I never thought you would, for I know what an unyielding heart you hide under that lovely exterior, dearest Menoë," drawls Prince Nikonos.

The collaborators, unmasked!

I have to get Temnos as far away from here as fast as possible before they discover the passage.

The huge Hall of Scrolls is famous for being a vast maze of aisles and cubbyholes and side alcoves, as convoluted as the Ribbon Market, a good place to hide. I squeeze past Temnos, grab his hand, and pull him along as we hurry down the dim corridor.

Suddenly a lamp appears, illuminating Queen Serenissima herself hurrying down the passage in our direction.

"Gracious Mother!" Temnos cries, then claps a hand over his mouth, aware that he spoke too loudly.

"Your Highness." I press fist to chest and bow. "I have Prince Temnos. Your Highness, the king has been murdered, and I fear a conspiracy between Prince Nikonos and Lady Menoë. You can't go back to the Playwrights' Pavilion."

"Of course not." Her face seems wax-pallid as she looks past me to Temnos, half hidden behind my body. He's so small, and he's breathing hard, his lungs taxed to the point of breaking. "You must come with me, Temnos. I've been looking for you. I hoped you would remember your father's secret plan, and so you have, clever boy. You are so very much Kliatemnos's child."

"Where did you come from?" I ask as I realize she appeared so abruptly she can't have approached us from the Hall of Scrolls, because the passage runs straight along the entire length of the wall and so we would have seen her light much sooner.

She pushes Temnos in front of her. Her lamp's golden aura of light spills along the wall as I watch them hurry away from me, shadows curling around her.

There is blood on the back of her dress.

Her hands are bloody.

They vanish down a side passage leading into one of the pavilions. I scramble after her, but before charging into the space she just entered, I peek past the passage's concealing tapestry. Beyond lies another warden's chamber. This one displays nothing but masks: savage cat masks, crocodiles with toothy jaws hinged wide, joyful butterflies.

She sets the lamp on a table and beckons to the soldiers who await her. "Take us to Prince Nikonos."

Prince Temnos grabs her hand and says, "Gracious Mother, I'm so glad we found you."

"Yes, come with me, Temnos. It will all be over soon."

She and the soldiers hurry out, and I race into the room on their trail, only to stop dead as my eye catches on a rumple of clothing in one corner of the room. The body of Lord Elotas has been tossed on the marble floor like so much discarded trash.

Temnos's mother knew. She is part of the conspiracy.

But there cannot be two queens.

I don't even know what I can do but I can't bear it. I walked him straight into the trap. I grab the lamp off the table and dash back into the passage.

When I reach the tapestry that opens into the warden's chamber of the Playwrights' Pavilion I set the lamp on the floor, lie flat, and ease up the bottom of the fabric. No one is looking my way. Nikonos has a hand on Menoë's elbow and her face is twisted in a grimace of pain. He presses harder, and laughs when she still doesn't cry out.

"Your ability to endure pain is remarkable, dearest Menoë," he says in a silky voice whose malice makes goose bumps rise on my arms.

She doesn't like him at all. She hates him.

How did I not see it? Everyone told me I was wrong, and yet I refused to see it.

I hated Menoë because she is Lord Gargaron's willing

424

accomplice and because I hate Gargaron for what he did to my family. I hated her because she married my father, who didn't even have the decency to scorn and deride her as a woman who could never take the place of my mother.

But she is not the villain. She was the spy placed in Nikonos's camp by Garon Palace.

And Nikonos's camp has found her out.

The queen enters, twisting Temnos's arm to force him forward just as Nikonos is wrenching Menoë's in the most agonizing way possible. She shoves the boy toward Nikonos. "Here he is, as I promised. We will have healthy heirs, not this useless weakling."

Nikonos draws his sword and stabs Temnos through the gut, then again under the ribs, and a third time with a merciful slash across the throat.

Free, Menoë scrambles for the door, only to have Queen Serenissima grab her by the hair and yank her to a halt so hard that Menoë crashes to her knees. The queen does not even look at the last twitches of her dying son as the stolen spark that kept him alive fades from his body. All she can see is Menoë kneeling at her feet.

"Oh, Cousin, you purred and laughed and pretended to confide all your secrets to me, but you never told me the truth, that your first husband caught you in bed with another man—your own cousin Nikonos!—and punished you as you deserved."

Nikonos laughs. "You were so contemptibly easy to seduce. I'd hoped my good friend Stratios would kill you and save me the trouble, but he had too much pity."

"If you call what he did to me merciful," spits Menoë.

She slams her shoulder into the queen's legs and jerks out of her grasp. Serenissima grabs at her again and where her hand fastens on Menoë's dress the fabric rips, tearing apart to expose Menoë's skin. The soldiers hastily avert their eyes, as it is forbidden for lowborn men to see the bare flesh of a highborn woman. But I can't look away.

Menoë's torso is hatched with fierce white scarring, and her right breast has been mutilated and has healed over in a mass of shiny seams like someone chopped bits out of it before giving up.

"I'm surprised your new husband can bear even to touch you, as grotesque as you are," says Nikonos with a harsh laugh, "but I suppose a baker's son isn't choosy."

"His behavior is closer to the gods' than yours will ever be! His is the courage and intelligence that forges our army. You are a spear made of reeds, an ornament for show."

He slaps her.

She doesn't back down in the face of death and humiliation. "You and everyone at the court of East Saro knew Stratios was a cruel man who loved to torment me. You seduced me with pretended kindness and sympathy because I was naïve and unhappy. You are the one who should be ashamed, not me. I'm tired of being told I should be ashamed that people abused me!"

Everyone is enthralled by Nikonos's towering rage and Menoë's imperious contempt.

When the Rings open a path, you have to take it.

I dash out and dump my lamp of burning oil over the piles of books and scrolls.

Flames leap up, gathering strength. I throw the lamp at the queen as hard as I can, and it hits her right in the forehead. Screeching, she releases Menoë, who sees me and bolts my way. I grab another lamp, throw it at the soldiers, its hot oil spattering as they flinch back. Burning pages float as ash into the air. I tip over tables to block their path, then shove Menoë past the tapestry. We race down the passage. When she seems determined to run all the way to the Hall of Scrolls I grab her roughly and drag her into the warden's room of the Masks Pavilion.

We stumble to a panting halt beneath the yawning crocodile masks. She tugs the ripped fabric of her dress up to cover what cannot be unseen. Her gaze catches on the dead youth, and her jaw sets.

"Stupid creature," she mutters, and I don't know if she means Lord Elotas or Prince Temnos. Or me. "We have to run down to the Hall of Scrolls. We'll have a better chance of hiding there."

"Running to the Hall of Scrolls is what they'll expect us to do. We're going to crawl out a window, hide on the roof until nightfall, and creep out over the wall."

"How are we supposed to get out windows too high even for men to reach? Much less onto the roof? And over the wall, at night? It can't be done."

"I'm an adversary, Lady Menoë. I can do it, and without leaving any trail. So if you trust me to save you, tell me now."

26

We lie flat atop the roof listening to the shouts and stomps of people searching the Hall of Scrolls, the pavilions, and the Archival warehouses. For a long time I brace myself for ladders thrown up against the pavilion and soldiers swarming over to find and kill us, but instead we hear scholars being arrested on suspicion of harboring a fugitive. Carriages arrive and depart, taking with them our queen and new king.

My heart is a mire of self-loathing. Why didn't I listen to Kal and go straight to the Heart Tavern? How could I have led that poor child to his death?

It's easier to lash out at Menoë.

"How did you get those scars?" We lie side by side, like lovers in a bed, speaking in intimate whispers.

"Your father asked me the same question. I liked that he didn't pretend not to see them."

"I'm sure he's seen worse. How did you get them?"

"Why do you think I killed my first husband?"

"Because he caught you in bed with your cousin?"

"They always blame the woman, never the man who led her there."

"You didn't have to go."

"What if I told you Prince Stratios was a cruel man who all his life was able to get away with brutalizing and murdering whomever he wanted?"

I wish I could rub Temnos's blood all over her highborn face. "I'd say he's no different from the rest of your kind."

But she's not listening to me as she presses a hand to her mutilated breast. "I meant to be obedient because Grandmama told me we needed the alliance. I would endure much more for her sake."

"Then why did you kill Prince Stratios?"

"Because I discovered he was lying to me. He wasn't going to ally with Grandmama. He was colluding with Nikonos all along, plotting to help him take the throne from Kliatemnos." An expression like that of a person who can't look away from a rotting corpse deadens her beautiful eyes. "Nikonos knew how bitterly unhappy I was at East Saro's court, how alone and friendless, how vulnerable. He seduced me by pretending to be a sympathetic ear, but all along it was part of a plan to disgrace me in order to make sure I could never make a bid for the throne. He'd made a wager with Stratios and his foul circle of companions that he could prove me a whore. And I was, wasn't I?"

The last thing I want is to feel pity for her, but I do. I pat her hand to show sympathy, and she flinches away like my touch scorches her.

I want to shout, *I don't like you either!* but I don't. Instead I ask, "Why didn't you tell King Kliatemnos that his brother was conspiring against him with the enemy?"

"I did tell Kliatemnos, and Serenissima too."

"You didn't suspect Serenissima was in on the plot?"

"No, I never did," she replies bitterly. "Why would I? Her own son is the heir."

"*Was* the heir," I mutter, but she isn't listening. She's already forgotten about him.

"They refused to believe the ruler of East Saro was their enemy because they were the ones who had arranged the two marriage alliances, me to Stratios, and Nikonos to Stratios's younger sister. Afterward Nikonos convinced them I was nothing more than a jealous and vindictive viper who murdered both my husband and his young bride out of spite and shame."

"You killed Nikonos's bride too?" It's my turn to flinch away from her.

"No, he just thinks I did. But I'm glad I killed Stratios and I only wish I had done it sooner."

431

"Why agree to marry into one of the other kingdoms at all, if marriage is so dangerous for a young, friendless bride at a foreign court?"

"Because that is the risk we have to take. You run the Fives, Spider. You have to take risks to win."

"What do you win?"

She stares at me like my words are gibberish, and of course they are.

What do they win? The ruling families of old Saro and conquered Efea win everything: the gold, the armies, the fleets, the land, the power.

"I don't want to talk about this with a mule like you who can't hope to understand. You aren't as special as you think you are just because Kal fancies himself in love with you—his big rebellion!"

The words don't even annoy me. I turn my head to look her right in the face, and I smile.

She stiffens and in a huffy whisper says, "Where are we going?"

"To the Warrens."

"You can't take me there!" She sucks in a breath as if someone has just kicked her in the gut. "That's a terrible, dangerous part of town!"

"You only think so because Commoners live there. Do you know what I think is a terrible, dangerous part of town? The part where a twelve-year-old boy is handed over by his own mother to be murdered, just so his uncle can claim the throne without fearing an innocent rival might grow up to become a man."

Her glare would kill a lesser adversary but I have lost all feeling and all fear. I am numb with rage and revulsion, much of it pointed right at myself. All I care about is reaching the Warrens and not thinking about whether Kalliarkos has survived the day. With this, my thoughts slam into a wall. I can't go any farther down that path.

The last of the afternoon passes, and the sun sets.

As soon as we get over the wall and onto the streets, we hide behind the pillars of a portico so Menoë can strip from the towering architecture of her hair all the wire rods, pins, extra braids, and ribbons that have turned it into a sculpture. Let free, her hair hangs silky smooth and straight down her back like the miraculous seaweed tresses of the goddess Hayiyin.

"I'll braid it while you strip all the finery from your gown. Use the pins and ribbons to repair the rips. Can you do it?"

She's trembling, having gotten sunburned and dehydrated from our time on the roof. "Of course I can do it! You must address me as 'my lady.'"

I want so much to slap her. Instead I take calming crane breaths, and discipline triumphs. "My lady, stow everything else in your sleeves in case we have a chance to exchange it for less conspicuous clothing."

To my relief she does as I ask. She's too smart not to.

Once we have finished, we scuttle along side streets until we reach the lantern-lit Avenue of Triumphs. I press her back into the shadows while I gaze along its length, trying to figure where and when to cross. Oddly, Efeans swarm the boulevard in huge numbers, carrying jars of water on their heads or pushing wheelbarrows filled with bricks and stacks of ceramic pots and bowls. People wearing the white belt that identifies them as individuals willing to exchange sex for money sashay past the foreign soldiers guarding the intersections, distracting them with smiles. Street sweepers make their slow way as patrols on horseback get caught behind them, and while the soldiers shout at the old women to get out of the way, they don't hit them.

Whatever the invaders might be willing to do, it's clear the conspirators have commanded there shall be no violence. They don't want their city to burn down the first night they rule it.

"That's what's wrong with you Commoners," Menoë hisses. "You just give in without a fight. Look at them all, out and about as if nothing has happened, offering their wares to anyone who asks."

"If you think so, then you're not very observant." I am sure Ro and his allies are behind this influx of Efeans onto the streets. "Do you see any children? Do you see any food? That's all being kept safe behind walls. These people are both slowing down the military patrols and spying on them. If necessary, the bricks in their carts can become weapons."

She pauses, examining the avenue with new interest. "I never thought of that. How do we get across?"

With her hair braided into a single rope, her ripped clothing crudely pinned to hide her gruesome scars, and the decorative wings and eye paint wiped into oily smears on her skin, she no longer looks like a palace lady. But she is obviously a Patron, and as far as I can tell, all the Patrons have fled the streets, even the lowborn and servants. The moment we try to cross one of the monumental avenues a soldier will spot her as standing out from all the Efeans and foreigners, but the only way to reach the Warrens without circling down past the harbor where the enemy ships lie in wait is to cross the Avenue of Triumphs.

I scan the people on the boulevard and pick as my target a group of about ten women hauling bundles of palm fronds and baskets of reeds like they're headed to a building site. Waving at Menoë to stay back, I sidle onto the street and lag back through the foot traffic until the women reach me, splitting around me like river waters around a rock.

"Honored Ladies," I say quickly, before they are past, "I need your help to get the woman I am with to a safe haven."

They halt and make a show of shifting bundles and baskets, switching the heavier and lighter burdens between them, the sort of thing people do when they are carrying burdens a long distance. "If she's hiding she must be a Patron doma. Why would we help one of them?"

"Because Efea will rise."

A knife blade flashes next to me. Before I can throw up an arm to protect myself, the woman holding it slices through the string that binds her bundle of palm fronds, and they fall in a rustling noise to the street. Soldiers look around as one of the other women begins screeching at her companion in Saroese.

"Clumsy girl! Pick it up!"

The foreign soldiers don't know that Efeans never speak Saroese among themselves, and that her shouting therefore is a ruse to make them think it's an ordinary disagreement. They watch for a short while, because they're bored, but women disputing about the tasks of everyday life can't hold their interest. Making an exaggerated business of gathering up the fallen vegetation, the women kick the fronds closer and closer to the side of the street. Once the group drifts close enough it is simple for Menoë to slide out of the shadows into our midst. A woman shoves a disorganized mass of fronds into Menoë's arms, and she clutches them awkwardly, concealing her face, as we start walking again. I'm given a basket that clacks softly as it shifts, and when I peek beneath the linen cloth layered on top I find I am carrying a load of fish-gutting knives.

"Where do you need to go, Honored Sister?" asks the eldest of the women, speaking in Efean so Menoë cannot understand.

"The Heart Tavern, to meet Ro-emnu."

"Are you one of Ro's sweethearts?"

A few snicker, and one says, "Who is Ro? Oh! The poet!"

"No, I'm not one of his sweethearts."

My interrogator isn't satisfied. "What obligation do you owe to this doma?"

When I hesitate she orders us down a side street, marching past a loitering patrol of soldiers wearing the hawk of East Saro. She says, in Efean, "Speak, or we will hand you over to the invaders."

I can't think of anything except the truth. "She's my father's wife. My father is General Esladas."

At the name Esladas, Menoë glances toward me, because it's the only word she's so far understood. A strange emotion settles over the women like the ripple of a boat's wake through still waters. In their glances at me I see calculation, interest, suspicion, and disapproval.

My interlocutor looks me in the eye. "Honored Sister, I am called Ibi."

"I am Jessamy, Honored Lady."

"What circumstances bring you here I do not know, but if you wish it, we can bring you by yourself safely to the Heart Tavern and leave the doma to the mercy of her own people."

How tempting her offer sounds. How easy to lose Menoë and never be called to account for it, for I can lie and say I never saw her. Father's ties to Garon Palace severed with no blame attached to me.

But I will not be one of them. I will not act as they did. It's true I am half Saroese, for that is the heritage my father gave me. But I am not a Patron and I never want to be one, not anymore. Not after everything I have seen.

"It would dishonor my father's courage and loyalty to Efea to abandon her," I say, even as I wonder if she is pregnant and if it's true the child, if a boy, could become king in time. "Anyway, Lord Kalliarkos saved the life of the poet, and she is thereby included in the obligation Ro-emnu owes to Garon Palace."

"Very well."

Deep in my heart I sense my companion is pleased that I have chosen the Efean way of shared obligation rather than the selfish violence of those who conquered this land a hundred years ago.

In the districts where Patrons live all the gates are closed, but throughout the city enough Efeans walk the streets that soldiers on patrol take no notice of another group of Efean women busy about the never-ending work of serving foreign masters. Once we reach the twisting alleyways of the Warrens the patrols disappear, and the gates to each household stand open. People sit in their courtyards looking out onto the street as runners dash from one clan house to the next bearing messages. People watch us pass with an interested air, for what the soldiers missed they see instantly: Menoë in our midst, struggling as her exhaustion and the unfamiliar experience of carrying a burden combine to unsteady her.

From fountain to fountain in the order of the menageries we spiral into the center of the Warrens until we reach the tomb spider fountain. Young men loiter here, pretending to practice a dance in the open space before the closed gate of the Heart Tavern. Ibi approaches a narrow slit in the wall. Murmured words pass between her and someone inside, and the gate is opened.

Our companions take the fronds and the basket of knives, and Menoë and I enter alone.

I've never been here at night. A few lamps burn but the shadows hang heavy, although the tables and benches are more crowded than I've ever seen. The smell of lentil stew makes my stomach growl.

I scan the gathering for a familiar face but it's too dim. People look our way but no one greets us or makes the slightest move to help us along.

Menoë leans against a wall, pressing a hand against her forehead. "I'm going to faint if I don't get a drink," she murmurs. "Get me wine, Spider."

"I'm not your servant!"

She snaps upright, and a hand jerks up as if to slap me before she catches herself and rubs at the smears on her face, the residue of her fancy cosmetics. "I like your father better than I like you."

She rests a hand on her belly.

Before I can scream at her that my father will never, ever love her, Mis appears, wending her way through the tables.

She hugs me and says, "Come with me."

Then she sees Menoë. Her eyebrows fly right up her face and her mouth drops open in such a comedic figure of surprise that I would laugh if I hadn't just been witness to the deaths of several boys, two scholars, a child prince, and a king.

"Mis, if you've heard the news, and I know you must have, you'll understand why we have to get out of the city. I remember what you said yesterday about not fighting their war, and I'm sorry to bring a woman here who you don't want to help, but—"

"Come with me, Jes," interrupts Mis. "You too, Doma Menoë."

"Who are you to speak so familiarly to me?" She eyes Mis as if my friend is a crocodile gifted with human speech.

"I ran as an adversary in Garon Stable. But people like me aren't important enough for people like you to notice, are we?"

Without waiting for a response, Mis turns and leads us through the supper tables. Here and there people salute with their cups, acknowledging me, and one young man offers his cup as I pass. I gulp down a blessedly cool swallow of creamy goat's milk. Then I take pity on Menoë and offer her the cup. She recoils, as if I had offered her a mug of scorpions instead, so I gladly finish it myself and with a smile of thanks return it.

The small terraced semicircle of seats and tables where the mural of the Mother of All presided when I was here before looks oddly blank until I realize the image has been painted over, as if in preparation for a house-to-house search. In my visits to Ro I have never ventured beyond it, but Mis leads us through a gate into a maze of passages so narrow I can't tell if they are open-air corridors in a giant house or alleys in the most crowded part of the Warrens.

Mis ushers us down an arched corridor and past a curtain into a bowl-shaped courtyard surrounded by a circular terrace of seats and, above them, high walls that almost block out the sky. I was never in the true Heart Tavern at all, because this is it. By lamplight I see that the walls are painted with a larger version of the mural: the Mother of All seated as a procession of people approaches Her from either side. There are three other curtained entrances, and an unusual number of elderly women—a dame council—sitting on the terraced seats listening to the woman standing at the center.

"Mother!" I whisper, shocked into speaking out loud. I want to charge over to her as I used to when I was a little girl, anxious for her comforting embrace, and the sheer force of my relief at seeing her alive and healthy makes me realize how tightly I've wrapped away my fears these last months.

Menoë looks stricken as she mutters, "I didn't know she was so beautiful."

Mother is holding a fat and precious baby against her hip as she speaks to the dames. Her mellifluous voice never rises and yet effortlessly carries to all who need to hear it. When she speaks it is impossible not to listen.

"How long do you think the new king can control the foreign soldiers who put him on the throne? The city is quiet now, but I believe the calm will not last. It is my advice that first all the children be sent out of the city to their kin in the countryside, but in small groups so the Saroese do not suspect. If Efeans flee in a rush, the invaders will panic. They'll use the turmoil as an excuse to loot the city and abuse, enslave, and kill the inhabitants. This is how the Saroese behave in their wars overseas, for I have heard firsthand accounts of their uncivilized behavior. But if the invaders—and our new king—believe we are docile, then our movements won't be checked, for now."

"This way, Doma Menoë." Mis leads us down a passage and holds aside a curtain to reveal an alcove tucked into the retaining wall.

In the shadows the servants of Garon Palace stand crammed together. I see Darios and even Talon, a slim shape at the very back like she's trying to hide all trace of herself. What I don't see are any of the Efean adversaries and servants from Garon Stable.

Beneath a single lamp a frail, ancient woman sits slumped on a couch, toying absently with a pearl-studded gold bracelet like it's a scrap of ribbon. She glances up wearily, looking like a defeated old woman forced to weep for lost loved ones one time too many. When we step forward she drops the bracelet as from suddenly nerveless hands.

"Menoë! Oh goddess in her merciful glory! I feared the worst!" She begins to weep in the most undignified manner, quite unlike an imperious royal princess.

Menoë runs to her and buries her head against the princess's leg. Sobs shake her whole body. "Oh, Grandmama! He made a fool of me again. I hate him. *I hate him!*"

I slip back past the curtain to find Mother. She has to hide from them, and yet Menoë has already seen her. How could everyone be so careless?

"Jessamy? Is that you?"

Mother appears in the passage, having abandoned the dame council midspeech.

"Oh, Mother," I cry, and after all I do run to her and hug her—as well as I can with an infant in the way.

The obstacle is Wenru, the sweetest-faced and chubbiest baby you could ever see until he recognizes me and his expression takes on an entirely too-mature look of calculation. He thinks a moment, clearly considering ways he can get rid of me, then opens his mouth and wails.

I grab his ear and hiss, "Shut up!" in Saroese.

He shuts up.

"Jessamy!" Mother scolds. "Your movement startled him, that's all!"

She holds him out to the young man who stands behind her. I'm aghast to see Ro-emnu accept the baby with the ease of a person accustomed to the child. Ro looks sleek, assured, and pleased with himself, like the disruption in the city is the best part of a thrilling play he's concocted.

"You liar!" I push into Ro's space as Wenru turns his little face into Ro's shoulder, hiding from me.

"Poets only speak truth, sullen schemer." He strokes the baby's head to soothe him, but it's the lazy smile he turns on me that feels like a caress. "That is the obligation we hold in service to the Mother of All. If poets lie, we lose our gift."

"You promised you would take her to a safe haven!"

"And I did. I brought her home to her own people."

"Jessamy, please remember your manners," says Mother in her kindest voice, which means she is annoyed.

I flush at the reproof.

She takes my hand and smiles, and it's as if the sun has come out. "Do not fret yourself. All is well. I am myself now. I insisted that Maraya and Polodos leave the city some weeks ago, so they are well out of the way, for which we can thank the money you sent to us. What of you, Jessamy? I can tell you are in good health, but there is a shadow in your eyes."

"Yes, Mother." But I'm not sure I want her to know the truth of what I've done.

"However, you and I will have to speak later because there is much to accomplish tonight."

"That's right," says Ro cheerfully, handing Wenru back to Mother. "Lord Kalliarkos called in the debt I owe him. We're going to smuggle his family and retainers out of the city."

"Where is Kal?" I ask.

Mother looks sharply at me, guessing everything from my tone and my use of his name.

Ro frowns. "I told him not to do it, but of course he wouldn't listen. Once we had the others safe here he took two Garon soldiers and returned to the Fives court to look for his uncle Gargaron. But they never came back."

27

Ro and I work our way through the alleys of the lakeside Market District, headed for the King's Hill. He pushes a cart filled with caltrops, nails bound together in spiky tangles that we can throw in front of vehicles and horses if need be. The caltrops are concealed by twists of straw, but I can hear them shift and knock together like all my doubts. Three long sleeveless servant's vests lie folded on top, borrowed from Berenise's people and weighed down by a covered pot of red coals and a sealed jar of oil.

"You shouldn't have come," Ro says. "You should go back so we can get you out tonight with the others."

"You know I'm not going back. Why do you even bother to say it?"

He halts, sets down the cart, and before I realize he means to do so, takes my hand in his. There's a heat in him I never expected, and it sparks too much warmth in me.

"Jessamy, if this doesn't work—"

I shake him off, troubled by the sound of my name on his lips. "This isn't the time."

"Will you ever think it's the time?" he says.

"No."

I can tell I've hurt his feelings, but I start walking anyway. We have to go faster. It's taking too long.

He lifts the handles of the cart and comes up beside me. "It's still a bad idea for you to be out here. Too many people know your face."

"You have an exaggerated opinion of my fame. Anyway, I'm disguised as a boy."

His gaze skims down and then up the short linen keldi whose hem brushes my knees, the overly large vest meant to hide my breasts, and the cap crushed over my bound-up hair. "No, you aren't."

When he glances away, hearing a noise, I wish he would look back at me. Instantly I'm furious at myself for being flattered by his attention, for allowing a boy's flirting look to distract me from the urgent life-and-death seriousness of this expedition.

"I told you to stop, Ro," I mutter, yet I can't help but feel out of balance. I go on in a harsher voice, because my face is still burning. "Why did you agree to come? You don't love our Patron masters."

"My obligation to Lord Kalliarkos will not be fulfilled if he is killed when I might have done something to prevent it. And I intend to be quit of all obligation to him."

"How are you getting his people out if all the city gates are guarded?"

"We Efeans have our own secret gates and hidden ways."

His answer reminds me of the other question I need to ask but whose answer I'm afraid to hear. Yet I can't allow fear to control my steps, not now, not ever, so I blurt it out.

"Why were none of the Efeans from Garon Stable at the Heart Tavern? Like Gira and Shorty?"

"They were, but the dames decided it was better to send them home to their families. Ah!" He chortles in a way that makes me grind my teeth. "Were you afraid that Lord Prince Captain Kalliarkos showed his true ugly face and left them behind?"

"I wasn't!"

"You were! Or at least you feared he might have. Ha! I will say this for him, so noble and righteous as he is: he brought everyone out of the palace and the stable, Patron and Commoner alike."

Now I feel worse than ever, hating myself for doubting

Kal. I fear that he is captured and already dead with a sword through his gut. Like Temnos.

When Kal and the two soldiers left the Heart Tavern, Ro sent trackers with them, people Kal can use to relay messages or to scout as they look for Gargaron. A band of Ro's accomplices shadows us along rooftops, ready to pull us out if we're spotted. Other groups like the women who saved Menoë and me brave the streets, delivering goods to locked-in Patrons hiding in their compounds while at the same time gathering intelligence.

Ro taps me on the arm and I step back against a wall and draw the dagger they've given me. A youth pads out of the darkness—the fourth person who has found us and delivered news. Ro listens intently to a whispered message, then sends the lad on his way.

"What did he say?" I ask impatiently.

"There's a tracker with news from Kal waiting for us in the plaza of the City Fives Court."

It's like the start bell has rung, and we need to get up the ladder onto the court before it's too late. I push off the wall, ready to run. "Let's go."

He yanks me to a halt. "Why not leave Lord Gargaron to his fate? Let the Patrons murder each other. What's it to us?"

I roughly twist my arm out of his grip. "Ask me again when Kal is safe."

449

"Who are you, Jessamy?" he says to my back as I stride away. "Who are you loyal to, really?"

I keep walking, because it's easier than admitting I no longer know.

A winding street leads up to the saddle of high ground linking the King's Hill and the Queen's Hill. Between the two, the City Fives Court stands as a dark bulk, lightless and empty. Soldiers patrol the surrounding streets but give only a glance at a young man pushing a cart beside a boy carrying a jar of oil, which I position to conceal my chest.

A youth slides out of the night and falls into step beside us, a slim girl who, like me, is dressed as a boy. She's carrying a basket of dried fish so pungent I try not to breathe through my nose.

"Ro! Thank the Mother I found you. Did you get the message Kal sent to the Heart Tavern?"

"No. It must have come after we left."

"He hoped you would come. With the adversary." Her gaze flashes toward me, and I wonder how she came to feel so comfortable with Kalliarkos that she can refer to him in such casual terms.

"What's your news?" I ask, more sharply than I intend.

She looks at Ro, and he nods. "We got word that Lord Gargaron was taken prisoner at the Fives court and conveyed under guard to Garon Palace. So Kal's going in to try to rescue him. He says the adversary will know the route to take."

"Very good. Tell our spotters to hang back and spread out

in case we need to make a fast retreat, and then return to the Heart Tavern and give your report to the dame council."

I add, "If we're pursued, it would make sense to have people place obstacles in the streets, overturned carts, slippery fish, things like that to help us get away."

Ro coughs. "I think we know what we're doing, Spider."

The girl slinks into the shadows as a group of Efean men cart barrels across the Fives court's plaza in front of us. There's just enough moon and lantern-light that a subtle hand signal passes between the leader of the men and Ro. We fall in at the end of the line as the group heads up the King's Hill toward the high slopes where the most noble Patrons have built their palaces. When a soldier calls to us to ask our business, the group's leader replies in stumbling Saroese that we are bringing water to fill the cistern in the barracks behind the king's palace. Higher up on the hill Ro and I split away and head toward Garon Palace along quiet lanes I've come to know well.

Fortune favors us. The lamps along the lower end of the street aren't lit, and the closed gates of the stable aren't guarded.

However, lanterns blaze at the main gate into Garon Palace. Wagons heaped with furnishings, fabrics, and chests of belongings stripped from the pavilions and storerooms are lined up on the street outside. A buzz of activity still hums from inside, and men wearing the hawk of East Saro stagger out to dump more goods into the wagons. Nikonos's allies are looting the Garon riches.

"This way," I whisper.

We lodge the cart off to one side at the nearest intersection and put on the calf-length servant's vests. I pull on my Fives trousers beneath, in case I have to climb, as Ro pours oil over the straw.

I tie the third long vest around six caltrops. As we creep noiselessly into the stable, its eerie silence and complete abandonment make me feel I have entered a tomb. There's enough light from over the wall and from the stars and moon that we reach the bathhouse without tripping on anything, but past the entry curtain it is pitch-black.

"Hold on to me," I whisper.

"At last!" he murmurs, tucking a hand along my waist, and I want to kick him for that too-sweet tone. How can he joke?

Instead I lead him through the changing and washing chambers to the inner pool.

"You have to stay here, Ro, and guard this end."

His fingers tighten on the fabric of my vest. "I'm coming with you."

"No. I need you to guard our backs. If there's trouble, come through the tunnel to warn me. If you don't, then I'll know it's safe to come back."

He releases me. "Or that I'm dead and your enemies are waiting to kill you."

"I'm hoping they'll refrain so I can kill you myself."

"Not up to your usual standard, Spider, but not bad under the fraught circumstances."

As I start stripping down to my undergarments, he adds, "What are you doing? Oh."

For once he says no more. But I hear his breathing, which seems a little unsteady; his presence is so intimately close and yet impossibly distant because my head is too in the game.

With my own clothing rolled atop my head and the caltrops rolled up in the spare vest so they don't jab me, I descend into the pool and cross underneath the wall. The shush of ripples sloshing against the rim is the only sound as I ease out on the palace side. In total darkness I dress, then tiptoe onto the porch and hide behind the statue of Hayiyin exactly where I overheard Menoë's and Nikonos's whispers the first time I came here. Where I misunderstood everything. My wet hands might as well be coated in Temnos's blood.

I have to let go of what I can't change and concentrate on this trial.

Light burns in the public pavilions and storehouses, and that's where most of the noise is coming from as the soldiers continue their looting. Lamps bob in the garden like fireflies, moving away up winding paths back toward the main gate. As they fade I glimpse lights through the foliage from the direction of Kal's pavilion. I trace the memory of the path in my mind, then set out along the branching walkways until I find the tree that I spied from. After setting down the caltrops, I swing up.

The branch gives me the height to see across a bend in the path. Three private pavilions stand in a row, each raised on stilts and with a long balcony. Kal's pavilion lies dark and abandoned but on the balcony of the pavilion next to it two soldiers bend over the railing, rigging up a hanging rope. Gargaron stands with shoulders square and chin high, arms bound behind his back. He's not looking at Prince—now King—Nikonos or at the two soldiers guarding his back, one of whom is Sergeant Demos.

"I will give you one more chance," says Nikonos. "Lead me to your niece and nephew, and I will allow you to live. Don't you think that's a bargain?"

"No."

"Everyone knows you murdered your own relatives to elevate yourself to your current position as head of Garon Palace. Why show such loyalty to the niece and nephew who stand in your way?"

"I think it unlikely I can ever adequately explain loyalty to a man like you, my lord, to whom it is obviously an inexplicable concept."

Nikonos laughs. "To what are you loyal, Gargaron? To your own ambition! Nothing more."

"I am loyal to Efea. Your brother was a weak king, on that we are agreed, but you have handed us over to our worst enemies. You are nothing but a mule to be driven by them. As long as my niece and nephew are alive, they can restore legitimate rule."

"With what soldiers? The dregs of the Royal Army are outnumbered and on the retreat. Not even your pet general can save them. We will box them between sea and land and annihilate them."

"So his opponent believed at the battle of Maldine and yet Esladas prevailed." Gargaron's cool confidence is impressive in its own way.

I notice three shadowy shapes stretched along the pavilion's roof, just as I hid months ago when I eavesdropped on Kal. Blades gleam softly where moonlight gilds their edges. They must mean to drop onto the balcony to cut Gargaron free.

Nikonos begins to pace, his tone peevish as if he's just now realizing he can't break his rival and it's ruined his pleasure in the confrontation. "My agents are even now handing out ale in the West Harbor District and spreading the rumor that Garon Palace engineered the bread shortages to benefit your profit margin. The accusation that you personally murdered King Kliatemnos will send the good citizens of Saryenia rioting all the way up here, where they will find you trussed up by your arms. They will doubtless rip you limb from limb, uproot this lovely garden, smash these delightful pavilions, and burn your remains with the debris, a scene I'm terribly sorry I will have to miss because I would enjoy it so."

Gargaron sighs as might a man grown bored of a yapping dog who won't shut up.

Nikonos halts abruptly. "Unless you cooperate with me, it will be a painful and humiliating death worthy only of the jeers it will receive when I commission a play depicting the fall of the traitors of Garon Palace."

He theatrically cups a hand to an ear. A burr of noise clings to the night, like the distant roar of a stormy sea against rocks. "Can you hear that? I do believe the mob is already climbing the King's Hill. This is your last chance to spare yourself a gruesome death. Tell me where your niece and nephew are."

"No." Is Gargaron aware of Kal? Or does he think he is going to die and intends to go with honor and dignity intact?

"King Nikonos? We've finished our sweep of the compound. There's no one here," calls a man from inside the pavilion.

"Secure him over the edge." Nikonos goes inside, his voice drifting faintly as he hurries away. "Is my carriage ready? We must be far clear when the mob arrives."

The footfalls of the new king and his retinue fade.

We can't wait any longer. I push backward off the branch, flip, and land on my feet with a thump that I hope Kal notices as he did last time. A caltrop in each hand, I dash around the bend. I'm not a soldier but that's not my job. I'm here to create a distraction so the people with swords can do their work.

I throw the caltrops at the men setting the rope: the first

bounces off the railing and the second glances off the shoulder of one of the men hard enough that he recoils with a cry. Of course the men on the balcony all look my way.

Kal and his companions drop from the roof, taking the guards by surprise from behind. A melee breaks out. Two more soldiers burst out of the pavilion onto the balcony.

I leap up to grab the lower edge of the balcony with one hand, clutch at the hanging rope with the other, and give it a flip that wraps it around the neck of a soldier. When I let go of the balcony's rim my full weight on the rope drags the man over the railing, legs kicking. He smacks headfirst into the ground and sprawls unmoving. Kal has Demos pressed back against the railing but the sergeant is cutting with the speed and precision of an experienced soldier and Kal is barely able to block the blows. I grab a fallen caltrop and toss it. It just brushes Demos's back but that's enough to break his concentration. He flinches, and Kal slashes inside and cuts him down.

A shrill whistle from beyond the pavilion calls an alert. "Trouble! Over here!"

Neartos is one of Kal's companions. He slices the rope binding back Gargaron's arms, and the four men swing over the railing and drop. Kal of course hits the ground with a tuck and roll to absorb the shock, flowing right up onto his feet like any good adversary, but his uncle slams too hard and yelps in pain.

More guards swarm out onto the balcony. We run. As I pause to scoop up the remaining caltrops, a spear rattles through leaves and hits an arm's length from me, followed by a second that kicks up dust at my heels.

"Jes! Hurry!" Kal shouts.

I sprint down the path, slide past the bathhouse curtain behind them, and in my haste accidentally kick over a bucket as we pass through the washroom. The clatter resounds like thunder in my ears, a signal to anyone searching for us.

"Jes, you go first," says Kal.

Gargaron snaps, "No! Neartos goes first, to make sure the way is clear for you, Kalliarkos."

"No," I say. "Kal goes first because Ro is waiting and will trust only him. Then you three, and I'll bring up the rear. Go!"

We wade in, and I drop the caltrops behind me in the watery tunnel. The twisted nails won't stop anyone but they might draw blood.

We climb out the other side into darkness.

"Ro?" I whisper but I feel his absence in the chamber. Water drips to the floor from our wet clothes. I'm a little giddy, and I want to grab Kal and kiss him, just once, just quickly, but Gargaron's presence hangs like a sword between us.

"This is all very well," says Gargaron in the tone I imagine he uses when he's been given a platter of unappetizing food, "but how are we to get out of the stable?"

"Uncle Gar, do you think for one moment Grandmama would have built a stable for me to practice in if there wasn't a bolt-hole and a secret passage in case someone tried to assassinate me?"

I almost laugh at Kal's unexpected bluntness, at the cool way he throws Gargaron's machinations back in his face. But of course it isn't funny at all. Shouts and whistles, muted by the walls, remind us that we're still in danger.

"Let's go," I say.

Fingers brush mine; he squeezes my hand.

The canvas at the entry scrapes.

"Jes? Do you have them?" Ro whispers.

"Yes."

"Excellent. When I heard the commotion I ran out and set the wagon on fire to draw their attention down the lane. I've lined the closed gate entrance with the rest of the caltrops."

Murky echoes rise from the pool. People are searching the bathhouse, and ripples stir along the rim, lapping as water is displaced on the other side. I nudge Kal.

"In the Fives court, under Traps," he says.

Lamplight and alarms rise around us as we run across the courtyard and into the unlit Fives court. The stable gate creaks open. Men shout as they stumble over the caltrops. But Kal and I know the court intimately, and our pursuers do not. We lower ourselves through a hidden trapdoor into a stone-lined tunnel while soldiers are still blundering around trying to find the entry gate to each obstacle.

With the hatch closed firmly behind us Kal lights a lamp tucked into a niche in the wall.

"This will bring us out near the Grain Market," he says. He commands Neartos to advance at the front and the other soldier to act as rear guard, then starts down a flight of stairs.

Gargaron gives Ro that thin smile meant to cow his opponents, and Ro stares flatly back at him, not giving way. Both men know they've been dropped into a tiny bubble in which, for once, their respective positions in life matter nothing. They're like two hungry predators, circling as they study their opponent for a single hint of weakness.

I shove between them to break off the contest. "Move," I order, as my father would. "My lord, if you will, follow Lord Kalliarkos."

Gargaron gives me a long, measuring look, then starts after Kal, favoring his right leg.

"Why did you return to save me if you believe I've wronged you?" Gargaron asks his nephew.

"Because I'm not you." Kal halts and holds up the lantern to fully illuminate his uncle's face. "Did you kill my father and grandfather?"

"As it happens, I did not, and I am willing to swear in the temple to that effect. Mining accidents happen, and so does death in battle. It was the gods' will."

It's the lie he could have told my father: *I did not kill them. I sent them away and now no one can find them, but there's no help for that. It was the gods' will.*

I'm sure he's lying.

Kal nods as at an answer he expected. "We need each other, Uncle Gar. Efea needs us."

"We need to keep moving," I say more curtly than I intend.

Yet I can't help but wonder: Is Kal still this naïve, or is he—as Ro predicted—slowly sliding into the role his position mandates for him, in which every brutal calculation he makes is devised to maintain and increase his power?

For a bit we trudge without speaking. Not a breath of sound disturbs the stuffy air of this long-sealed tunnel. I'm grateful for the silence as I stare at Gargaron's back because Ro's words ring in my head:

Why not leave Lord Gargaron to his fate? Let the Patrons murder each other.

I have a knife. I could plunge it into his flesh and end the power he holds over Kal, over me, over my family. But his soldiers would defend him. I can't put Kal in that position.

Yet Ro's accusations might as well be shouts: *Who are you, Jessamy? Who are you loyal to, really?*

I can't see how these Rings will open, not for me. I can only see them unfolding for everyone else.

The passage lets out by a ladder through a secret door set into a fountain alcove behind a bank of public latrines. An alarm bell is ringing, and above us, on the King's Hill, we hear the growling noise of a mob in full rampage.

Gargaron sags onto the ground to massage his right ankle. Kal sets the lamp down beside him, then orders Neartos to scout the nearby streets and report back.

"I'll go too," says Ro. "Some of my people have to be around here." He vanishes down the dark lane.

Kal hasn't yet closed the door, and he tugs me back inside. We are crammed so close I accidentally step on his foot.

"Ow!"

"Repayment for the splinter," I whisper, hoping Gargaron and the other soldier are too far away and too preoccupied to overhear.

Kal brushes a finger along my palm in a way that makes me shiver. "I suppose I deserve that."

"Exactly what is it you think you deserve?" I tease, but the moment I speak, the words seem too light, too joking, for this awful day. Hoarsely, I go on. "I was so afraid you were dead."

I run my hands up his chest. He's wearing coarsely woven laborer's clothing but the pleasure of touching him is all silk, and he makes a soft sound in his throat as I lean in to kiss him.

Every complication falls away. There is only his mouth testing mine, my body pressing against his, the way his fingers slide up my bare skin under the loose cloth of my vest to trace the curve of my ribs like the brush of desire....

A cough and soft words cause us to shove abruptly apart,

like illicit lovers in a play caught by an untimely entrance, but it is only Gargaron and his guardsman conversing.

Kal raises my hand to his lips and kisses my damp, dirty knuckles. "Ask me again when we're safe. Did the scheme with my sister and Temnos work?"

At first I can't answer because my mouth goes dry but I have to tell him. I won't hide my fatal miscalculation. "Your sister is safe, but Prince Temnos is dead."

"What happened?"

He wraps his arms around me, and in the shelter of his embrace I find the courage to tell him the story, each step of that terrible journey a shard of glass I have to bleed on yet again.

"I was so sure Menoë was the villain when it was Nikonos and Serenissima all along. The queen sacrificed her own son to stay in power. I don't even understand how a mother could do that. I led Temnos to his death because I wanted to think the worst of Menoë even when everyone told me I was wrong."

"Jes, it's not your fault. *They* killed him—not you."

I shake my head. "I could have saved him if I'd just listened."

"We're not done yet, Jes. It's not over. And it's going to be ugly. It's not like poor Temnos is the first or will be the last to die."

"What did your grandmother intend to do with Temnos?"

"Nothing. He wasn't a threat to anyone. She promised me he'd be exiled to a distant estate to live in peace."

Lies are the air children growing up in palaces learn to breathe. But I can't tell him that.

Ro whispers from the darkness outside, "Can you two cooing lovebirds leave off? We need to move now, while the street is clear."

I step out of the passage first, and Kal closes the opening behind us. The light from the lamp seems so bright that I rub my eyes. Neartos has also returned, and he helps Gargaron to his feet.

"You have boats enough for everyone, as you promised?" Kal asks Ro.

"And a secret shoreline departure point so we won't be caught leaving the city?" I add.

"We Efeans have a lot of things Patrons don't know about. Just remember, once I've saved you and your people, Kal, you and I are quit of obligation. After this anything goes"—he looks at me, and holds my gaze just a little too long—"and nothing is off-limits."

Kal slaps him on the shoulder like it's a joke, and although Ro smiles in answer, the twist in his lips tells me they will never be friends.

But poets may not lie lest they lose their gift.

So it is that much later that night I sit in the prow of a rowboat out on the vast waters of Mist Lake. Stars shine in the cloudless heavens, mirrored in the still waters. Threads of mist wind like the ghosts of ancient mazes, dissipating as the wake of our passage rolls through them. Ro and Kal work the oars behind me, their backs to the shore we are approaching. Seated on a pile of fishing nets, I hold the lamp to light our way.

They're talking, Kal in an expansive mood and Ro coaxing the words out.

"Nikonos acted too soon. The populace doesn't want foreign soldiers on its streets."

"No, indeed, the populace really doesn't," Ro agrees, like he's speaking a language Kal can't hear, and yet I say nothing.

"The coming battle will break apart old loyalties and force lords and generals to take sides," Kal goes on. "We have General Esladas in command of the Royal Army, but Nikonos has the armies of old Saro. If Thynos can turn West Saro to our side with his marriage, then that will weaken Nikonos's alliance. We know what a ruthless, power-hungry man he is. We have to depose him before he ruins Efea."

"Deposing such men must always be a noble and righteous goal," agrees Ro.

A little flotilla of boats precedes us, and although we left the city in total darkness so as not to be spotted from the walls, now lantern-light floats like spark-bugs on the water. Mother is in the boat right ahead of us, a scarf looped over her hair and draped to conceal her face. I wanted to be in the boat with her but dared not call Gargaron's attention to her in such a way. She's holding Wenru while Mis, seated beside her, carries Safarenwe.

The murky night slowly lightens to gray. Ahead a reed-choked shoreline rises out of the fading darkness. Figures appear, men and women holding spears and swords. I brace myself for trouble, but then I see they have Efean faces. We've reached the village we visited months ago, where Tana and Inarsis were born.

General Inarsis steps out of the ranks as Princess Berenise's boat bumps first onto the land, for naturally she must be in the lead. Her regal self-possession has been restored now that she knows her grandchildren are safe. Temnos means nothing to her. Menoë sits beside her, head high but face pallid with exhaustion, and Gargaron sits upright and stony-faced in the stern. He has not made a single complaint about his badly swollen ankle.

Garon stewards splash onto the shore from the other boats and hustle forward to help their nobles disembark more elegantly. The Efeans stand in masklike silence as the highborn Patrons are escorted past their ranks to the wagon in which they will ride to the village.

Out on the water we in the last two boats wait until the wagon rolls away. Only then does Mother's boat put in to shore. Inarsis extends a hand to her. As she takes it and alights, the hundred lamps carried by the Efeans sway forward as if offering homage to a queen. Once her feet rest on solid ground Mother looks back to make sure my boat is coming in. The tilt of her head causes the scarf to slip, and she tugs it back up.

That's when I see, past her, that the last knot of Patron

servants has only just begun to walk after the others. That's when I see that Gargaron evidently decided to hang back despite his sprained ankle, either because he wants to keep an eye on me and Kal or because the disciplined ranks of armed Efeans and the reverence of the lamps have drawn his attention, for he is alert at all times to such details.

That's when I see he's seen her.

Recognized her.

He doesn't move. He doesn't speak. But his gaze seeks me out where I sit holding the lamp that guides us.

It's like a spill of cold water drenching me.

"Are we there?" Kal glances over his shoulder from the rowers' bench, his smile as bright and welcoming as the promise of day.

"Yes," I reply even as my courage falters and then, in a fury, rages back to full fierce strength.

Stepping off onto the land I meet Gargaron's furious gaze. I give him a thin smile, making sure he knows that I saved my mother. That I defeated him.

I should stop there. I should.

But I don't.

I flash him the kiss-off sign, just to rub it in.

He stiffens and turns away.

He'll wait to make his move to go after her, he'll devise a cunning scheme, but it will be too late when he does. It's already too late.

I see what all the Commoners know and the Patrons are blind to because they can perceive only their own image in the mirror of power: The coming battle will undermine Patron rule. And when it does, those who have been trodden low will lift up their faces. Hands that have toiled so long under the lash of harsh masters will reach for weapons of their own making. Those whose hearts have been buried deep will climb the stairs into the light.

Efea will rise.

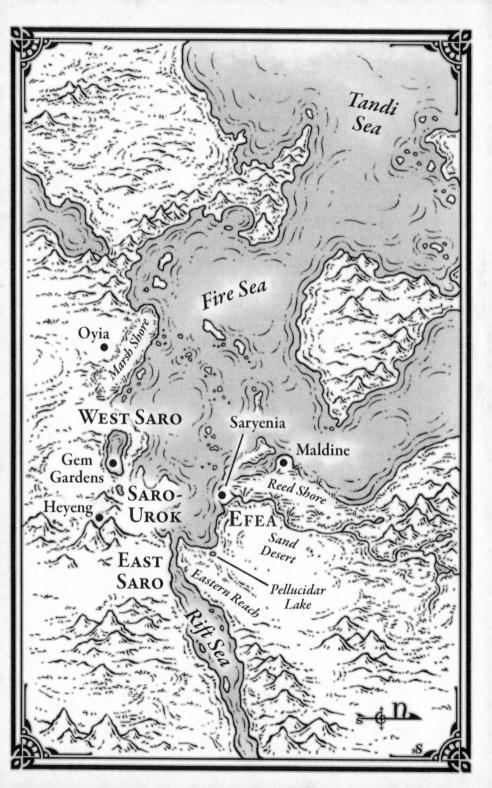

Tandi
Sea

Fire Sea

Oyia

Marsh Shore

WEST SARO

Saryenia

Maldine

Gem
Gardens

Reed Shore

SARO-
UROK

Heyeng

EFEA

*Sand
Desert*

EAST
SARO

Eastern Reach

Pellucidar
Lake

*Rift
Sea*

ACKNOWLEDGMENTS

Huge thanks to the fantastic team at Little, Brown Books for Young Readers, and to my fabulous editors, Andrea Spooner and Deirdre Jones. Special thanks to Nafiza Azad, Justina Ireland, Dani McKenzie, and Wendy Xu for reading the penultimate draft and making comments. This novel was inspired by athletes and activists, their hard work, their passion, and their vision.

For more information on *Poisoned Blade* and the Fives or Kate's other series, or to sign up for her new-release e-mail list, the author invites you to visit her website at KateElliott.com, or you can follow her on Twitter @KateElliottSFF.

DISCUSSION QUESTIONS

1. Like many athletes in our own world, Jessamy receives celebrity status and accolades that cross social classes. How does she use that celebrity to her advantage? How does her training in the Fives help her off the court?

2. How are Saroese women and Efean women treated differently within their individual social groups? How are Saroese women treated by Efeans, and how are Efean women treated by the Saroese? Why do you think these differences exist? What are some historical parallels in our own world that demonstrate this kind of discrimination?

3. In *Court of Fives*, Kalliarkos seemed to reject the practices, ideals, and methods of the royal family. Does he feel like the same person at the end of *Poisoned Blade*? How is he the same person that Jessamy fell in love with in the first book, but also a very different person after his time with the army?

4. What are some of the differences between life in the city of Saryenia and life in the Efean countryside that Jessamy encounters during her tour? How do these differences affect her thinking about her Efean ancestry and her Saroese ancestry? Does Jes consider herself more Efean or more Saroese?

5. Code-switching is the practice of switching back and forth between two or more languages, or between two dialects of the same language. It can also refer to switching between "identities" in cultural and interpersonal situations. How is code-switching essential to Jessamy's survival? Do you ever use code-switching in your own life?

6. In the world of Efea, every body has five animating souls: the vital spark, the shadow, the self, the name, and the heart. In *Poisoned Blade*, we see the transference of the vital spark from one body to another with Prince Temnos in the palace gardens, with Cestas at Crags Fort, and with Kalliarkos on the battlefield. How are each of these transferences similar and how are they different?

7. Jessamy appears to be following in her father's footsteps when she becomes a spider scout, but she also harbors a deep resentment of his abandonment of their family in *Court of Fives*. Are there people in your life who you both love and hate sometimes? Can you see their point of view even when you don't agree with them, as Jessamy can with her father, who she respects deeply?

8. By the end of *Poisoned Blade*, Jessamy and Bettany are both participating in their own rebellions. How do these protests differ? How are they alike? Do you agree with (or at least empathize with) Bettany's choice to leave her family for good? Can you draw a parallel between Bettany and the character of Beth in Louisa May Alcott's *Little Women*?

9. *Poisoned Blade* is a sequel to *Court of Fives*, meaning the author had to incorporate information from the first book into the second to remind readers about key characters and plot points. Which places incorporated this information most effectively, and what techniques did the author use? Does the information come to readers through dialogue? Description? Flashbacks?

10. What do you think will happen in the final book in the Court of Fives series, *Buried Heart*, now that the Saroese king has been murdered and the Efean revolution is beginning?

In this epic conclusion to the Court of Fives trilogy,
Jessamy is at the crux of a revolution.
Can she bring together two sides that have despised each other
for over a century?

Turn the page for a sneak preview of
BURIED HEART.

Available July 2017

I **stand poised on** the shore of Mist Lake like an adversary gathering focus before a Fives trial. South across the waters, too far away to see from here, lies the city of Saryenia from which we just escaped. A rhythmic sound drifts out of the dawn haze that obscures the horizon: the drums of a fast-moving war galley.

"Do you hear that?" I say. "The new king is already hunting us."

The boat I arrived in rocks wildly as its two occupants—Lord Kalliarkos and the poet Ro-emnu—jump out onto land and scramble up to either side of me. Kal takes my hand, the touch of his skin a promise against mine, and gives me a smile that makes my heart leap. Ro glances over, gaze flicking down to our entwined fingers, and looks away with a frown.

"We've got to get you out of sight," I say to Kal, reluctantly shaking loose from his grip. "And get my mother to safety where your uncle can never find her."

My mother has already disembarked. We are the last people out of the flotilla of now-empty rowboats in which our party fled the murderous new king. Surrounded by local Efean villagers, Mother is speaking to them with such an appearance of calm dignity that no one would ever guess how desperate our circumstances are. As the three of us run over, the villagers leave her and race past us to the shore, carrying baskets and fishing nets. They shove the boats back out onto the water.

"Are they abandoning us?" I ask as we rush up to Mother.

"Not at all, Jessamy. They are risking their lives to aid us."

"By fishing?"

Ro breaks in with his usual needling. "The sight of Efeans

hard at work to enrich Patron treasuries always lulls our Saroese masters."

"By placing their own bodies between us and the soldiers," Mother goes on. "It isn't only military men wielding swords who defend the land and act with courage."

I look back again, viewing the scene on the lake with new eyes. "That's very brave, especially since they're unarmed."

"Doma Kiya, we need to get moving to the shelter of the trees," says Kal to Mother, offering her a polite bow with hand pressed to heart.

Although his words and tone are courteous, Mother's usually gentle expression stiffens into a stony-eyed mask. "I can see that for myself, my lord," she snaps.

Kal is taken aback by her hostility, and so am I.

Irritation and impatience clip off my tongue. "He's helping us!"

Kal looks from my mother to me and, still with his courteous voice, says, "I'll scout ahead to make sure my uncle isn't lying in wait in the trees to capture you."

He races away while we follow at a brisk walk. Mother holds my infant brother Wenru while, beside her, my friend and former Fives stable-mate Mis carries Wenru's twin sister, Safarenwe. All of the other Efeans have either gone out onto the lake or have left to escort the wagons conveying the fugitive Patrons of Garon Palace, who own this estate and its surrounding villages.

"Maybe the soldiers will pass by," I say with another anxious look toward the lake. The shape of a mast coalesces in the mist. Oars beat the water in unison as the warship speeds toward us.

"Seeing only dull Commoner fishermen and farmers, not bold conspirators who just rescued the new king's rivals from certain death," murmurs Ro.

"Don't speak of such matters in front of Lord Kalliarkos, Ro-emnu," says Mother, with a warning glance at me.

"Kal won't—"

"Enough, Jessamy. Keep moving." Her tone scalds.

Kal waves an all-clear from the edge of the orchard and ducks out of sight before the war galley can get close enough to spot his Saroese features and clothing. The fig and pomegranate trees aren't particularly tall but they are bushy enough to conceal us. As the others push forward on a wagon track through the trees I pause to look back one last time.

While most of the rowboats have dispersed out onto the water, six have made a rough circle with a large net between them, blocking the approach to the shoreline where we landed. But the galley cuts straight through the little flotilla. Two of the boats flip, and the others rock wildly as their occupants struggle to keep them from overturning. Oars slap the heads of people in the water to jeers from the oarsmen. Arrows streak out from the deck. Most slap harmlessly into the water but one hits a hapless swimmer in the back. The armed men crowded on the deck shout excitedly and laugh as the victim's head sinks beneath the surface. It's a game to them.

The drum beat ceases. The galley plows through a stand of reeds with a rattle of noise before dragging to a stop in the shallows exactly where we just disembarked.

A man steps up to the rail of the ship.

It is the new king himself, once Prince General Nikonos and now the man who murdered his older brother and innocent young nephew so he could seize the throne of Efea. From this distance I can't fully distinguish his face although I know he resembles Kal in having regal features and a golden-brown complexion; they're cousins, after all.

Nikonos calls out in the voice of a man used to shouting over the din of battle. "The Garon estate lies beyond the trees! The man who brings the corpse of Lord Kalliarkos or Lord

Gargaron to me I will raise to become a lord! As for the rest of the Garon household and any who shelter them, show no mercy to traitors!"

I sprint after the others. Thorns from the pomegranate branches scrape my arms. Mother has been jogging along at the rear but she slows to a halt, puffing as she struggles to catch her breath. The others stop too, Mis supporting Mother with a hand under her elbow.

I charge up. "It's Nikonos himself. Right on our heels."

"Honored Lady, I'll take the baby to lighten your burden," says Ro.

To my consternation—because I should have asked first—Mother hands Wenru over to the poet. After a moment of disgruntled squirming, my infant brother settles into Ro's arm with an expression of un-babyish disgust.

The sounds of snapping branches and men cursing at thorns as the soldiers push through the trees chases us onward. We emerge at a run from the orchard and hurry through grain fields toward the stately roofs and walls of the main compound, built for the Saroese stewards who supervise the estate with its rich fields, groves, and fishing. A path lined by trees leads to the northeast, toward an Efean village.

"Shouldn't we head toward the village?" I whisper urgently.

"My grandmother always keeps an escape plan in reserve," says Kal. "There's a merchant galley hidden in a backwater river channel beyond the northern fields for just such an emergency as this. She and the rest of the household should already be boarding it."

"In other words," remarks Ro, because he just can't stop himself, "you Saroese nobles expect at any moment to be murdered by your own relatives."

Kal touches my arm as a warning to not bother answering.

"This way," he says in a tone that reminds me of my military father, a reminder that Kal fought a campaign in the desert and commanded a squad of spider scouts.

We splash through a shallow irrigation canal and race across another stretch of fields.

"Do you visit here often?" I ask in a low voice, sticking beside him.

"Twice a year with my grandmother. When I was a boy I would play on the hidden ship and pretend I was a sailor on the high seas."

I grin at this innocent memory, and without breaking stride he bumps a shoulder against mine, just a tap. Despite the danger we're in, it's exhilarating to keep pace together, feet hitting the ground in perfect time.

Mudbrick reservoirs rise at the end of cultivated land and the beginning of marshier ground where bushy-headed papyrus sways over our heads. Fresh wagon tracks in the earth mark where the Garon fugitives passed only moments ago, so it's with shock that we emerge onto the bank of a backwater river channel to find the dock empty.

The merchant galley is gone.

Except for an embroidered blue silk shawl fluttering in the branches of a sycamore, there's no trace of the Garon household, of Kal's grandmother Princess Berenise, his sister Lady Menoë, his uncle Lord Gargaron, nor any of the fifty relatives and retainers who escaped with us out of Saryenia. Nothing except three village rowboats bumping against the pilings with neatly folded fishing nets inside, and the two abandoned wagons.

"How could they have left without me?" says Kal, a hand on his neck like he's trying to stem the bleeding from having his throat cut.

We stare, all too stunned to ask the same question. Safarenwe gives a fussing cry, and Mother takes her from Mis, soothing her with kisses. Wenru remains uncannily silent in Ro's arms.

Mis points back the way we came. "Look!"

We turn. Shock tightens to a new stab of fear. Threads of smoke rise in the distance. They thicken to columns and then boil up into fierce black clouds.

Nikonos's soldiers are burning the estate.

The tops of papyrus start thrashing: soldiers following our trail.

"I found fresh wagon tracks!" a man shouts in Saroese.

Kal and I instantly scan our surroundings. The channel has been dredged along the steeper bank to give enough draft for a galley to dock, while the other bank is a shallow marsh-land choked with reeds. We glance at each other with a flash of shared understanding.

"I can swim underwater to hide in the reeds," he says.

I nod. "We'll pretend to fish in the boats."

He doesn't protest that we'll become targets while he hides. We both know this is the only way. I grab his wrist and even with my mother right there give him a quick kiss, as a promise.

If his gaze slides to meet Ro's in challenge, it happens so fast I am sure I have mistaken it. But then Ro says, as if in retort, "Don't you fear crocodiles, Kal?"

"The ones on two feet are sure to kill me, so I'll take my chances."

He slips into the water, vanishing without sound or splash. I run to the end of the dock and yank the shawl out of the branches so our pursuers won't guess that Patron women have passed by here. By the time I race back, Mis and Ro, with Safa-renwe, are already rowing away as Mother, holding Wenru, waits for me.

We push off. Mother gives Wenru to me and takes the oars. She handles them with an adeptness that surprises me until I remember she grew up in a rustic village far from sophisticated Saryenia. Wenru clutches at my vest like he's afraid I'm going to toss him overboard. A pair of ducks flutters up noisily from deep within the reeds. I can't see Kal from here but he must have surfaced and startled them. The thrashing in the papyrus comes closer as men shout, having heard the quacking. Ahead of us, Ro and Mis glide behind a thick stand of reeds. We're too far behind to have a hope of concealing ourselves.

Mother stops rowing and takes up a net as five soldiers burst into view and stamp out onto the dock. She flips out the net, which flares like a flower blooming, strikes the water, and sinks. The movement draws their attention.

"Hey, Sergeant! Let's catch some Efean delicacies for our supper," calls one, his accent that of a man from overseas, not a locally-born Patron.

I hate the way they stare at us as if they are hungry and we are food. If only I could slam my oar into their ugly faces.

Mother whispers, "By no sign show you can understand them."

Wenru stirs, stout infant legs shoving against my chest as he twists around to look their way. He sucks in a breath, prelude to a scream.

In Saroese I snap, "You should be ashamed of yourself, you little rat."

Our gazes lock. His face is as brown as my own, and his eyes so black they are shadows dropped into his heart. A flicker of irritation passes across his face, and I'm once again sure that an unknown self resides in my dead brother's body.

I lower my voice to a whisper that brushes his perfect little ear. "I know you aren't what you seem, but to Saroese soldiers you look like an ordinary Efean baby. They will throw you into the river to drown. If you betray my mother, I will pin you to the dirt and let the vultures eat you alive."

Mother is staring at me, eyes wide. But the net twitches, distracting her, and she briskly hauls in two fish.

From out of sight a man calls, "Here's mule tracks, Sergeant! Someone went this way with animals, maybe the ones used to haul the wagons."

"You two!" The sergeant points to the man who was just calling out to us and his nearest companion. "Bring in those two women for questioning."

"But Sergeant, they say the rivers here are infested with monsters that eat people."

"Use the boat. You others, follow me."

He and two other soldiers hurry off on a track that leads behind the crowds of willow and sycamore shading the opposite bank. The two remaining soldiers, arguing with each other in the tone of very nervous men, climb into one of the boats.

"Switch with me." I thrust Wenru into Mother's arms, the boat rocking as we change places. "I need my hands free."

"What do you intend?"

"I don't know yet."

I row as Mother uses the shawl to sling Wenru to her hip. I'm not as skilled, so the oars skip over the water a couple of times. The soldiers gain on us. We skim past a clump of reeds into a backwater overhung by trees where Mis and Ro have paused to wait for us.

I gesture at them to keep rowing upriver. Something large in the water passes beneath us and rocks the hull of our boat. I'm so startled I yelp out loud. Beyond the reeds the soldiers shout in excitement; they think I'm scared of them, and they're right about that, too.

A hand emerges from the water to tap the side of our boat, then Kal's head emerges. He gulps air.

I murmur, "Two soldiers in a boat behind us. No one else in sight. They're scared of crocodiles."

"Distract them." He dives.

I turn the boat and start back the way we came.

"Jessamy, we should follow Ro-emnu and Missenshe, not expose ourselves like this for some reckless plan."

"Father trained him. Kal knows what he's doing."

The soldiers have come up so fast it takes only three strokes for us to skim past their bow.

"Good Goat!" One laughs. "The luscious fruit drops into our laps."

Reaching for our boat, they don't notice Kal launch out of the water on their boat's other side. He grabs the gunwale with both hands and uses his weight to tip them.

Alone he can't overturn it, but I shout, in Saroese, "Crocodile!"

Their panic and flailing does the rest. The boat goes over with a huge splash. One man goes under and never comes back up as his comrade churns the murky water with his arms, struggling to keep afloat in his stiff leather armor. I slam an oar down, clip the side of his head, then slam it down again, stunning him momentarily.

He goes under, dragged down as if by a mauling crocodile. Thrashing disturbs the water. Bubbles fleck the surface, staining red. I balance in the boat, an oar in my hand, ready to strike. I'm breathing so hard I can't catch my breath.

A head breaks the surface: Kal, alive, expression grim and yet satisfied. A body bobs up briefly, rolls over to flash the dead man's slack face before the heavy leather armor drags him under. Kal grabs the gunwale of our boat and tosses his sword in. The blade gleams, already washed clean by the river water. He dives under twice more, retrieving the soldiers' swords, then mires their boat in the reeds so it can't be seen from the shore.

"May the blessings of the Mother of All give mercy to the living and the dead," Mother whispers.

She and I throw our weight to the opposite side as Kal hauls himself up and over the gunwale, flopping gracelessly atop the now tangled net. He's dressed in the clothes of a laborer, and the cloth of his keldi—the knee-length skirt Efean men wear—is plastered to his muscular thighs. I glance away, only to find Mother examining me with a frown.

As we drift out from under the overhanging branches of a giant sycamore, Kal straightens up. The stark sunlight gilds his face, making him look like a hero on the stage despite his dripping wet clothes and bedraggled hair. His grave expression fixes on me, but there's a wild light in his eyes that unsettles me and yet also sets my heart pounding.

Hoarsely he says, "Ask me again when we're safe, Jes."

My cheeks flush as if I've been burned. He said those same words when we escaped Garon Palace with his uncle, when we caught a moment alone in a secret passage to kiss in a way I have never kissed anyone before.

Was that only last night?

Mother taps my arm as if she's angry. With *me*. "Jessamy! We must get out of here. The others will come looking for their comrades."

Irritated by her unrelenting hostility to Kal, I start rowing after Mis and Ro, who are now out of sight around a bend in the channel. Smoke billows up in the distance, accompanied by shouts from the searching soldiers. A bird whistle pulls my head around.

"There," says Mother.

Ro is waving at us from partway up a tree. I maneuver the boat in beneath branches. We rustle through bulrushes and bump up against the other boat, which is tied to a post in a hidden inlet. Three Efean sentries armed with sickles help us out onto the bank, paying particular attention to Mother, whom they address as Honored Lady. Kal greets each by name, and it's clear they know who he is from his occasional visits to the estate and aren't surprised that he recognizes them.

Ro tests the heft of the captured swords. "How did you get these?"

"The crocodiles took their tax," I say, hoping to get Kal to smile, but his grim expression doesn't lighten.

Ro makes a fist of his hand and bumps the side of Kal's fist in a gesture Efean men make with each other. "Well done."

The unexpected mark of respect startles a grin out of Kal after all.

"Thank you for saving our lives, Lord Kalliarkos," I say with a meaningful glance at Mother.

"Your quick thinking served us well, my lord," says Mother, finally sounding more like the gracious, accommodating woman I grew up with rather than this angry, mistrustful person I don't recognize.

"My thanks, Honored Lady," says Kal cautiously.

But she's not done. "We must also thank the Honored Poet, Ro-emnu, for arranging our passage out of Saryenia. It was astoundingly well managed, especially with so many people to transport in secrecy."

"My thanks, Honored Lady," Ro murmurs with downcast eyes, and spoils the pretense of humility with a sidelong look at me, making sure I've heard my mother praise him.

Kal says, "I hope you know how indebted Garon Palace is to you, Ro."

"I do know."

An awkward silence follows.

I catch Mis's eye, and she comes to the rescue by handing over one of the bundles she's carrying. "Here's your Fives gear, Jes. Darios grabbed it when they evacuated Garon Stable. Now what? We can't hide here."

"That's right," I agree. "Nikonos isn't going to give up searching. Is there a plan?"

One of the sentries says, "We were sent by General Inarsis to look for the Honored Lady and bring her to shelter."

Instead of waiting for Kal's order, which he normally would give as one of the Patron masters of the estate, all five Efeans look to Mother, who nods agreement. If Kal is offended at being bypassed he gives no sign of it as we leave one of the swords with the two sentries remaining on guard at the inlet. The third leads us along a concealed path through a tangle of overgrown vegetation. Of course, despite our frantic situation, Mother has brought the two fish in a basket, just as if we are returning home with our night's supper to a happy family.

I blink back tears, remembering the days when we four sisters would sit in the courtyard at dusk as Mother embroidered: Amaya writing poetry and practicing speeches from plays, Bettany muttering about injustice and hypocrisy while her sisters ignored her, me counting the moments until I could escape to run the Fives, and Maraya studying for the Archives exam she hoped to take one day.

"Where are Maraya and Polodos?" I ask in Efean, with a glance at Wenru. He's looking around like he's trying to figure out where we are and where we are going.

"They stayed in Saryenia at the Least Hill Inn. That way they can listen to the gossip of foreign soldiers and pass on intelligence."

"As spies? That's dangerous."

"We are all fugitives now, Jessamy. We are in danger no matter where we are. Anyway, you said Bettany and Amaya are on their way to the city by ship."

"Yes." I'm not yet ready to break her heart by telling her what really happened with Bettany.

"So Maraya will be there to shelter them when they arrive." She pauses, then goes on sternly. "Was calling your baby brother a little rat your idea of a jest? Because I am not laughing."

Nothing is worse than Mother's disapproval but I don't know how to explain my suspicions or whether she'll believe me.

"Don't think I didn't notice that you spoke to Wenru in Saroese rather than Efean. I've raised enough children to know his behavior is unusual and even at moments disconcerting."

We plod along, her expectant silence as she waits for my reply like a hand tugging insistently on my arm. What if I don't warn her that her infant son is actually dead, and whoever resides in his body has a chance to betray her because she's not on her guard? To protect her, I have to try.

So I say, in Saroese, "There's a huge poisonous snake about to drop out of the trees right onto your heads."

Wenru's head snaps back in fear, but Mother has heard the lie in my voice, and her gaze stays on the baby and his slow confusion as he realizes what I've just done. He tucks his head down like he wishes he could turn into a turtle with a shell to hide in, and says "ba ba ba" in the most unbabylike voice.

Mother stares at him as if he has turned into a snake. In Efean, she says, "Jessamy, what is going on?"

Our guide raises a hand for silence. Concealed by a stand of trees we look across well-kept gardens to an empty Efean village.

The guide murmurs, "Move fast and keep your heads down."

We dash along a wagon track that takes us into the center of the village where stands a simple Fives court. I hear soldiers speaking Saroese, their voices far too close, and I gesture toward the gate into Pillars, thinking we can hide in the maze. But a burly, threatening man steps out from behind that very gate, sword drawn, to halt us in our tracks.